Also by Elizabeth Helen

Beasts of the Briar

Bonded by Thorns

Woven by Gold

Forged by Malice

Broken by Daylight

Frozen by Stardust

stolen BY shadows

ELIZABETH HELEN

Bloom books

Published by Bloom Books, an imprint of Sourcebooks
1935 Brookdale RD, Naperville, IL 60563-2773
(630) 961-3900
sourcebooks.com

Cataloging-in-Publication data is on file with the Library of Congress.

Printed and bound in the United States of America.
VP 10 9 8 7 6 5 4 3 2 1

To Graeme,

Lyra and Elias have faced the Baron. So have Lance and Eira. Thank you for letting us borrow him for the Briar.

THE ABOVE

Emberwood Forest

KEEP OAKHEART

Shrine of Nymphia

CASTLETREE

The Sun Colosseum

SOLTIDE KEEP

The Equinox Pass

The Suadela Sands

THE ENCHANTED VALE

The Great Chasm
Voidseal Bridge
KEEP WOLFHELM
Queen's Reach Monastery
Mount Lumidor
KEEP HAMMERGARDEN
Meadowmere Forest
Sylvanita Lake
THE BELOW

Chronology

AGE OF THE COSMOS

Years unknown

A glorious time that is shrouded in mystery. Very few fae who lived in this age still remain today. It is said the Above hung from a canopy in the cosmos. All the light, magic, and goodness of the world emanated from the Gardens of Ithilias, which contained a celestial rosebush.

A young fae woman named Sira desired to create her own realm and stole one of the heavenly flowers. She fled the cosmos and, using the might of her stolen rose, forged a new realm known as the Below. In the dark, Sira was able to use the rose to breed creations of her own, monsters crafted of darkness and rot.

For the treacherous act of stealing the rose, Sira was forever banished from the Realm Above. Enraged that she and her creations were not accepted by the Above, Sira waged a great war. Sira's creations mercilessly attacked the fae of the Above. Though the fae were courageous, they knew not the ways of war. Sira destroyed the Gardens of Ithilias, and all that was good and beautiful in the world fell to darkness and despair.

AGE OF THE VALE

0–1025

A young fae woman named Aurelia, filled with courage, was able to save four roses from the Gardens of Ithilias. Infused with the roses' magic, she forged a new world consisting of five realms. The first four realms—known as Winter, Spring, Summer, and Autumn—became safe havens for the survivors of the Above. In the fifth realm, Aurelia grew a magnificent tree that housed the four roses. The tree, known as Castletree, channeled the last light of the Gardens of Ithilias and provided strength and stability to all. So grateful to Aurelia were the survivors of the Above that they named her queen, and the land of Castletree became known as the Queen's Realm. She appointed a high ruler to each of the seasonal realms and blessed them with celestial magic from the sacred roses.

Queen Aurelia was a dauntless and spirited ruler who was determined to see her people thrive. More powerful than any other fae, she was able to change the world around her, including the shape of plants, animals, and even other fae. Under her rule, the world she created, known as the Enchanted Vale, prospered and great civilizations flourished.

However, peace was not to be, for down in the darkness, an enemy schemed. While Aurelia ruled five lands of light and prosperity, Sira's realm was one of darkness and rot, and her only subjects were her monstrous creations. Sira began to manipulate fae from the surface realms into joining her, promising them power and ancient magic. Using the first rose stolen from the Gardens of Ithilias, Sira threw herself into creating armies of darkness.

Attacks from the Below against the Enchanted Vale became more frequent until finally war broke out. The Gloaming War raged for hundreds of years. Desperate to end the suffering of her people, Aurelia and the high rulers devised a plan. The first high ruler of Spring, High Prince Rafael, was a masterful blacksmith and believed he could craft weapons of immense power if only he could access ore from the Above. Though the fae had lost their way to the ruins of the Above, Aurelia and the high rulers traveled across the Enchanted Vale in search of fallen shards from their first home. After a great journey, they recovered five shards, and from this, High Prince Rafael extracted ore enough to craft five mystical weapons: the Sword of the Protector, the Hammer of Hope, the Trident of Honor, the Lance of Valor, and, most powerful of all, the Bow of Radiance. Aurelia put an enchantment on all five weapons so that they could only be used by someone who possessed one of the queen's tokens, necklaces blessed by her magic. Without a token, anyone attempting to wield the weapons would find their blood turning to rot. Aurelia gifted the weapons to her loyal high rulers, keeping the bow for herself. With the aid of these divine weapons as well as the Queen's Army, a dedicated force of soldiers, Aurelia was able to keep her realms protected.

Sira's forces were defeated, but her spirit was more enraged than ever. Sira turned to a new source to try to regain power. With dark and perverse magic, Sira was able to open windows between the worlds. She used these to seek a greater power than any in the Enchanted Vale. In her search, she found Malekai Furiondemius, Baron of the Green Flame, a godlike entity who traversed the paths between universes, conquering whatever lands he desired. Though

Sira's window was not powerful enough for the Baron to step within this world, he began to fill her mind with ambitions. Together, they designed plans to claim the Enchanted Vale for their own.

As the Gloaming War finally came to an end, Aurelia bade the Queen's Army return to the monastery they called home and recalled the divine weapons, for they were only to be used in times of war. The only exception was the Sword of the Protector, which she allowed High Princess Elowyn of Winter to keep. She named the High Princess of Winter Sworn Protector of the Realms, with the instructions that if she were ever unable to rule as queen, the Sworn Protector of the Realms would serve the Vale in her place.

Aurelia's closest confidants reported that she had lamented that the centuries ruling the Vale and the memories of battle weighed heavily on her.

AGE OF THE MISSING QUEEN

1025–1450

Queen Aurelia disappeared. Although grief blanketed the lands with the loss of the beloved queen, four new high rulers inherited the realms: High Prince Erivor of Winter, High Princess Isidora of Spring, High Princess Sabine of Summer, and High Princess Niamh of Autumn. The realms maintained stability and peace. Four princes were also born during this age: Keldarion of Winter, Ezryn of Spring, Daytonales of Summer, and Farron of Autumn.

In the Below, Sira was lost to her envy of Aurelia's beautiful realms and creations. She desired above all else to create the perfect entity: a child of her very own, one who would put the rest of the world to shame. After beseeching the Baron, he granted her greatest wish, impregnating her with a child: a fae of the Below and of the Green Flame.

Growing up in the Below, Sira's young son, Caspian, was raised to inherit his father's magic, the power of the Green Flame. With Aurelia gone, Sira turned her attention to her new goal: finding a power that would allow her to open a gateway between this world and the Baron's so Caspian's father could step through and join them. Sira envisioned a future where she, Malekai, and Caspian ruled not only the Below but the surface realms as well. She even dreamed of rebuilding the Above and ruling the land that once shunned her.

Though full-out war was avoided, tensions remained high between the Below and the surface realms. High Prince Erivor of Winter and his wife, Princess Runa, devised a plan to incapacitate the Below's forces. They intended to take back the rose that Sira once stole from the Gardens of Ithilias. Without such power, the Queen of the Below would no longer be able to create her monsters.

Erivor and Runa's valiant attempt ultimately failed. Although they were successful at gaining the rose, they were ambushed before they were able to escape the Below. Erivor and Runa survived the attack; however, the rose was lost. Without the rose in her control, Sira's power was significantly weakened, and many of her creations became feral, no longer answering to any master.

Meanwhile, Sira's young son lived within the boundaries of his birthright: as half his blood was tied to a demigod from another world, Caspian was not able to stray far from the Below. He tested these limits as much as possible, including visiting the human world, where he was befriended by a young couple with secrets of their own. Caspian developed the mysterious ability that would one day become his namesake: control over thorns.

In Summer, High Princess Sabine passed Summer's blessing and the title of high ruler to her eldest son, Damocles.

AGE OF THE WAR OF THORNS

1450–1501

High Princess Isidora died while passing Spring's blessing to her eldest son, Ezryn. Prince Ezryn inherited the throne of Spring.

Sira, enraged by the loss of the rose and her lack of power, devised a plan to not only find the rose but weaken the surface realms forever. She sent her now grown son Caspian undercover to gain the trust of the four realms while secretly doing her bidding.

During a fateful Rainbow Eclipse Festival held at Castletree, Caspian appeared at the door, distraught and hurt. He implored the high rulers to take pity on him, despite the fact that he was well known as the son of the Queen of the Below. Claiming to have escaped his mother's clutches, he promised intelligence and aid to the surface realms in their plight against the Below. As Sworn Protector of the Realms, High Prince Erivor chose to imprison Caspian.

However, Erivor's son, Keldarion, desired to trust the Prince of the Below and convinced his father to set Caspian free—under his watch, of course. Keldarion, eager to prove his worth, believed Caspian could have the answers to many of the problems they faced. The young Winter Prince desperately wanted to succeed at the mission his parents had failed at: retrieving the stolen rose that was lost somewhere in the Below.

Caspian began to immerse himself in Keldarion's life, attending functions with him, training alongside him, and even befriending Keldarion's companions, the princes from the other realms. Keldarion's most trusted ally, the High Prince of Spring, however, never warmed to Caspian. The Prince of the Below played his role dutifully, assisting Keldarion but also secretly using his thorns to return to the Below, reporting to Sira. Though Keldarion attempted to maintain a strictly neutral relationship with Caspian, the tenacious spirit of the mysterious Prince of the Below captivated him. Little by little, harsh words gave way to lingering glances, and talks of strategy became long conversations late into the night.

However, Keldarion was betrothed to Lady Tilla of Spring. On the day of their wedding, he fled the altar. He was intercepted by Caspian, where the two admitted their feelings for each other and were intimate for the first time. While this occurred, the Below launched an attack on the capital of the Winter Realm, Frostfang. Caspian was blamed for the attack and banished from the surface realms.

Against the wishes and advice of all those around him, Keldarion refused to believe Caspian would betray him. He followed Caspian to the Below where they decided to continue working together to find the lost rose. Keldarion took up residence in Cryptgarden. The persistent feelings and newfound intimacy between Caspian and Keldarion continued to grow. Within each other, they found solace and a connection like neither had experienced before. As their search for the rose persisted, passion and partnership evolved into a loving relationship.

In Autumn, High Princess Niamh passed Autumn's blessing to her eldest son, Farron.

Down Below, Keldarion and Caspian made a fae bargain of everlasting love, with the fateful words, "Let me take no other but you. If one day, my vow shall prove false and I lie with another, let them serve you in repentance until you tire of them as I did your heart. And if ever there is no love between us, let this bargain melt away like snow under rain." This particular bargain was specific in its terms that it could not be rescinded; it would only break if no love remained between the two. Under the terms, should either of the fae princes lie with another, that person would magically be sent to the other and fall into a thralldom, intent only to serve the one who had been betrayed until they said otherwise.

Desperate not to lose her son's allegiance, Sira took Caspian to visit the Fates so that he could see the pain Keldarion would cause him in the future.

Despite the vision, the Prince of the Below and the Prince of Winter continued their mission and were ultimately successful: they found the lost rose. Keldarion organized an elaborate celebration in Frostfang.

Worried that she was losing control over Caspian, Sira decided to organize a betrayal of her own son but wanted to frame the surface realms. She planted a member of her inner circle in the Winter army and had them pose as a loyal soldier. Then she had her servant reveal condemning information to Keldarion's closest confidant, High Prince Ezryn, outlining Caspian's true allegiance to the Below. Ezryn took Keldarion's army and attacked Cryptgarden, destroying much of the city. Keldarion led the army away and told Caspian there was a mistake and the soldiers had arrived at his command, unwilling to reveal that Ezryn had ordered the attack. Distraught, Caspian still agreed to attend the celebration.

At the great celebration when Caspian was supposed to be recognized for his loyalty to the surface realms and for retrieving the lost rose, the Prince of the Below ordered a vicious attack against the capital. Princess Runa of Winter was murdered during the siege, Frostfang was occupied, and Prince Keldarion was kidnapped. Thus began the War of Thorns.

Battles scoured the land. Autumn faced a deadly fight against a goblin force that ended with a mudslide destroying both armies. The Great Scriptorium of Alder was destroyed during an attack on Coppershire. Spring was able to hold its borders, but nearly the entire royal family of Summer, save Prince Daytonales and Princess Delphia, were killed during a siege of Hadria, the capital of Summer. Prince Daytonales inherited the blessing of Summer. High Prince Ezryn of Spring rescued Keldarion from his imprisonment in the Below.

High Prince Erivor led a valiant assault on Frostfang with intentions to liberate his people. He successfully recaptured the city but was felled in the process. Keldarion inherited the blessing of Winter and the title of Sworn Protector of the Realms.

With newfound power, Keldarion sought revenge against his old ally, the newly dubbed Prince of Thorns, Caspian. With incredible power, the two fought across the Anelkrol Badlands. The battle caused massive damage to the area, including the creation of the Great Chasm, a deep and vast canyon that revealed tunnels straight to the Below. The rose was caught in the turmoil and destroyed.

Ultimately, the surface realms were victorious. Caspian and Sira survived the war and returned defeated to Cryptgarden.

A year passed with Castletree being overseen by the four young high rulers: Keldarion of Winter, Ezryn of Spring, Daytonales of Summer, and Farron of Autumn. Recovering from the war, the realms lacked true leadership as all four of the high rulers struggled to rise to their positions.

AGE OF THE CURSE

1501–1526

An enchantress appeared at Castletree and cursed the four high princes for their negligence. The curse forced the princes to spend each night in the form of hideous beasts as well as tying their life forces to four enchanted roses. The more time passed, the more the roses wilted. If the roses were to die completely, the curse on the princes would be complete, trapping them as beasts forever. Ashamed and hopeless, the four princes hid away, waiting for the day they could break their curse: when they found their fated mate and that person accepted the bond. Stewards were appointed to rule the four realms in the princes' absence.

Down Below, Sira adopted a child and raised her as her own. Ever ambitious, Sira discovered the curse and once again saw an opportunity to claim the Enchanted Vale for herself. Slowly, she began to put plans in place for her complete and utter takeover. Caspian grew a great briar bush around Castletree, causing the Queen's Realm to become known as the Briar. His thorns wrapped around the once-powerful tree and were believed to suck the vitality from its roots.

AGE OF THE ROSE

1526—

A young woman from the human realm discovered the Enchanted Vale and found herself at Castletree…

Dramatis Personae

ROSALINA O'CONNELL

daughter of George and Anya, fated mate and wife of Keldarion, and fated mate of Ezryn, Daytonales, Farron, and Caspian

Curious and wistful, Rosalina O'Connell spent her first twenty-six years living in Orca Cove, a small town in the human world. When her father went missing, Rosalina accidentally wandered into the Enchanted Vale while searching for him. After finding herself imprisoned by a fae prince, High Prince Keldarion of Winter, Rosalina bargained, wiled, and worked her way to freedom, finding peace and acceptance in the fae realm. She later discovered she was half-fae and daughter to the missing queen of the Enchanted Vale. Rosalina is fated mates with all four of the high princes, as well as the Prince of Thorns, Caspian. She married Keldarion in the Winter Realm before the magic of a bargain made between Keldarion and Caspian whisked her away to the Below, where she is currently Caspian's thrall.

GEORGE O'CONNELL

husband to Anya and father of Rosalina and Wrenley

An accomplished archaeologist, George O'Connell lost his wife, Anya, twenty-six years ago and has spent most of Rosalina's life searching for her. This obsession caused him to be an absent father. When George found his way to the Enchanted Vale, it set him on course to make amends with his daughter while finding clues to his wife's whereabouts. George has developed a strange illness and sense of forgetfulness. He is working on reassembling the fragments of a magical rose once stolen from the Gardens of Ithilias, which may turn the tides of the war.

ANYA O'CONNELL/QUEEN AURELIA

wife to George and mother of Rosalina and Wrenley

Anya went missing twenty-six years ago. She is said to have been an outspoken and free-spirited woman who loved her work as an anthropologist and was known to collect trinkets from around the world. Rosalina has discovered that Anya is also Queen Aurelia, the queen of the Enchanted Vale. Aurelia is known for creating the Enchanted Vale, her immense bravery, and her love of language. She disappeared five hundred years ago and is currently Sira's prisoner in the Below.

SIRA

Queen of the Below, mother of Caspian and the Nightingale

One of the first fae who hailed from the Above, Sira coveted the ability to create. She is responsible for stealing a rose from the Gardens of Ithilias, creating monstrous creatures such as goblins, and waging war on the Above. She rules from her tower in the Below, forging dark pacts with a god from a different world and raising her two children: her son and her adopted daughter.

CASPIAN

the Prince of Thorns, son of Sira and Malekai Furiondemius, brother to Wrenley and fated mate of Rosalina

Child of the Queen of the Below and an evil god from another world, Caspian has never felt a sense of belonging. He strives to manipulate others to maintain a sense of control in a life where he has almost none. Caspian has the ability to control thorns, a power only wielded by three others in history: Queen Aurelia, Rosalina O'Connell, and his adopted sister, the Nightingale. Hated by many fae of the surface realms, Caspian has caused his share of chaos, including several supposed betrayals against Keldarion and the creation of the Great Chasm. Caspian has lost himself to the Green Flame and is currently keeping Rosalina as his thrall as he plans to dominate the entire Vale.

WRENLEY

the Nightingale, adopted daughter of Sira, adopted sister to Caspian, daughter of George and Anya, sister to Rosalina, and fated mate of Kairyn

Wrenley was born to Aurelia, the queen of the Enchanted Vale, while she was imprisoned by Sira. Due to a bargain made by Aurelia, Wrenley is forced under Sira's command. Dubbed "the Nightingale," Wrenley becomes a vicious assassin, helping to fulfil Sira's nefarious plans. Prince Kairyn of Spring is a close ally to Wrenley. She has a tumultuous relationship with Rosalina, her estranged sister. After destroying the Bow of Radiance, Wrenley disappeared.

KELDARION

High Prince of Winter, Sworn Protector of the Realms, son of Erivor and Runa, and fated mate and husband of Rosalina

Keldarion first received Winter's blessing during the War of Thorns. The majority of his reign has occurred while residing at Castletree, as he was cursed only a year after his coronation. Though known for his temper and standoffish nature, Keldarion has proven he will do anything to protect those he loves, even if he has to destroy himself in the process. After Frostfang was nearly destroyed by the Prince of Thorns, Keldarion finally realized what he needed to do. He wed the love of his life, Rosalina, and consummated their relationship, thus breaking his curse and coming into his true power. Though this turned Rosalina into the Prince of Thorns's thrall and sent her to the Below, Keldarion has faith that his wife will save herself and Caspian.

ERIVOR

late High Prince of Winter, husband of
Runa and father of Keldarion

Erivor was a renowned leader to the citizens of not only Winter but all the realms. He was felled during the War of Thorns while leading the force that would eventually recapture Frostfang.

RUNA

late Princess of Winter, wife of Erivor, and mother to Keldarion

Runa was lauded for her wisdom and beauty. Stories say icy rain fell across all the lands of Winter when she was killed during the siege of Frostfang.

IRAHN

warden of Voidseal Bridge, brother of
Runa, and uncle to Keldarion

Irahn lived in the wilds of Winter as the warden of Voidseal Bridge. He was killed by Sira during the Battle of Voidseal Bridge.

EZRYN

former High Prince of Spring, son of Isidora and Thalionor, brother to Kairyn, and fated mate of Rosalina

Ezryn was once a famed warrior across the Vale. He was praised for his martial prowess as well as his talent for command in battle. Ezryn dutifully served under both his parents. High Princess Isidora willingly passed Spring's blessing to her son. Unfortunately, overcome with the new power within him, Ezryn accidentally killed his mother in the process. While living at Castletree, Ezryn was cursed by the Enchantress for the malice he bore in his heart. Years later, Ezryn fell in love with Rosalina and discovered she was his fated mate. When the curse began to break, he was once again overcome with power; his fear of losing Rosalina as he did his mother only caused the magic to grow more out of control. After destroying Spring's sacred grove and nearly killing Rosalina, Ezryn was arrested by his own soldiers. His throne was usurped by his brother, and he was banished from Spring. Ezryn has traveled around the Vale, offering restitution for the pain he has caused. During the Battle of Voidseal Bridge, he finally found forgiveness for himself, broke his curse, and reclaimed the blessing of Spring.

ISIDORA

late High Princess of Spring, wife and fated mate of Thalionor, and mother to Ezryn and Kairyn

Isidora was the beloved High Princess of Spring. She wore a helm of starlight silver and wielded a broadsword of the same metal. Though she had a stern and imposing disposition, it is said she was the only one to show true empathy and understanding to her youngest son, Kairyn. It was with great pride and resolve that she passed her blessing to Ezryn, believing he would be the greatest leader Spring had ever seen, though she was not able to see that wish come to fruition.

THALIONOR

late Prince of Spring, husband and fated mate to Isidora, and father to Ezryn and Kairyn

Thalionor was known as a powerful soldier and inspiring commander. However, after the death of his fated mate, Thalionor succumbed to his grief, unable to serve as steward of Spring without the assistance of the majordomo Eldor. Eventually, Thalionor's state worsened, and he developed strange physical symptoms. He was killed by Caspian, an act Ezryn has sworn revenge against the Prince of Thorns for.

KAIRYN

High Prince of Spring, Emperor of the Green Rule, son of Isidora and Thalionor, brother to Ezryn, and fated mate of Wrenley

Kairyn always lived in his brother Ezryn's shadow. Quiet and introspective, Kairyn was never the soldier or leader his brother was. After witnessing their mother's death at Ezryn's hand, grief drove Kairyn to challenge him in the rite, a duel that ended in Kairyn's defeat and exile to Queen's Reach Monastery. There, he uncovered the corruption of the high clerics and met Wrenley, a woman from the Below who offered him the glory and acceptance he craved. With her aid, he overthrew the clerics, rose to power, and later usurped Ezryn's throne. His ambitions turned to Summer, but he lost everything when Dayton reclaimed Hadria. Shamed, Kairyn returned to the Below. When Wrenley vanished soon after, Kairyn spiraled into despair and became a hollow servant to Sira. She eventually transformed him into an underfae as a show of loyalty to Faustrius. Rosalina, Ezryn, and the princes of Castletree freed him and took Kairyn back into their care. Now, Kairyn seeks redemption by helping George reassemble the magical rose from the Gardens of Ithilias.

DAYTONALES

High Prince of Summer, son of Sabine, Ovidius, and Cenarius, brother to Damocles, Decimus, and Delphia, and fated mate to Rosalina

Daytonales, referred to as Dayton by his friends, never thought he would be the High Prince of Summer. As a third-born son, he spent his days enjoying fights in the arena, drink, and the companionship of beautiful people. However, after most of his family was killed in the War of Thorns, Dayton was forced to assume the title. Deemed a drunk and a dullard, Dayton hid away in Castletree, allowing his young sister to serve as steward. Dayton was cursed by the Enchantress for his avoidance. However, Dayton's relationship with Farron and Rosalina has reminded him there are things worth fighting for. With the help of Rosalina, the high princes, and the citizens of Summer, Dayton reclaimed his throne from the Green Rule. However, he was killed in the aftermath by Wrenley. Farron resurrected him using the Green Flame. Dayton struggled with this realization and with Farron's reliance on this insidious magic.

SABINE

late High Princess of Summer, wife of Ovidius and Cenarius, and mother to Damocles, Decimus, Daytonales, and Delphia

Sabine was a descendant of the Huntresses of Aura and the former High Princess of Summer before she passed the blessing to her eldest son, Damocles. Sabine was known for her fierce love for her husbands and children as well as her fearless nature. She was killed amid the siege of Hadria during the War of Thorns. Many say her spirit still shines in her daughter, Delphia.

OVIDIUS

late Prince of Summer, husband of Sabine, partner to Cenarius, and father to Damocles, Decimus, Daytonales, and Delphia

Ovidius was a great warrior, a stern man who loved his family fiercely. He was killed amid the siege of Hadria during the War of Thorns.

CENARIUS

late Prince of Summer, husband of Sabine, partner to Ovidius, and father to Damocles, Decimus, Daytonales, and Delphia

Cenarius was beloved across the realm for his ability to light up a battlefield, a tavern, or a strategy meeting with a joke or song. He was killed amid the siege of Hadria during the War of Thorns.

DAMOCLES

late High Prince of Summer, son of Sabine, Ovidius, and Cenarius, and brother to Decimus, Daytonales, and Delphia

Damocles was a legendary hero of the Enchanted Vale. Some said he was the most powerful warrior to walk the realms. A serious and determined leader, he loved his family and wished to see them achieve the glory he knew they were capable of. He took particular interest in Dayton, wishing him to reach his full potential. Damocles never shied away from a fight and always resolved to face battles head-on. He was killed amid the siege of Hadria during the War of Thorns.

DECIMUS

late Prince of Summer, son of Sabine, Ovidius, and Cenarius, and brother to Damocles, Daytonales, and Delphia

Like his older brother, Decimus was a great warrior and skilled gladiator in the arena. He often had a playful rivalry with his younger brother, Dayton. He was killed amid the siege of Hadria during the War of Thorns.

DELPHIA

Princess and steward of Summer, daughter of Sabine, Ovidius, and Cenarius, and sister to Damocles, Decimus, and Daytonales

The youngest-born of the four royal families across the seasonal realms, Delphia was only a small child when most of her family perished in the War of Thorns. With her brother residing in Castletree, she was forced to serve as a child steward of Summer. Such responsibility has made Delphia wise beyond her years, though she still possesses the boldness of her parents and brothers. She became close friends with Eleanor when the young Autumn Princess served as a ward of Summer.

FARRON

High Prince of Autumn, son of Niamh and Padraig, brother to Dominic, Billagin, and Eleanor, and fated mate of Rosalina

Farron was a reluctant leader when his mother first passed the blessing of Autumn to him. He carries the weight of many failures in leadership during the War of Thorns and was cursed by the Enchantress for his cowardice. However, Farron learned the strength of his heart through his love for Daytonales and his fated mate, Rosalina. With Rosalina's love, Farron was able to break his curse and help his people. After his mother perished in a battle outside Coppershire, Farron has become anxious about losing more of his loved ones. He traveled with Caspian to the Below where he met Malekai Furiondemius, Baron of the Green Flame, and accepted a mysterious power. With this new magic, he was able to bring Dayton back to life. Now, Malekai Furiondemius lives in Farron's head, reminding him exactly what the cost of such magic is.

NIAMH

late High Princess and steward of Autumn, wife of Padraig, and mother to Farron, Dominic, Billagin, and Eleanor

The former High Princess of Autumn, Niamh believed her son Farron would be a great ruler and willingly passed the blessing on to him. She served as steward during his reign but was still treated as the true ruler and held the loyalty of the people. She died in battle but was able to see her son become the leader she knew he could be.

PADRAIG

Prince and steward of Autumn, husband of Niamh, and father to Farron, Dominic, Billagin, and Eleanor

Jovial and lighthearted, Padraig is both a talented war commander and a loving family man. After the death of his beloved wife, Padraig assumed the role of steward to assist his son in ruling Autumn and does everything he can to protect his people.

DOMINIC

Prince of Autumn, son of Niamh and Padraig, and brother to Farron, Billagin, and Eleanor

A young prince, Dominic is the twin brother of Billagin. The brothers have had to learn to defend themselves in times of strife. They have trained to be spies and now pride themselves on their skills at navigating deadly terrains, even the Briar.

BILLAGIN

Prince of Autumn, son of Niamh and Padraig, and brother to Farron, Dominic, and Eleanor

Dominic's twin brother, Billagin tries to maintain an optimistic attitude, even in times of peril. The twins were entrusted with leading George O'Connell across the realms in search of his missing wife. When George fell ill, they dutifully saw him back to Coppershire and watched over him.

ELEANOR

Princess of Autumn, daughter of Niamh and Padraig,
and sister to Farron, Dominic, and Billagin

The youngest member of the Autumn royal family, Eleanor, or "Nori," serves as a ward in Summer. Fascinated with the macabre, Nori often gets herself in trouble when she conducts arcane experiments. Close friends with Delphia, the two princesses rely on each other when the rest of the world seems against them.

MARIGOLD OF SPRING

A proud and boisterous woman, Marigold once directly served High Princess Isidora and helped raise Ezryn and Kairyn. Now, she serves at Castletree. Before she was freed from the curse, Marigold spent her nights as a raccoon. She loves Rosalina fiercely and will do anything she can to help her. Marigold has reconnected with her old flame, Eldor.

ASTRID OF WINTER

Despite once being cursed to turn into a hare at night, nothing can dim Astrid's upbeat attitude. She is proud of her position at Castletree and loyally serves Keldarion and the other princes. Astrid was Rosalina's first friend at Castletree and continues to be her close confidante.

ELDOR OF SPRING

The majordomo of Keep Hammergarden in Spring, Eldor, or "Eldy," dutifully serves the royal family of Spring. During Thalionor's stewardship, Eldy completed the majority of tasks as Thalionor was suffering with the grief of his wife's death. With Rosalina's help, Eldy was able to escape the occupation of Florendel by the Green Rule and now lives at Castletree with his beloved, Marigold.

FAUSTRIUS, LEADER OF THE ELDERBLOOD

One of the first fae of the Above, Faustrius followed Sira down to the new world she created, the Below. He allowed her to turn him into an underfae. He and his people were not accepted on the surface and the first high prince of Winter froze them all in ice. The Elderblood were broken free when Caspian and Kel created the Great Chasm. Now, Faustrius seeks vengeance for his people and has allied himself with Sira.

AQUILA, PRIESTESS OF THE ELDERBLOOD

Aquila once worshiped the stars before she chose to follow Sira down to the Below. Now one of the underfae, Aquila serves as Faustrius's second-in-command. They desperately wish to reclaim the rose stolen from the Gardens of Ithilias so no one can ever use it to steal their wills.

PART 1

thrall

PROLOGUE

West bank of the Nile, outside Luxor

1905

FRANCIS SHIFTED THE WEIGHT OF THE BRASS VASE IN HIS ARMS, SWEAT running down his spine like the Nile itself. He could hardly breathe. It wasn't just the desert heat that made the air thick down here; it was the dust, the smell of old stone and things that should've stayed buried. The flickering torchlight stretched shadows high up the carved walls, granting the painted figures an eerie, shifting life.

Around him, the salvagers laughed and jostled each other, as careless with the treasures as they were with the cards and whiskey they spent their nights on. But they'd promised Francis a share of the profit if he helped them carry things, so he tried not to complain too much.

Clyde Webb, the ringleader, had a face of sun-beaten leather and a silver watch he never took off, as if that gave him some kind of fancy shine that made him worth respecting. He was the only one with a gun, and that made him king down here. His right hand, Roy Berker, round-faced and always chewing something, had been prying out gold inlays from the shattered coffin and stuffing them into a burlap sack.

The man tied up across the chamber wasn't laughing.

"You don't understand what you're doing!" Grover—or was it Glenn?—strained against his ropes. He was one of the fancy archaeologists they'd found digging up this spot. "This tomb belongs to history. You're desecrating the final resting place of Horemheb—"

Clyde snorted, inspecting a gilded mask before tossing it onto the growing pile. The shadows seemed to crawl over him like a snake. "Never heard of him."

Francis hadn't either. Didn't care to. The past wasn't worth much when you were scraping by in the present. Clyde explained it all, simple and true. They were actually *helping* the archaeologists, who would stuff all this junk behind a glass box only to have rich people stare at it. But if *they* took it, then it would be of real benefit to real men. Honest, hardworking men like Clyde.

And if Francis didn't complain and carried his weight, he'd get a whole two percent of the profits.

A gust of air stirred the dust by the entrance, and Francis glanced up. He didn't like being underground, thinking of all that sand above him. They'd descended so many steps, it felt as if they could have gone all the way to the center of the earth the way Mr. Verne went on about.

Another gust of wind blew back his thick, copper hair. It smelled fresh, nothing like the air down here. Was someone up there?

There'd been two other people with the archaeologist: a little boy a few years younger than Francis, maybe twelve at the oldest. And a woman. He'd only seen a flash of her as she slipped away, but she'd been beautiful, with enormous eyes, long brown hair…

Well, at least the woman and the kid had escaped. Clyde only needed one of them to tell him if any more treasure existed in these parts. Had she and the boy come back? If so, they were idiots. Nothing a woman and a little boy could do against three grown men.

Francis shifted the sack of loot higher on his shoulder as Clyde jerked the archaeologist up by the ropes around his wrists. "Time to go, Professor," Clyde said. "We've got enough to take a load up."

Roy slung a bundle over his back. "Should gut this place proper before we move on. Could get another few rounds of treasure."

"This could be Horemheb's tomb!" the archaeologist—Gus? Maybe his name was Gus—red-faced and furious, yelled. "The evidence in this tomb could help the theory that Horemheb was the one who restored Egypt's religious beliefs after the Amarna period. And I don't think I need to describe the enormity of that prospect. It was when Akhenaten promoted a cultlike worship of Aten instead of the—"

"Sure, sure." Clyde cut him off with a wave of his hand. "A real important dead guy. Not so important they bothered to write about him in the paper though."

Francis sighed and followed them up the sloping tunnel, away from the flickering torchlight and into the cool bite of evening. As he stepped out, the desert stretched before him, endless and quiet, all burnt orange fading into blue. The wind hissed through the dunes. He didn't enjoy it out here. His eyes landed on what he liked the least.

The columns.

They jutted from the sand like something out of a story, half-unearthed, half-lost, their surfaces carved with strange figures with too-long arms and animals for heads. The light of the setting sun turned them copper, while the moon washed their edges silver.

It didn't sit right with Francis. How had one man, one woman, and a kid managed to dig this much out? The sand in this part of the valley had swallowed people whole. And yet somehow, they'd dragged a king back into the world, only to have Clyde and his crew turn him into a payday.

"Drat," Clyde said, spinning around and patting his shirt pocket. "Watch must have slipped off while we were down there."

"The boy can go and get it." Roy roughly ruffled Francis's hair. "His legs aren't tired yet."

Francis sighed. His legs *were* tired, turned near jelly. How many times were they going to go in and out of this tomb? There was still a lot of treasure down there.

A few yards away, the camel shifted on its tether, stamping at the sand. Lanky, dune-colored, and moody, she eyed the horizon with disdain. The archaeologist gave her a sad look. "Cleo," he muttered under his breath.

Clyde snorted. "You name all your camels after queens, Professor?"

Gerald—yes, it was definitely Gerald—set his jaw. "Just the ones with more dignity than you."

Francis bit the inside of his cheek to stop from smiling. Foolish move, talking back to Clyde, but he had to admit, he liked Gerald's spirit.

"George!"

A sharp cry split the air, and all Francis could wonder was *Who the dickens is George?*

"Anya!" the archaeologist—Gerald, or George, Francis supposed—yelled.

The woman appeared at the edge of the rocks, her hair wild, her boots kicking up sand as she sprinted toward them.

She wasn't armed. No rifle, no knife, nothing but fire in her eyes.

Fear pricked through Francis regardless.

George turned to him, Clyde, and Roy. "You're all fucked now."

Anya threw something small and metal, glinting silver in the moonlight. It landed with a clatter at Clyde's feet. A coin? No. A pocket watch. Clyde's pocket watch.

Cleo reared up, braying and thrashing against her tether. She must have been spooked, maybe by the watch, maybe by Anya's sudden charge, but in the chaos, the rope snapped, and one thousand pounds of furious camel bolted straight for Clyde.

The salvagers shouted, scrambling back as the beast barreled forward.

Damn, she's clever, Francis thought.

But where was the boy? Francis looked around, then spotted a smudge behind a nearby pillar. The little boy. There was something strange about him. He wore his dark hair too long, brushing his shoulders like a girl. And his eyes…they weren't a color Francis'd ever seen before. Purple as a violet sunset.

Francis averted his gaze, a chill shuddering through him.

He should tell Clyde the boy kept hovering around…but what harm could a little kid do?

Anya darted toward George.

The gunshot cracked through the air before Francis saw Clyde raise the revolver.

Anya's body jerked, then she collapsed to her knees. She pressed a hand to her side, fingers coming away dark with blood.

George screamed, the sound raw. Francis's stomach twisted.

It just wasn't right to shoot a woman, even a crazy one like her.

Clyde barely spared her a glance. "Damn fool," he muttered. He kicked his watch aside, reloading his gun.

Francis swallowed hard, shifting on his feet.

The desert was still again.

Except for Anya, who closed her eyes, muttering to herself, hand clasped over her wound.

Clyde strode up to Anya, pressed the barrel of his rifle to her head. "Now, you gonna behave, broad? Let Roy put those ropes on your wrist, and we'll think about letting you live."

Anya heaved in a ragged breath, still clutching her wound. Roy marched forward, tugging a rope between two meaty hands.

"Get away from her." A voice cut through the night air as the little boy stepped out from behind a pillar.

Fear curled through Francis. Fear he couldn't explain. He

dropped his bag and staggered back. It didn't make sense. He was just a boy, younger than him.

Clyde and Roy didn't appear afraid though. All they did was laugh. "Go sit like a good boy beside your father," Clyde sneered, "and maybe you won't experience your first beating."

They turned to where George had been tied up—but he was gone. Francis's eyes widened. George was now standing next to Cleo, a knife in his hand, ropes cut. He raced toward them, arm pulled back, and slugged Roy in the face.

"I'd rethink that if I were you." George's voice was low, deadly.

"Want to get shot too, tough guy?" Clyde raised his weapon, his hands shaking a little. He tilted it to the little boy, still standing eerily still. "Or better yet, your son?"

The little boy quirked his head. "That's not my father," he said softly. "My father is… Yes, Father. We could."

"Caspian, no!" Anya snapped her eyes open, panic crossing her face for the first time. "I'm alright. See? I'm alright."

But the boy—Caspian—wasn't looking at her. He'd closed his eyes, muttering to himself.

"Caspian!" Anya screamed and sprang up. She moved her hand away from her side. The wound didn't look as bad as Francis had first thought.

"I said to stay down, woman," Clyde roared, grabbing her by the shoulders.

"And I said to get away from her," Caspian said. He opened his eyes. They weren't that violet sunset anymore. They were green.

And, by grace, they were glowing.

Clyde screamed, stumbling from Anya as green flame erupted

across his hands and surged up his arm. Flesh blistered and peeled away, revealing stark white bone. His screams turned ragged. He dropped to his knees, the fire devouring him. He threw his head back, his silhouette flashing white-hot before the flames vanished, leaving only a heap of bones and ash.

Francis hadn't even had time to blink.

"W-what is this?" Roy stammered, wiping his nose from where George had slugged him. "A curse? The mummy's curse? Please help me, God, I—"

Caspian stepped forward, eyes still glowing. "Your gods can't help you now."

More of those flames sprouted at Roy's feet.

Francis had never seen that color of fire before. He stumbled back, head shifting from side to side, but there was nowhere to go, nothing but an empty desert.

But surely that would be better than here.

Roy's scream, choked and broken, sounded almost worse than Clyde's. Francis was closer to Roy than he had been to Clyde. Close enough to see how Roy's flesh bubbled and burst as the flames crawled up his arm.

Crawled so slowly.

He's making sure he suffers, Francis realized. Confirmed it when he saw the cruel, satisfied smile on the boy's face.

"Caspian, stop! This isn't you," Anya snarled. She faced the archaeologist. "Hurry. Get Cleo."

The boy ignored her, focused on Roy. Francis had to get out of here before the kid finished off Roy and turned to Francis for his next plaything.

"Enough!" Anya roared. Something broke out of the sand around the boy. Giant snakes. No, not snakes. Vines, beautiful vines, blooming with golden roses. They shot toward the boy.

He raised a hand. Flames leapt from them, spitting onto the briars, wilting the roses and turning the vines to dust in an instant. "This doesn't concern you."

Francis started to run, but the first step he took, his leg sank knee-deep in the sand. He attempted to scream but inhaled a mouthful of dust, then he couldn't see.

The sand around him was *moving*. He tried to quell his panic. Away. He had to get away.

He fought his way through the storm, but the sand swallowed his steps, dragging him deeper. His footing gave, and he slid, sliding back down to the center.

A flash lit up his vision. Probably not a good sign. But like a moth drawn to candle flame, his eyes were drawn to the light. He came upon Roy, just as the flames were devouring his face.

Francis threw up in his mouth. He was next, no doubt about it.

There was so much sand swirling about, he couldn't find a path. He ran, smacked into a pillar. His head ached, vision swimming.

Then he saw what was in the eye of the storm—Caspian, the little boy. He stood at the squall's heart, screaming. Or laughing. Francis wasn't sure. Flames circled him too, but they didn't seem to devour him like they had Clyde and Roy. These flames appeared to be dancing with joy.

A powerful wind lifted Francis off his feet. He gripped the pillar, digging into the old carvings to keep from getting dragged away and swallowed by the sand.

There was a flash in the air, not green light but gold. A woman.

Not a woman. An angel, with wings of pure radiance.

An angel come to save him.

He blinked, and she was gone. But now the woman Anya was in front of the boy, a hand shielding her eyes as she took deliberate steps toward him.

"Get away," the boy cried, panic lacing his words, then slower, softer, "The world belongs to the Green Flame."

"That is not what you desire, Caspian," Anya said, kneeling before him. "That is not your heart talking."

The wind picked up, so strong, Francis could barely hold on to the pillar. It pulled in great waves from the surrounding dunes, sliding sand down into the entrance of the tomb, burying it. *At least I won't have to climb back down all those stairs.*

"You are kind and loving and brave." Anya grasped Caspian's hands.

"I can't stop this," the boy wailed. "He's in my head."

Green flames crawled up her arms too, just like Clyde. Just like Roy.

And it must have been hurting her real bad, because she grimaced and let out a pained groan. But she didn't let go of the boy's hands.

"Remember who you are, Caspian." She dropped her forehead to his, and the flames curled in her beautiful hair. "Trust yourself to find the way and..."

He was crying, Francis realized.

"I c-can't."

"Say the words, Caspian. You know them," Anya gritted out. She sounded in a lot of pain.

Sand sank faster, gathering around Francis's feet. He gripped the pillar and climbed.

"Yes, you can. I know you can," Anya yelled. "You control your own destiny."

The little boy screamed, and the sandstorm got worse. Lightning flashed within it, green lightning, and Francis couldn't see the sky anymore. But he couldn't focus on any of that. The sand kept rising, and he wasn't a very good climber.

"Trust yourself to find the way," Anya cried. "When the path is lost..."

"When the path is lost," Caspian repeated slowly, as if each word was difficult, "the journey..."

"You can do this," Anya said.

Francis took her words as his own encouragement, kicking, trying to get out of the rising sand. But his legs became trapped. He tried to kick free, couldn't.

The desert was going to swallow him whole.

Sand rose around Anya and the boy too, the flames trying to consume her, but she didn't let go of his hands.

"The journey begins..." the boy said and released a long breath. And when he blinked his eyes, they weren't green anymore. The flames were gone. Caspian shook his head. "I can't stop this storm!"

"Then we'll find our way out," George cried. He rode atop the camel, breaking through the haze. "Together!"

"George!" Anya said, standing. "You brilliant fool!"

"We'll never make it out of this!" Caspian yelled. "The sand is going to bury us."

"Don't worry, kid," George said, grabbing the back of Caspian's shirt and lifting him up. "This old girl always knows her way out of a storm."

"You and that camel," Anya scoffed but winked at him.

George put Caspian in front of him, one arm on the reins, the other wrapped protectively around the boy's waist.

As if that boy wasn't a monster who had just done...*that*...and was actually his son.

George spurred the camel forward, abandoning the woman. As for Francis, the sand was near up to his chest. As far as deaths went, suffocating beat burning, he supposed.

Someone grasped his arm, yanked him clear out of the sand. Before Francis knew what had happened, he was bouncing on the back of the camel behind the archaeologist.

"W-what are you doing?" he cried.

"We don't leave anyone behind." George reached past the boy in front of him and patted the camel's neck. "Come on, girl. You know the way."

Cleo bleated and tore through the storm.

~

Francis awoke to a crackling fire and a clear night sky. The winds had died down, and he must have passed out on the camel. What had happened?

A storm. A real bad storm.

The archaeologist sat next to the fire and stirred a pot over it. Cleo, Francis's new favorite animal, lay resting. Anya had a notebook in her lap, scribbling away. Relief flooded Francis. She'd made it back. She hadn't been on the camel, had she? And nearby, the little boy was whittling a piece of wood.

They didn't seem at all concerned that he was there.

Did any of that even happen?

"Ugh, this is awful." Caspian threw the wooden piece onto the sandy ground.

Francis peered at it, not quite ready to let these strange people know he was awake.

George placed the stew down before the boy and picked up the wooden piece. He squinted his blue eyes at it. They were mighty blue eyes. Now that Francis thought about it, this man looked too young to be the boy's dad. "This is supposed to be Cleo, right?"

"Yes," the boy mumbled. "I was going to give it to Anya, to thank her for..."

"Oh, don't be so hard on yourself." George smiled and ruffled the boy's hair in a much nicer way than Roy had ruffled Francis's. "I'd say it's rather cute. It's got character."

"Did I hear my name?" Anya placed her notebook down and went over to them.

"This is for you," Caspian muttered and wiped his nose. Something dark, maybe blood, ran from it.

Anya took the camel from George, and a huge smile appeared on her face. "I love it," she cried and embraced the boy.

He stiffened, as if he didn't know what a hug was, before he carefully wrapped his arms around her.

"Can I give you something now?" Anya asked, pulling back.

The boy nodded.

"Hold out your wrist," she said.

Caspian did, and Anya hovered her fingers over it. She had

beautiful hands, long and delicate. Everything about her shimmered with beauty. Like an angel. And by the way the archaeologist stared at her, he thought so too.

"Hold still," Anya said, and a band around the boy's wrist glowed.

Glowed with beautiful golden light.

But Francis had seen enough weird stuff today not to question it.

The light faded, and a golden bracelet appeared around the boy's wrist, inlaid with roses.

"Is this like a bargain?" Caspian gasped.

"No, it's a gift." Anya opened her palm to reveal the wooden camel. "You have shaped this. Now shape yourself, Prince of the Below. You decide what to do with the magic you bear."

The boy smiled, and he waved his hand. From the ground sprouted a briar with a purple vine and black thorns.

The next day, the family—Francis supposed even if the boy wasn't their son, they were a family—dropped him off at a port with enough money for a ticket back to England. And he was so glad about it.

But as Francis stepped onto that ship, he vowed one thing.

He was never going to rob a mummy's tomb again.

1

Rosalina

I HAVE NO NAME.

No soul.

But I have a heart.

It belongs to him.

Everything that I am belongs to him.

The Prince of Thorns.

2

Rosalina

My days in the dark are beautiful.

He is like the stars, twinkling in and out of sight, his cool radiance the only light I need.

He doesn't speak much. I long for his touch, for the feel of his skin against mine. But he's always out of reach.

Sometimes, he visits my room. It's filled with pretty things, like a bed draped in gauzy curtains and large jewels hanging from the walls that fill the space with a soft violet glow. But when he enters, it's as if even the light bows before him. I fall to my knees, pleading and sobbing for a kiss, an embrace, a touch.

He doesn't answer. He just stares, his eyes shining like emeralds.

3

Rosalina

"Do you miss the sun?"

The sun? What use do I have for the sun when the mere sound of his voice fills my entire body with heat?

It's the first thing he's said to me in…

Well now. I don't know.

It's hard to tell time in the dark. I don't sleep much. How can I sleep when I know he is so close yet out of my reach? My thoughts are utterly consumed with him. My hero. My god.

Hmm. There's a word for this.

Ah yes, that's it. It slipped my mind.

Love.

I love the Prince of Thorns. This is the single, most irrevocable truth of my spirit.

I love the Prince of Thorns.

My fork clatters to the plate, still reeling at his words. We sit at a dining table in the halls of his palace, known as the Gem. Perhaps the food is good—it's a thick stew of mushrooms and roots, topped in a bloodred sauce—but I don't taste food. It is unimportant when all my senses must be focused on him.

He smells of lavender and rich earth and appears as if carved from the moon, pale skin draped in a cloak of the darkness between the stars.

He sounds like joy feels.

As for how he tastes…

I shift my body forward, eyes fluttering shut—

The Prince of Thorns snatches my chin. My heart near tears from my chest. How he feels! How he feels is like fireworks exploding in my chest and a choir singing and—

"The sun," he says sternly. "Do you miss it?"

"No. I miss you," I breathe.

His gaze softens. "I miss you too."

I can barely contain myself. I am a panting, scrambling, tearful mess as I fall to his feet, tearing at his cloak. "Have me. I belong to you—"

He sends me back to my room.

4

Rosalina

I HAVE A FRIEND DOWN IN THE DARK. WELL, SHE'S NOT MY FRIEND—the only friend I need is the Prince of Thorns—but she tells me I'm her friend.

I suppose that's nice.

Her name is Heidigog. She's about three feet tall, with pale green skin like a sprig of sage, huge yellow eyes, and three sharp teeth that glint when she smiles.

She's a goblin.

I think the Prince of Thorns must have sent her to me. She helps me dress in the morning and always lays out the most luxurious dresses crafted of black silk brocade and jewel-toned silks. She knows how important it is that I look my best for the Prince of Thorns. I tell her that often.

Heidigog has a little stool that she stands on to comb my hair. It's comforting. Familiar.

Sometimes, we walk around the halls of the castle. She asks me if I'd like to listen to the harpists play. I say no. She asks me if I'd like to play a game of moonlight mastery. I say no. She asks me if I'd like to read in the library. I say no.

I only want to wait for the Prince of Thorns.

So we end up wandering the halls. She holds my hand as we walk, as if she's afraid I'm going to drift away. Her hand is small and warm, and she shuffles when she walks like a duckling. Her favorite place is the gardens.

"Where you come from, the gardens are all different, aren't they?" she asks. "Up-up there, you grow flowers, not stones, right? No gems at all?"

I take a few steps along the path of shattered quartz, walking deeper into the garden. It's bathed in the cold glow of an unseen light.

Sunshine. The Prince of Thorns asked me about sunshine. There's nothing such as that down here.

He asked me if I missed it.

Do I?

I shake my head, mind buzzing uncomfortably.

Here, the garden is a jungle of jewels. Plants carved from vibrant stones grow from shiny onyx soil. Clusters of ruby berries hang from twisted obsidian vines, their surfaces catching the strange light so they gleam like drops of blood. Jagged amethyst petals twine with emerald leaves. A cluster of diamond thorns rises nearby, and I fight the urge to test the sharpness of a prickle on my thumb.

There is no scent here. No perfume of daisies or lilacs, only the cold, metallic tang of mineral and stone.

Heidigog stares up at me expectantly.

Right. She asked me a question.

Flowers.

I remember flowers.

I remember a rose the same color as a blushing cherry blossom, one like the sea encapsulated, a rose the orange of a maple forest, and one as sapphire as a frozen lake. I remember golden roses blooming all around me, over my skin, along my heart—

I squeeze my eyes shut. My brain feels itchy.

"Yes, we grew flowers," I mumble.

Heidigog shuffles back and forth on her wide duck feet, scratching at her dress with long fingernails. "I used to live in the Briar before scuttling down here. Have I told you that before, hmm-hmm?"

Maybe she did. Heidigog tells me many things. I'm not a very good listener. But I'm listening now.

"Me and Brother Bugu lived out on Spring's edges, we did. Used to creep-creep close, just to look at all the bloomies. Crows, they were pretty! And the petals—soft, so soft! Like clouds on my fingers! Never gonna forget them, never ever-ever."

My face feels funny. Oh, I'm smiling. That's nice. I don't smile much, not unless the Prince of Thorns is around.

This must be a good story.

Heidigog must be a good friend.

She tells me more, about the great planters filled with blooms of red and purple and yellow flowers that sit on the windowsills of the pink houses in the Big City. I tell her of a path of cherry blossoms leading to the keep. Oh, maybe I made that up, but it sounds nice.

We walk farther into the garden. Ahead of us, at the center, a tree stands, its trunk carved from moonstone. Its branches hang heavy with dangling chains of opals and pearls.

"Pretty," I say.

I reach forward, running my fingers over one of the glistening branches. It hums beneath my touch, lifeless and living all at once.

"This is a good tree," I say quietly.

Heidigog comes up and takes my hand. "I'm as happy as a grinjaw dog with a whole hind to hear you say that. I've been thinking you don't like nothing at all. Nothing at all but His Highness!"

Oh, my brain is itchy again. Heidigog is wrong. I don't like anything else. Nothing else matters but the Prince of Thorns.

I let Heidigog lead me out of the garden but turn back once to stare at the moonstone tree. I suppose I was right before. It is a good tree.

And I know good trees.

5

Rosalina

We have nicknames for each other, Heidigog and me.

I call her "Heidi."

She calls me "Rosalina."

I don't know where she came up with it, but it's pretty. I like when she calls me Rosalina.

My name is Rosalina.

That sounds nice.

I'm sad when Heidi goes away, because then I forget.

I don't want to forget this name. It feels important.

I should write it down.

There are a few things in my room, things the Prince of Thorns didn't give to me. They are not special, just boring things that I had before my true life began.

But I think one of them was a book. A book with paper. I can write the name Heidi gave me on the paper.

I walk over to the wardrobe in my room. The bag is stashed behind all my beautiful new dresses. I pull the leather satchel out and dump the contents on my bed. A heavy book falls out, along with a pen filled with ink, a jar with some stinky cream, a hideous gray cloak, and a ridiculous stuffed toy of a lion with wings. Why do I have these things?

Men gave me these items. My stomach roils. The idea of anyone besides the Prince of Thorns fills me with disgust.

I grab the pen and open the front cover of the book.

What was I doing with this again? Writing something down.

Well, bother. Now I've forgotten. It must not be important, because the only thing important is the Prince of Thorns, and I would never forget him.

I'm about to close the book when my eye catches on the flowing script. *The Complete History of Autumn's High Rulers.*

No interest to me. Yet…

My fingers flip to the back of the book, to the final entry, searching the name. *Niamh.*

Hmm. Was I expecting to see something else?

I slam the book shut and quickly start shoveling everything into the bag. My hand lingers on the stuffed toy.

How silly. A winged lion. Perhaps the Prince of Thorns would find this sweet. Heidi certainly will. Maybe I'll keep this out. Just this one thing.

I lay it on the bed, right by my pillow.

Rosalina.

The name pops into my head all of a sudden.

Ah, right! That's what I wanted to write down. Heidi's nickname for me.

It really is too important to forget.

6

Rosalina

"I UNDERSTAND NOW," I TELL HEIDI THE NEXT MORNING AS SHE SWEEPS my hair into a tousled bun upon my head. I'm wearing a dress of black lace with a collar of multicolored jewels around my neck.

"Understand what?" she responds in that squawky tone she gets when she's concentrating.

"Why the Prince of Thorns will not have me. It's because of this." I hold up my left hand triumphantly.

Heidi narrows her yellow eyes and stares at my finger. "Because of that scrawny little grabber of yours?"

"No, because of what I'm wearing." I wiggle my fourth finger. "This ring!"

"Ah, yes-yes, pretty thing. If you want to toss it, I'll take it, oh yes!"

"No!" I snatch my hand to my chest, then lightly caress the silver band and diamond snowflake. I take a steadying breath. "Ever since I came here, I've been wearing this ring. I didn't even think about it. But of course, it's making the Prince of Thorns sad. I remembered last night that someone else gave it to me. So I need to show him I'm willing to take it off."

It had happened late at night—or what I've started to think of as night. I'd been lying in bed, arms around the winged lion toy. Sleep evaded me, which was unusual. Usually, I easily drift away with thoughts of my sweet prince. But this time, I kept swirling the ring round and round my finger. I haven't even thought about it at all since coming here. It's felt like an extension of me, like part of my own skin.

But then I remembered.

Someone else gave it to me. Someone who was *not* the Prince of Thorns.

I spend the rest of the day sitting on the edge of my bed, staring at the door. Despite Heidi's cajoling to visit the "bloomies" again, I remain rooted to the spot.

There is nothing more important than the Prince of Thorns.

I *belong* to him.

Holding my hand in front of me, fingers splayed, I examine the ring. It is a pretty thing, as Heidi said, with a delicate silver band adorned with diamond snowflakes, garnet roses, and a beautiful sapphire in the middle.

When someone uses magic, I can feel it in the air, crackling and shivering. When I move my hand *just so*, the diamonds and sapphire catch the gemlight, and it looks as if that feeling of magic was captured and trapped in the ring.

My thoughts start buzzing again, faster than ever. I squeeze my eyes shut, but it doesn't help. I can *see* things in my mind's eye, hear voices…

Fae of Winter…visitors from across the realms…

A snow-covered courtyard, filled with people looking at me.

We are gathered here today…

Arm in arm with an older man with shining eyes and the warmest smile I've ever seen.

To celebrate the union…

Three figures standing upon a dais. Their faces are shadowed, but I feel *something* radiating from them. Something familiar. Something lost.

Of High Prince Keldarion of Winter and Princess Rosalina—

Another figure comes into view. Him I can see clearly. He's the tallest man I've ever seen, with broad shoulders and long, white hair that flows down his back. His eyes shine with starlight, just like Caspian's.

This is a wedding.

My wedding.

And this *thing* on my finger is a wedding ring.

A feeling of disgust so visceral roils through me that I swear I may vomit. That fae, that *High Prince Keldarion*… How could I ever wear a symbol of his upon my body? I tug the ring off. He is nothing but a pathetic gnat in my journey to true love with the Prince of Thorns.

No wonder the Prince of Thorns has scorned me so! All this time, I've been wearing this hideous thing on my finger. I must get rid of it. Destroy it. Burn it until it melts into a puddle—

My door swings open, and the Prince of Thorns strides in.

He is resplendent in a cape of purple violet, with eyes of glowing green. Distantly, I remember that I used to think he moved like a cat. Now, he is a panther, every motion thick with a predator's confidence.

He walks over to me, close, so close, and stares down. "Your maid servant reported that you wished to speak with me."

I need to give him the ring. Need to tell him…need to tell him…

Flicking my eyes up, I hold his gaze, no matter how terrifying it is in its beauty. "My prince, I remembered something."

"Oh?" He looks to the door, his attention as fleeting as the wind.

"It's about High Prince Keldarion."

He jerks his whole body back toward me, and his lips curl. "What of Keldarion?"

"We fought him together. On the mountain."

He raises a brow. "Something of the like."

My breasts heave with my rapid breath, but I need to get the words out. I won't survive if he continues to scorn me, continues to avoid me like I'm some mutt he dragged in from the rain.

I belong to Caspian. He must understand that.

Clinging to the torrent of memories, of words and images assaulting my mind, I grab hold of one. "You said you would make me your queen. That the Enchanted Vale would worship me as I worship you."

He says nothing, simply wavering from foot to foot as if he were more shadow than man.

"But I cannot be your queen if I am left alone day and night to wander your halls like a lost specter. Let me help you. Let me serve you. It is my purpose. Together, we can make you king of all the Enchanted Vale and Keldarion nothing more than a smear of blood upon the snow."

The Prince of Thorns stays quiet for a very long time. Oh, what I would give to hear the voice within his head, to understand what thoughts race through that glorious mind.

When he finally speaks, Caspian's voice is raspy and hypnotic. "I suppose I have been treating you like you're something precious, haven't I? A treasure locked away in a chest. But if you're my treasure, then I should wear you like a crown and let all gaze upon you."

I wet my lips, core tightening at the darkness in his words.

"Kneel."

My self-constraint gone, I fall to my knees in a clatter, chest heaving, hand knotted in my skirt so as not to clutch at him.

"Kiss my boots."

They're covered in mud, but I don't care. I shower his filthy boots in kisses, caking my face in dirt. The mud tastes woodsy and damp, like rain-soaked leaves and fallen acorns. He's been outside the Below.

He's been in Autumn.

Long minutes pass as he lets me clean his boots with my lips, until my knees ache and my tongue tastes of leather and soil. His gaze presses down upon me like a weight.

Finally, he snatches my jeweled collar and hauls me up, cutting off my air until I'm gasping for a breath.

"Do you miss the sunshine?" He lets go of the collar.

My voice is a rasp. "I do not miss the sunshine. I am a creature of darkness and will forever scorn the light as it scorned my prince."

"Good." His cape whips my body as he turns away from me. "Because I will be bringing you back into the sun, and you must not fall in love with it. I shall send Heidigog to prepare you. It's hot where we're headed."

I stay rooted to the spot, one hand on the raw skin that my collar dug into, one hand to my mud-caked lips. I shall never wash.

I'm to travel with the Prince of Thorns!

Unconsciously, one of my hands drifts down to my pocket. Oh, there's something in it.

The ring.

I forgot to give it to him.

Oh well. Perhaps I'll keep it. Just for a little while.

7

Rosalina

I love traveling with the Prince of Thorns. He wraps me tight in his briars, my skin pressed to his, and for those brief moments when we're whipped through the earth, it is as if we are one body.

Those are the only times he holds me.

Sometimes, he'll touch me. We walk arm in arm to dinners. When others are around, he likes to graze his fingers over my shoulders or bring a lock of my hair to his nose to smell.

When we are alone, he looks at me as if he hates me. As if there's a great tiger standing between us, and it's all he can do to turn and run.

So I hold fast to those moments when we're entangled, two hearts beating as one among the briars. Our own secret world.

We travel all over. Along the River Gami that runs all the way from the Briar through Summer. Up into the Ribs to speak with harpies. To troll camps deep in the north. To gargoyles that perch in the mountains of Spring. To bands of wild goblins in Autumn.

I learn things, and I write them in my book, over the pages of the high rulers of Autumn. I don't know why, but something compels me to pay attention. That this is *important*, in the same way Heidi's nickname for me is. And it's catching too. Most of the time, the Prince of Thorns calls me Princess. But sometimes, every so often, he'll call me Rosalina.

I write lots of useless things in my book, like how we're gathering armies of rogue creatures from around the Vale to come to the Below. How it will take weeks for them to reach us. How many seem to hate Sira, but the Prince of Thorns is making them great promises for allegiance.

I write important things too. Like how he prefers the white sauce on his potatoes to the red sauce. That he's not very good at sleeping and often cries out in the night—but I'm not to go to his chambers when he does that, because he gets very angry. And that sometimes when I say things that make him sad, like "I love you," his eyes flash from green to purple, just for a second. I don't like to make him sad, but I do like when his eyes are purple like that.

When we're home in Cryptgarden, I no longer dine alone or only with the Prince of Thorns. Now, we eat at a huge obsidian stone table with Sira, his mother. Often, two horned fae will join us, Faustrius and Aquila. Faustrius has gigantic antlers like an elk, and though he's very polite to me, I can't help but feel a curdling rage in my belly every time he speaks. Aquila doesn't talk much. Heidi says, "One side of her face is pretty as a bloomie. The other looks like a rat snuck into the boiler." I have to say, Heidi's right. Aquila still has her long, emerald-green hair on one half, clear skin and a full mouth. But the other side is angry red scars and patchy hair. Someone really mean must have hurt her.

Sira doesn't seem to like me much. She doesn't talk a lot at dinners, but she watches her son. I don't talk a lot either, so I watch her watch him. It's like she's observing a faucet dripping into a bucket one drop at a time. *Drop drop drop.* Just waiting for the whole thing to overflow.

I write about Sira in my book. Things about how she slips off by herself much of the time. She rejects Faustrius's requests for counsel. When she's lost in thought, her hand drifts to her shoulder and scratches idly at her back. All ridiculous things to write in a book, but my mind feels itchy when I don't.

The Prince of Thorns is too busy for me, so I still spend lots of hours with Heidi. Sometimes, we wander outside the Gem, all the way into the city of Cryptgarden.

Heidi talks to me about the bloomies she's seen up on the surface, and I promise to bring her some when I next travel with the Prince of Thorns. Though usually where we go, there are no flowers to be found. I like listening to Heidi's stories. When she tells me about her life in the Briar, her adventures with Bugu, or funny things she sees in the castle, it's as if an empty well in my chest fills right up. I wish I could have more stories.

But no one else in Cryptgarden likes to talk to us. I wonder if they have empty wells too. A malaise hangs over the city in the way the light hangs: no one knows where it comes from or why it's here, only that it drifts like a fog through the alleys and into our bones.

Maybe we're all ghosts here.

8

Rosalina

The Prince of Thorns and I sit on a fallen log near a bog. Frost clings to the tall grasses, and chunks of ice float in the marsh, but the sun is shining beautifully, basking everything in light. I wish I could stretch out and soak my whole body in the rays, but I fight the urge. He doesn't like when I search for the sun.

We're on the border of Winter and Spring, though I can't remember which realm this log sits in. All I know is the Prince of Thorns negotiated with a coven of bog witches: ugly things with gnarled fingers and hair made of marsh grass with eyes that can see straight through to your bones. They're on their way to Cryptgarden now, to amass with the rest of Sira's gathering army.

The Prince of Thorns and I share a wedge of hard cheese, passing it back and forth, not talking.

"You and I are mates, right?" I say it absently. Just because I felt it in my heart, and I wanted to say it.

The cheese falls from his grip and into the boggy mud beneath his boots.

"Bother," I chide. "That was good ch—"

The Prince of Thorns is upon me, shoving me flat against the log, his entire body covering mine. His eyes flash not green or purple but a muddy black, like bog water.

"You mustn't ever say that aloud. Do you understand me?"

"But why? It's true, isn't it? We're mates—"

He covers my mouth with his hands, the weight of his body near suffocating. "Stop it. Stop it right now. My mother cannot know that, and her spies are everywhere. Do not ever say it aloud. Do you understand?"

I blink, then a smile curves beneath the touch of his palm. "What will you give me to keep the secret?"

His chest heaves, and he looks at me as if I'm crazy. Maybe I am. Who am I to negotiate with one who is a god?

He licks his lips. Looks around. I can practically hear his thoughts rumbling like an avalanche. Then he closes his black eyes and nods as if he's figured it out.

Slowly, he shifts forward. I feel every place our bodies touch, the movement so slow, I may expire from the pure ecstasy of it. His breath is warm on my skin. Achingly unhurried, he brings his face to mine and, ever so gently, lays a kiss on the very corner of my mouth.

"Please, Princess," he purrs, "be a good girl and keep our little secret."

"I swear," I whisper.

I touch the corner of my lip, right where he kissed me. For this, I would do anything. For this, I would raze the realms.

9

Rosalina

SOMETIMES, I DREAM.

I dream of flowers, of rose bushes bursting with blue and pink and turquoise and orange blooms, with stems of deep purple. I dream of wandering through briars thick with these colorful blossoms, of getting lost within the branches.

These dreams make me sad.

I always wake to a tear-soaked pillow, my throat raw with sobs. There's only one thing that calms me down. I drift over to my wardrobe and pull out the leather satchel, laying everything out on the bed beside the winged lion. I flip through the pages of my book, wrap myself in the gray cloak that once I found ugly but now looks like mottled snow, twist the lid off the jar and smell the rich, floral scent, and I hold tight to that silly lion.

It's the only way I sleep anymore.

I try so hard not to do it. Last night, I put everything in the wardrobe and locked it, promising myself I would sleep with only thoughts of the Prince of Thorns. But in my dream, there were new roses this time, great golden blooms that reached for the sun. And I must have felt sadder than ever, because I awake to Heidi shaking me, her yellow eyes filled with concern.

"You's alright, Rosalina? You were squawking and wailing like a wee baby! Must've been a nasty dream."

"I... I dreamed of flowers," I mumble, wiping the tears from my cheeks.

"Of what-what?"

"Of flowers," I repeat.

"What's a flower? Some kind of tasty thing? Some kind of shiny thing?"

I wave my hand in the air, signaling the purple gemlights to turn on and illuminate the room. "Flowers. You know, bloomies? You love them?"

Heidi shakes her head. "Don't know what a flower is, nor a bloomie. But they must be scary to get you all wiggly like that. Don't you worry, Rosalina! I'm here for you! I'll be watching, so you can sleep safe and sound."

I narrow my eyes. Heidi loves flowers. It seems an awful strange thing to forget.

But I suppose I've forgotten stranger things.

10

Rosalina

"I didn't mean to! I'm sorry! I'm sorry!"

Great, heaving sobs rack my body. I wrap my arms around myself, rocking on my knees, trying to gain some semblance of control, but I can't stop my tears. I've upset him. Made him angry. Stupid, idiot, useless—

The Prince of Thorns gives a silent yell and begins tearing at my briars, ripping them straight from the ground.

They're covering my bedroom, cracking through the floor, jutting through the bedframe, and curling around the wardrobe. So many beautiful golden briars, bursting with golden roses.

I didn't mean to. I really didn't mean to.

But I woke up, and my brain was itchier than it's ever been. Usually, I can soothe the feeling by being near the Prince of Thorns, but this was like prickles planted in my mind. *How* could Heidigog forget about her bloomies? She talks about them nonstop. Water lilies on ponds, daisies in a meadow, even the fuzzy catkins on willow trees. She might miss the flowers of the surface more than I miss the sun—

I don't. I don't miss it. Don't miss anything. And I've made him *mad.*

A wail escapes me, and I try to help him, pulling at my own briars. Thorns snag my flesh, and blood runs down my hands.

"Stars sake, Rosalina," the Prince of Thorns snarls and dashes over to me. He falls to his knees and snags my wrists, examining the torn skin. With an exasperated sigh, he rips two ribbons of fabric from his shirt and binds both of my palms.

I sniff. "I–I didn't mean to cause trouble."

He doesn't let go of my wrist. "Why did you do this?"

"Last night, I mentioned flowers to Heidigog. And…and she couldn't remember what they were. But we've talked about them before. When I woke up, I had the feeling that I could *make* a flower and show her. And if I showed her, she would remember… But when I started, it…it…"

"It what?"

"It felt so good I couldn't stop," I whisper. "It was like…stretching after being cooped up in a seat for hours."

The Prince of Thorns lets loose another sigh and shakes his head, tendrils of black hair falling in his face. "This magic of yours—it's dangerous. Do you understand? You could hurt yourself."

"I don't care," I wail. "I have to use it, or I might die—"

"You could hurt *me*," he snarls, and his eyes flash with phantasmal green. "You must promise me you won't do this again. Promise me."

A buzzing sounds in my head, like a hive was just turned upside down in my brain. My lip curls, and I avert my gaze. I don't want to look at him right now. He can't make me promise that. He can't, he can't.

He yanks on my wrists hard. "Rosalina, listen to me. You must promise—"

"No," I snarl.

The Prince of Thorns goes still. Very still, like the soul has left him and there's only a husk. The shadows in the room gather around him like a cloak. Warmth seeps from my blood.

I try to pull away from him, but he tugs my wrists again. "Listen to me, Rosalina O'Connell. You are *mine*. Mine to control. Mine to do with as I please. You *will* obey me. Do you understand?"

He's right. I am his. I belong to him.

"Yes," I whisper.

He continues to slither before me. "So if you will not make me a promise, then you will do one better. You will make me a bargain. By thorn and shadow, by oath and will, you are bound. No magic shall stir in your veins, no power shall rise at your call, unless I grant it. Swear it, and let the bargain take hold."

Shadows coil around me, cold as the light of his eyes. The air seems to still, to wait.

I am his. To control. To do with as he wills.

"By thorn and shadow, by oath and will, I am bound," I breathe. "My magic is yours to command, unless you grant me leave."

Now the air quickens, then hums. Two black steel cuffs materialize around my wrists, carved with thorns and roses.

His smile is slow, dark. Victorious. "Good girl. How I love when you obey."

With a sweep of his cape, he exits the room, leaving me with my briars and my cuffs.

The Prince of Thorns took something from me. But he gave me something greater.

My full name.

Rosalina O'Connell.

And alone in my room, with only my tears and my briars, I will admit it to myself.

I miss the sun.

11

Dayton

Hadria is changing. It still doesn't look like the city I grew up in, but it's no longer claimed by the sea. Not since I returned from Winter and called the tide back out.

Hand braced on the wall of Soltide Keep, I stare out over Hadria. In the two fortnights I've been here, there's been notable progress. The fae Rosie transformed into sirens have come back to help rebuild, and the citizens of Aerantheis are using their legs to assist on land.

With resources at an all-time low in the Vale, I'm still awed that Winter, Spring, and Autumn all sent their most skilled craftworkers to help in the restoration effort. No, it will not be the same city as before. We'll build more canals for the sirens to swim in. Instead of being purely Hadrian architecture, we'll have a blend of the sea and the other seasonal realms.

Something about it warms my heart: everyone coming together

to make the Summer Realm better. It reminds me of Rosalina, how she somehow saw the goodness in all us princes.

Rosie.

I miss my Blossom so much it aches. It kills me not knowing how she's doing. But I can still feel our bond, so I know she's alive. And unlike the last time she was taken from us, this was her choice. It's where she needs to be. The best thing I and the other princes can do is concentrate on strengthening the four seasonal realms so we're ready to take on the Below.

Keldarion has been rallying the scattered people of Winter. The legend of the prince who defied a volcano and tore the stars from the sky is spreading fast across the Vale. And I have to admit, even I get a little tingly when I think of it. It was pretty fucking awesome, and standing with my brothers protecting Winter is one of the greatest things I've ever done.

Ezryn has traveled to Spring with Rosalina's father, George. They have the best forges to work mythkarite and hopefully repair the rose. Everything hinges on that. Once we can control the goblins and Sira's other creations, we'll have a way to seize the Below.

That is…if Rosie's accomplished her mission and somehow recused Cas from his own mind. Because all our armies won't be enough to take *him* down. Not when he's trapped by the Green Flame.

I, unfortunately, can relate all too well. My mind flashes to my bed, soaked with sweat from nightmares of the day I attacked Ezryn. Whispers still cloud my mind.

I shake my head, clearing my thoughts. *Caspian's not here. He can't control me.*

As for Farron...

Farron is in Autumn.

Hissing through my teeth, I turn, gaze landing on the coral throne: spires of pink and crimson coral twisted together. It's never looked warm or welcoming, and it especially doesn't now. I mean, there are barnacles on the armrest, and those give nasty-ass scrapes.

But it's not the fear of a scratch that's kept me from sitting on it since I've returned.

I can be the leader Summer needs. Wield the blessing well. But what if I wield it *too* well and I lose myself to the Green Flame again—

"Day?"

I turn and breathe out a sigh. My little sister, Delphia, stands in the doorway to the throne room. Her curly hair is windswept. She must have been flying around on her winged horse, Drusilla, who is big enough to ride now.

Trailing behind is my sister's ever-present shadow, Nori, her nose stuck in a book, thin mouth in a frown.

"Del, Nori, I didn't expect you here," I say. "Thought you'd be gone a couple more days."

"Of course we surprised you," Delphia mutters, then looks up at me with her most formal expression. "Well, High Prince, we finished our mission early. We found them. They've made a camp in the Starweaver Mountains."

"Seriously?" I move closer. "You located the rest of the Queen's Army?"

The Huntresses of Aura have been searching the Enchanted Vale for the sector of the Queen's Army that first left Queen's Reach

Monastery when Kairyn took over. They're one hundred strong at least, and having them on our side, with their skills, would surely aid in our fight against the Below.

"Well, it didn't matter." Delphia's shoulders slump. "They *hated* us."

Nori raises her nose from the book and slams it shut. "It wasn't that they *hated* us. They didn't respect us. There's a difference."

"Seagull, sky rat," Delphi moans. "Same thing. They wouldn't come back with us."

"What did they say?" I ask, stepping closer to my sister but still keeping a distance.

"They refuse to follow any master but their queen."

"But Rosie—"

"We told them all about Rosalina," Delphia continues. "They said it was a rumor. Especially when I couldn't lead them to where she was."

"Rosalina will come back," I say.

"Statistically, the odds of surviving the Below are low," Nori says. "Especially under a thralldom bargain. I mean, even the queen herself has been down there for twenty-five years. Rotting alone in the dark..."

"Eleanor," Delphia hisses, smacking her on the shoulder. "You're talking about his mate and his mate's mother."

"Right." Nori looks at me unbothered. "Which is why, because I've met Lady Rosalina, I do believe she'll return. It's unfortunate it wasn't before we found the Queen's Army."

"But Rosalina is not without allies. Matron Valeria wanted you to have this." Delphie reaches into her satchel and pulls something out. It's a magnificent horn. She steps closer and drops it into my palms.

The body is gold, polished to a soft, sunlit glow. Silver metalwork twists over the surface, curling like vines, inlaid with delicate roses. The mouthpiece is shaped in the form of an open bloom, the bell flared wide.

"No matter where they are in the Vale, the Huntresses of Aura will hear it," Delphie says. "And they will come."

The weight of her words settles between us. It's the kind of thing that could change everything. "I'll take good care of this," I promise. "And now that you've returned, I have to head out."

"To Autumn?" Nori looks up.

It would be nice to see how Farron's doing in his quest to push back the goblins of the Briar that leak into Autumn. "Spring first," I say. "Then Autumn."

Delphia turns to go but looks back at me over her shoulder. "When you return, I want to see you, Day. It feels like you've been avoiding me."

I swallow in a dry throat. "I haven't, Del. I've just been so busy restoring Hadria." A lie she sees right through. But keeping my distance from the last blood family I have is the only way to keep her safe from me and the monster I've become.

Delphia nods, then raises a dark brow. "When are you finally going to sit on it?"

I shrug. "Was thinking about it. Still feels like Dammy's. Fear I'd sit down and hear him laughing at me from the world beyond."

Delphia shakes her head, but Nori looks me straight in the eye with that familiar Autumn gaze. "I don't think so."

"You didn't know Damocles very well." I grin.

"No," Nori agrees, opening her bag and swapping her book for a small leather notebook. "But he knew you."

"What are you holding?"

"A diary Farron kept during one of the summers he spent here, years ago," she says, flipping through it.

My cheeks heat. "Are you sure you should be reading that? Because I'm betting it's not exactly suitable for children—" I cut off, thinking of all the very inappropriate things Fare and I have done in Summer.

Nori's scowl deepens. "First, I'm not a child. Second, I'm only reading because I wanted to learn all I could about Summer to help in its restoration. My brother happens to be painfully detailed."

"That's true," Delphie says. "Best way to fall asleep after a long day. She starts reading one of his eight-page descriptions of a weed bursting through the cobblestone or the meaning of a statue and I'm out."

It's so classically Farron. The shy Autumn boy kissed by Summer's heat. It's like remembering someone who doesn't exist anymore.

"Third," Nori continues, "I know how intercourse works, but thankfully the most vivid my brother got in his description was something about how his untouched petal bloomed and opened, spread apart by the sea's crushing waves."

"I threw up in my mouth a little at that part," Delphie says.

"Okay, okay," I say, waving my arms. "Enough of that. Why did you bring this out?"

"Oh, here it is," Nori says and begins to read. "*I shouldn't be surprised Daytonales wasn't there to see me off. The empty seat beside me in the carriage looks like a specter. The ache in my heart—*"

"The lamenting goes on for sixteen pages," Delphia says, reading over Nori's shoulder. "Skip to the part about my brother."

"But Farron's misery is just so dark and delicious." Nori sighs, flips the page, and continues to read. "*Despite all that, I still believe the words his brother, High Prince Damocles, spoke are true: 'Dayton is a fool.'*"

I turn away, because I already know this part of the story. I heard my brother speak those words when he wasn't aware I was listening.

"'*But I know my brother. His spirit is wild and untamed, like the fiercest of Summer storms,*'" Nori continues to read.

I stop and turn. Because this I hadn't heard. I'd left trying to spare my own feelings. But had my brother been saying something nice about me?

Delphia takes the book and stares me in the eye, reciting the last line. "'*Yet there is a warmth and a light in him that can shine in any darkness. He may stumble, he may falter, but within him lies the potential to ignite a path of glory.*'"

"A path of glory, hey?" I say and smile, then stare out at the sea. "That's a big ask, big brother."

Delphia comes up beside me and takes my hand. And despite the fear coursing through me, I let her. "We'll do it together. Now get your big butt on that throne."

I give a long, dramatic sigh, then march toward the coral monstrosity and fall into it.

Damn, it really is as uncomfortable as it looks. Regardless, I laugh. "Guess you were right about me again, Dammy. One last time."

12

Farron

Briars snag on my clothes and pull on my hair. I keep running, shoving myself deeper into the thicket, holding my arms up to shield my eyes. Branches snap beneath my boots, and wilted roses float from their stems.

Another scream shatters the air, as clear and violent as the last. Rosalina's scream. I've never heard her so terrified, in such pain…

I have to get to her. My vision tunnels, heart pounding, lungs burning as I dive deeper and deeper into the Briar. She's somewhere in here. Someone's hurting her. *Killing her.*

My skin is tattered ribbons by the time I fling out into a clearing. Blinking against the blaring sun, I peer around. There's nothing but dark fog hovering over the ground—

Not fog. Shadow.

And from the shadows, a figure forms, a gargantuan woman

with tendrils of darkness wisping out from her skirt like tentacles. Her hair is a black cloak behind her, and her face is elegant and cruel. Lightless, joyless eyes peer down at me, and her mouth curls into a smile.

"Welcome, Farron, Autumn blood. Are you ready to join your family?"

Sira, Queen of the Below, laughs, the sound blowing her shadows away and revealing a sight that staggers me.

I fall to my knees, reaching out, hand grasping empty air—but there's nothing to hold on to.

Huge, snaking briars jerk in awkward angles from all around her. Pierced on the ends of her barbs are my family. Father, Billy, Dom, Nori…hanging like puppets who have had their strings cut. On the other side, a thorn pierces through the chest plate of Ezryn's armor. His helmet lies upside down below him, filling with blood from the dripping slice across his neck. Keldarion hangs limp beside him, impaled through the stomach. His lifeless eyes stare upward, mouth agape in a silent scream.

"Did you think you could save them all?" Sira cackles. "You couldn't even save *her*!"

A briar spears through the ground right in front of me.

Rosalina looks like a paper doll, blowing in the wind. Her face is pale, long hair waving in the breeze. But a thin streak of blood runs from her perfect lips. I follow its trail, down her chin, along her neck, over the crest of her bosom—

To her ribs, which are splayed open by a jagged thorn.

Sira laughs. The sound assaults me on all sides, ringing between the briars, hitting me like arrows.

I throw my hands over my ears and squeeze my eyes shut. This can't be happening, this can't, this can't—

I rock back and forth in the mud, the sickening smell of wilted roses assaulting me along with Sira's relentless laughter. I open my eyes, begging to be anywhere but here, but only see Rosalina's dangling corpse before me, hanging like wet laundry.

"What do I do?" I cry out. "What do I do?"

"There's only one way to protect them!" a voice calls in response.

I know that voice. Joyful and bright as a Summer afternoon. The epitome of a hero.

A streak of green light arcs above me as someone leaps over my head. The figure skids to the ground before the limp dolls that were once my family, and when he stands, silhouetted in emerald flame, he is like the sun rising itself.

Dayton twirls his dual blades and flashes me a smile. "Save them, Farron, like you saved me."

Then with a burst of flame, he scythes his blades through the briars. My family falls to the ground, then Kel and Ezryn and finally Rosalina.

I rise on shaky legs. Their bodies are wrapped in Dayton's green fire, and it's as if a warm breeze has chased away the chill. One by one, they stand, smiles on their faces, eyes burning with emerald hearths.

"You did that," Dayton says. "You can protect them all. Just remake them as you did me."

I thought it was Dayton's fire…but my hands burn with flames. I saved them?

I saved them.

Now, a new voice says, one that comes on the wind, *you must kill the one who hurt them. You must kill Sira.*

I turn my attention to the woman cloaked in shadows. She's not laughing anymore. In fact, she looks terrified at the growing inferno surrounding her.

But it wasn't her shadows who killed my family.

It was briars.

His briars.

My teeth clench so hard, a muscle pulses in my jaw. Great waves of fire leap up, licking and snarling with a twist of my hand.

"I will burn all the Briar to the ground," I say lowly, "until the Prince of Thorns is nothing but ash upon the wind."

A blaze erupts around me, the hiss of flame mixing with screams, so many screams my skull is thick with them, and I—

I awaken in a cold sweat. My heart thumps so loudly, I rub my chest to make sure it's staying put.

My room is dark except for the large moon hanging outside my window, casting ghostly shapes upon the floor. I reach for the water glass beside my bed, but my hand trembles so much, it clatters to the ground.

It was just a dream. A dream like the one I had last night and the night before and the night before that. A dream like I've had every night since Rosalina sank to the Below.

Rosalina is gone, and Dayton will not smile at me like that again.

I'm shivering, but I can't stay in here. It feels suffocating, as if there's not enough oxygen. I cross to the balcony and open the door, stepping out into the cool night. I'm only wearing sleeping trousers, so Autumn's night wind sends goose bumps skittering across my chest.

With a sigh, I collapse on the railing and stare out over my realm. The moonlight plays over Coppershire and the realmlands. Hills of heather glow in the silver light, their usual purple hues muted. Beyond the quiet farmlands and woods, where the land fades into mist, the Briar looms at the very edge of the horizon.

It is a jagged scar, destroying my home.

I should burn it down. I could do it. Raze the entire wicked place with green flame, killing every goblin that lives within. How would Caspian like that? His precious Briar nothing more than ash?

But what of Castletree?

My thought pulls me away from images of smoke and fire. Caspian's bloody briars are the only thing holding Castletree up. Without them…

A low rumble followed by a whistle sounds behind me, and I jump. Someone's bundled in a cloak, fast asleep by the door to my balcony. I would never have noticed them if it weren't for the snoring.

I walk over and kick my brother's boot. He jerks awake, snatching his falchion from its scabbard and leaping forward. I duck out of the way. "Steady there, Aeneas, great warrior!"

Billy—I know it's him by the pattern of freckles across his nose—blinks as he recognizes me, then lowers his blade. "Hah hah, very funny."

I cross my arms. "Mind telling me why you're armed and holed up on my balcony? Do you not have a perfectly good room with a *bed*?"

Billy gives a sheepish grin and shrugs his shoulders. He meanders over to the railing and assumes a position much like mine moments ago. Except he's at the age where he's all arms and legs, gangly as a willow tree's branches. "Oh, you know. Dom and I are just looking out for you."

I peer around the balcony, searching for another shape.

"He's watching your front door," Billy mumbles.

I run a hand over my short beard and level my brother with a watchful gaze. "Care to explain why you two are standing guard?"

Billy stares out across the horizon. Fae age slowly in adolescence compared to our human counterparts, but I can't help but think he and Dom have grown up so fast in the last few years. But what other choice do you have? War steals the innocence from us all.

"We thought…you seemed like you needed someone to look out for you, Fare. You've been a smidge on edge lately." Billy turns to me and flashes a crooked grin. "So we're here to keep you safe."

Words catch in my throat. "Oh, Billy." I wrap an arm around him and tug him close. He smells like cloves and pumpkin and memories. "You don't worry about that, okay? Keeping us all safe—that's my job."

13

Keldarion

THE WIND HOWLS ACROSS THE ENDLESS WHITE HORIZON AS I RUN. Snow whips against my fur, sharp and biting, but I hardly feel it. My paws dig deep into the ice-crusted powder, pushing forward, relentless. The hunger for movement, for escape, is a gnawing thing, but no matter how far I run, she is always there.

Rosalina.

I can't stop seeing her. Her voice is in the wind. Her scent clings to the frozen air. And Cas, curse him, lingers like a shadow at the back of my mind, tormenting me with all the things I should have done differently. All the ways I failed him. Failed her.

I snarl and push harder, leaving deep gouges in the ice. If I run fast enough, maybe the memories won't catch me. Maybe the ghost of her warmth won't reach into my chest and tear me open all over again.

The storm howls louder, a beast of its own. Ice shards spin through the air, but I don't stop. Not until the land changes, shifting from rolling drifts to jagged peaks jutting from the snow.

I slow, breath misting in the thick clouds around me. Justus told me to meet him here. But why? This is the middle of nowhere, nothing but unending white and the silence of the frozen expanse. Yet I know I'm in the right place.

I shift.

Pain lances through me as my form bends and twists, bones snapping and reforming, fur withdrawing into skin. The cold bites, but I ignore it. My clothes were strapped to my back, and I move quickly, pulling them on. The thick cloak and furs help, but they do nothing to chase away the unease curling in my gut.

Where are you, Justus?

A figure steps from behind a jagged rock, Justus's form barely visible against the misty snow. His expression is unreadable, but his eyes gleam.

"I've found what I was looking for," he says. "When you've been alive as long as I have, your memories start to feel like dreams."

"And what exactly were you looking for?"

Justus gestures me forward. "Come and see."

I follow him. The peaks around us twist into strange, jagged formations, and something shifts beneath the ice. Not only cracks and fractures but shapes.

Ruins.

High columns and pillars, half-buried in ice, stick out of the earth. Their surfaces are carved with sigils. The further we walk, the more the ruins reveal themselves, winding across the frozen landscape.

I glance at Justus. His face is unreadable, but something flickers in his eyes. Something ancient.

Aeneas.

The first High Prince of Summer. That's who he truly is.

My breath fogs in the frigid air. "What is this place?"

Justus doesn't answer. Instead, he places a hand on a pillar, fingers tracing the faded markings. "A memory," he says at last. "One I thought lost."

We step up to the remnants of a building, its entrance half-buried beneath thick sheets of ice. Light filters through the cracked walls, illuminating dazzling runes carved into every edge. These symbols must form words, but I can't read them. Though I do recognize them.

From the note of the underfae assassin.

It's the language of the Above.

A round table stands in the center of the chamber. Five faded circles are etched into the ground around it. I step closer, brushing a gloved hand over an engraving. A leaf. Beside it, a rose.

"This was once known as the Celestial Landing," Justus says, his voice reverent. "A portal Aurelia created in hopes to one day return home."

I straighten, the weight of his words settling on my shoulders. "And you needed all the high rulers and the queen to make it work?"

"Aurelia was able to open it on her own," Justus says. "But without her, its power comes from the divine weapons."

"Just like Kairyn theorized," I continue. "It's why he wanted them so badly."

I glance down at the circle beneath my feet, the designs eroded by time. A snowflake, its edges chipped and broken.

"It took a great deal of magic to make these work," Justus murmurs, tracing his fingers over the faded symbols. "Far more than any single high ruler could muster."

I exhale, my breath clouding before me. The Celestial Landing. A portal between realms.

"All this time, I knew it was here," Justus continues, "but I couldn't recall how we powered it. It's been coming back to me slowly, and I've finally remembered!"

I frown. We've spent the last few weeks researching, trying to decipher if it's possible to reach the Above. Kairyn theorized there might be ancient forges there, ones where we could work the mythkarite, the metal ribbed along the stars I pulled down. It's the same metal used to craft the divine weapons we carry in our tokens. George is working with what mythkarite was liquefied from the volcano's lava. As for the rest…no forge in the Vale is powerful enough to melt it.

Not anymore, at least. The divine weapons were forged in the Vale, crafted by the first high ruler of Spring, Rafael. Justus explained how Rafael had carried with him a gift from the Above: a single flame from the Forge of Onaulion, the same kind of fire Faustrius had used to awaken the volcano in Winter. But Rafael used such a flame not to destroy the Vale, but to save it. His final remnant of the Above was spent forging the divine weapons.

But now…if there is a way to repair the weapons here in the Vale, I can't fathom it. So we'll need a forge beyond my imagining.

And for that, I need to find a way to the Above.

I cross my arms, my gaze flicking back to the faded sigils on the ground around the table. "Don't suppose this could work with three weapons?"

Justus's expression darkens. He doesn't need to say what he's thinking. I already know. Rosalina's bow is shattered. So is my sword, both broken by Faustrius's blade.

"The danger would be too great to try," Justus says, his gaze lingering on the crumbling portal. "Far greater than we can afford. If it didn't work, we'd risk losing some of the most powerful fae in the Vale."

"This was one theory on how to defeat Sira, not our only," I say, turning from the table. "But there still may be answers here."

I let my gaze drift to the ruined walls. There, carved into the stone, are depictions of islands floating in the sky with fae suspended beside them. Behind each figure is a pair of wide, tapering wings that flare outward, symmetrical down to the patterns etched within them.

Justus steps beside me, his fingers ghosting over the carving. He shakes his head. "We fae forgot how to fly in the Vale. There was no need. Not like up there. Such a different world."

Is that true? Did the fae once have wings? Or are these an old man's ramblings? The underfae don't have wings, but perhaps that's another thing they sacrificed in their change to become Sira's monsters.

I study the image, my thoughts drifting to Aurelia. Is this why she loves birds? Some forgotten longing for what we lost?

Another carving catches my eye. Five powerful fae, each holding a divine weapon and an amulet in their hands. They are clad in magnificent armor, unlike anything I've seen, even in the Spring Realm.

A pang of sorrow grips my chest, and I shake my head. "If only we could get to the Above, we could forge armor like this again."

Justus exhales, his eyes focused on the ancient warriors. "Ah, we forged great armor in the Above," he murmurs. "But this…this was something different."

His hand drifts to his chest, pressing against the place where a token once lay, fingers splayed as if searching for a presence long gone. Then, with a slow inhale, he lifts his palm outward, fingers curling into a fist before unfurling, releasing an unseen weight into the air.

A strange sensation stirs inside me. A call, waiting for an answer.

I touch the snowflake token on my chest. It should be Farron, the scholar, in these ruins. Rosalina, whose intuition never fails her.

I can't help but feel like I'm overlooking some hidden truth. The heart of all these questions.

But maybe I'm searching for the impossible.

There's no simple answer to winning this war. No simple way to get Rosalina and Caspian back.

I'll do what Rosalina taught me—protect my realm. Protect all the realms.

I don't need the Sword of the Protector to win this war.

I just need us. Together.

14

Ezryn

"I've told you ten times now, Tilla. I don't know how to fix an airship. If you need repairs, you're going to have to ask Kairyn."

Tilla levels me with a glare. At least I'm pretty sure it's a glare. I know her well enough to sense the fury radiating from beneath her dark gray helm. As steward of Spring, she cannot take it off in front of anyone but her family.

We stand in the small storage room turned sleeping quarters at the back of Draconhold Forge. This has been my, Kairyn's, and George's home for the last four weeks since we left the Winter Realm. Our makeshift mattresses are filled with itchy straw, and the heat of the nearby hearths makes for sweltering days, but it's not such a bad setup. At night, when all the smiths have gone home, we creep out to work. Draconhold is the only forge in all the seasonal realms with strong enough equipment for our needs.

Tilla's the one person in Spring who knows we're here. Given her role as steward, she deserved to know everything that had transpired—the rose, the underfae, our new missions. She visits often to keep me abreast of the efforts to rally Spring's forces, but she's not thrilled about my decision to stay hidden in Draconhold while we continue our work. I understand, but this is what's best for all the realms now.

George, Kairyn, and I stay out of sight during the day. At night, we creep out to visit the communal kitchen, where we find jugs of water, flatbread, and—if we're lucky—half-filled carafes of coffee. Then, by moonlight, we work on rebuilding the rose.

The rose that Sira stole from the Gardens of Ithilias. The rose she used to create and control her monsters. The rose that, once rebuilt, we can use to bind their wills to our own. Then, even from afar, we can help Rosalina.

Rosalina. The mere feel of her name in my mind is enough to quicken my heart. What is she doing now? Is she safe? Hurt?

I squeeze my eyes shut, thankful Tilla cannot see the play of emotions beneath my helm. Rosalina held fast to her courage, and so must we.

"Are you listening to me, Ezryn?" Tilla snaps, and I realize I haven't been. "I'd rather throw myself into the heat of a forge and let my armor melt around me than ask Kairyn—"

"Ask me what?"

My little brother walks in and leans against the doorframe. His giant form fills all the space, and the horns that jut from his brow are so large, they nearly skim the ceiling. He takes a bite of a mango with his sharp canines and flicks his bloodred gaze from Tilla to me.

His massive size, I'm used to. He was always taller and broader than me anyway. Even the horns, I've become accustomed to. But his eyes…

Though they swirl like the coals in a hearth, they're softer than I expect. So much gentler to look at than the dark void of the helm he previously wore.

At Kairyn's presence, Tilla leaps back and points her morning star at him.

"Are we still doing this?" he sighs and ambles to his too-small straw mattress before collapsing on it. "You *are* aware I'm currently unarmed?"

In fact, he hasn't touched his weapon since we reached Draconhold. Our mother's sword, the one he wielded to protect me in Frostfang, rests untouched in the corner of the room.

"Doesn't matter. I'm sure you'd love to cave my chest plate in with those horns," Tilla retorts.

Kairyn doesn't respond; he rolls over and faces the wall.

I may be getting used to Kairyn's appearance, but I know he's not. Every time he catches his horns on a doorframe or accidentally knocks something over with his skin-colored tail, a great silence overcomes him. Not sadness or rage.

Shame.

I can't blame Tilla for holding a grudge. Kairyn did take over our city, imprison her and all the other refugees fleeing Florendel, and force her to fight in his twisted games.

After Keldarion called down the stars and stopped the volcanic eruption from destroying all of Winter, it was long days before I left Frostfang. During that time, I deliberated what to do with Kairyn.

Leave him to rot in Keep Wolfhelm's prison? Even I cannot say his acts are not deserving of such a sentence.

But Spring's past has been filled with blood and pain and vengeance in the name of justice. If I don't end it, then who?

So we began letting him have supervised time out of his cell. He ended up following either me or Marigold around like a lost duckling. It was George who took him under his wing, asking him to assist in the lab. "He's knowledgeable on these ancient metals and as skilled a blacksmith as I could ask for," George told me. "Besides, I hear he means a lot to my daughter. So he means a lot to me."

George's youngest daughter. The one who consumes Kairyn's thoughts every time we sneak out of the forge to get some fresh air and he hears a bird call.

His mate, Wrenley.

I turn to look at my brother. Since being turned into an underfae, he has not donned a helm, nor does he wear any armor. Now, he wears only ragged trousers and a skintight, white undershirt streaked with oil and dirt. He must have been assisting George at the hearth.

When it was decided that George and I would travel to Florendel to complete the forging of the rose, it was he who suggested Kairyn accompany us. "I need an assistant. And he needs a friend."

The O'Connells and their relentless compassion.

George, as he tends to be, was right about Kairyn's skills. With his years of research at Queen's Reach Monastery and a near obsession with the ancient world, Kairyn has an array of knowledge about mythkarite, an ore that comes from the Above, responsible for the creation of the divine weapons. It is like magic turned stone. When Kel created the star shower, he called down an entire boulder laced with the stuff. We extracted the rare ore and brought it here, but even the fires of Draconhold were not hot enough to melt the raw mythkarite.

I suppose we should thank Faustrius, the zealot leading the underfae. If he hadn't poisoned Mount Rhuvenmark with fire from the hearth of the Above, the volcano would never have erupted. And the lava would never have landed on the boulder, creating a perfect pool of liquid mythkarite. Not a lot, but just enough for us to repair the rose.

Thoughts of Faustrius and his underfae have me peering out the door into the smithy. George sits at a workbench, hunched over, sweat dripping down his brow as he works. The steel container of mythkarite and the shards of the rose lie before him. It's almost complete now.

I breathe a sigh of relief, seeing him at ease in his work. Given the attempt on his life, I'm nervous to let him out of my sight.

Tilla lets loose an angry exhale, the reverberation of the helm making her sound like an angry bull. I turn back to her, refocusing my attention. Right. She'd come tonight to tell me of an engine issue with one of the ships in the air fleet. Spring has requisitioned the ships once used by the Green Rule.

"Look, Tilla, I don't know what else to tell you. Kairyn's the one who oversaw the creation of all the airships. He could help—"

"I will *never* accept help from that traitor," she snarls, then faces Kairyn. I can practically see lightning bolts surging out of her glare into his back. "You've always been a shit, and you'll always be a shit."

"Be fair," he sighs and rolls over to peer at her through his dark lashes. "The last few years, sure, but I wasn't *always* a shit."

I lift my helm slightly so I can knead the bridge of my nose, hoping to stave off a headache, and wonder if it's too late to switch places with Dayton. I'd much rather be in Hadria, working with Delphie and Nori. Wrangling two teenage girls would be far preferable to *this*.

Tilla groans and hooks her morning star back to her belt. "Look, Ez, I don't even want to be dealing with this. I told you I'd be your steward until you found a new high ruler. Well, you've got a helm and a blessing and a whole realm in need of some hope. Instead, you're hiding away in here. You've got to deal with this!"

I lay a hand against the doorframe and stare out at the halls of Draconhold. I never imagined coming back to my beautiful city like a rat, sneaking around at night, stealing bits of food, and hiding from the light of day. But then again, I never imagined coming back to Florendel at all.

I was banished. How can I face my people after letting them down so completely?

My gaze shifts to Kairyn, twirling his half-eaten mango in his hands. And if I cannot fathom standing before my citizens, how could Kairyn? He who betrayed them and everything Spring stands for?

Tilla puts a hand on my shoulder, urging me to look at her. Her voice softens. "Ezryn, I served your mother loyally. And when she made you high prince, I truly believed we could be in no better hands. I *still* believe that. You and Kel and Dayton and Fare may be idiots, but you're good idiots." I hear a kind smile in her voice. "But you're living my dream right now. Working with magic ore to craft an ancient weapon? That's my passion! Instead, I'm living *your* dream. Rallying the people of Spring under a common cause. One of the main reasons I never wanted to marry Kel was because I didn't want the life of a royal. Now you're forcing me into it."

"You're right," I murmur. "It's not fair. I'm sorry."

"Spring needs you, Ezryn."

"I'll think about it—"

Tilla slugs my arm *hard*, and I regret not wearing my full suit of armor. "Well, think fast, because I'm tired and I miss my forge. And I need my damn ship fixed."

I rub my bicep, already seeing a bruise. "Okay, okay. Kairyn will meet you in the dockyard tomorrow night—"

"I'm not meeting him alone," she cries, then crosses her arms. "He's likely to strangle me with that weird tail of his."

We both turn to Kairyn, who's sitting up. He gives an intentionally creepy grin and flicks his tail.

I gesture out the door. "We can't both go. It's not safe to leave George alone."

"Well, good thing a new bodyguard just arrived."

The voice fills the small storage room with warm bravado. I shift to the sound, and my chest beams with brightness.

Standing in the doorway, skin bronzed from the sun and with a giant smile on his face, is my brother by choice, Dayton.

15

Dayton

THE BARE SKIN OF MY BACK IS ITCHY FROM THE STRAW MATTRESS, AND I can't seem to get comfortable. It's bloody hot in here, and not the bright, beautiful warmth of Summer, where it feels like you're being warmed from the inside out. This is the cloistered, stifled heat of sitting too close to a fire with no open windows.

This sorry excuse for a bedroom is far too small for me, even though I'm the only one in it right now. During the day, while the sun shone overhead and Draconhold Forge swarmed with workers, we locked the door and stayed hidden in the dark. The smell of four grown men who had been working by a hearth all night is *not* for the weak of stomach.

I arrived yesterday evening. My heart sparked with joy to see Ez and George again after these four long weeks apart. I filled them in on all the progress in Hadria, and they told me about their work on the rose. Truthfully, it felt a bit like joining a long-standing club and not knowing the rules. George, Ez, and even Kairyn were all so in sync, feeding off one another's energy and finishing each other's sentences. I could barely keep up when they started on the properties of mythkarite.

I'll admit, my fist still itches to slam into Kairyn's face every time I look at him. But I owe him for keeping Ez alive when I was doing everything I could to kill him in Keep Wolfhelm.

Squeezing my eyes shut, I force away the memory, reminding myself Caspian's not here. *He can't control me. I am myself. Caspian has no power over me here.*

When will Ez be back? He and Kai left at the break of nightfall to do some repair work on one of the airships. It's just been me and Papa all night.

George barely spared me a word, immediately heading back to his workbench, muttering how he's closer than ever before. I tried to help him, like I'd seen Ez and Kai do, but he kept telling me I was in his light.

"You're making me nervous, hovering about like that! I'm so close to the end now, boy. Go find something else to do," he said with a wave.

Alright, so smithing isn't my forte. I passed a couple hours trying my hand at juggling hammers. Then when they kept crashing on the stone floor and George yelled that I was "breaking his concentration," I switched to playing with the bellows. It was entertaining at first, until George reminded me that they were *not* to be used as giant accordion lungs.

Now, I'm back here, in this cell of a bedroom, counting down the minutes until Ez returns.

If Farron were here, he'd have found a way to occupy himself. George would have loved him as an assistant, or he'd be reading a book on smithing and trying it himself. He always finds something interesting, no matter where we are.

Stars, I miss him. Miss his incessant curiosity. Miss the way he made me want to see the opportunity in things.

We could be together now if I hadn't told him—

But I needed to leave. If Farron wasn't going to fight for himself, why should I?

I only hope he's okay.

"Eureka!"

I jolt up and sprint out into the smithy.

"I did it," George whispers. He's got his dirty hands laced through his hair, standing back with eyes wide as saucers. Staring down at...

At the rose. All the shards, welded together, forming a perfect, intact rose.

A strangled gasp escapes him, then tears flood down his cheeks. "We did it. We did it!"

My chest bubbles with laughter, and I sprint over, grabbing George by the shoulders. "You did it!"

Joyous cries escape us as we leap up and down, hugging each other, slapping each other on the back. George pulls away and spins in a circle, rubbing his face with his hands and staring outward in disbelief. "It's done. After all this time..."

"We've got you, Rosie," I say. "We've got you."

George drifts over to the workbench and looks down reverently. A glow emits from the rose unlike I've ever seen before: bloodred and radiant. I follow his gaze. It's the most extraordinary thing… living and yet not, the way magic lives and yet it doesn't.

"Do you feel it?" George whispers. "The magic emanating from it?"

I stand beside him and inhale.

Power rushes through me, a breath of wind and fire and frost and earth—an energy so vast, so boundless, I can hardly comprehend. It thrums in the air, crackling along my nerves like a thousand unseen sparks. This isn't just magic. It's something ancient and knowing, something that *sees*.

But I can see too.

This small object has enough power to change the fate of the Vale.

It must be returned to its rightful master.

The light dims, the embers in the hearth shifting from orange to a glowing green. My vision tunnels, edges turning black, mind filling with an emerald haze. My fists open and close of their own accord.

George's smile falters. "You alright, son? You look a little green around the gills—"

I snatch George by his shoulders and throw him as hard as I can against the nearest wall. His body slams against the stone, and he crumples to the ground in a heap.

"Soon the world will be made right," I tell his motionless form. I reach into the glowing red light and close my hand around the rose. My lungs expand as if I've inhaled the storm before lightning strikes, my fingertips tingling, my heart pounding in rhythm with the flower's silent, radiant pulse. The air tastes of iron and roses, of something forbidden and divine.

I hold the rose before me, watching it catch the glow of the green flames now bursting in the hearth. "The world will be made right once the Prince of Thorns burns it to ash."

16

Rosalina

It's another perfect day.

The Prince of Thorns has me wrapped tightly against him as his lovely briars twine around us and we travel up, up, up.

We break through to the surface. Dusky clouds dot the sky, and there's a faint drizzle. The raindrops are cold and refreshing on my skin. At least the clouds block the sun, so I don't have to worry about looking at it.

He doesn't like when I look at it.

But I inhale, and the sweet scent of fresh blooms and rain-wet stone fills the air.

Spring. We're in the Spring Realm.

I know this, though I'm not sure how.

A terrible image flashes across my mind. Eyes like the richest soil, a jaw covered in stubble that scratched my cheek as he kissed me.

I shake my head, clearing the dreadful thought. Why would I want anyone to kiss me other than the Prince of Thorns? I touch the corner of my mouth where his lips touched mine. Such a special day.

"What are we doing here?" I ask.

The Prince of Thorns has made a suspended chair of briars, legs dangling down. "Waiting for a delivery, darling. Mother wants this thing *so* badly."

A delivery. How exciting! I'm sure whoever gets to deliver this thing to the Prince of Thorns is very lucky indeed. We're in a small forest outside a grand city. I pace beside him, my slippers stained brown from the soft earth, the hem of my dress mud-splattered.

There's a crunch in the briars, but looking at it would mean turning my attention from the Prince of Thorns, and that is something I cannot do.

"What do you think of our guest, Princess?"

The Prince of Thorns has asked me to do something, so do something I must. Observing the figure, I notice he has the same bright green eyes as my prince, but that is where their similarities end. This fae is tall, far taller than Caspian, with long golden hair the color of the sun. Where Caspian is lean and lithe, this man is broad. He wears no shirt so I can see his muscles ripple as he moves.

And he walks strangely, an odd gate to his stance, as if he's a puppet on strings.

Something about it makes me terribly sad.

"Well?" the Prince of Thorns prods.

He's beautiful, I think, but somehow, I know better than to say that out loud. Nausea curls within me. How can I even think that?

Think that when the most beautiful, perfect man in existence sits right above?

But now that I've had this thought, I can't banish it. It's taken root inside me. I can't tear my eyes from him. There's something else. His scent…it's the same as the stuffed lion on my bed.

A man standing in a crowded market, trading a vendor a coin, and tossing the toy into my hands, the most brilliant smile on his face…

But the man coming toward us now isn't smiling.

"He's like…" I quirk my head, answering my master. "He's like the sun."

The Prince of Thorns chuckles and leaps from the branches toward the stranger.

But he's not a stranger. I feel it inside me, this root growing. He's like the sun. Like daylight.

The Prince of Thorns stands before him, and the man drops something into his outstretched palm.

It's a rose.

Not one of the beautiful roses I dream about but a strange, almost glassy thing, with red petals and silver filigree along the stem that shines in the dim light.

My whole body goes cold. My mind begins to scream at me: *Sira must not get that rose. Sira must not get that rose. Sira must not get that rose.*

Holding my hand out, I notice I'm shaking. Neither the Prince of Thorns nor the man pay attention to me.

He did it. O'Connell. My name. My father's name?

But why? Why can't I remember?

Why does it matter? It doesn't matter because it doesn't involve the Prince of Thorns.

He'll never be saved if—

I shake my head. It feels like wandering through mist within my mind.

The Prince of Thorns pockets the rose in the sleeve of his cloak and walks to me, looping an arm around my waist. My mind soothes. It feels so good to be close to him.

"Now that my thrall has served his purpose, he's only a liability," the Prince of Thorns muses. "You see, my father could intervene and turn him against us. The only choice is to dispose of him. Submit, thrall."

The man drops to his knees, golden hair falling across his face. Green flames sprout in a circle around him.

Caspian tilts his chin. "Goodbye, Sunshine."

Yes, the Prince of Thorns agrees with me. He's like the sun. Like daylight. *Cas called Dayton "Sunshine."*

My body trembles. My mind hums. I'm about to vibrate out of my skin. There's too much light in my vision, bright and green and terrible.

"Let your last moments in the Vale be with the awareness of how you failed everyone…again," the Prince of Thorns hisses.

And then the eyes of this man—Dayton, his name is Dayton—flash from green to teal.

Teal like waves under the burning sun, like a siren's tail glittering beneath the sea. The eyes of a man I love.

His scream tears through the rain as the green flames writhe up his body. I feel as if it's my own. Because it is passing through our mate bond, this connection that can fight through anything.

A fire blooms bright in my heart, burning away the fog that has clouded everything that I am. Like a dam being broken, it floods into my consciousness.

My mates. Dayton, Farron, Ezryn, and Keldarion.

Caspian.

My mission here.

All my memories return.

17

Rosalina

I CANNOT DWELL ON EVERYTHING THAT HAS HAPPENED SINCE I WAS sent to the Below. How much time has passed? It feels like a half-remembered dream.

I need to save Day.

My first instinct is to sprout forth my briars, but I feel heavy black binds around my wrists. *Of all the stupid bargains to make, Rosalina O'Connell!* Not that I can blame myself when I was under that spell.

Magic won't help me here, and I can't let Caspian know I've broken past being his obedient little servant.

I tear my gaze away from Dayton, try to block out the pain pulsing through our bond, and instead lay my hand on Caspian's chest. "A waste," I say.

Caspian tilts his chin down at me. His eyes are so green. "What's a waste?"

"Don't you think he could still be useful, my love?" I ask. "A high prince under your command. You're far more powerful than your father if it came to it."

"Rosie, no!" Dayton screams, voice breaking. "This isn't you! Let him end me!"

Shut up, I say in his mind. *I know what I'm doing.*

Dayton blanches. Caspian lets the flames dull to a simmer. He lays a hand over mine. "You're trembling. Does his pain hurt you?"

Of course it does. He's my mate, I think. But instead, I look up at him sweetly. "A little."

Caspian chews his bottom lip, looking between Dayton, who has collapsed on the ground, and me.

"I was afraid of this," he says. "His death might break you. And I don't have the time to put you back together. Perhaps you're right. He can be useful in the future."

Purple briars rise to coil around us.

Dayton stands on shaking feet. I can feel him readying his blessing. *No!* I shout in his mind. *You can't beat him, not how he is. Tell everyone Sira is amassing an army of all her wicked creatures of the Vale. I'll get the rose back, I promise.*

Dayton grits his teeth. *I'm sorry, Rosie, I failed you.*

Tears fall down my cheek. I hope the Prince of Thorns doesn't notice. *No, Day, you set me free.*

Tears fall from his eyes too. *My love for you is an endless sea.*

The briars pull us under, but I shout to him through our bond, desperate and wild, *I love you, I love you, I love you. Even more than I love the sun.*

PART 2

caged beasts

18

Ezryn

My legs burn from the squat position I sank into hours ago, but I haven't been able to move. I still can't; my body feels frozen, my heart pounding a sluggish rhythm against my ribs, as if it's too much effort to even beat.

In the corner of the smithy, Kairyn is a flurry of movement as he wields a hammer with deadly accuracy, assaulting a wooden dummy. I'm surprised his voice isn't raw from the guttural roars that have been tearing out of him.

And in the moonlight that filters through the maw of Draconhold Forge, Dayton paces, leaping every time he catches his reflection in a shield or the glint of a sword. Terrified of the man staring back at him.

George left. I didn't stop him. No point. He doesn't have anything anyone wants anyway.

We'd figured out what had happened by the time Dayton returned. I'd healed the worst of George's wounds—a gash to his head and a dislocated shoulder. But nothing can heal this.

It's gone.

The rose is gone.

Our one hope for turning the tide against Sira, for being able to help Rosalina while she's trapped Below…

Gone. In the blink of an eye.

Amid Kairyn's roars of frustration, I hear Dayton mumbling to himself. He paces like a caged animal, turquoise eyes wide and unseeing. "He wasn't even here, and he could control me. He yanked my strings from across the realms. What is this body? Nothing but an effigy for his use. A fake, that's what I am. A wraith who cannot trust my own hands."

Kairyn lets loose a banshee-like howl, throwing a hammer, shoulders trembling. "All for nothing! I could have told you! She's unstoppable. Nothing will ever change that. What Sira wants, she gets, by blood and by force. Useless to hope. Why did I think…"

I need to say something. They need me to say something.

But what can I say? They're right. Dayton is a pawn on Caspian's board. Whatever move we make, Sira's there waiting. Who am I to offer them hope? I am leader of the rats alone.

"Are you three still in here moping?" a voice calls from the entrance of Draconhold. Slowly, I crane my neck to look, the mere act like moving through sludge.

George stands there, backlit by moonlight. He looks tall from this angle, sapphire gaze sharp and warm at the same time. He must have found a stream, for he's washed all the dirt from his face and clothes.

"Where were you," I say, not even able to manage the inflection of a question.

"Never you mind that. It's far too dark in here. Let us get some light."

None of us seem capable, but George strides in and gathers lanterns on the workbench, filling the space with a warm, golden glow.

We are as still as Kairyn's abused dummy, merely watching this human man bustle around. He leaves for a few minutes, then comes back from the communal kitchen with some sliced mango, four cups of steaming coffee, and a plate of polvorones—which I know he didn't find in this kitchen. *Where were you exactly?*

With a deep sigh, he settles on the workbench, then gestures to the empty space around him. "Come now, join an old man."

I don't know how I'm going to eat, but I can't resist the smell of coffee. My legs creak as I stand and shuffle over to the seat opposite him. Kairyn sits in a huff beside George, nearly tipping the bench before it settles back down.

Dayton wanders over but stays hovering in my peripheral, as if he's afraid to get too close.

"So we're in a spot of trouble, aren't we?" George says with a mouthful of polvorón.

"This isn't trouble, George," Kairyn growls. "This is defeat. Something I'm all too familiar with now."

"Without the rose, all our plans are futile," I say.

George nods and takes a large slurp of his coffee. "Well, not all our plans. I'd say one seems to be going exceedingly well."

I raise a brow. "Oh?"

"My daughter's plan. You said you heard her voice in your mind, did you not, Dayton? That means she's no thrall." A mischievous twinkle lights in George's eye. "She's an inside agent."

"Yeah, well, she's on her own. Again," Dayton growls. "We were supposed to save her. Instead, I've only endangered her more."

"Then I suppose we'll have to find other ways to be helpful," George says.

Kairyn gives a loud snort. "What else is there? We've got a possessed gladiator, a prince with no power, and me." His red eyes flash downward. "A bloody demon."

"Come now, that's not the attitude we need right now. Let's hear some ideas. Ezryn?"

George fixes his gaze on me, but I look away. There's nothing to say.

"Dayton?" George turns to him.

"Kairyn is right," Dayton mumbles. "We're worse than Sira's monsters."

Silence fills the chamber, sharp and acrid. I welcome it, this discomfort. It is what we deserve—

Slam! George thumps his coffee cup down so hard on the workbench, it sloshes everywhere. "Now, this is quite enough! It is not becoming of three members of royalty to be so disparaging when so many others are rising to face hardship greater than we can imagine."

All three of us are on edge by his sudden movement, too shocked to reply.

His eyes crinkle, his gaze softening. "Look, boys. I've done terrible things in my life. Things that will haunt me until my last breath. Do you know what kind of monster I saw in the mirror, sitting alone in my cabin in Orca Cove after my daughter sacrificed herself for me? I saw a man who abandoned his child. And there is no greater shame than that."

He rises to his feet, circling us, his presence heavy, his voice steady. One by one, he meets our eyes, holding us there.

"But do you see me whinging in the dark? Well, yes, but only because I'm stuck with *you three*." A flicker of humor, gone as quickly as it came. "No. I made peace with my evils. I faced them. I looked into the eyes of those I hurt and *apologized*. And then I spent every damned day trying to live in a way that would make my daughter proud."

He stops, turning to us fully.

"Now it's your turn. Stand up and wipe the blood off your pride. You think you've lost everything? No. You still have a choice. Make the right one."

I realize I haven't blinked in minutes. I give my head a shake, the weight of the helm comforting.

Kairyn lets out a slow exhale and runs a hand through his hair, across his horns. "You make it sound so damn simple," he mutters, voice quiet but edged with something sharp. "Like we just decide to be better, and suddenly we are." His crimson gaze flicks to George. "What if it's not enough?"

There's something raw in his voice, as if he's afraid to believe in the possibility George offers. Hope is dangerous. Hope can break a man worse than defeat ever could.

"It's not simple, Kai. And it's never enough." He lets the words settle, heavy between us. "Nothing you do will change what's already been done. No apology, no grand gesture, no amount of regret will rewrite the past. But that's not the point."

He gestures at all of us.

"You don't do it because it erases the wrongs. You do it because it's right. And because if you don't, you'll wake up one day and realize you've let the worst parts of yourself win."

He grabs Kairyn's hand and squeezes it.

"Spring is the season of rebirth. For new beginnings. It's never too late."

My brother doesn't respond but looks to where George clasps his hand. Then he puts his own over it and gives a terse nod.

Magic shimmers in the air, and we turn to the entrance of Draconhold to see the golden wolf. Moonlight illuminates the pearly shells and coral laced in his fur as well as the leather bag strapped to his powerful back.

"Where are you going, Dayton?" I call.

"To Autumn," the wolf responds. "George is right. Neither Farron nor I can change what happened. If this is our fate, then I would weather it together."

A smile breaks across George's face. "Run! Run like the summer's wind!"

Kairyn, George, and I move to the entranceway to watch Dayton lope away from the forge and out of the city proper. Silence falls over us when he disappears from view, but it's not the sharp quiet of earlier. It is the contentment of hope.

"And you, Ezryn?" George asks. "What will you do?"

I cast my gaze across Florendel to where Keep Hammergarden

sits, surrounded by cherry blossom trees. "I suppose it's time I walk the Hall of Vernalion once more."

"Oh good." George turns. "Because I've been to the keep and told Tilla to prepare for your coronation."

19

Rosalina

There are details in Sira's dining room I've never noticed before. During the haze of my thralldom, my focus so intent on the Prince of Thorns, everything around me became a blur.

Now, sitting at Sira's long table in the Tower of Nether Reach, I take in every detail, just as I did on the journey here. It was a half-hour trip from Cryptgarden, pulled in a carriage by a pack of grinjaws, the hyena-like canines that serve the goblins.

I never opened the curtains in the carriage before. But this time, I did. The scenery was mostly gray rock, sometimes enclosing us in vast, jagged tunnels, other times giving way to sheer cliffs with nothing but darkness yawning below. Now and then, we'd drive past glowing mineral veins in the rock that would light the entire carriage up, fractured rays scattering across the velvet seats, as if we'd driven straight through a kaleidoscope.

I pressed my face against the cool glass as a forest of tall crystals glittered outside, a reminder that even in the dark, light persists. A light I'll find in the Prince of Thorns again.

When I tried to show Heidigog the glowing trees, all she did was shrug. She's seemed so sad lately. Here in the dining hall, I swivel to look at her standing behind me in deference. There's a weight to her shoulders. That hasn't always been there, has it?

I look around. The dining hall is cavernous, its vaulted ceiling lost in shadow, the obsidian walls flickering with a pale glow from the mounted lanterns. We sit at a long table made of bloodred wood, a bowl of soup before each of us. Velvet chairs enough for an entire party line each side, but there's only me and *her.*

Sitting at the head is Sira, Queen of the Below.

It's really not fair that someone so terrible is so damned beautiful. Her high cheekbones are as sculpted as blades, her hair a midnight black. It's as straight and silky as a shampoo commercial, the kind of hair I was so jealous of as a teenager. A crown of blackened silver spikes rests upon her brow. Even her gown, a gunmetal gray threaded with green, seems alive, shifting with the smallest flickers of light.

She doesn't smile, and I'm glad of it. Somehow, she seems more sinister when she smiles.

Unable to stand her stare anymore, I ask, "Where is the Prince of Thorns?" I glance to the empty seat beside me where Caspian usually sits. We are often summoned to meals with Sira, but this is the first one where he hasn't been in the carriage with me or met me at the entrance to Nether Reach.

Sira doesn't respond for so long, I wonder if I've turned invisible.

Then she cricks her neck, and her gaze refocuses on me with slightly less intensity. "My son's duties are taking him far longer than usual. He'll join us shortly."

I nod and place my hands in my lap. This might be for the best. Since seeing Dayton, I've kept my thoughts my own, but the closer I am to Caspian, the harder it is. There are still traces of that bargain in me that want to fall back into my devotion to him.

This meal, with my mind so clear, could be the perfect opportunity to learn some things about Sira, as long as I can manage it while pretending to be Caspian's thrall. It's the state in which she finds me the most appealing.

At least Caspian hasn't given Sira the rose yet. He keeps it tucked tight in his cloak. *Why hasn't he handed it over? Sira must not know he has it.*

"Are you going to stare at your food all night or eat, girl?" she says, leaning on one of her armrests.

I nod and turn my attention back to the soup in front of me: a bland gray thing with a swirl of white in the middle. I have no idea what it is, only that it's tasteless. Maybe I should be grateful for that. I shudder to think of what Sira's favorite food is.

Dutifully, I sip my soup. It's cold.

When I finish, I look up at Sira with my best thralldom gaze.

Sira motions for her goblin servant to clear our dishes. Heidigog grabs mine and takes it to the kitchen. Another goblin places a platter of charred eel and blood-drenched marrow before Sira. Beside it, a goblet of obsidian nectar swirls. My stomach roils.

"Oh, don't look so disgusted," Sira sneers. "I had something special prepared for you." She snaps her fingers at Heidi. "You, goblin. There's a special plate for my son's pet in the kitchen. Atop the marble platter. You'll know it."

Her words are not comforting, but when Heidigog places the platter down in front of me and lifts the lid, all I can do is gasp.

It's a whole pizza, glistening with bright red tomato sauce and bubbling white cheese. I've never seen anything like this in the Vale.

"This is what you ate in the human realm," Sira asks as she leans forward on her elbows, smiling, "isn't it?"

"Yes," I say. I'm confident she won't poison me; I'm much too useful to her alive. But something wrong twists in my gut.

"Go on," Sira urges. "Try it."

I glance to Heidigog, whose yellow eyes narrow. She gazes down at the pizza like a human might look at a cockroach. As tasty as it looks, I don't want to eat it. But Caspian's thrall wouldn't say no to Sira, so I can't either.

I grab a slice. It's cold, despite the steam rising from it. The crust is slippery...

But with Sira's ever-watching eyes following my every movement, it's all I can do to bring it to my lips. I bite down, and the pizza dissolves into inky black shadows.

I cough and sputter on the smoke. Heidi gives a great gasp, whirling her short arms and knocking the tray lid to the ground with a clatter.

The pizza on the plate dissipates into a cluster of shadows. Illusions. Like the fake vial she created within Mount Rhuvenmark to deceive Caspian.

"Oh, you have the same expression as your mother when she's

been fooled." Sira bursts into a laugh, whether in genuine amusement or simple cruelty, I can't decide. "You know, in the Above, Aurelia and I used to play these little games on each other all the time. She once tricked me into eating a delectable moonberry pie, but it tasted of mud. Then I covered the soles of her feet with thistlebind. She stuck to everything for a week." Sira lets out another string of laughter.

Were my mother and Sira once *friends*? I couldn't imagine playing those kinds of pranks on someone I cared about.

Sira's laughter fades, and she taps her chin. "Aurelia always thought herself so clever. I got the best of her in the end though."

My hands clench into fists beneath the table; she's speaking of the bargain she used to trap my mother. Perhaps if I can get her to speak more of it, I'll find a loophole. Fae bargains are all about their wording. "The Prince of Thorns told me your magic far exceeds even the queen's."

He never said that, but she's vain enough to believe it. A smile spreads across her face. "Of course it does. It's the reason your mother came to me, to learn a power only I understood."

"To save my father's life," I say.

"To bind one's life to another." Sira stands, gaze faraway. "Everything in our world is woven together by life and spirit. You need to pull back the veil from your mind to see the threads."

"Can the Prince of Thorns do this?" I ask. What I want to know is how she did it. The more I learn of her powers, the more we can undo her.

"Perhaps, but he is a child of the Below," she says. "The fae of the Above have an easier time of spotting what would stay hidden.

We can see the spirit of things as you see mist rise from a lake in the morn. But the light on land makes it harder to see."

A part of me understands what she means. I've seen the souls of fae when I reached across the oceans to connect to the sirens and when I turned the Deep Guard to snowy owls. I saw the threads that make up Astrid when I tried to turn her back from hare to fae. But I've never tried to see the spirit of other living things in the Vale: the trees, the flowers, the grass. Or Castletree itself.

I itch to try it, but with Caspian's bargain holding my magic at bay, it's nothing but a prickling beneath my skin.

"We'll see how Castletree holds up once we take the surface," Sira continues. "Perhaps if you keep being so good, we'll let it stand. It'll need redecorating, of course, and the Queen's Tower needs to go. The only magic left in the Vale will be mine and my son's."

My stomach twists, and I try to control my breathing. The thought of Sira touching Castletree sickens me. I feel vulnerable without the comfort of my magic simmering below my skin.

Sira, still smiling, waves her goblet. "This is empty."

The other goblins have returned to the kitchen, so Heidigog dutifully steps forward and grabs the bottle of inky nectar. The first few drops land in the goblet, the consistency more like oil than wine. Then Heidigog's hand slips. The bottle tips too far, and nectar splashes over Sira's sleeve.

For a moment, silence. My pulse pounds.

Sira sets down her goblet with eerie grace. Then she flicks her fingers. Shadows slither from beneath her chair like living smoke, curling toward Heidigog.

The goblin whimpers, stumbling back. "I–I'm sorry, Your Majesty. Please, I—"

Sira barely looks at her. "You are a disgusting disgrace."

Her shadows strike.

Heidigog shrieks as the darkness wraps around her wrists and ankles, lifting her off the ground. The tendrils squeeze, twisting and tightening as if testing how much she can take before her bones snap.

No, Heidi! I clench my fists under the table, nails digging into my palms. My breath comes fast, shallow. I'm supposed to be Caspian's thrall. Powerless.

If I give myself away, I'll never get the rose back from Caspian. This is about so much more than just one person's pain.

If I move, if I so much as flinch wrong—

She will know I've been lying. Know I'm not just another broken thing in Caspian's collection.

Heidigog lets out a thin, choked cry. The shadows wind higher, curling around her throat.

Something inside me snaps.

I lunge from my seat, throwing myself between Sira and the goblin, arms outstretched. "Stop!"

Sira's eyes flash, sharp as cut obsidian. "*You* would question my judgment? Why?"

Heidigog falls to the ground, trembling.

I stare at Sira. "Because she's my friend."

Sira smiles. "Then you'll be more than happy to take her punishment."

A shadow lashes at me, and all goes dark.

20

Rosalina

I wake with a start, body heavy, my vision swimming in and out of focus. The dining hall is in ruins—plates shattered, goblets overturned, the remnants of food strewn across the floor like the aftermath of a storm. The air is thick with the scent of spilled nectar and something fouler, acrid. My dress is torn, the hem now in frayed strands. My head throbs with a dull pulse.

A whimpering noise reaches me.

Heidigog.

She cowers in the corner, her yellow eyes wide, but she's not looking at me. Her gaze is fixed on something behind me.

I do not turn. I know who it is.

Instead, I swallow my fear and keep my expression vacant as Sira steps toward me. "What is your purpose?" the Queen of the Below snarls.

I blink, feigning confusion. It's not hard with my head still ringing. "To serve the Prince of Thorns. I belong to him."

Sira *tsks*, tapping a finger against her lips. "Evēn as his thrall, you are disobedient. And disobedience cannot go unpunished."

She turns as footsteps echo through the hall. The presence that enters is unnatural. A cold weight settles in my gut. The air grows thick with magic that shouldn't exist in this world anymore, like dust and rot and things buried beneath the earth for too long.

"This is Vespera, the Abyssal Sorceress," Sira purrs, gesturing toward the figure that steps into the dim light. "She has a unique power. One you'll get to experience."

I try not to shrink back, though every fiber of my being screams at me to run.

Vespera's skin is a strange shade of pale blue. Her dark hair coils and shifts as if caught in a breeze no one else can feel. And her teeth…rows of razor-sharp fangs, her gums slick with black, oozing blood.

She tilts her head, voice curling around me like smoke. "The hood or the mirror?"

I inhale.

I do not know what the hood entails, but I do not want to lose my sight, to be trapped in darkness. My words are barely a whisper. "The mirror."

A smile unfurls across Vespera's face, slow and knowing. From within the folds of her dark cloak, she draws a tarnished mirror. The handle and rim are engraved with butterflies, their delicate wings warped into something twisted.

She steps closer, holding it up before me. "Stare into the mirror, and do not look away. For if you do, you will write what you see into truth."

Stare into a mirror. I can do that. I take it in my hand.

The edges of the mirror glow red. Jagged light crackles from the glass.

I scream.

The pain is immediate and searing, like something burrowing deep beneath my skin. *Don't look away*, I remind myself. *Don't look away.*

I force myself to stare into the mirror's glass surface. Farron appears in the reflection. My heart races. He's running across a battlefield as a troll's spear impales him through the chest. Then beside him is Day, his eyes glowing sickly green, plunging his blade into Ezryn's back.

Pain blossoms through my body as if I too have been struck. I cry out, my breath ragged, my hands trembling.

"Look away at any time, Rosalina," Sira croons. "Vespera stole this mirror from Philiris, Fate of the future. Now the power of destiny is in your hands."

No.

It can't be true. I control my own destiny.

And still, the visions come.

Keldarion, my husband, stands alone in Frostfang. Thousands of Winter soldiers lie dead around him. Dark creatures swarm him, an unending tide of the Below.

A scream tears from my throat, echoing through the chamber. My knees buckle against the cold floor. The rest of me follows, shaking and splintering.

Then I see her.

My mother, strung atop great green crystals, her body lifeless. Caspian holds out his hand and forms a glowing portal. A giant of a man with flowing white hair steps through, ears too long to be a fae of the Vale. *Who is that?*

I can't watch this anymore. I am breaking. Shattering. Another vision slams into me like a dagger to the heart—

My father, falling into a chasm of great briars and bark.

My breath hitches. The mirror nearly slips out of my trembling hands. Pain surges, too much to bear, as the visions keep coming, relentless. A spasm jolts through my fingers, and I clench hard around the handle. Surely it must be almost over…

The visions start again. The same ones, over and over and over again. Every few rounds, new horrors get added to the rotations. Astrid and Marigold crushed beneath the falling rubble of Castletree. My sister speared by shadows.

I want to look away. No one controls my fate but me, and yet… I cannot risk them. Not my mates, my friends, my family. I will exist forever in this nightmare.

I don't know when I started screaming, only that my throat is raw from it, eyes blurred with tears of sadness and pain. I feel every death that flashes in this mirror as if it were my own. Over and over and over and—

The glass shatters.

A briar spears through the mirror, splintering it into shards of light and darkness.

I fall to the floor, gasping. Silence crashes over the room, thick and heavy. A storm waiting to break.

And then I hear it.

The slow, deliberate step of boots against stone.

A part of me thinks I'm still trapped in the nightmare because the figure in the doorway is too terrible to exist.

Shadow and fire coil at his feet, writhing and snapping like caged beasts. The air around him crackles with power, wrath barely restrained. His eyes burn, twin coals of fury, bright green against the abyss of his face.

A monster of night made real.

The Prince of Thorns has returned.

21

The Prince of Thorns

I'M NOT PARTICULARLY WORRIED ABOUT THE FEELINGS OF OTHERS.

Rosalina, my mate, is the exception.

Her pain, her sorrow, courses into me through our bond until there is a single thought in my mind.

I will not rest until everyone who hurt her has suffered tenfold what she has.

The mirror shatters on the floor. One of Vespera's torture devices. I know it intimately, as I do the hood, the crown, and the string.

My mate gasps, her beautiful gown torn, face wet with tears.

With a deep snarl, I pierce Vespera with my gaze. Thorns sprout, dragging her to the ground, and shadows gag her sickening mouth. With a clench of my fist, an inferno of fire sprouts around the witch.

She's a creature of torture, so a painful death would only delight the old crone. Better to kill her quickly.

"Stop," Sira snarls. "I command it."

My shadows and thorns and fire fall away. The bargain clamps down on me, controlling my every whim. Ragged breaths claw out of my throat.

Vespera writhes on the ground, clutching the burned flesh of her spindly legs.

"Vespera will be invaluable in the war to come," my mother says and strolls over to the grand table, righting a goblet and pouring nectar. "It was I who called her up. Surely you can appreciate a little torture."

It wasn't Vespera who hurt my mate or me all those times. Over and over. It was *her.*

Queen of the Below.

Kill her, a deep voice rings in my mind. *Kill her and ascend to your throne as lord of the Below. Take the fae woman as your queen.*

Finally, something we agree on, Father, I answer.

A ball of fire appears in my palm, and I register the moment she sees the reflection in her goblet. Quick shadows snap up to block my attack and send the flame careening across the dining hall.

"You would not—*will not* harm me," she stammers, changing from a question to a command at the last second.

Clever.

That bargain stills my hand, and I snarl through my teeth.

"What was that?" Sira's eyes are wide, watery. "You would never hurt me. My son?"

I huff and begin to pace. "Your son hesitated to kill you because he had a soft heart. Thankfully," I say with a smile, "your command to embrace the Green Flame burned away all parts of him. I would gladly pike your head outside this tower."

"Why do you care so..." Sira clutches her heart, then her gaze shifts to Rosalina. "She's your mate."

A voice inside me screams. Terror floods my being.

Not for myself. No one in the realms or all the worlds could harm me.

But for her.

Sira's stare is furious as she pierces mine. "Kill her."

"Caspian!" Rosalina cries.

A scream echoes in my mind from somewhere deep within. No, not a scream. An answer. Calling out to her. Her name.

"Cas, I love you," Rosalina says, staring at me. "You'll never hurt me."

"It doesn't matter what he wants," Sira snarls. "He is under my control. Kill her."

All I know is this—every ounce of my power, every flicker of magic in me, was made to protect her. To protect my mate. So even as the barbs of the bargain pierce deep and thoughts of her death strike like arrows through my mind, I grit my teeth. "No."

It's like two fibers of my being are at war with each other, and I have just enough strength to keep them at bay.

Sira blanches. Then that beautiful face, so similar to my own, shifts into a snarl. "I commanded it. You are under *my* control."

Fae can only make bargains with other fae, right? It's my mate's voice, invading my thoughts. Even within my head, she sounds weak. But as I look at her, I see she's assessing the situation. Searching for a way to help me.

What a good little queen you are, I purr in her mind. Then I turn my attention to my mother.

"I am the son of Malekai Furiondemius, Baron of the Green Flame," I say, prowling forward. "I am half fae…and half something greater. Power that the fae of the Above can only dream of. And the strength of that blood will not be commanded. You do not have control over me as you do Aurelia."

Sira stumbles back. "Kill her," she snarls. "Kill your mate."

The more this new command beats against my willpower, the more it lessens her other commands. Do not harm her.

"Kill her? Keep the witch alive? Or do not harm you? What is your command, Mother?" I snarl. "Because you can only hold one, and I could kill Rosalina in the same sweep of fire that would devour you."

My mother's lip trembles.

"Choose." Flames grow at my feet, lighting every inky space of this cursed tower in green.

Sira finds her back flat against the wall.

"Choose, Mother," I growl.

"Y-you…" she gasps. "You will not harm me."

"Pity," I say.

With a snap of my fingers, Vespera erupts into a pillar of ash, the smoke turning a sickly blue gray as her rotten corpse burns.

I look down at my mother. "Kneel before me."

Her eyes widen in indignation. "*I* am your queen. You should kneel before *me*."

I raise a dark brow. "Is that a command? By all means, change it."

Her breath is raspy, fury near unkept, but inch by inch, Sira drops to her knees.

I regard her for a moment before turning to my mate. Then I

scoop Rosalina into my arms. She's barely conscious. I hiss through my teeth. *I will have vengeance for this.*

With heavy steps, I carry her toward the door, her little goblin attendant scurrying at my feet. I pause and look back over at my mother. She's still on the floor.

Good.

"If you lay a hand on her again, Mother, I fear nothing in this world could keep the green flame from burning through your pitiful fae bargain and consuming you."

22

Rosalina

A sharp stab of pain shoots through me, and I squeeze my eyes shut. The mirror. Green flames…

The Prince of Thorns.

A hand brushes the hair from my brow. The scent of lavender sweeps over me, and I shift over sheets that are so soft, they feel like water flowing over my body. My whole being feels relaxed, as if some primal part of me knows I'm safe.

Blinking open my eyes, I see the Prince of Thorns leaning over my bed, his unnatural green stare fixed on me.

No, I'm not safe. An illusion of a memory.

This isn't my bed. It's his. He brought me to his chambers.

Caspian holds my gaze, then slides a hand down my neck. "Your heart's beating so fast." He says it like a question. "When did you break out of the spell?"

"I—"

"You can't lie to me, Rosalina." He pulls his hand away and stands.

"When I saw Dayton."

A low rumble sounds in the back of his throat. Jealousy? "I knew that was risky." He shakes his head. "It doesn't matter. Thrall or not, you won't get far in the Below without your briars."

I chew my bottom lip. He's right. Slowly, I sit up, realize I'm now wearing a silken nightdress. I throw my hand across my chest. "Did you…?"

A slow smile curves over his face until he finally says, "No, Heidigog changed you. Couldn't have you in those tatters."

"She's alright then?"

"You would care about the goblin," he says, though not unkindly.

This is the most he's spoken to me since I've come to the Below. Perhaps having a doting thrall grew tiresome for even the Prince of Thorns.

"But you know," Caspian continues, tilting his head, long strands of dark hair covering his brow, "it wouldn't matter if I had been the one to do it. I've seen your body. Tasted every inch."

"Really? The Green Flame didn't burn those memories away from you too?" I ask, remembering what he said of Caspian's soft heart.

He kneels on the side of my bed. "No fire in the world could burn away the feeling of being inside you."

The intensity in his gaze shocks me. I know that stare. *But what about your love for me?*

"You were afraid today," I try.

"You're very breakable," he replies. "As you've pointed out, I lose you, and I lose my ability to rule the Vale. My father's blood may give me an edge over Sira, but it makes it tricky to live anywhere but here."

"It's more than that," I challenge him.

"You're my mate, Rosalina. I don't like people touching what is *mine*."

I'm not sure why it comforts me, the thought that our bond holds strong, even when he's like this. It feels more like possessiveness—and, judging by the way his gaze sears into me, lust—than the love I once knew from him. But if those emotions are there, perhaps the others are buried deep inside.

There were flashes of purple in his eyes. He's still in there. I just don't know how to bring him back.

But first, I have to concentrate on what I can control.

My eyes search his room until I land on his cloak discarded in the corner. The cloak in which he's hidden the rose.

If Sira gets that, we have no hope.

But without my magic, there's no way for me to escape with it.

Idly, I finger my beautiful wedding ring and think of Kel, Ezryn, Farron, and Day. I hope they're alright. It feels like there's a brand crawling over my skin as Caspian's eyes track my every movement. A plan begins to form in my mind. "I don't just belong to you," I say lowly.

He lets out a low breath and crawls closer to me. My body heats at his presence. *It's because I know he's still in there.*

"How come you never touched me?" I ask. "Even when I begged?"

He shrugs but doesn't answer, instead tucking a curl behind my ear.

"Tell me."

"I meant it, Rosalina." He leans in, breath hot over my neck. "You are to be my queen. I would not have you any less of mind."

I hold out my wrist. "But you would have me less of power?"

He chuckles and touches the cuff where his bargain binds my magic. "Not forever. Just until you accept your place by my side."

I tear my wrist away. "You know my heart will never fully belong to *only* you."

In an instant, he hooks an arm around my waist and flips me to the mattress. Then he prowls over me.

But this is not the Caspian I remember.

This is the Prince of Thorns. Every movement he makes is predatory, calculated. The power Cas kept so locked inside radiates off him in waves. I could get drunk on the feeling of that power if I'm not careful.

He drops his head, trailing his lips a breath away from my skin as he travels lower down my body. He inhales, as if he could get as drunk on the scent of me as I can from him.

"I'm not a fool. I know you hate me," he says.

I take his face in mine and draw him closer. "You once told me you would know me in any form. Caspian, Prince of Roses, I will love you in any form."

And maybe it's the light, maybe it's my own delusions, but I swear for a moment his eyes flash purple.

So I kiss him.

I breathe him in as he tugs me flush against his body. He makes a desperate male sound in the back of his throat, and I tangle my hands in his hair.

With a strong hand, he grabs my thigh and hoists it up over his leg so I feel his hard length press against me. "Cas," I sigh against him.

He huffs a breath and pulls away, kneeling on the bed and peering down at me. "Don't call me that. Don't delude yourself into thinking that's who you're kissing. Look at my eyes, Rosalina."

They're green.

His smile widens. "If you choose to stay in this bed, then I am going to fuck you. And it will not be the sweet, tender way *Cas* did. You are mine. To play with. To torment. To use."

"What about your bargain?" I breathe. "Are you willing to lose me for one night of pleasure?"

He tilts his head. "I can control myself when I need to. Staying means you accept that. Choose, Princess."

My chest heaves in my throat. He's a beautiful nightmare, lust and power radiating off him.

But maybe there's a way for me to save him and the rose.

Will our love, my touch, be enough to pull him from this haze?

And if not… What if he did lose control? Would I have time to grab the rose before his bargain with Keldarion took over? I could whisk the rose away to safety.

This is possibly the best and worst idea I've had yet.

And it only requires sleeping with the Prince of Thorns.

So I take my hand and draw the strap of my nightdress lower, revealing the curve of my breast. "I told you. Any form."

23

The Prince of Thorns

A THRUM OF SATISFACTION COURSES THROUGH ME AT HER OBEDIENT little smile. "Perfect." I smirk, then stand off to the side of the bed. "Now, kneel and suck my cock."

It's cute, the immediate flash of defiance in her eyes. That pitiful thrall the Winter Prince sent me would have slobbered on me from dawn to dusk had I let her.

No, that didn't interest me at all.

Not like my real Rose.

Keeping my eyes locked with hers, I draw the laces from my tunic and drop it to the ground, then unlace my pants and step out. My cock is already impossibly hard, as it always is around her.

Her gaze turns appreciative, and she stands.

"Naked, please," I tell her, holding up a palm.

She drops her nightdress in a pool at her feet, and I take in every inch of her perfect body: the heavy swell of her breasts, nipples pink and perked, the lush dip of her hips. There isn't a mark on her.

No one will ever touch her again.

She saunters toward me, looks at my cock, then back at my face. "What if I've reconsidered?"

I stroke the nape of her neck softly, just enough to leave her wanting more. "I could force you to watch me fuck one of the depraved fae of Cryptgarden. You'd love that."

Stop or I'll die. The memory of her voice in my mind is still so loud. The last time I was with someone other than her…

Or him.

"That would be just as painful for you as it is for me," Rosalina says. "No one else's body makes yours feel like mine does."

Unfortunately, she's right.

"Okay, Prince of Thorns," she says, looping her arms around my shoulders. "Let's make a deal."

"My queen," I purr. "Already negotiating."

"I'll obey your commands, but every time you give me one, I get to say, 'I love you.'"

"A lie." I trail my tongue along her throat. "But if imagining I'm him is what it takes to have your body, then lie all you want."

"Deal."

"Princess." I press on the crown of her head. "On. Your. Knees."

She drops to the ground and looks up at me with those bright, brown eyes. My cock twitches. Fuck, all these weeks of having her so close and touching her have been torture. To give in now…

It's dangerous.

But I can't resist.

Her soft hands grip my thigh, and she runs her tongue along my shaft, teasing.

"Enough," I growl, grabbing the back of her head and shoving my cock down her throat.

She lets out a surprised gulp before eagerly swallowing me. I give a low groan, immense pleasure coursing through my body. God, she's so fucking good.

I pick up my tempo, roughly fucking her throat, and she matches my pace, nails digging into my thighs to hold herself steady. "Just like that," I sigh.

My cock spears the back of her throat, and she falls back, coughing.

"Too much for you?" I ask.

She throws her wayward hair over her face and stares at me. "I *love* you."

I turn away from her dangerous game. I should send her away. She's a threat to my power.

And the only way to secure my rule.

The one thing in this world that matches my fire's need to burn, to control…is her.

How much I *want* her.

"Cas, what next?"

She says my name like a prayer.

"Get on the bed."

She does, and I crawl over her.

I let my hand trail to her throat, just tight enough to remind her who she belongs to. Her back arches, that perfect body trembling, already on edge from pleasuring me.

"Are you enjoying this, little rose?" I murmur. My mouth ghosts over her jaw, down her neck. I want her *desperate* for me.

Her moan resembles *yes*, but that's not enough. I still her with a look, and her breath hitches as if she's seen something divine. Or terrifying. Same difference.

"Say it," I command, tone dropping to a growl. "Tell me how good I am to you. Tell me who I am to you."

She hesitates for a second. And gods, that second is agony.

Then she gives in.

"You're," she gasps as I roll my hips against hers, pulling another helpless sound from her throat, "you're my mate."

"More."

"You're beautiful," she breathes, eyes fluttering shut. "Powerful. You make me feel like I'm—"

"Yours," I finish for her, sinking my teeth into the pulse at her neck, just enough to sting. It leaves a mark on her. She whimpers, clinging to me, melting beneath the pain-pleasure edge.

"Yes," she moans. "Yours."

That's it. That's *exactly* it.

"I know," I whisper against her skin. "Say it again. Say it like you mean it."

And when she does, when her voice breaks on the word *yours*, when her fingers dig into my back like I'm the only thing anchoring her to this world, I give her everything she's asking for.

And everything she doesn't know she *should* fear.

I sink my cock inside her.

She cries out, teeth biting into my shoulder.

She feels like everything I've ever wanted. Everything I need.

She's the sun burning away every shadow lashed around my heart. *Rose—*

"Cas, Cas, Cas," she cries, grabbing my face, searching for something she won't find.

Someone she'll never find again.

I begin to move, savoring the sweet feeling of her wet heat. Magic coils beneath my skin, electric, barely leashed.

"I love you," she says again.

"You're mine," I remind her, trying not to lose myself too deeply in her.

She gasps, her body arching into mine, and her fingers clutch the back of my neck.

"You feel that?" I murmur, brushing my lips against her temple. "That's me, little rose. Inside you. Around you. *Under your skin.*"

She nods. Her lips part to speak, but I catch her chin between my fingers and tilt her head, forcing her to meet my gaze.

"Say it," I command again. "Say what I am."

"You're..." She falters, dazed and aching, and it makes me smile. "You're my prince."

"Mm-hmm." I drag my mouth across hers, slow, possessive. Not a kiss, not yet. Just a promise. "Not *a* prince. Not who you remember. *The* prince. Say it."

"The Prince of Thorns," she breathes.

"That's it, Princess. I will keep you like this forever."

A gasp shudders out from between her lips.

"Do you want that, Rosalina?"

She nods.

"Say that too. Say you want to belong to me."

Her leg hooks over my hip, drawing me deeper. "Yours. I want to belong to you."

I believe her.

Because I know that is a part of her truth. A piece of her heart that is mine. I just have to make her *all* mine. Burn out all traces of her other mates.

She uses her leg to flip us, and I let her, simply because the sight of her body above mine is divine. I caress her breast, then drag a hand down, rubbing her clit. She moans, sighing into the touch. Her inner walls clutch around me.

"Yes, like that." She presses a palm to my chest, right over where my heart should be.

"Caspian," she whispers. Not *my prince.* Not *the Prince of Thorns.* Just *Caspian.* "Come back to me."

I still.

The green fire snarls in my veins. The shadows twitch like agitated crows. Thorns break out from the ground and curl closer.

I could bind her wrists. Or better yet her mouth, so she stops saying such things.

Snarling, I grip her hips and rut harder into her. It doesn't matter what she says. I need to make her forget everyone but me.

But she looks at me like I've already lost.

"This is who I was always meant to be," I snarl, catching her wrist and pulling her flush against me. "The Green Flame *freed* me. I will make you the queen he never could."

"No," she says, voice shaking. "It *changed* you."

She tries to pull away. I don't let her. Vines of shadow lash out and circle her waist, not tightly yet. A warning.

"You will love this version of me," I whisper, dragging my fingers up her arm. "You don't have to fix me. You will join me."

Her face twists into a glare, and I still my movement, save my cock twitching inside her.

"You are nothing but your father's puppet," she says. "Caspian was brave. I want the man who used to laugh. The one who told me his dreams. The one who kissed me like he wasn't sure he deserved to."

In the deepest dark of the Below, when I thought I would never see light again, all I could think of was you.

Something in me stutters. The flame inside flickers.

She sees something and dares to hope.

She places her hand over mine.

I want to tear it away.

I want to let it in. *Save me, Rose.*

My mouth finds hers. I kiss her like she's air and I've been drowning in fire. She kisses me back like she's trying to put the flames out.

And for one moment, one *terrible* moment, I remember who I was.

And I *hate* it.

I pull away from her, the green fire roaring again.

"You shouldn't have done that," I whisper.

Her eyes shine. "I'll do it again," she says. "I'll keep doing it. Until you remember."

I let the shadows dissipate. "Leave."

She doesn't, her body still intertwined with mine. "I'm not finished."

A smile curves up my face. I'm done with games, and it seems so is she. "I can't promise to be gentle with you. But I can promise that you'll come so hard, you'll feel it for days."

Her thighs tremble around me, and she stares me down as she mouths, *I love you.*

She dared to try and fix me. She kissed me like I was him, like I was still that boy with trembling hands and a voice that cracked when he said her name.

I hate her for that.

I love her for it.

It hurts worse than any blade, any torture I've ever endured.

"You think you can heal me?" I growl, slamming her back against the bed, my hand braced beside her head, thorns breaking through the mattress. "That your soft words and sad eyes will unmake what I've become?"

She stares at me, lips parted, chest rising with each breath. She doesn't answer.

She doesn't need to.

Because I already know, and it makes me furious.

"You want the man I was?" I snarl. "Then take what's left of him."

I kiss her, rough and hungry, like it's a punishment, like I can shove all the confusion and grief back down with the taste of her. She gasps against my mouth, but she doesn't push me away. Her grip tightens, claws into my skin, and I drag her harder against me.

We make love like it's war.

Every movement is a battle between what I am and what I was. Between what I want and what I've become. My shadows crawl over her skin, thorns curling around us.

My hands knead her soft breasts, twisting her nipples as her nails claw down my back.

"Caspian!" She cries out my name, the old one, and I freeze, just for a moment.

Rose, I'm not.

I'm not him.

Unable to stop touching her, I bring her to the edge over and over until she's shaking, breathless, tears glistening on her cheeks. She's hurting. And I'm the reason. And still…her body answers mine.

She's so wet, my cock easily slides in and out. My fingers are sloppy as I circle her clit.

She feels good. She feels like home. And I ruin her anyway.

When she shatters beneath me, I hold her too tightly. I press my mouth to her throat and breathe her in and pretend I can keep her as she is, soft and trembling and mine.

And why can't I?

"Come inside me, Cas," she gasps, still shaking from her high.

Ahh, she'd love that, wouldn't she?

To be sent to her precious Winter Prince. And while the thought of sending her to him, used and spent and covered in me, has some sort of pleasure…

I want to keep her more.

"I'm never letting you leave." I slip my cock, near ready to burst, out and step away.

Keldarion will never have her again.

24

Rosalina

The shadows have stopped moving.

The thorns have retracted from my skin.

My body aches, and my lips are still swollen from his kisses. I sit up as the Prince of Thorns crosses the room. He picks up his discarded cloak.

"This is what you wanted, isn't it, love?" He tosses the cloak over to me. "Couldn't keep your eyes off it."

How did he know?

He lazily pumps his cock as he watches me search through the folds of the fabric. Empty. *Empty.* He must have moved the rose.

The Prince of Thorns lets out a pained groan as cum spills over his hands. He sighs and stares me straight in the eye. "Would have rather emptied that in you. Guess I'll have to start getting creative to make that icy bastard fall out of love with me."

My eyes drift to the frosted thorn bracelet on his wrist.

Kel will always love you, I say in his mind. *As I will.*

He either doesn't hear or ignores me and wanders to the attached privy.

A long sigh escapes me. My plan didn't work.

Why do I feel this way?

I should be furious. Sickened. I should be screaming at the moon for ever believing he could be saved.

But instead, I press my hand to one of the thorns that broke through the mattress.

Because for a moment I saw him.

Not the Prince of Thorns.

Not the green fire god with eyes like molten emeralds and a voice that cracks the sky.

Caspian.

The man who once touched me like I was something precious. The man who saved me again and again. The man who stopped me from creating a darkness in my own heart, who bore that burden for me. The man who told me he feared his own magic and what might happen if he ever lost himself.

He lost himself.

And now I'm standing in the aftermath.

I drag my knees to my chest and try to breathe.

But the way he touched me, the way he looked at me, just before he pulled away… He *was* in there.

One thing is clear. I am the only person in the Enchanted Vale capable of breaking the Prince of Thorns.

And if I can break him, I can put him back together again.

The door opens and he steps out, looking immaculate. He snatches the cloak from my hands and fastens it around his neck. "You think my mother didn't feel the rose as soon as I brought it to the Below? She commanded me to hand it over."

My stomach drops. Sira has the rose? No. No, it can't end like this… "Why hasn't she used it then?"

He huffs a breath. "Controlling the will of all her creations is a monumental task. It takes a great deal of magic, even for my mother."

"It's why she's been getting you to gather her creations here," I say. "Everyone she got you to barter with to come to Cryptgarden under the promise of an alliance. She's luring them here to take control."

"Exactly. She's making them promises of creating more of their kind, more riches, more power. She's holding a gala soon where all may gaze upon the rose's splendor. But it's all a front to have them in one place."

The pit in my stomach grows wider. She'll steal their wills in one sweep. We don't have much time.

The Prince of Thorns grips my jaw before dragging me into a kiss. "Don't leave this room. I have to go. One of your mates is causing trouble."

And with that, briars spring from the floor and carry him away.

25

Farron

My realm stretches out before me, a quilt of purple heather hills, golden and red groves, and bright gray sky, the clouds thick but still bursting with a chilly light.

I wonder how we'd appear if one was looking down upon us, the way the gods supposedly looked down at the fae of the Above. Or how the fae of the Above would have looked down on the surface if any had been able to remain in their home. I imagine we could spur fear even in the hearts of such so-called gods.

Every battalion in Coppershire and the surrounding forts under my command has rallied to my side. We march as a united front, armed with lances, spears, bows, and fire. Most of all, fire. Magic wielders line the perimeter of our ranks, and those who can't spark a flame wield torches and carry canisters of oil.

Our enemy lies before us, a deep violet scar across the horizon. The Briar.

My steed, a pure black mare except for one white sock, is uneasy but stays the course. Never in my time have I known the cavalry of Autumn to be so jumpy. This must be a bad apple. I'll switch her out upon our return to Coppershire.

Normally, I ride Thrand, the great elk. But he's gone rogue of late. As unpredictable and changeable as a storm. He won't come close to Coppershire anymore, instead wandering the woods nearby like a ghost from some legend of old. I don't understand it. Perhaps the horrors of battle changed his disposition. Regardless, he's no more than a wild animal now.

My hand stiffens on the reins. My palm is still covered in ash from the burned remainders of the letter I received this morning. Sealed with Tilla's signet and written in George's handwriting, it is unfortunately no hoax. The rose is in Caspian's possession. George didn't go into detail of how it was stolen, but it doesn't matter.

That path is lost to us.

No more waiting. While we've been milling about on the surface, Rosalina has been in Caspian's hands. Now he has claimed our one hope of securing her freedom. I will not stand by while the Prince of Thorns weaves his many webs around the Vale.

I'll throw an entire sea of Autumn soldiers upon the Briar. Burn it to ash. Smoke Caspian out, then kill him myself.

Flanking me, Dominic and Billagin, dressed in golden armor, ride matching gray mares. With Dom wielding a hand axe and Billy a falchion, no one would know they have not yet passed the cusp of manhood. My father begged me not to take them, to leave them with him in Coppershire. But the twins are sons of Autumn. They must witness our glorious victory. Besides, they're safe with me.

The Briar looms ahead, a vast, writhing expanse of dark purple thorns stretching across the land. It shimmers in the cold light, bristling and alive. The air near it tastes of copper and rot, and even the wind dares not pass through.

The earth trembles beneath us, a slow and pulsing beat—*doom, doom, doom.* It's as if thousands of war drums are pounding below the surface.

Then the first gate blooms.

It erupts from the ground ahead, a tangle of blackened thorns arching and knotting into a circular gate. Thorns like claws. Vines like veins. At its center yawns a swirling black void.

A second gate blooms. Then a third. A fourth.

Each bursts from the earth with the sound of thorns shrieking as they grow. I've seen a gate similar to this before, one created by the seed Caspian gave us for his revelry day party.

I ignite the Lance of Valor from the queen's token. *He's near.*

From the first gate pour creatures the color of old meat and moldy bread. Goblins. Dozens of them, hundreds. Rotting bark for skin, sharp teeth in too-wide mouths. Some crawl on all fours; others sprint on backward-bending legs. Their armor is a mockery—scraps of bone, stolen metal, helmets made of hollowed-out skulls. Their eyes glow yellow and bright, like frogs peering out of a swamp.

A larger goblin emerges riding a snarling grinjaw with a broken mandible. He points at our ranks and lets out a roar.

The horde screams back and charges.

There's a tug on my arm, and I turn to face Dom, his golden eyes flashing. "We should try to lure them out of the Briar. We can't fight in there. That's his territory."

I shift away from him, then raise the lance high and shout to the battalions, "Burn the Briar to the ground! Go, now! For Autumn! For the Vale! Charge!"

Flames roar to life along the front line as our mages advance. Bows notch. Oil canisters roll. The fire is coming.

But even fire must fight to survive in the Briar's shadow.

My soldiers rush forward, pushing back the first ranks of goblins, driving them into the Briar. The smell of smoke assaults my nose as a barrage of flaming arrows takes hold in the brambles.

My brother stares at me with a betrayed expression. "I do not fear death, little brother," I say, "nor should any who stand with me. I control who lives and who dies, because I control the flames. The Briar will burn, and Caspian will be ashes within it."

Then I crack my reins and surge into the fray.

My army crashes against the Briar like a golden tide. Arrows scream through the sky, torches fly, oil slicks the ground. The first line of goblins shriek and scatter as flames lick the outer edges of the thorns. The Briar itself seems to wail, a low, keening sound that rises from the brambles, as if the land resents our presence.

It's like entering a forest. The towering briars swallow daylight. Thorns slash at my skin and armor, and walls of violet and black twist around our flanks. It is a labyrinth within. My horse shudders beneath me, but I urge her on. Out of my peripheral, I see soldiers trapped between pockets of briars and fire. The goblins know this terrain. They scramble along the thorns like insects, springing from above, tearing men from their horses with jagged knives and shrieking laughter.

I spear one monster through the throat, another through the gut. Blood spatters the ground. The light that makes it through is fractured, strange—purple and orange and flickering as if the realm can't decide what time of day it is.

A roar shatters the air.

Something massive barrels toward me: a goblin that's twice the size of the others. It's the one I noticed earlier, mounted atop a grinjaw with a dangling mandible. It swings a club.

I try to dart out of the way, but it's too late.

Crack.

Pain explodes across my shoulder as the club hits me. I fly from the saddle, slam into a patch of thorns, and roll hard onto the scorched ground. My horse bolts, screaming.

The goblin grins down at me, its mouth a mess of drool and shattered teeth.

The Green Flame answers my call before I realize I've summoned it. It bursts from my outstretched hand, cold and unnatural, glowing emerald against the violet thorns. It wraps around the goblin and its mount, swallowing them whole.

They don't even have time to scream.

When the fire fades, only bones remain, charred black and smoking.

My soldiers freeze, staring at me. "Fight," I rasp. "Keep fighting!"

They obey.

I stagger to my feet, giving myself a shake, ready to unleash another spray of fire, when a silence rings through the battle, an unnatural hush in the middle of the storm.

A new thorn gate slashes upward from the ground. This one grows slower, more deliberate.

From its center steps the Prince of Thorns.

Sleek, composed, without a hint of armor. He wears a fine tunic embroidered with silver thread and a cloak of black velvet draped over his shoulder. He moves like he's stepping onto a ballroom floor, not a battlefield.

His eyes find mine across the chaos.

And he smiles.

"Farron, princeling, so grateful you could join us. You've been quite obnoxious of late, murdering so many goblins living on your lands."

My jaw tightens so hard, I think my teeth may crack. I take off toward him at a run, lance raised.

He doesn't even flinch. "Now, I do have the most nagging feeling you're not here for a dinner invitation. Do I perhaps have something you want? Like this?"

A shadow appears beside him—a figure, tall and curved as an hourglass, with waves of hair formed by curling tendrils of smoke.

Rosalina.

I stop. *It's only an illusion.*

Caspian smiles at my hesitation anyway. "Or this?"

He holds out his hand, the shadows twisting into the shape of a rose floating over his palm.

Another illusion, but it doesn't make it any less true. He *does* have what I want. And I will kill him to get them back.

The shadow of Rosalina puffs away into smoke. Caspian drags a finger along the rose, ever so gently disturbing its form. "Do you know how I got this little treasure?"

I stagger toward him, knuckles white on the lance. "You stole it like the beggar prince you are."

Caspian clicks his tongue. "Oh, tut-tut, Farron. So rude. And you're a guest in my home! No, it was *given* to me." He narrows his eyes and smiles a serpent's smile. "Dayton is such a beautiful puppet, isn't he?"

Dayton. My chest tightens. No. He used Dayton again. Took control of the Green Flame within him and twisted it to his will, like he did in Frostfang. "I'm going to kill you."

"What a fickle heart you have. And I thought we had a connection." His emerald gaze blazes with mockery.

A growl starts at the bottom of my belly and works its way up my ribs and through my throat. He thinks no one can stand against him. But I too have the Baron's power. Malekai Furiondemius knows his trueborn son is a wicked, reckless monster, so he chose *me* to wield his magic. I am a conduit of the Green Flame. And I will make the Prince of Thorns rue the day he challenged me in my realm.

I prepare to charge Caspian, wreathing my lance in emerald fire.

Caspian only glances to the horizon, bored. "It appears all your ranks are well within the Briar now. As lovely as our time together has been, I have places to be. Princesses to fuck. Gladiators to manipulate. You know, important things."

The Briar begins to scream.

Not with sound but with movement.

The earth beneath my boots lurches. Thorn walls twist and convulse, writhing like serpents disturbed. Above, violet brambles rupture, splintering skyward, then crashing down in jagged bursts, sharp as spears.

The Briar is *alive.*

And it's hungry.

My soldiers cry out. One is impaled clean through the chest, lifted off the ground like a rag doll. Another disappears into the tangle, his golden armor vanishing in a sea of thorns. Blood mists the air.

The battlefield collapses into pandemonium.

"Shields!" I roar, though I know it's useless. There's no direction to defend against. The attack is coming from everywhere. Above, below, behind. What briars we burned earlier are immediately replaced with new ones, the brush springing up around us in violent bursts.

A thorn javelin rips through a young footman, and he crumples, mouth open in shock, already dead. He couldn't have reached peak manhood. Couldn't have been older than Dom or Billy.

Another wall of briars explodes up between my ranks, cutting off my vanguard from the rear guard. Dom. Billy. They were right beside me, weren't they? But I can't see them. Can't hear them.

"Dom!" I shout, turning in a circle, lashing out with fire, trying to burn a path through the thorns. But for every thatch I destroy, five more rise in its place. "Billy!"

The Briar has become a battlefield of shifting corridors, transforming my army into scattered, panicked fragments.

A soldier crashes into me, his face shredded, blood pouring from gashes along his neck. He grabs my shoulder, gasping. "They're coming from the thorns!"

Before he can finish, a hook-shaped vine pierces through his chest and yanks him backward into the dark.

I stagger, my heart rabid.

This isn't a battle anymore.

It's a massacre.

"Farron!"

One of my brother's voices. I can't tell which one, but I rush toward the sound. In the chaos, I smash into two of my soldiers. There're hands on my shoulders, my face. I search beneath the helms. It's them, Dom and Billy, their matching eyes mad with terror.

"We have to get out of here," Billy yells. "Order the retreat before we're all dead!"

My brothers' fear is infectious, and I feel it stealing my breath, turning my legs to water. Looking around, I see soldier after soldier strung up like bloody banners, waving upon their thorn flag posts. Caspian, asserting his dominion over my realm with my own dead men and women.

No. I cannot give in to fear now. I must find my valor.

And to do that, I need to reach the most sacred space within my heart. The part of me that always gives me courage. That has given me hope and lit up even my darkest days.

The ember of the Green Flame.

I slam my hand to the ground. *I do not fear death.* Green fire erupts from my palm, carving veins of flame into the earth like a thousand roots cracking through stone. *Death cannot touch those who stand by my side.* My vision narrows to a pinpoint of power—my heart, my breath, my very soul threading into the weave of life and death.

Come back to me.

I reach out to the bodies strung up on the thorns, the soldiers torn apart in the bramble's maw. I feel them—thin, silken strands of their essence—frayed but still present.

With a cry, I *pull.*

Green flames explode across the battlefield. Every corpse I reach ignites in a fiery resurrection. One by one, they jerk upright, limbs twitching, armor clanking, eyes blazing with emerald fire. They pull themselves free of the thorns. Their wounds still gape. Blood still seeps from their mouths.

But they rise.

Dozens of them. Hundreds.

The Green Flame obeys me.

I do not fear death.

I've done it. I've done it. I've done—

One of them turns. It's the boy, the one on the cusp of manhood.

His eyes are wide open—green and gleaming—but they do not *see.* They stare past me, blank and hollow. The soldier stumbles forward with a jolt, head cocking to one side like a broken doll.

One lets out a wet, gurgling moan.

Another snaps its own neck into place with a sharp, unnatural *crack.*

They are not the same as Dayton, who awoke with his heart still filled with sunshine.

These are…these are…

These are wrong.

"Farron!" Billy shouts. "What's happening? It's the Battle of Coppershire all over again! Perth Quellos…when he raised the dead…this is the same thing!"

"No, no, I'm not like him!" I shout, but my voice is lost in the growing din. How did this happen? Is it because I didn't take enough care? Because I didn't lovingly retie their threads as I did Dayton's? There was no time, no time…

The risen turn, their bodies moving in staggered, jerky rhythm, arms reaching. Not for the enemy. For *us.*

The Green Flame surges in my chest, but something yanks at it, pulling it away from me.

A laugh slithers through the air. Caspian's voice, silky and triumphant. "Oh, Farron. What a lovely gift. You really are too kind to offer your entire army as my thralls!"

I spin, but I can't find him. A shadow casts over me. I look up.

There he is, above us, suspended in a cradle of thorns. Vines coil around his arms and legs, holding him aloft.

I feel it then—my connection to the soldiers unraveling, slipping through my fingers.

He's taking them. Just like he took Dayton and me at Frostfang.

I scream and clutch at the flames burning in my soldiers' hearts, trying to reel them back to me, but they won't answer. The flame still burns, but the will driving it is no longer mine.

Baron! I cry in my mind. *Help me!*

There's only a painful, echoing silence.

Dom swings his sword wildly at the encroaching horde of our own risen army. "They're everywhere. We're surrounded!"

Goblins pour in from behind the undead ranks, cackling and snarling, closing the circle. My brothers press against me back-to-back, blades up, panting.

Above us, Caspian lifts one elegant arm. A sword grows in his hand, long and gleaming, made of vines twisted around a thorned core. It hums with magic, bleeding shadow from its edge.

He levels it at me.

"Now," he says, voice sharp with joy, "I will make you suffer."

I don't know what else to do, so I close my eyes. The last thing I see is Caspian arcing his sword down toward my neck.

A torrent of icy wind erupts at our side, followed by a shower of dagger-sharp icicles. Goblins and risen soldiers alike scream as they're pummeled to the ground. Caspian is flung back amid the storm, landing in a heap at the base of his briar tower.

A massive shape leaps over me and the twins and lands in a spray of ice and ash before us.

Two ice knives form in Keldarion's hand as he turns to face me, his long, white hair blowing, his eyes blazing with blue fire. "Farron," he snarls, "you are a fucking idiot."

26

Keldarion

I CAN'T REMEMBER THE LAST TIME I FELT SO *FUCKING* ANGRY.

What was Farron thinking? No forewarning to any of the other realms. No strategic planning. No backup. Just a full-fledged assault on the Briar.

I might expect this recklessness from Dayton or even Ezryn if the mood strikes him wrong. But from Farron?

He was always the one to keep us in check. Now, he's run headfirst into a mess there's no way to clean up.

If it was just his own life, that would be different. But he's brought legions of soldiers. Brought his *brothers*.

If we survive this, I am going to *kill* him.

With a roar, I cast my arms out, creating a barrier of jagged icicles to encircle myself, Farron, and the twins. It won't stop the Below's army, but it will slow them down.

I level a heated glare at Farron. "What were you thinking? If I hadn't shown up, you'd be dead right now!"

The only reason I'm here is because Padraig still possesses a mote of sanity, which Farron seems to have lost. Farron's father used the enchanted door between Castletree and the realms' keeps to find me in Frostfang. He was panicked, sputtering about how Farron would not come to his senses. I've summoned reinforcements, but even our fastest platoon, the Kryodian Riders, will take hours to cross the border. I don't know what's happened to his soldiers, but I'm Farron and the twins' only hope of getting out of this.

"I had to do something!" Farron yells. A goblin scrambles between two prongs of icicles but ends up with the point of Farron's lance between its eyes. He pulls the lance out with a squelch. "They stole the rose."

"I know," I growl, cutting the throat of a grinjaw as it struggles over the icicles, no mind for ripping its own belly on the sharp points of ice. "I received a letter. And do you know what I didn't do? Wage a *fucking* assault without telling any of my allies!"

Farron hisses through his teeth but doesn't respond. His brothers exchange nervous glances but remain occupied, holding back any goblins that clamber over the barrier. The boys have grown so much since their messy assassination attempt on me, all that time ago.

We can't stay in this icicle ring forever. Already, cracks are forming as the Below's army smashes into my pillars. An Autumn soldier, golden armor still gleaming though spattered with blood, makes a gargling sound as he attempts to leap between two icicles. I'm about to pull him into our protection when I see his eyes are burning with Green Flame, and his throat is slit to the point where his head wobbles upon the neck. My stomach lurches. *He should not be moving.* What happened to Autumn's soldiers?

I don't have the heart to lay a blade to him, so I throw up my hand, and a gust of wind shoots him back. There's no time to delay. If I can't figure out how to get us out of here, we'll be overrun in—

A quiet descends over the Briar, accompanied by a darkness that feels like nightfall. The chittering of the goblins, the moan of the Autumn soldiers, the clatter of metal against ice… It all vanishes.

And I know, deep in the core of me, that there is only one person in all the Vale capable of commanding such a silence.

Cold dread shivers through my body. Selfishly, it was the only thought running through my mind as I sprinted through the door of Keep Wolfhelm into Castletree and then into Keep Oakheart. *How could you do this to me, Farron?* Not how could you do this to your father. To your brothers. To your people.

How could you put *me in* a position to come here, knowing who I am most likely to find?

When I arrived at the battle, I came with an ice and wind so strong, it covered my vision with Winter's might. But I knew who I'd struck. Known it in my bones, even if I wasn't able to admit it to myself.

There's no running from him. I've never been able to, no matter how hard I try.

He's here.

As if the mere thought of him is a curse, a briar spears through the ground beneath me, wraps around my ankle, and whips me under the earth.

Cold dirt sails over my skin as I'm thrown flat on my back upon the blood-soaked surface, outside my icicle barrier. The sickening scent of goblin sweat and fae innards overwhelms me. I give my head a shake and press up on my elbows, trying to orient myself.

Horrifying faces surround me: the slobbering maws of goblins, their eyes even more bugged out as they take me in. Their steeds froth at the mouth, dagger-sharp teeth covered in jagged pieces of flesh. But worse of all are the blank stares of the Autumn soldiers, their bodies in various states of mutilation. Many have puncture holes or thorns stuck through them. Others have the crude goblin weapons embedded in their skulls or armor. The chittering and moans begin again, the sight of me working them into a frenzy—

"Do not touch him."

That voice.

It shudders through me. A voice that has calmed me. Emboldened me. Whispered words of love that I could never quite believe.

The crowd shuffles back. I stagger to stand and form new ice knives in each hand, even though I know they won't do any good. I wouldn't be able to use them on him anyway. Not after everything Rosalina's risked to save him.

The army parts, forming a path before me. Like darkness made to dance, he strides forward. There's snow in his black hair from my gust of wind, and his cloak is disheveled and covered in leaves, but he's still the most beautiful man to ever walk the Vale.

He stops several yards away from me. Afraid to get too close? Afraid to look me in my eyes?

"Keldarion," he says, and that's it. My name, his entire thought.

"Caspian," I say, his name, my entire thought.

A new silence beats like a heart between us. Could this be—

He laughs, long and low and cruel. "Caspian! Caspian! Oh, both you and Rosalina are so obsessed with that name. Call me what I truly am. The Prince of Thorns."

Can one die of a broken heart? Has it happened before? Because I swear I may be the first fae in the Vale to succumb to such a thing.

But something keeps me drawing breath.

The pure, feral rage of hearing *my wife's* name in *his* mouth.

My body shakes. My muscles tense. The ice daggers shatter into deadly shards beneath my grip. And the words tear out of me in a threatening roar. "What have you done to my wife?"

Caspian takes a few strides forward, whatever pretense I assumed moments ago long gone. "Oh, Kel, do be assured, she's well taken care of." He strokes a hand down his chest before landing between his legs and making a lascivious gesture. "As long as *I'm* taken care of."

Rage climbs up my spine like a blade. Before I can think, I'm throwing ice shards straight at that hand. A briar leaps from the ground, knocking them away.

"Kel, manners! Though you're so similar to your wife, aren't you? She has no manners either. Constantly panting and slobbering over me. Like a dog. Guess you're both beasts. Except you were easier to tame! Doesn't matter what I do for my sweet Rosalina. She'll crawl on all fours after me, begging for a drop of my—"

"Liar!" I bolt forward, charging straight at him.

"Kel!" Farron yells.

Caspian flicks his gaze over my head. "Don't kill the Autumn princelings. It was so kind of Kel to build a cage for them. Keep them in there."

There's the rustle of goblins and soldiers, and I hear the ting of metal and the boys crying out, but I don't look back. My vision has tunneled on Caspian. I leap for him—

Briars snag my wrists and pull me to my knees. Thorns bite into my skin, and I feel the hot rush of blood dripping down between my clenched fists.

"Oh, I'm many things, love," Caspian purrs, crossing the space between us with feline grace, "but I'm no liar."

I'm too shocked to move when Caspian grabs the back of my head and thrusts my face against his groin. Even through his pants and the surrounding stink of battle, I can smell her on his cock. The sweet scent of her mixed with his earthy musk. The combination is aphrodisiacal, sending my mind into a haze.

Caspian jerks his hips away, then grabs my head and forces me to look up at him. A line of black rot drips from his nose. He doesn't bother to wipe it away. With a gentle smile, he says, "I am your wife's god."

I scream, a yell as primal as the Vale before the fae descended. Wind and snow gather around me, mixing with a torrent of green and orange flame. Farron's voice screams my name over and over, and I know he's fighting to get to me, but I will cover all the Briar in frost to keep the Prince of Thorns from Rosalina—

Caspian steps back and gazes at the growing storm, a flash of apprehension in his eyes. "Well, I do say this has been a most productive afternoon. And since you've been served up on a silver platter"—he drags a lustful gaze over me—"I can't resist taking a bite."

Briars wind round and round my entire body until I'm ripped under the earth and dragged into the dark.

I could resist. Explode with power as I did when I called down the stars.

But Caspian's taking me exactly where I want to go.

To my mate.

27

Farron

THE ICE BARRIER ENTRAPPING ME AND THE TWINS SHATTERS. THORN gate after thorn gate erupts out of the ground. The goblins and my soldiers—my Green Flame wraiths—shuffle through. Caspian doesn't bother to look at me as he takes his army and mine and disappears.

I stagger forward, collapsing to my knees on the churned earth that swallowed Kel.

The soldiers came at my command. Keldarion came to save my life.

Caspian took them all.

And left me a survivor to ensure my suffering.

My hands knead the dirt as if I could order it to bring Kel back. The blood-wet mud swirls in front of me as my vision stops focusing. The silence that fills the empty battlefield is replaced by a mild buzzing.

I sit.

Outside of the buzzing, there are other muffled sounds. My brothers' voices. They're attempting to give orders to Autumn soldiers who escaped death. Ones who have crept out of the briars like goblins long living here.

Snow begins to fall. No, not snow. There is no Winter prince in Autumn anymore. It's ash from our useless fires, now burnt out.

I shall stay here, I think, until the ash covers me completely.

The voices outside my buzzing are getting louder. *What do we do*, they beg. *Stand up, please. Farron, we need help.*

It's as if they're speaking from the other side of a forest, muffled and lost between the trees.

Eventually, they go away.

My eyes burn from the drifting smoke, but I cannot blink. Perhaps I shall sink into the earth like Kel.

In that faraway manner, I hear a new sound. Heavy hoofbeats and a familiar bleating. An elk's call.

Then my brother keeps saying a name that weighs on my mind.

Dayton.

Dayton! they cry.

And all at once, it rushes back at me.

The buzzing stops, my vision clears so the pools of blood in the dirt stop swirling, and I feel the pain in my shoulder, the burns on my skin from my own flames where I took no care.

Whirling, I turn to look.

Dayton sits atop Thrand, my elk steed, his long blond hair half pulled back, the rest waving in the slight breeze. He wears a black tunic with the colorful embroidery along the cuffs and neckplate that is common in Spring. Dust from the road has settled in the creases of his face, but even so, he rides with the majesty of a high ruler.

Dayton's eyes dart around, taking in the scene, concern overtaking his expression. He hops down from Thrand, giving the elk a reassuring pat on the neck. Dom and Billy stagger up to him. Without a word, Dayton pulls them to his chest.

They embrace him, shaking. His shoulders heave as he hugs them tighter. "Thank the gods you two are alright. Coppershire looked empty. Couldn't find Paddy or any of you. I had no idea where you'd all gone, but he came running out of the forest and seemed to be able to follow the scent." Dayton jerks his chin toward Thrand.

I wonder if I've succeeded and have started sinking to the Below like Kel, for I can't seem to stand. Dayton doesn't look at me. I can only imagine how this ghost of me has disappeared in the ash and smoke.

Dayton wastes no time. After pulling away from my brothers, he's adopted the full mannerisms of a high ruler, ordering the remaining men to search for survivors, then to rally to him. Dom and Billy cling to his words like they're prayers.

I stay there in the dirt for what may be eons, watching him. I cannot go to him, and I cannot run. Perhaps I died when that goblin hit me with the club. A corpse so pathetic, even Caspian did not wish it for a thrall.

A curl of smoke passes between us, then Dayton's turquoise eyes flash through the murk. He sees me. I know because a pulse of lightning jolts up my spine, as it always does when he stares at me.

What will he do? Scream? Banish me from my own realm? Or worst of all…turn away?

He surges forward, moving with lethal intent, the way he does in the arena when going in for a kill.

Perhaps he's decided it would be a mercy to end me. And he would be right.

But instead, Dayton falls to his knees before me, cups my face, tears shining in his eyes, then gathers me in his arms.

And I weep for the first time since I was reborn. Weep for the lives I've lost. My soldiers. Dayton's.

My own.

28

Dayton

I LIFT MY FIST TO KNOCK ON THE DOOR, THEN DROP IT. A HEAVY SIGH escapes me.

Night has fallen over the Autumn Realm. With its mixture of stone and dark wooden paneling, Keep Oakheart has always given me the creeps after sundown. It's not like Soltide, where even at night, a breeze drifts through the open windows off the ocean, and moonlight drips through skylights in every ceiling. Here, it seems the suits of armor decorating the halls may come alive at any moment.

But there's no retiring to the warmth of a guest room. I need to speak with Farron.

We were silent on our journey back from the Briar to the capital. I got bits and pieces of what happened from Dom and Billy and the rest from the handful of soldiers who survived the slaughter.

Kel's gone. A nauseating wave of grief and fear somersaults

inside me, and I swallow, trying to force it down. Kel is the Sworn Protector of the Realms, and he's gone. What are we to do now? I'm a third-born son, not meant to be high prince—

I squeeze my eyes shut. Those thoughts are no longer welcome.

But still… I'm barely used to embracing the role of high prince. Kel's the one who's supposed to be looking out for the entire Vale. Farron and I will need to make our way to Spring as soon as possible to create a plan with Ezryn.

But there are things to see to here first.

Thankfully, most of the cavalry's mounts survived. Horses don't obey orders as well as men and had been quick to flee the Briar. We'd rounded many of them up and were able to transport the surviving soldiers back to Coppershire.

Farron drifted off as soon as we crossed into the keep, and I'd let him go. In this state, trying to keep him by my side would be like trying to hold a breeze.

I'd seen the twins to their father though. I won't forget the look on Padraig's face as he embraced his two youngest sons. Tears of relief ran down his cheeks as he pinned them both to his chest in a hug.

"Farron?" he asked, voice barely a croak.

"I'll look after him," I replied.

"Like you always have," Padraig said.

I think about that now with my fist hovering at the wooden door. It's not true, not really.

Farron's always been the one watching out for me. All those years in Castletree before Rosalina came, when we were hopeless, he was the only one who believed there could be a different future for us. He kept me from losing my mind to drink and loneliness.

How could I expect him to stop looking out for me, especially at the bitter end?

I rap my knuckles on the wood, then open the door.

Farron's sitting on the end of his bed, appearing much like he had in the Briar. Skin pale as ash, eyes vacant, that new, scruffy, red-tinged beard making him look like a stranger. His hands are in his lap, thumbs twirling over and over each other in an uneasy rhythm.

His hair is wet, and he's wearing clean, white linen, so he's washed. That's a start.

I click the door shut behind me, then step into the dim candlelight illuminating his room.

He drags his gaze to me but says nothing. I sit down beside him. Clear my throat.

Stars, I'm no good at this. Farron's the one who always knows what to say. Whenever I was upset or defeated, he'd find a way to cheer me up. And when it was his turn to be upset, well…

I'd just pretend he wasn't. Eventually, he'd be okay again all on his own.

But we're so far from okay, it might as well be one of Kel's stars twinkling off in the horizon.

And we aren't the same people we were from summers ago. Maybe that's what I've been hoping for, that we could fall into that easy pattern, the one where we'd both run away in whatever ways suited us.

I look at him now, this ghost of summer's past. He's not the same as he once was.

But neither am I.

That's okay.

No more running.

Gently, I bring a hand up to his face and tuck an auburn curl beneath his ear. "Tell me what's going on in that head of yours."

"It's quiet," he whispers. "It's all gone quiet. He chose Caspian over me."

My throat tightens. *He*. The *he* that is the strange feeling lacing through my bones and blood, keeping me together. The feeling that shouldn't be there—that means *I* shouldn't be here.

I fight the urge to grab Farron by the shoulders and insist he doesn't need the Green Flame. To rattle off everything incredible about him, the amazing things he's accomplished with his beautiful mind and his magic.

Instead, I wrap an arm around him and pull him tight to my body. He sinks against me. "We're going to get through this."

"How?"

How. That insatiable question. There's only one person who always has an answer for it, and she's deep below the earth, fighting her own battles. "I don't know. But as long as we're together, there's nothing we can't overcome."

Farron doesn't respond, so I sink to the floor between his legs so I can catch his downcast gaze. He is indescribably beautiful, even wrapped in melancholy. His damp hair curls ever so slightly, shimmering like burnished copper in the candlelight. He's sporting that short beard, the color redder than his hair. And despite all the ways we've changed, I've still got the constellation of freckles across his nose memorized. I can picture them with my eyes closed, my favorite set of stars.

Farron's thumbs continue to rotate around and around each other, body shivering as if a fever has taken hold. "I w-wanted to save them. I thought I could. Death cannot touch what stands at my side—"

I want to tell Farron he doesn't need the green flame. But I know the words will go unheard. To him, it's the only way he won't lose anyone the way he lost his mother.

I clasp my hands over his, stilling the movement. "Death is not our enemy, Farron, and we cannot fight it. But what you're feeling—that fear? I know it too. But it's only embers. Your love, Farron, is a raging fire. One that can light our way. Trust yourself."

"Trust myself?" Farron makes a pained sound. "I changed you, Day."

I grab his hands with such force, his wayward gaze finally focuses on me. There is no doubt in my voice nor my heart as I tell him with all the strength I can muster, "I'm not giving up on me. And I'm not giving up on you."

29

Farron

I BLINK, SLOW AND HEAVY, THE WAY ONE DOES WHEN WAKING UP after a long sleep. A shaky inhale rattles through my lungs.

Then I nod.

So many horrible thoughts assault my mind when I let the haze drift away. The bloodcurdling screams, the shatter and squelch of thorns through flesh and armor, the intense scent of lavender and intestines on the wind. And a guilt that scrambles with claws and fangs through my body, tearing at me with such fury, all I want to do is fade—

But…when I look down at Dayton…

It seems as if there's a dreamy glow emanating from him. And if I stay within it, nothing bad can touch me.

Dayton looks up at me with those earnest eyes. He's changed from his road clothes, but his hair is a matted mess. I imagine weaving my hands through it, untangling the golden strands, braiding the front pieces back so no part of his beautiful face is hidden. Regardless of whether he's clad in armor or candlelight, he looks the perfect hero.

No wonder he always leaves. Autumn is what becomes of Summer when it's time to die.

"I always come back," Dayton says.

"What?" *Where did that come from?*

"I'll always come back," Dayton repeats.

There's a single beat of silence, and then we are two magnets, pulled together, not daring nor wanting to fight against it anymore. Dayton runs his hands up the sides of my body, then twines his fingers through my hair. I trace the lines of his jaw, his cheeks, knowing them intimately yet needing to reassure myself all the same.

We stare at each other. Our breath mingles. Then we both lurch forward into a kiss, hungry and desperate and sad all at once. His body presses against mine. I kiss him like I need it, and I do. More than oxygen. More than sunlight. More than the beating of my own heart. As long as he kisses me, I am sustained.

I scoot back on my bed, and Dayton scrambles up to join me. Though I know he hasn't been to Hadria in days, he still smells of Summer. The whiff of salt and sunbaked stone mixed with the heady spiced scent of Autumn reminds me of our younger days.

We collapse onto the bed, kissing. My hands roam his neck, the muscles of his shoulders, the strength of his arms. He engulfs me in an embrace, his tongue dancing with mine.

There's a purity in the way he kisses me, basking me in that light of his that chases away the rest of the world. What would it be like, to live without fear, without war, without the threat of violence against all we hold dear?

The thought drags a raspy inhale from my throat, and I pull away.

"Fare?"

"What is good outside this?" I whisper. "Rosie's trapped. Kel's captured. I have poisoned us and—"

"No, no, no," Dayton murmurs and begins kissing my neck, hand stroking the scruff of my beard. "Are you crazy, Fare? There's *so* much good on the horizon. We just have to get there. I promise."

I tilt my head up, staring emptily at the canopy of my bed. "Like what?"

"Like...the next summer equinox celebration! It will be Delphie's turn to compete in the Luminae Games, following in her big brothers' footsteps. Can you imagine that? I'll be cheering so loud, you'll have to hold on to your ears."

An image drifts through my mind's eye. Dayton and Rosalina in the stands, hooting and hollering like mad people. Nori reaching out to grab my hand as she watches Delphia fight across the sands, the way I once watched Dayton when he competed as a gladiator.

A fantasy. As good as a fairy tale.

Dayton trails kisses along my collarbone. "And...what about the scriptorium restoration project? Nori mentioned it to me. Everyone working together to rebuild the greatest library the Vale has ever known!"

Another image. Me, sitting at a beautiful table carved of alder wood, stacks of books before me. Ezryn bringing samples of plants from the Spring Realm for me to catalog. Keldarion reciting all the stories told at the Festival of Tales so we can commit them to paper, never to be forgotten.

A future that will never come to pass. Not as the world is now.

"And…there will be weddings." Dayton kisses my chin, then up to the point of my jaw.

"What weddings?" I murmur.

"Well, ours, of course. And Rosie's. Pros of doing them all separately—you know, yours and Rosie's, mine and Rosie's, and yours and mine—is we get three parties and probably three times the number of presents. But we could also have one big wedding. I think the night of celebration would be worth it." Dayton pops up on his hands to stare down at me with the most ridiculous grin.

It's so hopeful, so absurdly optimistic, I can't help but smile myself, just a little. "Are you serious?"

"Come on. I'm not letting Kel get all the glory of being Rosie's one and only husband. And Ezryn can plan his own wedding. You know how Spring celebrations are. So stuffy."

It's such a lovely idea. The promise of a lifetime together, all of us.

But there's no path into that future for me.

My chest squeezes, and my heart starts beating too fast. I pull away from Dayton. He stares at me quizzically. He doesn't understand, but how could he? Despite the Green Flame, he's always known who he is. It never changed him, not really. Not like how it changed me.

My words come out short and clipped as I rush to get them out. If I don't speak now, I'm sure these thoughts will be stolen from me forever. "I'm so afraid, Day. So afraid I've lost who I am. I'm wandering through the flame and can't find my way out."

Dayton cups my face, his brow furrowed. "You're my Farron. Wise and clever and kind. You're not lost, 'cause I've always got you right here." He grabs my hand and places it over his heart. "Stay with me, and I'll lead you out. I'll remind you who you are."

I entangle myself with him, kissing and grabbing at his clothes, his hair, his skin, as if trying to become part of him. If only I could live in his heart. There, I'm wise and clever and kind. Not the clawing, fearful wraith of a man I truly am.

With each kiss, that wretched version of me feels further away. I settle, like sand shifting into place. I was never perfectly at home in Summer, nor was Dayton at home in Autumn. And Castletree always seemed to belong more to our ghosts—Dayton's brother and my mother.

But I feel at home now, wherever he is.

I ease off his shirt, desperate for the warmth of his skin. It radiates with sunlight, so strong maybe it can burn the evil parts of me away.

He follows suit, tugging off my tunic. I don't want anything between us, be it shadows or clothing. I tug off his pants.

His substantial manhood springs free, hard as steel. With quick, ravenous movements, I run my hand along the silken skin before clutching the base. A shiver of relief pours over me. This cock has always made me feel powerful when I need to be powerful, vulnerable when I need to be vulnerable.

Dayton throws his head back, letting out a low moan, then blinks his eyes open and stares at me. He smiles.

"I wish I could be the person you see," I whisper.

"Look through my eyes, Fare," he says reverently.

If only I could. Become such a part of him that our hearts

would beat as one, that I could bear his pains, even our thoughts intertwined.

We kiss again, then pull away, staring. I can see it in his gaze, the same desire burning in me. We need each other now.

Dayton trails a hand along my waistband before tugging off my trousers. Gently, he pushes on my shoulder until I'm lying on my back, then positions himself between my legs. He sucks two fingers into his mouth.

"I love you," he murmurs, then presses his fingers into my entrance.

A great sigh rumbles through my chest. Immediately, I relax for him, every muscle within me desperate for his touch. I picture the sunlight that radiates from him skittering across me. I know that's impossible, but it's a pretty thought.

Rays of pleasure beam through my body as I move in rhythm with Dayton's hand. I've craved him these last few weeks, though I wouldn't admit it to myself. Now, I'm desperate for more.

"So good, baby," Dayton murmurs. "That's right. Loosen up for me. I'm going to make you feel so good. Trust me."

I stretch my palms across his chest. "More. Please. I need all of you, Day."

His gaze flashes with intensity. We both know this is not the time for teasing or games. This feels like we're both reading from a spell or wielding a divine weapon together. Something sacred and powerful.

Dayton pulls his hand away, causing a shiver up my spine. "Whatever you wish." He grabs the base of his cock and notches himself in the entrance. The smallest amount of contact sends my stomach looping.

As he's about to press in, I rake my fingers down his chest. "Wait!"

Dayton quirks his head.

"Are you going to leave me again?" I breathe. *Like you did the first summer we spent together? Like you did all those nights in Castletree? Like you did on the starfield outside Frostfang? Because I would. I would leave me.*

But Dayton has never been one to heed my advice, and for once, I'm glad he can't hear my thoughts. He smiles and leans down, placing the whisper of a kiss over my lips. "Never ever. Never ever ever."

Then he straightens and plunges his massive length inside me.

I cry out, the sudden sensation of fullness a shower of sparks through my body. I loop my legs over his hips and move with him. It's an old dance but one that feels brand-new every time.

Dayton looks like a sea god from ancient Summer legends, his blond hair wild, skin sun-kissed as a bronze statue. He ruts into me with such power, I could imagine him standing atop a rock, splashed with white foam, commanding the waves to do his bidding.

He is the call, and I am the answer, my body responding to his with each movement. My breathing turns ragged, and I vary between clawing at the blanket and his skin, barely able to contain myself.

The rhythmic slap of his body against mine, our panting, the rustle of bedsheets—it is a symphony, spiraling around us more beautiful than any choir.

A feeling grows within me, something deeper than physical pleasure. The warmth that surrounds my heart, the one that keeps me safe. The tether that makes my life worth living.

It's not the Green Flame. No, it's something more powerful.

It's my bond with Rosalina, singing out with joy. And it's louder than ever before, a chorus rising between Dayton and me. It's light and music and magic and love. Pure love. I see it between our chests like a tiny sun, so full it's about to burst and shower us in starlight.

Dayton holds my gaze with his. "You stay with me. Follow me out, Fare. I'll lead you. Don't look back, okay? Don't look back."

I grasp his face. Lead me out of the flames. I can follow him, follow this light. There is a path for me—

He'd be dead if it weren't for me.

The voice rushes through me like an icy sigh. *No, you were gone. You left me. You were gone…*

The light blooming between Dayton and me fades, jolting into his chest. It dims, revealing…

A gaping arrow hole. The one left by the Bow of Radiance.

"Hey! Stay with me, Fare."

Dayton grabs my shoulders and squeezes hard. I shake my head. The wound disappears, revealing his skin, unmarred and perfect.

Leaning down, Dayton kisses me, murmuring over my lips, "You are my Farron. Stay with me. Through every season and every storm."

The light is gone, but so is the voice. So I do the only thing I can. I surrender to him.

It overtakes us together, the powerful, united release. Dayton roars a godly roar, his body emptying all his passion and pain into me. I take it willingly, my chest painted with my own evidence of our love. It is a tidal wave, dimming the emerald sparks still burning within me.

As Dayton collapses over me, I loop my arms around his neck and hold him tightly, burying my head in his hair and willing him not to feel the tears pouring down my cheeks. *Don't go. Don't go. Don't go.*

"Never ever ever," he mumbles sleepily.

We lie there entwined for a long time, until the candles burn low.

I know we should get up and wash, but I can't bear to move away from him. I stroke his hair, carefully untangling the knots with my fingers. His breathing turns steady and heavy as he teeters on the edge of sleep.

It was beautiful, that light that bloomed between us. For a moment, I wondered if it was possible that it was brighter than the Green Flame.

But though Dayton is a hero and as beautiful as his love is, he can't fix me.

I lift my hand, staring at it. *Can I fix me*?

A strange sound whispers through the room, a fluttering. Dayton jerks up, looking around with glazed eyes. "Huh? What's that?"

I catch sight of it in the candlelight. A small bird, formed of paper. It must have slipped in through the crack in my balcony door.

It looks the same as the one I received this morning, telling me of the lost rose.

Dayton snatches it out of the air and unfolds it. My heart shudders, and a deep sense of foreboding fills me. "I can't take any more bad news," I mumble.

Dayton smiles. "No, this is good news. It's an invitation."

"What?"

The candlelight flickers playfully in his turquoise gaze. "An invitation to the recoronation of High Prince Ezryn of Spring."

30

Ezryn

"Rise, Ezryn, son of Isidora and Thalionor, guardian of Hammergarden and the verdant lands beyond, as High Prince of the Spring Realm."

Tilla's voice radiates with command as she sprinkles sacred water over me, drawn from the river's highest point upon Mount Lumidor. My starlight silver armor clatters as I stand before the throne, crafted from the helms of my ancestors.

I stare into the visor of her helm. She gives me a reassuring nod. Then I turn and face the Hall of Vernalion. Face my people.

Everywhere I look, I meet the gaze of one of my citizens. They smile up at me. Some of their eyes are watery with tears, others' shining with hope—something sorely lacking in our realm of late. Flowers are woven into crowns upon their heads, young and old, men and women alike. A symbol of joy, of merriment.

Tilla steps beside me, her voice ringing through the sun-dappled hall. "Behold Ezryn, the Reborn Prince!"

The room is silent for a beat, just long enough for the words to settle in the air like drifting petals.

Then it begins.

A cheer swells, low and trembling at first, then rising to a rumble. The Hall of Vernalion erupts. Applause, stomping feet, joyous cries. The sound is thunderous but somehow still beautiful.

"Hail the High Prince of Spring!"

"Hail Ezryn!"

"Long may he bloom!"

The cheer catches. Through the windows, I spy the grounds of Keep Hammergarden filled with people. They begin dancing, scooping up the cherry blossoms that cover the ground and throwing them up into the air.

At the very front of the hall, I look to Dayton and Farron. Happiness shimmers in both their gazes as they clap. Next to Farron are Padraig, the twins, and Delphie and Nori. George looks up at me with such pride, a lump forms in my throat. Nearby, Marigold and Eldor are arm in arm, while Astrid gives the air a triumphant punch. Marigold wipes a tear away with a handkerchief, then waves at me. She turns to the person beside her—an acolyte who's made the journey down from the monastery—and points to me, mouthing, "That's my boy!"

In spite of everything going on, they have taken the time to gather, to witness this moment.

My heart swells and aches at once.

Rosalina and Kel. Cas. They should be here.

But I cannot hide in grief as I have before. Rosalina would want me to take my rightful place upon the throne. In her mother's absence, she is my queen, and I will do everything I can to protect her realms.

Tilla nudges my shoulder. "Welcome back, Ez."

I rock against her. After no small amount of cajoling from me and persuading from George, she agreed to remain my steward during the war. She's eager to return to her forge, and this is no minor sacrifice. But I need a trusted hand at my side. Besides, I'm pretty sure she never intended to leave and just enjoyed my insistent flattery before giving in and agreeing to stay on.

Gently, I raise my hand, drawing the applause to a close. My gaze stretches over my people. They have seen me win great glory in battle and help keep us safe during the War of Thorns. They have watched me fail, been as forced to endure my shame as I was.

And yet they have forgiven me. For those are the pillars upon which Spring grows, the foundation with which I will lead us.

Forgiveness and redemption. And hope, for blue skies when we're cold, rain when we're thirsty, and a bright, beautiful garden of a life for us all.

I have no speech prepared for my people, for no words in the common tongue could encapsulate what I need to say. So I pull from the ancient language of Spring, a song that was sung long ago, when the world was new and Rafael, the first High Prince of Spring, led our queen in creating the divine weapons. A time of rebirth. A time of hope.

My voice rings out in a clear, solemn tone:

Varenthiel cae miralune os theryan em elunoré. Yevanor sai liorin, aneth viala caelithar.

The slow rhythm and the words, older than Spring's grief, settle over the crowd. And as I continue the song, I picture the words sinking to the earth, drifting all the way to the Below to Rosalina.

May we rise in golden blooms and mercy reign. We are the reborn, forgiven by the breath of life.

~

Meadowmere Forest is always a place of beauty, but tonight it has been transformed into something out of legend. Trees rise like pillars, their branches woven with leaves adorned with sparkling paint. Every path has been swept clean and lined with blossoms, and glowing orbs hover, casting the clearing in a soft, dreamlike light.

The air is warm with the scent of fresh rain and green things. Not just flowers but soil, bark, new growth. Spring in its rawest form. And above it all, the quiet murmur of anticipation, threaded with bursts of laughter and music.

Hundreds have gathered to celebrate my coronation with food, drink, and dance. My people…they waited for me. They hoped. Now, they believe.

I will do right by them.

And that means there is no time to partake. I stand in a circle at the edge of the party with George, Tilla, Dayton, Delphia, Farron, Padraig, the twins, Nori, and Keldarion's steward, Eirik Vargsaxa.

While it may appear as if we are eating and making merry, we have spent the night planning and plotting.

"It is settled then," I say. "We cannot risk another full-out assault on the Below without leaving one of the realms defenseless. Voidseal

Bridge and Autumn's Briar border have proven that. Dayton, Farron, George, and I will leave on the morrow for the covert mission to locate Rosalina, Keldarion, and the rose."

"And we'll have the realms armed and ready to fight when you return," Delphia says, her voice booming with a command beyond her years.

I catch Dayton's and Farron's gazes. Despite the joyful music and being surrounded by those we love most in the world, a somber feeling pulses between us. We all know this is a fool's errand. George and I are risking our lives by traveling with them; Caspian has but to tug on the threads of their souls, and they could turn on us.

But it's been too long with no word from Rosalina. There's no one stronger of heart than her, but the Baron is not from the Vale, and he does not work with matters of the heart.

Besides, I've rescued Keldarion from the Below before, and Caspian too. I can do it again.

A glint of something in the dark of the forest catches my eye. Not a firefly or a painted leaf but the bright red of embers in the hearth, the ones that flicker right before going out.

"Come now. Plans are set. There is still time to enjoy the night," I tell my friends. "Go. Revel in the wonders of Spring. For me."

As they drift away to get food and drink, I slip into the darkness, becoming nothing more than a shadow among the trees. One of the trunks wavers, disengaging from the rest, and comes to stand before me.

Kairyn wears hardy clothes, made for harsh travel: leather boots, a large satchel, and a sweeping black cloak with a hood. His red eyes flash in the moonlight, horns curving around his head like the branches of a tree.

"I've come to say goodbye," he says.

My chest tightens. I asked my brother if he wanted to join me in Florendel, but he declined. The memories are too fresh, his shame too raw. He has remained out of sight from any of our citizens. I will not force him into the light.

"Where will you go?" I ask.

He stares to the north, eyes faraway. "To find Wrenley. She's out there somewhere. I don't understand what…what this means," he says, scratching at his heart, "but I need her to know she's not alone."

I think of that wildcat of a girl, moving through life like she's cornered, her back always against a wall. "What will you do when you find her?"

Kairyn's gaze turns skyward, through the trees, up toward Mount Lumidor. "I will return to Queen's Reach Monastery and serve out the remainder of my penance until my high prince deems me worthy."

A breeze rustles between us, carrying the smell of sweet water from nearby Sylvanita Lake. What does the grove look like now? It was once a place of immense beauty, but I drained the life from the earth. Has it regrown? Can a seed still manage to bloom even there?

Perhaps Kairyn and I will walk among the boughs of the willow trees once more. But for now, I rest my hands on the side of my helm and pull it off. Tucking it under my arm, I look at my brother with my own eyes. "Let us agree that you and I are finished doling out sentences for each other."

A muscle trembles in Kairyn's cheek. "Then perhaps, after I find Wrenley, I will continue to wander until I discover a new place to call home."

I touch his arm. "Home isn't always a location, Kairyn. It's a heart, singing the same song as yours."

Kairyn reaches over his shoulder, unstrapping the sheath at his back. He holds it out before me. I know it better than I know my own hands, for I have claimed more lives than I can count with it. Mother's sword. Kairyn's been holding on to it since the battle in Keep Wolfhelm.

"This is yours by birthright," he mumbles.

I take it. Draw the sword. Examine the beauty of its craftsmanship in the starlight. If I close my eyes, it's as if my mother's wielding it with me.

Then I sheathe it once more and hand it to him. "Keep it." I touch the small rectangular token at my neck, carved with cherry blossoms. "Now we both have something of Mother's."

Kairyn hesitates, then straps the sword on his back once more. He clasps his hand over mine. The words sound strangled from his throat. "Be well, big brother. May we meet again in a different world."

With that, my brother turns and strides into the forest, cape snapping behind him.

I stand there, watching him until he is nothing but another shadow among the trees. I think of the ballad I sang at the coronation. Of the final line.

Naeven tiras elarion sai liraen em variel.

Let the weary walk in light and find the song of hope.

31

Rosalina

My heart hammers against my chest so loudly, I swear all of Cryptgarden below me can hear. Taking a deep breath to steel myself, I continue tiptoeing the spiraling path. It winds along the mountain that Caspian's palace, the Gem, is built upon.

Ahead of me walks Sira, her dark cloak melding into the shadows that seem to follow her everywhere.

When I heard she'd left the Tower of Nether Reach, I tailed her through Cryptgarden and all the way up here. With my wits returned, it's time for me to do what I came here for. No one is infallible, and nothing is impossible. I will find a way to end this threat once and for all.

The path arcs onto a lookout point that gazes over the gem-crusted city of Cryptgarden. Dull purple light shimmers over the buildings and glints off Sira's tower in the distance. Sira seems to make a show of gazing over her dominion, then glances back the way she came.

I press myself against the side of the mountain and wrap my cloak around me. It's one of the items I found in the bag the princes gave me as I left. Kel must have packed this cloak; it's made of the thick, weather-resistant fabric worn by the Tundrafolk. On its outside, it appears nothing more than mottled gray and black, but when worn, it blends into its surroundings. Safely covered, I appear as an outcrop of the mountain.

As helpful as my wedding gifts are, the most wonderful thing about them is it feels as if there's a little bit of my loves with me. I can hold Aeneas, my lion plushie, and for a moment feel like I'm in my bed back at Castletree with Dayton. When I open the tin of healing balm, I remember what it was like to watch Ezryn prepare a poultice. Reading the handwriting in Farron's book of secrets, it's as if he's whispering in my ear, cheering me on. And wrapped in this cloak, I am back under the starlit sky in Winter, staring at my new husband. Absently, I twist the wedding ring on my left hand, willing it to give me strength. I'm close now.

It wasn't long after my thralldom broke that I remembered Farron's instructions about the book he'd packed. Under firelight, the innocent words fade away, becoming his handwritten notes, everything the princes knew about the Below. Farron had taken considerable care writing about the spiraling path up the mountainside, the lookout point, and the notch hidden among the rocks that opens a secret door.

That's where we're going now. To the heart of the mountain,

where a pool awaits, and within that pool, the god threatening to take over my home.

Even my thrall-muddled observations have helped this plan. The notes I scrawled were chaotic, but there was truth to be gleaned among the passages. Like how Sira takes this path nearly every day.

A fearful wave of nausea passes over me, thinking of what will happen if Sira discovers me, breaking into her most sacred place. But I can't spend all my time flitting around, pretending to be under Caspian's spell. I need answers.

Farron and Caspian shattered the crystals surrounding the Baron's pool. That chain reaction surged throughout the Below, all the way to my mother's prison. Though it destroyed her cell, a bargain still traps her in the Below. We have hindered Sira's plan to loose the Baron on our home, but we haven't stopped it.

It all ties here, to the pool. Each day that passes brings us closer to Sira's full-on assault, with every perverse creation of the Below at her command. She has the rose now. We're running out of time. I won't shut my eyes because I'm afraid of her darkness.

So when Sira turns from the lookout point and opens the secret door, I don't think. I slip behind her, as quiet as one of her pet shadows, and follow her into the heart of the mountain.

The passageway is pitch-dark, except for a few flickering torches here and there. I have to squint to keep sight of her silky black hair ahead of me. Away from the din of Cryptgarden, the whistle of my breath through my nose seems like a damned air horn. At least in such darkness, this cloak makes me all but invisible.

My foot kicks something hard. It rolls across the ground, making a *tingtingtingting* sound. I stop, every muscle going taut. But Sira doesn't turn around. Her pace has quickened now. The passageway opens to a large chamber lit by a soft green light—

That emanates from a pool in the middle.

An icy chill ripples up my spine. I've grown accustomed to the feel of magic in the air—a sparkly crackle—but this is different. Power pulses off the water in slow waves. Whereas Vale magic twinkles, then disperses, whatever this is seems to settle over the ground. A predator in wait.

With the added light, I look down to see what I kicked. Crystalline shards litter the floor, colorless and dull. Now that I'm looking, I notice them everywhere—spiking from the walls, cracked open like broken wineglasses, prismatic husks barely clinging to the ceiling. There's a graveyard of crushed glass lining the pool.

A smile graces my lips. *How did the great god enjoy Nori's little mushrooms?*

Sira's moving at a near run now, casting her cloak upon the ground. I meld against the remains of a large crystal, becoming another broken piece.

Sira doesn't stop walking when she approaches the pool. Instead, she falls in it, a giddy tone to her voice. "Darling, have I a feast for you today! Anchors upon anchors to fuel your spirit."

Then she takes a deep breath and dives down.

I wait, watching the ripples slow. Surely, she has to come up for air. As powerful as Sira is, even the Queen of the Below needs to breathe.

But she doesn't emerge. A minute passes, then what must be ten. I'm struck still, waiting for something, anything, to happen. Caspian had told me of communing with the Baron, but it was always at the edge of the pool. Could there be something else?

Something...below the Below?

A chill rips through me, and I involuntarily shiver, clutching Kel's cloak close. I didn't think a breeze could find its way in, but a cold's crept through my bones. It's different from the icy wind in Winter. This feels dark and murky.

Nervously, I wring my hands together. My fingers trace a ring on my left hand. I look down at it. Oh, it's beautiful, the diamonds forming a snowflake so clear they appear carved of ice. I rack my brain, trying to remember where I got it. Perhaps Kel slipped it in my bag, and I started wearing it during my thralldom.

I'm still trying to recall its origin when little waves ripple in the pool. Sira takes a gasp of air, then glides out of the water. Droplets fall from her as if she were coated in liquid emerald. She snags her cloak from the ground and wraps it around herself, turning to face the water once more.

The pool continues to swell. Another figure appears, not rising out of the water like her but *forming* from it. With each poised and certain step toward the edge of the pool, his body gains corporeality. A man approaches, though *man* seems an inadequate word. My chest tightens, because so does *fae*.

He is something else entirely. Tall and broad of stature, the figure wears slim-fitting black armor with jagged edges. Its finish is so sleek and oily, it reflects the green shimmer from the pool. His hair is the same bone-white as his skin, a color reserved for skeletons and spiderwebs. With a sharp jaw, cut-glass cheekbones, and long, pointed ears, everything about him seems ready to shred. Yet there's an undeniable beauty to him. A sickening beauty. The firework spray of lava from a volcano, a tsunami on the edge of the horizon, a flash of lightning on a rooftop.

Malekai Furiondemius, Baron of the Green Flame.

"That was good magic, my little thief," he rumbles. In a gesture that seems too gentle for his body, he runs a finger along Sira's cheek. "You have fed me well. The tether is strong."

"And strong I will keep it," she purrs. "The time nears. All my subjects are nearly gathered."

"And when they are, you shall bleed the sweet butterfly you keep in a cage for every drop of magic she possesses."

Icy terror grips my heart. My mother…

Sira darts her gaze away from him. "Are you sure? It is a great risk. If we rush the process, she could die, then—"

"Then you secure her child. Is she not with our son now? As lovely a consort as she would make him, if her magic is needed to open the door, so be it."

Sira's voice adopts a tremor. "Caspian won't be pleased if this is the path—"

"Caspian will do as he's told," the Baron thunders.

"He has been testing the limits of his power, testing my orders," Sira says. "You need to keep him in line."

"All children rebel against their parents at some point," the Baron says. "You only need remind him of the power you possess."

"Very well." She lowers her gaze. "I'll see to it that Aurelia survives long enough for the complete siphoning of her magic."

Blood rushes between my ears. We're running out of time.

The baron's body curves over Sira's, a crescent moon devouring the night. "Very good. Soon, we will be united. Your world, our home. And you shall have whatever you desire."

The Baron waves a hand, and sparks of green flash behind Sira, forming the outline of wings. Sira looks over her shoulder, a delighted smile on her face.

Suddenly, they fall, sizzling on the wet ground.

The baron turns and strides back to the middle of the pool. "My presence is needed elsewhere. Worlds beyond this one require my dominion."

Sira smooths a wrinkle in her skirt. "Very well. I must prepare for the coming revelry. All shall gaze upon the triumph of their creator."

The baron's body shivers like a lake caught in a rainstorm. "As soon they will gaze upon the triumph of their conqueror." With that, he dissipates back into the pool.

Heart thumping and blood rushing, I have to hold my breath as Sira turns and strides out of the chamber. I stay pressed against the crystal until long after her footsteps drift away. Even after I hear the groan of the secret door at the end of the passageway open and close, I force myself to count to one hundred before I move.

The chamber's gone dark besides the few lanterns, the pool having lost its luminous green glow. What did the Baron say? His presence is required elsewhere?

He's gone. For now.

I wring my cloak in my hands. Just as we feared. Sira is going to siphon my mother's magic all at once. How much time do we have? And what did all that mean, the talk of tethers?

I drift over to the pool. It doesn't look unusual. The baron can't be everywhere at once. And if he's disappeared for now—

Where *had* Sira gone? She couldn't have held her breath all that time.

There's something down there.

I snap my fingers over the water. No response. Gingerly, I lean down and dip a finger in. It's cool and clear.

There's no telling when the Baron will be back or if my absence at the castle will be noted. I came to the Below for a reason, so there's no point deliberating it.

I take a deep breath and dive in.

32

Rosalina

DOWN, DOWN, DOWN, I SWIM INTO THE DEEP. THE WATER IS CHILLING and so dark I cannot even see my hands in front of me. What am I looking for? The bottom? What if there isn't one, and I swim until my lungs burst? Or what if the Baron returns and bewitches me with promises like he did Farron?

There's nothing he can offer me that I cannot claim for myself, I think. *My home, my loved ones' safety—I will make it so by my own hands.*

My chest burns and my legs ache from kicking. I should have followed Sira's example and taken off my cloak, but the idea of being parted from it was too much.

I need to turn around before my lungs burst, but I've gone too far. There's no way I'll make it back to the surface before my air runs out. Stupid, stupid, stupid—

My hand hits something. Not the bottom.

Open air.

A current grips my body, and I'm *pulled* downward, where I plunge out of the water. I free-fall, gasping for breath and screaming at the same time. I smack hard against stone, jostled and bruised.

With a groan, I sit up and blink the water from my eyes. Above me, impossibly suspended in midair, is a vast pool of black water. Not held in a basin or glass, just floating. Waves ripple across its surface.

Is that the Baron's pool? Then where am I?

I spin in a circle. I'm in a dark, cavernous chamber, not unlike the one I came from. The only light comes from veins of gemlight threading through the rock—faint and bluish, like moonlight filtered through deep water. It flickers, as if unsure it wants to reveal what waits in the shadows.

Two towering obelisks rise on either side of me, jagged and black as midnight. They hum, low and deep. Though similar to the broken crystals above, these pulse with a different type of magic. A magic I'm more familiar with.

These aren't infected with the Green Flame. These belong to Sira alone.

Between the gemlight, the crystals, and the rippling water, I swear the reflections are playing tricks on me. Images flash on the surface of the obelisks. I shake my head and squeeze my eyes shut, but when I open, I still see them.

I drift closer to one of the obelisks, placing my hand on its smooth surface. Beneath my palm, visions flicker. A little girl playing with a doll made of straw. Then a man, laughing and pointing, standing under a shower of fireworks.

What is this?

I walk around the obelisk, staring at another side. An elderly couple lie in a bed, holding hands. A fight waged with sticks as children laugh and run through the alleys of a dark city. A small goblin, lying in a field of flowers, sighing as she stares up at the sun.

I stop. That goblin... It's Heidigog, reveling in her beloved bloomies.

She told me of this memory. It was so important to her.

But she'd forgotten.

My little thief.

Or...it had been stolen.

My heart thunders against my ribs as I turn to the other obelisk, searching the images. Two friends playing cards. A boy staring out at the ocean. A goblin with a grinjaw asleep in his lap. A young woman with light brown hair—

I narrow my gaze, trying to place her. Aquila, the priestess who helped Faustrius attack Voidseal Bridge. In this memory, she looks different. No horns or tail, and her hair and skin don't have that greenish tint. I can't tell what realm she's in, but she's sitting atop a white-roofed building, looking up at the sky and marveling at the stars.

All these images are precious memories. What has Sira done? Stolen them? Trapped them here? No wonder everyone in Cryptgarden is so bleak, always filling their days with drink and sex. Everything that's ever made them feel joy has been trapped in these crystals.

Just as I think I can't bear it anymore, another face flashes across the surface of the obelisk. One I know all too well.

My own.

I focus my attention, observing it as one would study a painting in a museum. I'm wearing a long, white dress and a veil, standing hand in hand with Keldarion.

I tilt my head. It looks…

It looks like we're getting married.

Tears prick my eyes. I touch the stone on my left hand as Keldarion takes mine in the obelisk and slips a ring onto my finger.

I'm married. *We're* married.

And Sira stole that memory from me.

The tears pour down my face, not from sadness but from *rage*. She has tried to take my home, my mates, my family. Now she steals straight from my mind. My *memories!* My precious, sacred memories that make me who I am! Has she taken anything more?

I run around the obelisk, searching the moving images. I don't recognize anything else, but there's one thing in common. Every single memory seems filled with joy.

You fed me well. The tether is strong.

What is this horrid thing? What is its purpose?

I don't know, but there's a rioting in my gut screaming at me that it *must* be destroyed.

My blood feels hot enough to melt my bones. I can't think clearly. With a roar, I kick the obelisk, wanting to crack it open, topple it over, shatter it once and for all. The only thing I shatter may have been my little toe. Yelping and rubbing my foot through my boot, I growl up at the hideous things. Anything can be broken.

I look around the cavern. Against the wall, I see a pile of

rocks. Grabbing the heaviest one I can find, I wield it like a mallet, pummeling the obelisk over and over again.

When my arms ache and the rock feels like it weighs a thousand pounds, I pull back, breath heavy.

It's tiny. Barely noticeable. But it sets my heart aflame.

A chip.

Anything can be broken.

My wrists burn, and I glower down at the damned bargain bracers trapping my magic. I'd need the full force of my briars to bring these down. Regardless, it's enough to realize it can be done.

I walk to the side of the obelisk where my memory is trapped. I stare into Kel's face. At my face, so happy and in love.

Now I know these exist.

And I won't forget.

I reach a hand up toward the floating pool of water. A current sweeps over me, sucking me into the dark. I kick and kick until I break the surface, then sprint away from the pool and up the passageway.

As I slip through the secret door, the air seems fresh by comparison. The earthy smell of Cryptgarden washes over me. Something else fills the air too. A loud, rhythmic chanting.

I drift over to the edge of the lookout and stare down at the city. A great commotion is happening down below. A parade, marching through the main street. Goblins, fae, and nameless other creatures hoot and holler, thrusting torches skyward. At the end of the procession, they're dragging someone. He's stripped near naked and bound in chains, his long, white hair flowing over his shoulders.

My husband.

33

The Prince of Thorns

Is there anything sweeter than the thrill of the hunt?

Oh, yes. Yes. Yes. Basking in the spoils. That is sweetest of all.

I lie on my side atop a perch I crafted of briars, just high enough that I can watch the entire parade. With one finger, I swirl the violet wine in my goblet, barely able to take my eyes off my trophy for a sip.

A procession of goblins, trolls, and fae caterwaul as they dance down the street. Shadows hop over the buildings from the swinging torches and gemlight lamps they carry. Someone's pounding a drum while another blows on a bone horn, the two sounds in complete dissonance.

And at the back, the hero of Winter pulls at his chains like a rabid beast.

I sit up and run a tongue over my top lip. The parade has not been kind to him. His clothes have been torn, leaving him fully bare besides a pair of ragged shorts. His muscles ripple beneath bruises and filth. On the sidelines, citizens jeer at him, though some make obscene gestures. A troll woman flashes her breasts.

Shadowed by his matted hair, its usual starlight-white now streaked with dirt, his eyes flash with rage. A beast, through and through, but a calculating one. Given his power—like all the high rulers—originates from Castletree, his magic is lessened down here. But I'm sure if he was so motivated, he'd see the entire city covered in a blizzard.

Yet he's not fighting back.

Perhaps he thinks this is the only way he'll get to see my precious Flower.

I cannot wait to break him.

Leaping down from my perch, I await the end of the parade. We're at the southeastern corner of Cryptgarden. No usual prison for my pet. Oh no.

I want everyone to be able to come and gaze upon the High Prince of Winter. Witness this great and powerful man brought low. To the Vale, he was the Sworn Protector of the Realms, but I always knew he had the heart of a beast. And this is where beasts belong.

With a flick of my cape, I walk beneath the wrought iron sign that reads MENAGERIE.

Two stone walls creep in on either side of me. Old stone covered in luminescent moss squishes under my boots. The air smells like honey and blood. A shiver runs up my spine as I suddenly realize how many eyes are on me. Not the creatures in the procession following me but the ones in the cages.

Rows and rows of bone cages infused with obsidian flank the path through the menagerie. Pathetic roars and howls sound around me. A small gryphon huddles in the corner of a cage, its wings clipped, coat dulled from bronze to beige. A pure-white stag paces in another, its antlers so big for the enclosure, it must keep its head permanently bowed. Behind the cages, there's a tiny glass aquarium where a siren keeps her pink tail coiled. This tank is so much smaller than the one she's shown in when it's time for her to perform.

I square my shoulders and keep my gaze forward. I don't enjoy looking at them, these sad, pathetic creatures. Miserable about their own existences. *So what? We're all caged here.*

Straight ahead lies the end of the menagerie: a steep drop-off down into the depths. Right on the edge sits a small cage, six feet by six feet, the bars double infused. The zookeeper stands beside it, a fae man who could honestly be mistaken for a ghoul for how ashen his skin is, how loosely it hangs from his bones. His eyes are dark caverns, but they gleam with delight.

He offers me a delighted smile, his one tooth barely hanging by a thread, as he opens the cage door. "What an offering for my collection, my prince!"

I don't acknowledge him. Instead, I spread my arms out as if welcoming Keldarion to a beautiful home.

This is what I wanted all those decades ago. For Keldarion to be at home with me.

He never could.

So I'll take away his option. He'll stay here, behind bars, trapped with me forever.

I notice the zookeeper has not taken the liberty of cleaning out the cage from its last inhabitant. The obsidian floor is covered in blood and filth.

Good. Let Keldarion know what happens to the beautiful and wild things when they fall.

The procession spreads out, forming a ring around the cage as Keldarion is dragged forward. His wrists are bound by steel manacles, held on a lead by a troll. The ugly creature gives a tug, and Keldarion falls to his knees, eliciting a chorus of laughter from the surrounding creatures.

But I'm not disappointed. Kel's shoulders shift, the muscles tensing in his legs and bare feet. He bursts up, tearing his lead out of the troll's hands. The chain clatters to the ground. Keldarion turns to run—

My briar pins the chain in place.

"Naughty, naughty. I see we chose appropriately." I gesture to the enclosure. "A cage for a wild animal."

Keldarion seems intent on proving me right, letting loose a beastly roar as it takes a trio of trolls to wrestle him into the cage. The zookeeper locks the door with a satisfied *click*.

Without waiting a moment, Kel spins, grabbing the bars with his bound hands. His eyes find mine. My first instinct is to look away, but I hold his gaze. Why not?

I have nothing to fear from Keldarion, High Prince of Winter. He is mine now.

"Listen to me, Cas," he says, voice raw, hurried. "This isn't you. This is the Green Flame. The baron's using you like he used Farron! Fight it!"

I can't stop the laugh that bubbles out of me. "You are a fool.

You dare equate me with that pathetic princeling? You are as stupid as you are trapped."

How could I expect Kel to understand? My father will offer anyone anything if it means getting what he wants. If Farron thinks he is of any importance to Malekai, it is because he has been deceived. Just as my mother has.

She has no idea that when her usefulness is up and my father steps into our world fully, completely, she will be his first casualty.

Though I suppose maybe Kel should understand this. Betrayal.

He was so good at doing it to me.

"Caspian!"

A voice rings out from behind me. I turn to see Rosalina gliding through the circle. All eyes of the procession follow her, not even attempting to hide their lustful gazes. But they know, just like the beast in the cage, she is *mine*.

"What's going on?" she asks calmly. I can tell she's doing her best to seem composed, to play the part of lovely little thrall for the onlookers, but her cheeks are bright red, her voice a near pant. She's been running. Sprinting, even.

With a sweet smile, she takes my arm, feigning that look of love as she gazes up at me. So tricksy, my future queen.

"A new prisoner?" she asks and looks to the cage.

And this is where her acting can only get her so far.

For in that moment, when she and Kel catch eyes, every truth in her shines through. Horror. Grief. Fear.

Love.

Love so deep and endless, it threatens to drown me.

A chill whistles between my ribs. She will never truly belong to me as long as he lives.

I look to Keldarion, gazing upon her as if she were every star in the sky. I could do it, and no one would question me. Kill him right now. Destroy the High Prince of Winter with a single blow.

Loving you was as easy as the first fall of snow.

I shake my head. But how could I cull such a wonderful new addition to the collection? I will keep him here, my pet. *Mine.*

Rosalina tears her gaze from Kel and grabs my arm. Her nails bite into my flesh, unnoticeable to anyone else but sharp and painful. "What is this place?" she hisses under her breath. "It's horrible. You would hate this."

"Beautiful things hate the dark," I answer back. "So this is where we keep them until they learn to love it."

She bares her teeth in rage. My own little beasty. "Set them free. All of them. Kel included."

"I can't do that, Princess." I yank out of her grip and stride away from the cage, waving a dismissive hand. "Enjoy your new abode, Keldarion. Tomorrow, you and I will play. And I will teach you the true meaning of pain."

34

Keldarion

My spine is aching and stiff, but I refuse to move from my curled position in the corner of the cage, arms wrapped around my legs, head buried in my knees. It does not matter what they throw at me, the words they jeer. I will be as uninteresting and immobile as a rock.

The scum of the Below will not get their pleasure at the expense of my pride. For I feel no shame in my ragged appearance or state. I went to the aid of the mate of my mate, and I would do it again, regardless of the outcome.

There is no day or night in the Below, just the ever-shifting purple and gray sky. I assume it must be what surface realms would call the small hours, for the crowd that had gathered around my cage has wandered off. Finally, there is silence, punctuated only by the occasional whine of another trapped beast.

I may be near naked, covered in blood and filth, humiliated and shamed, but nothing they can do to me is worse than seeing Caspian like this. He begged me not to let him become the monster he's spent his life fighting. I failed him.

Is there a part of him left, crying out within? Caged as I am?

I am exhausted, my chest heavy with sorrow, but there is no sleep to be found here. Moving as little as possible, I lift my head and blink. I was right. All the onlookers have left. The menagerie is lit with the soft gemlight that punctuates the Below, captured in iron lampposts and glowing naturally from the ground. In the nearest cage, I can only make out a mound of icy-blue feathers. One of Winter's rare frostbirds that live on glaciers?

Everything about this place feels sick, a macabre imitation of the surface.

It wasn't always like this, I remember. Decades ago, when I lived here with Caspian, Sira never walked the streets of Cryptgarden. Caspian kept many friends, some of which were goblins, and though he loved and craved the seasonal realms, he would never have allowed the imprisonment of creatures this way. His collections were limited to plants, which he tended to like they were his children.

There is beauty here, glimpses of it, caught in the gemlight. But there is no sense of hope like there once was. The people have given in to the darkness.

"Kel?"

I nearly leap from my skin. That voice! "Rosalina?"

I peer through the murk but can't see her. There's a shuffle beside a nearby cage, and Rosalina steps forward, shedding the cloak I gave her. Beneath, she's dressed in black pants and a matching top with billowing sleeves cinched at the wrists, the bodice tied with a loose bow.

"Rose." I seize the bars, heedless of the ache in my muscles. Immediately, she places her hands over mine and looks up at me with such sorrow, my heart breaks.

"Are you okay? What have they done to you?" she gasps.

"It doesn't matter." All I want is to stroke her face, wipe away the tears threatening to fall, but my manacles make it impossible. "What are you doing here? It's not safe."

"I'm safer than you are," she says in typical stubborn Rosalina fashion.

Pride washes over me. My brilliant girl. She said she could break free of the thralldom, and she did it. Even now, dressed in darkness and sorrow, there is a ferocity to her.

I could stay here forever, just staring at her.

But we don't have forever. "How did you get away from Caspian?" I ask.

Her eyes shine with steely purpose. "The Prince of Thorns is not as infallible as he pretends. I think having you here has put him in a mood. He's stalked off somewhere alone. And I've learned how to get around this city unseen. That cloak you've given me has come in handy." She shakes her head. "Listen, Kel, I don't know what Caspian's planning for tomorrow. Your magic is weakened in the Below, so far from Castletree, but surely you can summon a frost cold enough to break these bars. There are places to hide—"

"No, Rosalina." I kiss her fingers through the slats. "I'm not leaving. This might be the opportunity we've been looking for."

She gives me an exasperated expression. "What are you talking about? He's going to torture you!"

"I've survived his torture for decades. But being close to him, to you…maybe together, we can remind him who he truly is."

Rosalina doesn't say anything, but she stares at me, deep and wondering. Her gaze flicks to her wedding ring. "My husband."

"My wife," I whisper back.

A soft smile appears as she leans toward the bars. "My reckless, brave, stubborn husband."

I meet her, my breath a caress across her mouth. "My reckless, brave, stubborn wife."

The cold bars press against my face as I kiss her, slow and savoring. My body warms with each pass of her lips over mine. It's as if she's giving me strength. Though the light of Castletree simmers like dying ashes, her touch is a breeze, blowing me back to life.

Clattering my manacles against the bars, I stretch my fingers to caress a lock of her hair. Soft and perfumed. I want to say she is too delicate, too perfect for this place, but I know better. My Rose makes a home wherever she goes.

She mumbles my name against my lips, reaching through the bars to grab my neck. I am too filthy, too ruined, for the likes of her, but she doesn't seem to care, kissing me as if starved. And are we not starved for each other?

A growl sounds deep in my throat, the taste of her driving the primal parts of me to madness. Perhaps I should reconsider her escape idea. I could freeze these bars until they shatter, then snatch her into this cage and fuck her like the beast they've made me.

But I resist. Because one day, we'll be free of this, our trials only memories of all we overcame to be together. And I will stand with my strong, beautiful, lovely wife upon the boughs of Castletree. A queen and her king.

Hoots and hollers sound from the entrance of the menagerie, and torchlight flickers in the distance. Drunkards, stumbling toward us, clattering an iron pipe along all the cages, eliciting angry roars and growls from the poor beasts trying to sleep away their existences.

"We're here to see the Beast of the Briar!" a goblin's voice carries. "Great Prince Keldarion! Where are you?"

I squeeze Rosalina's hands. "Go, before they see you."

"Kel—"

I kiss her one more time, hard and fast and filled with what strength I have left. "Go," I urge again. "Whatever tomorrow holds, we'll face it. For him."

She looks at me once more with that fierce expression, then slips into her tundra cloak and disappears into the night. My Rose, with her many thorns.

I return to my position, curled up against the wall, to wait away the hours until Caspian comes for me. I must steel myself, become more unbreakable than the Sword of the Protector.

For no one can hurt you quite like the one you love.

35

Ezryn

"This damned thing won't stay put," I grumble, pushing on the horned headpiece attached to my helmet. Never mind that one of the short horns, resembling an ibex's, keeps drooping, but the helm is heavy, nothing like the Spring steel we use for armor.

"I kind of enjoy mine," Dayton says. He's got bull horns fastened to his skull with a special glue, his hair arranged to hide the fixture. He lowers his head and pretends to charge Farron. The tunnel, lit only by Farron's palmful of fire, creates a menacing glint off the top of his horns. "Makes me feel as though I'm one of the minotaurs we'd fight in the games."

"At least you all got *two* horns." Farron pokes at the single spiraling horn jutting from his forehead, the fringe of his hair hiding its attachment. "Why did Flavia say I only suited *one*?"

"Enough whinging," George says, sporting his own headpiece,

resembling elk antlers. "Judging by the map, we're nearly there. There's no time to lose focus."

Flavia, Castletree's seamstress, has outdone herself, transforming us from three fae and one human into a scouting party of underfae. With scavenged horns, she's crafted elaborate headpieces, and we're dressed head to toe in the thick furs, heavy armor, and mottled coats recovered from Voidseal Bridge.

Anywhere else, and we'd look ridiculous. But we aren't anywhere else. We're in their territory.

The underfae tunnels, leading deep into the Below.

Even surrounded by rock, the cold bites. Memories crowd my mind, and it's easier to focus on my drooping horn than drowning in them. To access these tunnels, we had to travel back to Voidseal, which meant facing all the destruction that befell here. All the lives we lost and the ones we took.

I spent a long moment, staring down into the darkness. There were barely any signs of the bridge I'd destroyed, as if it had never been there at all.

Without the use of the lifts, I had to sink my magic deep within the rock again, forming a makeshift staircase for us to traverse. But we found an open tunnel—one crafted by those horrible mole creatures perhaps—and crept inside. We know the tunnels lead to the underfae war camp. If we can find our way back there, I can navigate us to Cryptgarden. Thankfully, Farron knows this terrain too, and George seems to always be able to tell which direction Aurelia's in.

And Dayton's good for the muscle in case we need it. I'm anticipating a smooth journey until we get to Cryptgarden. From what intel we've collected, Sira's been gathering her forces in the city proper. That must include the underfae as well. I'm expecting an empty camp, but there's always a chance of scouts lurking nearby.

The slightest clatter of pebbles on stone sounds in my left ear. I don't turn or slow my movement. But I mumble lowly, "I believe we're being followed."

No need to exchange glances. We move as one, even George, pressing ourselves to the rock and ducking into the shadows.

We wait a breath cycle, then two, then three.

Two underfae round the corner from behind us. Each has a single horn, one on the right side of his head, one on the left, so they appear a matching set. They shuffle as they walk, dragging their boots.

Should I let them pass or intercept them now? Though the underfae are incredible warriors, these two aren't very big.

Just as I'm stretching my fingers up toward the token around my neck to summon the Hammer of Hope, Farron steps out, blocking their path.

"A little far from Coppershire, aren't we, boys?" Farron growls, putting his hands on his hips.

The two underfae immediately jump to straight-backed position. The dim light ripples over them, revealing youthful faces splattered with freckles.

"Billagin and Dominic, you two rascals!" George says, grabbing the boys by the shoulders. "What are you doing here?"

Well, that would explain the shuffling. Their boots are far too big. I disengage from the wall and round on them. "You two were not assigned to this mission. Do you understand how dangerous this is? You could have been caught or killed!"

"Ah, go easy on them, Ez. I'm sure they have a good reason for being here." Dayton flashes them a withering glare. "You better have a good reason for being here. Otherwise, you'll make me look like an idiot for standing up for you."

"Of course we do!" Dom says.

Billy crosses his arms. "You're right it's a dangerous mission. And we made a promise to our big brother we were going to protect him. So that's what we're doing!"

Farron pokes Dom's single horn. "How did you get all this?"

"While I distracted Flavia with my powerful charisma, Billy grabbed all the extra pieces, and we assembled it on the way."

"Powerful charisma?" Dayton snorts a laugh. "I thought Astrid was your one true love."

"Dom's still mourning her latest rejection." Billy puts a condoling hand on his brother's arm.

Farron rubs his bearded chin. "I appreciate the sentiment, but you have to turn around. We don't know what we're getting into down here and—"

"—and that's why you need us to look after you." Billy nudges Farron's shoulder, then trudges ahead. "So what are we waiting for? There's no time to lose!"

I blow out a long breath. "He's right. We can't send them back now. It's too close to nightfall, and we don't want them on the tundra alone. And we need to keep moving. Guess we've got two more in our scouting party."

Dayton and George seem elated to have the twins with us. I'm constantly reminding them to stay alert. Meanwhile, Farron's dragging behind.

I slow my pace so he catches up. "What's wrong?"

Farron keeps his gaze downcast, the long, spiraling horn jutting out before him. "I don't want to worry about the people I care about. It's such a heavy burden to carry."

This helmet has an open visor, so I'm able to stare at his face with my own eyes. To search the dark circles, the slump of his spine. "That's the price we pay for love, Farron. The worry, the grief. It is heavy." I place a hand on his shoulders. "But you are so strong."

"If I were strong, I could have saved them," he whispers.

"Who?"

"My soldiers. The ones I led into the Briar. Caspian killed them all." His gaze widens with horror, as if seeing something evil within his mind's eye. "No. I killed them. They were my orders. My responsibility."

I feel his guilt as if it were my own. How many people suffered because I willingly passed on my blessing? I stop walking and grab his shoulder, forcing him to look at me. "You will bear the scars of that decision for the rest of your life. But those scars are not there to haunt you. They are there to teach you."

Farron squeezes his eyes shut. "How can I ever trust myself—"

"Trust your scars," I urge him. "When next you are faced with a decision, they will ache. They will remind you. And you will make the right decision. Because that's who you are, Farron."

When he finally looks at me, his face is drained of hope. "That's the thing, Ez. Who even am I anymore?"

I place a hand on his cheek. "You are Farron, High Prince of Autumn. But above all else, you are a good person."

He seems like he might argue, but Dayton's voice interrupts us, ringing out from ahead: "Hey, we've got light!"

Farron staggers away from me and I follow behind him. The path widens, then opens to a glowing maw. I signal everyone to line the shadows against the walls, then creep forward.

The underfae camp lies before us. But it's not empty. It's bustling with people. Drums play, but in rhythm, not for battle. I catch sight of horned fae dancing, eating, attending to weapons. Food is being cooked over pits that glow not with flames but with crystals. They're stacked like logs and must be emitting their own heat, if the steam wafting from the cooking pots is any indication. Tents dot the grounds. This is not a transient camp, and there seems to be no packing or movement.

"I don't understand," I whisper. "I thought they'd all be gathered in Cryptgarden with the rest of Sira's army."

"Can we sneak around it? There are tunnels over there. Southward usually leads deeper into the Below, closer to Cryptgarden," Farron suggests, pointing to the back of the camp.

"Why waste such a glorious opportunity?" George asks. "We're going to need information on Rosalina's and Keldarion's locations. Perhaps someone here knows about the rose itself."

"What are you suggesting?" I ask hesitantly, because I know that O'Connell look. The one where they think they've just had a brilliant idea.

George straightens his horns. "I suggest we mingle." Then with that, he steps out of the shadows and starts strutting down the hill into the camp like he lives here.

My heart lurches into my throat, and I'm about to dive out there and snatch him back when I notice something. Rather I notice the absence of something.

No one's leaping up to arrest George. No one's sounded a horn. No one's paying him any mind. In a war camp, there must be dozens of scouting parties coming and going. He's just another ranger, returning home.

"Well, I'm not about to let an ancient human show me up," Dayton says. "See you down there."

Before long, Dayton, Farron, and the twins have followed George, heads up and assured, and I'm left alone, hiding in the darkness.

I let loose a sigh. Stealth missions have never been my strength. I've got a perfectly good hammer. This would be so much easier if I could just *hit* things.

"Here goes nothing," I mumble and walk out.

Natural. Confident. Nothing to see here. Except I'm fairly certain one of my horns is drooping. My steps feel awkward, movements wooden, as I stride into the camp. Or rather I attempt to stride. I'm more shuffling in my effort to seem ordinary.

It's as busy a camp as I've ever seen; I'd thought they'd unleashed their entire army on us at Voidseal. Where were all these soldiers stationed? Tall tents crafted of heavy canvas line the cavern, interspersed with cooking canopies filled with pots bubbling with stew and armories lined with spears, bows and arrows, and all manner of handheld weapons.

Yes, they're preparing for war, but there's life being lived here. A group of women are gathered around a crystal hearth, singing in an unfamiliar language. Away from the tents, two men toss a leather ball back and forth, heckling each other. *There are no children*, I notice.

The Eldraíth Ruvénir. That's what Faustrius called his people. The Chosen Fallen. The fae who followed Sira down from the Above to the surface. She had taken their faeness and turned it rotten, as she does with all creations. And now they are alone in the world.

My son. That's what he called Kairyn after Sira turned my brother into one of them. How lonely, to be the last of your kind. How beautiful a chance at a legacy must seem.

Out of the corner of my eye, I see Dayton's stationed himself at an armory, blending in by busying himself with a rope. George is at a cook tent and somehow got himself on stirring duty. Stars know where the Autumn brothers have scurried off to, but I can only hope Farron keeps his curiosity in check. We can't make ourselves conspicuous.

Which means I better find myself something to do, because standing like an idiot in the middle of the causeway is sure to bring about questions.

Ahead, I see an area populated by several firepits. Though, I suppose that's not really the right word. There's no smoke, no flame, only a soft glow from the heated crystals within. Cryptgarden uses gems for much of their architecture, but these are different than I've ever seen before. They must be some underfae discovery. In fact, when I look around the camp I spot more of the crystals: glowing in the place of torches, heating metal for smithing, and even powering a rope pulley system that moves supplies from one side of the camp to the other. Light. Heat. *Energy.*

My mind begins to whirr with the possibilities, and as much as I'd like to snag one to examine later, I have to keep focused on the mission.

Most of the crystal basins are surrounded by fae, but there's an unoccupied one. It's close to a pair of underfae sitting around another pit but—

I know them. How could I forget the man who arranged for Sira to turn my brother into a monster?

Faustrius appears like any other soldier, huddled toward the crystals' warmth. His red eyes are grim, the rough scratch of an untended beard across his jaw. His skin is blue-gray, the color of slate, and his large antlers are adorned with strips of colored fabric.

Beside him sits Aquila, the priestess who nearly killed Dayton. She's got her head tilted up, staring at the cavernous ceiling with a faraway look. One side of her face is still red and sagging with ruined flesh from when Farron burned her at the volcano. A few stray hairs poke out from her skull.

Quickly, I descend to the empty crystal pit, pretending to warm my hands with the radiant heat, but my concentration remains focused behind me.

"Enough, Faust! I can't listen to this anymore," Aquila quietly snarls. "It's beyond me why you even care. He's not one of us."

"Does it matter?" Faustrius says lowly.

"Of course it matters. Did his kin treat us with fairness? With mercy? No. We were frozen and left for dead. The High Prince of Winter can rot in that cage."

I blow on my hands and work to steady my breathing.

"No creature deserves to be kept in such conditions, even an enemy," Faustrius says.

Aquila lets out an exhausted sigh. "It's not a prison!"

"The menagerie is worse," Faustrius breathes. "What you cannot control, you cage. Is that not her way?"

"She wouldn't like you talking that way," Aquila responds in a singsong voice.

Silence echoes between them. Up close, I can hear the faint hum of the crystals. My own breathing sounds like a roar in comparison.

Finally, Faustrius murmurs so low, I barely make out the words: "It's concerning, Aquila."

"The rose?"

"The rose."

"She plans to use it," Aquila whispers. "Change all those gobbos' minds to jelly. They don't know it yet." She pauses. "You don't think she'd..."

"No," Faustrius says quickly. "She'll never turn it on us. She promised me."

"But still. All those poor gobbos." Aquila lets out a sigh. "War is war, Fausty. We're all players. And one day, when this is all over, we'll see it again."

"See what?"

I turn my head so I can catch sight of them out of my peripheral. Aquila leans over to Faustrius and grabs his arm, pointing up to the sky. "Whatever's up there. It's got to be beautiful, don't you think?"

"Of course it is. You know it is, Quill. One day, we'll walk among the clouds once more and earn back the right to fly among the stars."

"The stars?" Aquila asks. "Oh, those sound wonderful."

Faustrius gives a strange laugh, then knocks her on the unburnt part of her head. "You should sleep."

Aquila stands and stretches. "I must respond to her summons. She wants to know when we're moving the army to Cryptgarden."

Faustrius rises as well. "Put her off. It's bad enough you and I have to spend so much time there."

"She's going to be *ma-aad*," Aquila sings and prances off toward one of the southerly tunnels.

Faustrius walks past me, and I duck my head, busying myself with rubbing my hands above the crystals. The heat licks at my skin, but I don't pull away.

Keldarion is being kept in Cryptgarden's menagerie. That's all we need to know. Because wherever Kel is, Caspian won't be far. And wherever Caspian is, our Rose will be too.

And wherever our Rose is, trouble is sure to follow.

36

The Prince of Thorns

The aroma of frost greets me before I reach the cage.

Not real frost of course. Not here in the Below. But the echo of it. His scent.

Winter magic rotting in the heat. I breathe it in like it's perfume.

I would know his smell in my grave.

Cryptgarden is quiet today. It's as if the fae feel my approach and retreat into the shadows. For the best. I want to see him without an audience.

Later, there will be time for spectacle.

But now… Now, I want to savor this.

My boots are silent against the cracked cobblestones of the menagerie. I feel his magic long before I get close, that unbridled blessing pulsing with power.

Even caged, he's perfect.

He's sitting with his back to me, chained and shirtless. Filthy white hair hangs over his spine.

I step closer, dragging the shadows with me. My precious gift for him dangles in my hand.

"Kel," I say, tasting the name like wine.

He stiffens, a subtle tightening of his shoulders.

I smile.

"You know, I thought you'd appear more broken by now." I continue pacing in front of the cage. "But you're still so regal, even in ruin."

His eyes lift to meet mine, glinting with hatred and something else he won't name.

Desperation maybe. Memory. Love?

I'll burn all that out of him soon enough.

"You took your time," he says.

"And you're still speaking." I smile. "How disappointing."

He shifts, just enough for the chains to rattle. "I figured you'd prefer to hear me scream before you paraded me in front of your little monsters."

I laugh, low and sharp. Gods, he still has claws. Good. It's better when they make me bleed back.

"No, no." I crouch in front of him. "Tonight isn't about screaming. Not yet. Tonight is about presentation."

His jaw tightens. "You think humiliating me will win your war?"

"No," I murmur, brushing a strand of hair from his face. "I think collaring you will remind the realms who holds the leash."

His eyes flash, full of fury and the kind of fear that makes my blood sing.

I pick the lock with a slim thorn, step inside the cell, and hold up the collar before him. It unfurls like a serpent, woven thorns and black ice.

Kel's breath hitches.

"Don't," he says. "Whip me, beat me, but don't put that thing on me."

"But I made it just for you," I say softly.

He lunges, but not fast enough.

I catch him by the throat and slam him back against the wall. The shadows rise to hold him there. My hand stays soft, fingers resting against his pulse.

"You want to keep pretending?" I whisper. "Keep lying to yourself?"

His breath is hot. He glares at me, hatred and heat twisting behind those blue eyes. "I would rather die than kneel for you."

I lean closer. My lips brush his ear. "Oh, you'll kneel. And you'll look beautiful doing it."

And with that, I fasten the collar.

It clicks shut, thorns locking into place like a jaw around his throat. It's no bargain circlet, but it's still a display. A symbol.

He chokes, muscles tensing, fingers clawing at the collar, but it's already sealed. The leash glows into existence, stretching from his throat to the bracer around my wrist, pulsing with green fire.

Kel gasps and collapses forward onto his hands and knees, the barbs digging into his throat.

His head bows, hair pooling like snow around him. I drink in the sight of him.

"I'll parade you through the heart of the Below," I say. "Let them see you kneel. Let them see the High Prince of Winter, collared like an animal."

"You'll never keep me here," he snarls, head still bowed.

"I think I will." I crouch again, lowering myself beside him. My fingers trail through his hair. "You're mine now, pet."

His breath shakes. I can feel him fighting. Resisting. I let him.

Resistance makes it so much sweeter when they break.

"Later," I whisper, pressing a kiss to his temple. "You'll thank me."

~

I pull the leash tighter.

Not enough to choke him. Just enough to remind him it's here. That *I'm* here.

Keldarion stumbles behind me, barefoot on polished obsidian. His once-regal clothes have been reduced to scraps. His matted hair hides most of his face.

And still…he keeps his head high.

I hate him for it.

I ache for him because of it.

He walks like a prince even when I've stripped him of everything. Even when the thorns bite at his throat and every step sends a whisper of pain through his collar. The leash in my hand thrums with his resistance. His hope.

Gods, I should have broken that by now.

The courtyard of my palace is packed full. They came when summoned, as they always do: ghouls in twisted finery, false scholars with eyes like polished bone, would-be warlords dressed in gold filigree and decay. The citizens of the Below, my people, leaning over balconies of black stone to get a better look.

They know what this is.

They love a spectacle.

Rosalina walks ahead of me. The gown I had made for her is a masterpiece, dark velvet with green embroidery, a low back that shows off all that beautiful skin.

She looks like my queen, even if she still refuses to accept it. But with no magic of her own, she must play along. I offered her a promise.

If she does what I say, I'll keep Keldarion alive.

So she lifts her chin and walks beside me. But I see the way her hands tremble. How her shoulders tense when the chain scrapes stone. She's feeling every bite of Kel's pain as if it were her own.

Unfortunate thing about mate bonds.

And I can't decide if I admire her…or if it makes me want to shatter her as I will Keldarion.

It's so fun to see how your favorite things break and can be put back together anew.

I wonder absently if my mother will come.

She rarely descends from Nether Reach anymore, and when she does, it's only to commune with the Baron, preferring his company to mine. If only she knew my father covets her death as much as I do. He knows how dangerous she can be. I suppose even gods fear.

I glance toward one of the upper balconies of my palace, where she usually observes the gatherings.

Nothing.

Fine. Let her miss this. I don't need her.

We reach the base of my throne made of briars and ascend the steps.

I halt. The chain goes taut and Kel drops to his knees. He catches himself on trembling hands, glaring at the floor as if it insulted him. He says nothing, his breaths steady and slow.

The hall hushes.

I step forward, turning to face the crowd, and lift the leash. "Behold, High Prince Keldarion of Winter. Sworn Protector of the Realms. The fae who called down the stars. And now..." I pause, glance at him. "Mine."

A hiss of delighted laughter ripples through the courtyard, followed by whispers. Kel's shoulders tense.

I circle him, dragging the chain across my fingers. I want my citizens to feel this moment. To see how far a prince can fall.

"I brought you here not for celebration but revelation," I say, letting my voice rise. "Not to toast this conquest but to witness the cost of defiance. The seasonal realms thought they could take on the Below. They were wrong."

I stalk behind Kel. One hand tangles in his hair, lifting his head to show the bruises at his throat, the cut at his cheek, the long slashes along his shoulders.

Rosalina gasps, forming fists at her sides.

I ignore her and address the crowd. "If the most powerful of the high princes cannot defy us, then no one can."

Kel's breath sharpens.

I lean closer, whispering against his ear, "Tell them."

No answer.

Louder now. "Tell them you saw this coming. Gods know you

would never shut up about it. You knew what I would become. This was always my destiny."

He stares up at me, blue eyes blazing.

"Cas," he says, "I was wrong."

The leash goes cold in my hand.

He keeps talking. "I should have trusted you. Trusted our love. And yet even here, I find I love you still."

Laughter dies as the hall quiets. Rosalina's breath stutters.

I stare at him. And for a second, for one cursed heartbeat, I forget where I am.

If you love me, kill me. Kel, you should have killed me. Something wet streaks across my cheek.

He stares at me. *My love was too great to obey that.*

"Liar," I say.

Other voices filter in, laughter and murmurs from the crowd. They came to watch the Winter Prince humiliated. Not…whatever this is.

Keldarion shakes his head. "You can make me kneel. But you'll never make me lie."

His words land sharper than a blade between my ribs. Not hate but love.

Not the venom I craved. Not the fury I needed. Just that same quiet, pathetic love offered up, a gift he knows I'll never take.

Rosalina has been a bad influence on the High Prince of Winter.

And she's watching him now, eyes shining, like he's every star in the damn sky.

But there are no stars in the Below.

My jaw tightens. Green flames roar to life around me, surging up from the cracks in the stone. The crowd gasps.

Rosalina flinches. "Cas, it's alright."

But I don't look at her. I don't look at anyone.

Except him.

"You should have ended me when you had the chance," I snarl. "Because now you'll pay for every lie you called love."

37

Rosalina

No. *No, no, no.* I'd seen him, seen him there for a moment with Kel's words, tears running down his face. Cas, *our* Cas.

He's in there. We're so close.

But the more we push, the more we try to break him free, the more the Green Flame tightens its grip. The man before us is cold and cruel.

The Prince of Thorns.

Emerald flames erupt from the stones beneath his boots, coiling up his legs, around his arms, twisting through his hair. It's not as if he's wielding them so much as he *is* them.

The light they cast is wrong. All the Cryptgarden courtiers fall silent, fear gripping even them. A few on the outskirts start to run.

But I don't move.

Because Keldarion is still kneeling. And Caspian is staring at Kel like he wants to turn him to ash.

"Anything more to say?" Caspian lifts his hand. A whip of thorns forms, coiling with flame.

Kel doesn't flinch. He just looks at him, soft and unafraid, which only enrages Caspian more.

Look away, Rose, he says in my mind.

He knows I won't.

The whip snaps.

I know what comes next. Know how this ends.

But something else rises in me. A memory.

Caspian's voice, days ago, as he carried me away from Sira. *If you lay a hand on her again, Mother, I fear nothing in this world could keep the green flame from burning through your pitiful fae bargain and consuming you.*

Caspian would *never* hurt me. Some part of that lives in the Prince of Thorns. And if he would tear his own mother apart, what would he do to himself for causing me pain?

Break through the bargain?

Break through the Green Flame?

Time to find out.

The whip cracks just as I dive between Caspian and Keldarion, lashing across my skin.

Agony explodes through my body, white-hot and searing. The whip wraps across my back, fire biting into skin and silk and soul. I slam to the ground with a cry, the breath ripped from my lungs.

Everything goes silent.

I lie there, curled around the pain, gasping, feeling the heat sear through me like it's trying to brand me. But all I can hear is Kel shouting my name.

And then—

"R-Rose?"

It's Caspian.

His voice is soft. Shaking.

He drops the whip.

The last of the green flames flicker around him, then die.

38

Caspian

The burning has stopped. The embers are quiet.

Locked away where they should be.

The voices have stopped curling around my thoughts. There's only silence. Cold, aching silence.

And in that silence, I remember everything.

The destruction of Winter. Taking over the minds of Farron and Dayton. Battling Keldarion on the mountainside. Recruiting all manner of filth to my mother's side. All the soldiers in Autumn speared by my briars. Rosalina as my thrall and then my lover.

The leash. The collar. The way Kel's voice broke when he said he loved me.

Rosalina's scream as the whip struck her down.

She's not moving.

Rosalina lies on the obsidian floor, her back torn and blackened.

The scents of scorched silk and blood twist in the air. Her hands twitch once, then go still.

I can't breathe.

Kel's chained. Kneeling. The collar has bruised his throat purple. His arms are bound.

He's looking at her like he might shatter.

And I finally see.

I did this.

The weight of my actions hits me all at once, as if the mountain above Cryptgarden has fallen on top of me. Every word I twisted. Every command. Every time I looked away when my loved ones screamed, when they begged, when they pleaded that they still cared for me.

I fall hard to my knees. "Rosalina…" My voice cracks.

Her eyes barely flick to me, and she forces herself up with shaking arms. "Just a little clumsy," she breathes.

That undoes me.

The Green Flame seethes, reaching for my heart in a final hiss of defiance. Clawing at me, hungry, waiting to coil around my spine and make me forget again. Let me become fire and fury and nothing at all.

But I won't allow it.

Not now.

Not when I've already lost almost everything. Was that enough for me to break through?

I grit my teeth and reach inward, past the pain, past the rot. I find the cage I once built for the flame and slam the door shut, locking it with will alone. My body screams.

Smoke curls from my fingertips.

I rise slowly. The pain is unbearable. My hands are shaking. My knees threaten to buckle.

But I stand.

The courtyard is silent.

Dozens of eyes gaze at us. They're wondering what happened. I bare my teeth. I can't lose myself, can't let myself break yet. There's still a game to play.

"Get. Out."

No one moves.

So I raise my hand.

The shadows rise around me like wings, vast and furious. The green fire may be gone, but darkness always obeys. "I said *leave*!"

My voice shakes the walls, and the crowd scatters. They don't walk—they flee. Even the boldest of them cower. Good.

They should.

When the courtyard is empty, I collapse to my knees between them. Kel breathes shallowly, still chained, still collared. Rosie is limp, pain written in every line of her face.

I want to tell them I'm sorry, but I can't make myself say the words. It's not enough. It will never be enough.

So I raise my hand, and the thorns snake from the floor in silence. Gentle this time.

They lift Kel. They lift Rosie. They cradle them like something sacred.

And I carry us away.

39

Rosalina

A RIVER OF FIRE RACES DOWN MY SPINE, BUT I HAVE NEVER BEEN SO happy.

Tears of joy spill over my cheeks as Caspian's briars lift us up through the earth. A smooth floor, then a fluffy bed envelops me. I know where I am. This is my chamber in the Gem.

Caspian is bent on all fours, and I can tell from the way he's breathing, it's truly him. I share a look with Kel. Without speaking in his mind, I know what he's feeling. He's in pain, but the only emotion that flashes in those sapphire eyes is love.

I crawl over and place a hand on Caspian's back. He shudders beneath my touch. "Cas."

He rises, a flower unfurling to the first rays of the sun after a long winter. But as always, he's more beautiful than any bloom, even with his hair in wayward strands across his brow and cheeks stained with tears. Those eyes, so wonderful and *violet*, I could stare at them forever.

His gaze sears over me until he tentatively touches the thorn cuffs on my wrists. "I release you from this bargain."

The cuffs writhe, then wither to the ground. I gasp as if it's my first gulp of air after being underwater. Magic prickles along my skin. Without hesitation, I reach for Kel, feeling for the skills I learned from Ezryn and from carrying the blessing of Spring inside me, and send a burst of healing through him.

The wounds on his body begin to knit closed, and he grimaces. "No, Rose, heal yourself first."

I don't listen, just watch as he regains his strength. The tension in his brow fades. Caspian approaches him like a nervous cat. Slowly, he reaches forward and unclasps the collar. It clatters to the ground, disappearing into a cloud of smoke.

Caspian shrinks back, staring at the empty space as if it offended him.

"Come on, Cas," Keldarion says. "Admit it. It turned you on seeing me in that."

The words crack Caspian out of his shock, and he releases a laugh, wiping his eyes.

Keldarion places a hand over mine. "Enough. I am fine. Help yourself or I will not be able to bear it."

After being caged for so long, my magic is sluggish, especially after pouring so much into Keldarion. "My bag," I say. "Ezryn made a healing balm."

Keldarion stands and returns a minute later. I could cry with relief as he spreads it across my back. A cooling numbness replaces the burn, and I'm awash in the smell of honeysuckle and echinacea. It's almost as if I can feel Ezryn's touch across my skin.

"Help me, Cas," Keldarion orders.

Caspian stares blankly for a moment before crawling behind me. "I don't deserve to touch her. Not ever again."

"Cas," I say, hoping the soft sound of his name can convey all the words I want to pour into him. Words he might not be ready to hear.

But Kel is gentle as he says, "Start by holding her hair up then so I can get the top of her back."

This must be alright with him, because I feel Caspian's touch as he lifts my hair and Keldarion smooths the last of the balm across my shoulders.

Sighing with relief, I turn to them. Keldarion is still shirtless, hair gray with dirt, but happy. Cas is rich with splendor, yet he has the saddest expression on his face.

"I understand if you hate me," he says. "I never wanted to become this."

"But you did," I say. "To save Wrenley. You'll always do whatever you can to save those you love."

He glances at Kel. "You should have killed me."

I huff. "If I'm mad at you for anything, it's that request."

"I tried, Cas," Keldarion says. "I couldn't do it."

Caspian hisses in through his teeth and draws his knees to his chest. "You both need to get out of here. My magic is weak from taming the fire. Rose, use your briars and *go*."

We both stare at him. Say nothing.

"What if it takes me over again?" Caspian continues. "What if

Sira realizes I'm not under the Baron's control anymore? I'm still bound by her bargain with Aurelia."

"She can't command you to do more than one thing at once," I remind him.

"No, the Green Flame helped me resist that. Without that magic, I'm as vulnerable as your mother. She could command me to kill you. Kill you both. You need to leave. Besides, she has the rose. I *gave* it to her."

I exchange a look with Keldarion before I grab Caspian's head between my hands. "We're not leaving you, not ever. I came down here for you."

Keldarion touches Cas's shoulder. "We'll figure this out together. For now, have faith that Sira still believes you're under the Green Flame and us your prisoners."

He nods, the thought seeming to calm him. I weave my fingers through his hair.

"Then there's just one thing I need to know," he whispers, looking at us. "Do you think you could ever love me again?"

This answer resounds in my very soul. "I never stopped."

I cup his face, brushing soot from his jaw. He's really here. Really back.

I press my forehead to his, and a tear slips down my cheek. I kiss him, deep and slow. A kiss to remind him he's home. That no matter how far he fell, my heart never stopped waiting.

40

Keldarion

THEY BOTH SEEM SO DELICATE, SO SMALL EVEN, WRAPPED IN MY ARMS. I lie on my side, Caspian's head on my bicep. Rosalina's sprawled over his chest, and I curl around them both. Outside Rosalina's bedchamber, the dusky sky of the Below never changes.

Tomorrow, we can strategize. But tonight? Tonight, I hold them.

I didn't realize how comforting it could be to just exist here, listening to them breathe.

Sworn Protector of the Realms.

I start with them, these two whom I love more than anything in the world. And with their love as my anchor, I extend that protection across my realm and to the others, to Castletree and beyond. *Protect them. I'll protect them all.*

Caspian stirs, blinks up at me, then smiles. I have known the deepest frost and strongest fire, battled hordes and sharp blades, but I have known nothing as ruinous as his smile.

I lean down and kiss him. He sighs into my mouth. I know the horrors of what he did under the control of the Green Flame will haunt him evermore, but hopefully tonight, he realizes how safe he is.

Let Sira try to take him from us again.

Rosalina gives a soft yawn. She stretches on Caspian's chest, then rolls, falling between us. Caspian chuckles, the sounds lighting something inside me.

"Is it morning?" she asks sleepily.

"Not yet," I say.

"Good," she replies, nuzzling into me. "I'm not ready for this to end."

Caspian gently moves the hair from across her brow, then his gaze shifts to mine. "I don't want this to ever end. Thank you for coming for me. Thank you for *staying* with me."

Rosalina presses her lips against his. "I told you. I will love you in any form. Forever."

I take a deep breath and press on her shoulder so they're both looking at me. Gently, I trace Rosalina's jaw, then weave my fingers through Caspian's hair. "When the stars wove my fate, they made a tapestry of light and fire and winter, one that always ends with me loving you."

I kiss Rosalina, then him, but when I pull away, my lips are salty and wet.

Caspian sits up, tears flowing down his cheeks. "Those are the words…the ones you said all those years ago, in this very palace."

"And I still mean them."

He shakes his head. "The way you touched her face… I've seen it before."

"What are you saying?" Rosalina asks.

"It was the vision," Caspian says. "The one the Fate showed me. My mother twisted it to make me believe you never loved me…"

I sit up, bringing Rose with me.

"You never gave our words away, not that I would care anymore, knowing what I do," Caspian continues. "But I never realized… I was always in that vision, here with you both."

Rosalina smiles, so bright and beautiful. "This moment was woven in the stars."

He reaches out a shaking hand, cupping the nape of her neck and drawing her into a deep kiss. Then he pulls away and looks up at me through thick, dark lashes.

"Do you remember that once I swore I'd never fall for you?" I ask and pull him against me. "But you are in my blood now." I crush my mouth against his, and he responds, passionate, desperate, all the emotions that have been coursing through us since he was taken. "I will never be parted from you again."

41

Rosalina

"It's risky," I say. "If you get too close to Sira, she'll notice your eye color."

"Would she really notice that?" Keldarion asks, lounging on the bed. He's wearing a loose blue tunic and leather pants, both of which fit him perfectly. They're clothes he left in Cryptgarden decades ago, clothes Caspian never could throw out.

The three of us have been pacing my chamber all morning, trying to figure out a plan to get the rose back. We can't leave the Below without it. "Caspian is Sira's most precious creation," I sigh. "She'll notice."

"And you can't summon a little of the Green Flame to do your bidding?" Keldarion asks.

Caspian lays a hand against the doorframe, brow creased. "I don't dare. If I let even a flicker of that magic out, it'll consume me again."

I throw myself to the end of the bed, kneading the bridge of my nose. Keldarion rubs my back. "Think. We have an advantage. She doesn't know you're *you* and I'm *me*."

"You mentioned a revelry party, attended by all manner of creatures," Keldarion says. "To celebrate Sira's possession of the rose."

Caspian runs a hand through his long hair. "Yes. Sira's creations have scattered across the Vale. It was my mission to gain their allegiance with sweet promises. They've all gathered now."

"What kind of promises?" I ask lowly.

"That Sira would make more of their kind. This may well still be her intention, yet…"

"She's also going to use the rose to steal their wills," I say. "Not to mention how many memories she'll take in the process."

When I told Kel and Caspian about what I'd seen in the cavern, both their faces dropped in horror. "Did you know about this?" Kel asked Cas.

"No, but it explains why everyone's always so miserable down here. If all they have is memories of goodness and she steals even that, what is there to live for?" Caspian shook his head. "What might the people of Cryptgarden become, if only they believe there was still hope to fight for?"

His words have stayed with me. Could there ever be a future where the Below and the seasonal realms were not enemies, but united?

"This revelry day could work to our advantage if we gain possession of the rose," Keldarion says, tearing me back to the present. "All of her followers surrounding her. She'll never escape the Below once we control them."

The notion twists wrong in my gut. But is it any worse than ordering legions of soldiers to march into battle for glory and possible death? *At least the soldiers have a choice.*

I shake my head. "Will she have the rose at this revelry?"

"Definitely. She's touring it across all the cities of the Below. The Tower of Nether Reach will be the last stop," Caspian says. "My mother won't miss the opportunity to gloat, but there's no worse time to try to steal it. It'll be right out in the open, surrounded by thousands of creatures and fae."

"Or the best time." I sit up. "Sira will notice if it goes missing, no doubt. We only have to make sure she doesn't know it's *us*. There will be so many fae there. It could be anyone."

"But how would we ensure that?" Caspian sighs.

A knock sounds on the door, and Heidigog steps in, a tray of breakfast in her little green hands. "Oh! Didn't expect you here, Your Highness. And the prisoner! He's all polished up like a jewel-box doll!"

"It's alright, Heidi," Caspian says, raising a brow and staring at her. "In fact, your timing is perfect."

"It is, Your Highness? Queen Sira says I'm always skitter-scattering in late like a rat looking for cheese." Heidi places the tray down on the end of the bed, still eyeing Keldarion warily. If he's thrown by my goblin lady's maid, he doesn't show it, only taking a croissant off the tray and tossing it to me.

I bite into it but can't keep my eyes off Caspian. That expression, the slightly furrowed brow, the tilt of his lips. He's thinking. Actually, with that look, he's most certainly *scheming*.

A glint flashes in Caspian's gaze. "We get the rose by very obviously *not* stealing it."

I smile. The Prince of Thorns is back. The one who saved Castletree and made it look like a horror, who first whispered truths into my ear and made them sound like threats, who chained Farron to help him break him free.

Shadows pool at his feet. He opens and closes his palms, darkness coiling around his fingertips. "Caspian may not have loved playing with shadows," he purrs, "but the Prince of Thorns did, and he picked up a couple tricks from Sira."

The living gloom swirls around Heidigog, caresses her arms, her head, then winds higher, turning solid, catching the light…until she turns into a perfect replica of me.

Heidi holds her hands up, staring at her now pale pink skin, then rushes to the mirror. She touches her face, my brown hair. "Oh my," she squawks, still with her goblin voice. "I'm hideous!"

PART 3

Legacy of a god

42

Rosalina

I'VE PERFECTED THE DULL-EYED GAZE AND WANDERING AMBLE OF A thrall. No one blinks an eye as I meander through the outskirts of Nether Reach. Though the citizens of the Below aren't under a spell like I'm supposed to be, many share that same inward look.

It reminds me of working at the bookstore back in Orca Cove, where reality felt so gloomy, it was better to live inside my head. In lots of ways, these people—goblins, deserters of the surface realms, or fae born in the dark—are no more free than the animals in the menagerie.

I grit my teeth. If I don't succeed, they'll be worse off. If we don't get the rose, Sira won't just be stealing happy memories. If they're one of her creations, she'll steal their wills. And if they aren't, they'll be at the whim of what she orders her creations to do.

I took a grinjaw carriage from Cryptgarden most of the way to

Nether Reach but am now making the final stretch on foot to be more inconspicuous. The Tower of Nether Reach looms ahead, a thin, jagged tower resembling a stalagmite made of black glass. Beautiful and deadly, like its queen. I imagine Sira, pacing her balcony, looking out over the horizon. She built it to be as high as possible, yet it can never reach the surface.

A great weight falls over my shoulders with each step closer. Memories of when the princes and I were imprisoned at the top of the tower. My magic felt so far away. Even now, at the bottom, it feels sluggish in my veins. Is there an enchantment on this place, or is Sira's energy so strong here, it suffocates all other forms of magic? Regardless, I'm so much stronger than I was back then. My magic *will* answer me when I call upon it.

Sira's revelry day party is planned for the courtyard outside the tower, so I've come to scope it out. The more information I have on the setup, the easier it will be to pull off our plan tonight.

I grunt, heaving my heavy bag higher on my shoulder. I wasn't sure what the security would be like, so I brought everything in case. Kel's cloak and Farron's book of maps may be useful if I need to do some actual sneaking.

But it doesn't look like anything's being set up yet. The courtyard is empty, and there's only a pair of goblin guards—Truubo and Scrumpy—at the door of the tower. They give me a nod as I wander by, used to seeing me about these last few weeks. A party in a few hours and the preparations haven't begun? Marigold would throw a fit.

Just as I'm certain I'll have to come back later for my intel, my ear twitches. There's a sound in the distance, so soft I'm now doubting I heard it at all.

Sniffling.

Giving Truubo and Scrumpy a friendly wave, I walk the curve of the round base of the tower. A black stream trickles behind, and I follow its bank.

A woman sits curled over the edge of the water, thin strands of long, green hair dusting the stream. Her sage-green cheeks are shiny with tears. One side of her face is badly scarred, half her head bald.

It's Aquila, priestess of the underfae and Faustrius's second-in-command.

Why is she all alone, crying? I suck in a breath. I should turn around, pretend I never heard her. What do I care anyway? She attacked us. Her people sided with Sira. Her misery is not my problem—

Aquila lets out a pathetic wail, and my breath rushes out of me in a sigh. I creep over to her. She doesn't look up until I'm right beside her, crouching down at her side.

"Aquila?"

She gives a few sniffles as she attempts to compose herself. "Rosalina."

"Are you okay? I heard crying so I came over."

She takes a breathy gasp that sounds somewhere between a baby bird's call and a hiccup. "Imagine! Imagine! I never thought there'd be anywhere darker than the caverns we woke up in after we were frozen, but now we're here, even deeper in the gloom. And that's not enough to hide me!" She smacks the stream, causing ripples. "You catch a glimpse of yourself only to be reminded you're something horrible."

I follow her gaze down to the stream, to our reflections beginning to form as the glassy water slows. Who does she see? *Something horrible.* Is that who *I* see? Beyond her being one of Sira's many puppets, I barely know this woman.

Aquila lets out a laugh so riddled with grief, a pang hits my own heart. "This is what I deserve, isn't it?" She tears at the strands of hair left on her head. "I first got ruined when I forsook home. Now, I got this"—she drags a finger across the scarred flesh on her face—"because I helped ruin someone else's. That boy didn't want to become one of us. Who can blame him? We chose this. He was forced."

The boy? Oh. She's talking about Kairyn.

Aquila looks up at the strange sky above us, nothing but wavering mist, and in that moment, it leaps out at me.

Even with her horns, I recognize her now. The fae from the crystal, the one I saw sitting on white pillars staring up at the stars.

Maybe I know more about her than I think.

"Sira changed you," I whisper. "The underfae are her creation, like the goblins and harpies."

"Another one of her monsters," Aquila whispers in a singsong voice. Her gaze is still faraway, as if she could pierce the mist. "We followed her down from home. Traded our wings for a new world. Why did we do it? See, I don't remember. Don't remember home." She squeezes her eyes shut, tears creeping out as she gives a heart-wrenching laugh. "Isn't that just the worst thing you've ever heard?"

That memory of her birthplace, trapped within Sira's crystal... Sira doesn't stop at stealing from her citizens. Even those she's in an alliance with are collateral.

I shouldn't feel pity for Aquila. She and Faustrius tied themselves to Sira's cause. But still... I wish I could reach into the crystal and give her back that memory. It belongs to her, as Heidigog's bloomies and my wedding belong to us. If there were more joy, maybe everyone wouldn't be so content to hide away in the dark.

"Why am I bothering to talk to you? If it's not about Caspian, you don't even comprehend it," Aquila mumbles.

Right. I'm supposed to be a thrall, and though Aquila doesn't know me well enough to understand the effects of the spell, she knows I'm bound to Caspian. But I can't stop staring at my left arm, the smooth skin there.

"Look, Aquila," I say lowly, "I understand better than anyone that when we're frightened or hurt or sad, we aren't the people we wish we were. And I've seen how powerful a fresh start is." I reach into my bag and pull out the healing balm. "May I?"

Aquila stares at me intently, then sits cross-legged and shrugs.

I brush the few stray hairs away from her burned skull and cheek, then open the jar. I bring it to my nose, inhaling the strong smell of honeysuckle and echinacea. It's a safe smell, one that reminds me of nights draped in Ezryn's arms. In those moments, it felt like nothing from the past or future could ever hurt us.

Having used the balm on Kel, I know it's not powerful enough to heal Aquila's burn scars. But I held Spring's blessing inside me. I remember the paths of the flesh—how to knit, how to reform, and most importantly...how to renew.

It is Spring's calling after all.

With a gentle touch, I dab it over her hot skin. Magic whispers from my fingertips into the ointment, Ezryn's powerful mixture a conduit. I remember how it felt as the letters carved into my arm faded, giving me my own fresh start.

"A fae of Spring once told me that rebirth is all around us," I tell her as I work. "A seed becomes a flower, which lives its season, then breaks down to feed the soil in which a new seed will grow. An egg becomes a bird, which dies and turns into dirt, which houses the worm that feeds the bird. Nothing is ever stagnant. We change, we die, and we are reborn."

Aquila shivers beneath my touch. Her voice is a raspy breath. "Even now? We can be reborn?"

"Of course. And you don't need anyone's permission to do it." I pull my hand away, magic twinkling from my fingers like pixie dust.

Aquila blinks and hesitantly touches her face. Where once the skin was red and raw, it is now a pale green, smooth and brand-new as a meadow after the rain. She whirls, staring at her reflection in the glassy stream. "You healed me. Why?"

"Someone gave me a fresh start once. And I've seen a lot of wonderful things happen from a second chance." I shrug. "By the way, Sira doesn't, uh, exactly know I can do that."

"Our little secret. Besides, Sira won't notice I look any different. To her, we're all just one big failure." Aquila turns to me, her eyes going so big, she reminds me of an adorable frog. "Can you…can you do more? Change me back to how I once was?"

"I'm sorry. I don't think that's possible."

"Oh." Aquila runs an absent hand over her horn. "That's okay. There's probably nothing good on the surface anyway."

A pang of guilt hits me. How would things have been different if Thrainn, first High Prince of Winter, had accepted the Elderblood instead of casting them aside, then freezing them for centuries? I wish I could tell her how wrong he was. That none of the current rulers would send them away.

But we're on two sides of a war. Soldiers hiding in their opposite trenches, guns pointed at the other.

Though right now…

Right now, she's just a girl, and so am I.

I rummage in my bag and find Dayton's gift to me. Aeneas, the stuffed winged lion. He told me it would come in handy, and it has, providing me with so much comfort during my lonely nights here.

But I'm okay now. And Aquila seems like she needs someone.

"Here. It's not to keep, just a loan. He's been a pretty good friend to me, and, well, you seem like you could use a friend." I pass her the lion.

Aquila takes him. Carefully, she runs a hand over his mane, along his back, before finally tracing the large white wings. "This reminds me of home," she murmurs.

"Were there creatures similar in the Above?" I ask.

"Oh yes, that's one thing I remember," she says. "We'd dart through the sky together, sailing through the clouds and sunshine, and at night, we'd—" Aquila shakes her head. "I thought I was about to remember something, but it popped out of my head." Her hand goes to her horn again. "I suppose this is how Sira felt."

"What do you mean?"

Aquila makes the lion fly through the air, flapping his wings, and says in that idle, singsong way, "Oh, you know. With her sickly, little wings. She couldn't fly, not like the rest of us. Maybe that's why she wanted us all to fall with her."

"Sira had wings?" I breathe.

"We all did. But Sira's never worked. Faustrius told me she ripped them off herself. Plucked them as one would pluck the petals off a flower."

My breath catches. A fae, born among the clouds, unable to fly.

And when she fell to the earth, she made everyone fall with her.

Someone clears their throat, and Aquila and I both look up, startled.

Faustrius stands over us. Despite his enormous size and the shadows cast by his antlers, I hadn't heard him approach. How long has he been here?

"Aquila, we're needed in the tower," he says lowly. Then he stares at me. I want to turn away, but he holds my gaze in a bone-deep and ancient way.

The stories you could tell, I think.

But I don't ask him what it was like to know Sira before she tore apart the Above or what it's like now, to watch her attempt to destroy another world. Instead, I quirk my head to the side, adopting a glassy-eyed look, and chirp, "I must find Caspian."

He says nothing.

If someone wants to survive Sira's realm, they either become a monster or play the role of one. From the way he's looking at me, he knows which one I am.

But I'm not sure which role he's playing yet.

43

Caspian

LAUGHTER SLITHERS THROUGH THE SQUARE, SHARP AND SERPENTINE, curling between the crumbling stones of Nether Reach. The tower looms behind me, a black spire needled into the gray abyss above, ribbed with spires and lattices.

Today is revelry day. A celebration of Mother's conquest.

I lean back on my throne overlooking the courtyard. Crafted of shadows, my thorns all jagged points and flickering edges, yet it fits me far too well. The corporeal darkness coils around my shoulders like a lover's touch, disappearing into a waterfall of inky smoke.

At my feet, Rosalina perches on the first step of the dais, half-turned toward the crowd, half toward me. Her body glows, barely covered in slivers of silver and onyx silk. Her legs are draped to one side. She plays her role perfectly, fingers brushing up and down my thigh, eyes watching only me.

The perfect plaything for a prince.

My gaze lingers too long on the line of her throat, the dip above her hips, the curve of—

I force myself to look away.

It's a performance. All of it. The throne. The revelry. Her.

Me.

Across the square, creatures howl and cheer. Harpies dive through the smoky air, trailing ribbons of what might be cloth… or might be flesh. Goblins overturn wine barrels and guzzle what pours out. Trolls arm-wrestle on rock tables, shattering them with each blow. Even the wicked-eyed fae laugh and drink and twirl with a hazy glee.

And at the center of it all, on a pillar of dark stone, rests the rose.

Encased in its bell jar, it draws the eyes of everyone here.

It's going to be very tricky to draw attention away from that thing.

I sigh and shift my gaze higher. Above me, suspended by shadows, dangles a cage. Within it, the High Prince of Winter.

Keldarion is shirtless. Dirt smudges the hard planes of his chest, white hair limp around his face. A tattered rag clings to his waist. His eyes—gods, those eyes—burn with frost and fury.

He hasn't looked away from me once.

Playing your part oh so well, I purr in his mind.

The ghost of a smile tugs at the corner of his lips. He touches the collar that I returned to his neck. *Keep it in your pants, Cas.*

Funny. Rosie joins in our minds. *You both are so funny. Meanwhile, there's a gargoyle down there who hasn't looked away from my chest in five minutes.*

Only two thin strips of cloth cover her round breasts, and they hang so beautiful and big, her nipples poking through the fabric. I lick my lips. *Want me to impale him on a thorn?*

Rosalina shifts, turning her back to the gargoyle who finally blinks, drool sliding down his chin.

It's alright, Rosalina says. *He won't remember much.*

No, none of the creatures here will. Not with the lotus flower potion I added to the wine, one of my sister's many creations. The crowd will remember enough to help with the plan, sure, but the details of this night will always be misty.

Which is good, because I don't want anyone except for the three of us to recall what's about to happen to Rosalina.

I clench my fist on the armrest. Shadows ripple and hiss. A horn blares. Another barrel shatters. The crowd screams for blood, for music, for madness.

And I smile, cruel and cold and hollow.

Let the monsters believe I'm one of them.

Let Keldarion pretend to hate me. Stars know he has so much practice with it.

Let Rosalina pretend she's mine. Because despite everything I've done, somehow she still is.

Soon, the game will change.

And I'll burn this whole cursed tower down.

A hush ripples through the crowd. From a low balcony carved into the tower's obsidian wall, she appears.

Mother.

Sira steps out in a dark gown, her pale hands resting on the curved railing. Her hair coils around her head in a crown of braided green ribbons, her eyes catching the firelight like gems. Behind her stands Faustrius, her ever-faithful guard, his broadsword gleaming. Below her, the monsters of the Below raise their faces to watch their queen.

Including me.

"My children," she begins, voice like poisoned silk, smooth and unmistakable, "what a sight you are."

A ripple of cheers, snarls, howls. She waits, unmoved.

"Today, we celebrate the return of our influence, of our precious rose, not for its indulgences alone but for what it means. We are no longer the castoffs. The broken. The forgotten. We are the future."

The rose pulses beneath its glass. My jaw tightens.

"The princes of the seasonal realms sit on gilded thrones, fat with power and drunk on privilege. But soon, they shall kneel." Her gaze flicks toward Keldarion's cage, then returns to the crowd. "Soon, we will take back what was denied to us. Not just revenge but dominion."

The cheers swell. A goblin tosses a firecracker into the air; it explodes in green sparks. The crowd roars.

"With this rose," Sira continues, her voice rising above the din, "we shall create others. Children. Brothers. Sisters. An army. Eternal. Ours. Obedient."

Obedient, I think. *To her alone.*

She doesn't want freedom. She wants control. A land of puppets with her fingers on every string.

The crowd doesn't care. Doesn't know. The Prince of Thorns twisted her words so prettily when he invited them here. They scream her name, pounding feet and claws against the stone. It's ecstasy. Frenzy.

She lifts her hand in farewell, already turning from the railing. "Enjoy your festivities," she says, almost as an afterthought. "My son will ensure everything runs…as expected."

Then she's gone, vanishing back into the darkness of the tower, her long train trailing behind her.

Faustrius takes one last look across the balcony down at me. A warning in his glance, or something else. Can he see my eyes no longer shine with green, that there isn't a single flame bursting around me?

No, he's too far away.

Then he follows his queen inside the Tower of Nether Reach.

Of course she's leaving. She always does. This aspect—the drinking, the bodies, the noise—is beneath her. It's base. Crude.

She never understood how well I play this part.

I drain the goblet of wine beside me and rise from the throne. Shadows lick at my boots and curl up my spine in adoration.

Rosalina tilts her head, lashes low over storm-bright eyes. I press my mouth near her ear. "Be ready."

Her lips curve, just a flicker. And then I'm standing before my people, going to do exactly what they expect of me.

Drink. Dance. Fuck the night away.

The heir of the dark on parade. And if this works out, every eye in this damned place will be on my Rose instead of Sira's.

44

Rosalina

I'VE WORN CROWNS OF JEWELS AND GOWNS SPUN FROM STARLIGHT. I've waltzed with princes beneath moon-drenched skies, whispered songs in enchanted gardens, touched magic and realized it was real.

But nothing feels quite like this.

I kneel on the cold steps of a throne made of shadows with hundreds of monsters watching me. My knees ache. My spine burns. My dress, or what little there is of it, clings to my skin. One wrong move and it will fall away.

Good.

Let them watch.

Above me, Caspian shifts on the throne. I don't look up at him, not yet. I play the part: the courtesan, the possession, the beautiful broken thing that dark princes collect like trophies.

His voice curls in my mind, velvet and sharp. *Are you ready, Rose? We need to put on a convincing show. Turn all eyes away from Sira's prize.*

I'm ready.

He pauses. Then: *Whatever I say…I don't mean it.*

My stomach clenches, but I nod. *And you remember if I yell stop,* I *don't mean it.*

If you say it in my mind, he replies, *we'll know.*

Another pause. Deeper now. The space between heartbeats.

When word gets passed to Sira of him using me so publicly, she'll never believe we took the rose. Not to mention the fae will be too preoccupied to keep their eyes on an object.

I exhale. The rose. The plan. The risk.

The monsters around us don't know. They drink and cheer and leer at me like I'm already ruined. Like I'm already his.

And I am, in ways they'll never understand.

Caspian turns from the crowd. Shadows peel off his frame, casting long claws across the courtyard. His voice rings out, loud, cruel, and laced with triumph.

"Behold," he snarls, gesturing, "the heir to the Vale. My whore."

A cheer goes up, vicious and wild.

"She was once meant for light, for honor, for thrones of virtue." He circles me, letting the onlookers drink in the sight of me on my knees, barely clothed, silent. "But now she kneels to me. As all the Vale will."

The crowd howls, hungry.

"I will use her," Caspian says. "And destroy her as her husband watches from above."

Keldarion growls, grasping the bars, shaking them. Convincing performance, though I'm sure a true part of his jealousy is leaking through. It won't be easy for him to watch this, even knowing most of the fae will forget.

"I'll use her as I'll use the realms," Caspian yells. "We'll tear down Spring, burn Winter to ash, drown Summer in shadow, and grind Autumn into dust."

The monsters scream for it: violence, power, sex, blood. And I let my eyes lift to Caspian's, just for a moment.

They're burning with fury. Not at me but at this. At all of it. He hates that he was so close to becoming a part. His voice comes again, low and private, where only I can hear: *I'm with you. Every breath. Every second. We'll do this together.*

The cheers grow louder.

I don't know what I expect him to do next. Kiss me, claim me, drag me up into his lap and ravage me before the entire revel. I don't expect this.

Caspian grips the thin fabric on my shoulder.

And rips.

The sound is brutal.

And then I'm bare.

"Since you belong to me," Caspian purrs, "I'll choose to do whatever I wish with you."

The cool air hits my skin first, sending a shiver racing down my spine. My dress lies in tatters around me. My body, pale and flushed, gleams in the torchlight. Hundreds of eyes lock on to me. Hungry and leering.

I thought I'd feel vulnerable.

Instead, I feel—

Power.

A pulse of heat coils in my belly. A thrill, sharp and unexpected. I should be terrified. But Caspian's eyes are on me now, and they aren't vicious. They're mine.

Caspian steps in close behind me, his breath brushing my ear.

"So beautiful, Rose," he murmurs, so low only I can hear. "You steal their attention. You make them weak."

His tone changes again, louder, mocking and cruel for them.

"This is what their princess looks like now," he sneers, lifting a strand of my hair. "Naked. On her knees. Begging for the heir of the Green Flame."

His hands move next. Not gentle. Possessive. Calloused fingers skate down my ribs, over my hips, along the inside of my thigh. Just enough to make me tremble. Enough to make the crowd believe the lie.

It feels good. Gods, it feels *so* good.

But wrong.

Not because it's him but because it's here. Because of the eyes watching us. Because of the harpies licking their lips, the goblins clawing at each other, the revelers chanting for more.

And still… I arch into his touch, begging for him.

He bends close, his lips brushing my temple. His voice is low and calm. "You're doing perfect."

My eyes lift to the cage above.

To Keldarion.

He's shackled, shirtless and chained, but his gaze is unbroken. I expect fury. Rage. Maybe shame. But what I find instead makes my heart clench.

Hunger.

He wants me. Even like this. *Especially* like this.

Caspian sees me looking, and his jaw tightens.

Then he drops into the throne again, sprawling like a king at rest, one hand draped on the armrest, the other extended toward me.

"Come here," he says aloud, voice laced with wicked amusement. "Sit."

The crowd whistles and hoots.

I rise, every inch of bare skin humming with fire. I step up to the dais and climb onto his lap, my back to his chest. His hands settle on my waist, then roam. My thighs. My breasts. My throat.

The shadows ripple in delight, licking around our bodies like smoke. I let my head fall against his shoulder. He positions me like I'm nothing but a doll.

"I'm yours, Prince of Thorns," I gasp, playing my part as thrall.

"Perfect," he whispers in my ear. His fingers tweak a nipple so hard I arch into him. He slides a hand down my body before tapping my inner thighs.

"Cas, please," I moan.

He laughs wickedly. "See how she begs for me? She craves my touch."

More and more eyes are drawn to us, and with every one, Caspian coils tighter. I might get a thrill from this, but I can tell it's angering him, to have so many eyes on what's his.

Caspian shifts beneath me on the throne. There's the unmistakable press of him growing stiff through the thin fabric of his trousers. And gods help me, I react. Heat flashes through my core, unbidden and dangerous, shame and desire tangling like thorned vines.

His hands are everywhere. Stroking my thighs. Palming my breast. Fingers dancing over me like I'm an instrument he's claimed. Like my only purpose is to be used.

And the worst part is I like it. I really like this.

Even as my cheeks flush, even as the monstrous crowd leers and laughs, even as shadows swirl like eager tongues around my ankles, I burn for him.

And then he slides a hand between my legs.

I tense for a breath, and he feels it.

Shush, Flower, he murmurs in my mind. *Just me. Only me. I've got you.*

His fingers slip through my folds, finding where I'm already wet. I bite the inside of my cheek, hard. A moan claws its way up my throat, and I swallow it.

But he wants the crowd to hear.

He presses deeper, firm and deliberate. "So easy to break, this one. Look how wet she is just from my voice. The heir to the Vale, coming on my fingers like a common whore."

Our audience howls with laughter and lust.

I don't look at them. I can't.

So I gaze up, past the smoke and fire, to the cage above.

Keldarion watches me. His hands are clenched around the bars, white-knuckled. His chest rises and falls too fast. He doesn't turn away.

He gets what Caspian is doing. What I'm allowing.

And he understands that it's not real. That it *is* real. That I'm caught somewhere in between.

Caspian's fingers curl just right, and my hips jerk in his lap. A whimper escapes before I can stop it.

His voice is a weapon. "See how desperate she is to be taken? How eager she is to be ruined in front of you all?"

Then he whispers in my mind. *I'm sorry, Rose. I'm so sorry. I hate them. I hate all of them for looking at you. I'll kill every single one after this.*

He's furious.

I can feel it in his touch, in the rougher press of his palm, in the way he coils beneath me like a storm waiting to break. His jaw grinds, his teeth clench. *You are mine. Not theirs. Mine.*

And yet he keeps touching me. For them. For the lie.

For the plan.

I close my eyes, arch into him, and play my part. We have to for our home, for the good of the Vale.

My body trembles, and I grip his wrist as if it might break. He knows what this means. I'm about to—

His fingers curl inside me.

"Cas, I'm, I'm—"

Then he stops.

I blink up at him, heart pounding.

He grabs me. One rough hand tangles in my hair, the other gripping my waist hard enough to bruise. He pushes us to standing.

Still too many eyes on the rose, he says.

I follow his gaze. While we've drawn stares to be sure, still a huge crowd lingers around the pedestal.

Then he bends me sideways over the shadow throne. It's cold against my skin, my chest pressing against something solid, though it ripples like liquid.

I hear the sound before I feel it. Briars break out from the ground. They coil around my wrists, binding me in place, coiling like vines with minds of their own. They don't pierce my flesh, but they could. One twitch, and I know they'd bite.

The crowd goes feral. Chanting filthy encouragement.

They don't know I can control these briars.

Caspian stands behind me, his body hard and hot and furious. One hand spreads over my back, pressing me down. "This is the Princess of the Enchanted Vale. Bent and begging. Pretty and pathetic. *Mine.*"

The crowd erupts, drunk on violence and spectacle and sex.

But then, through the storm of it, his voice reaches me again—low and warm and real, right into my mind. *You're doing so well, Rose. I hate this. I hate making them see you like this. But I swear, I'm here. I'll never let them hurt you.*

I breathe in sharply. My hips twitch, needy, traitorous.

Use me, Cas, I reply in his mind. *I want you. I always do.*

"I love you," he whispers. Then he enters me, cock sliding all the way to the hilt.

It feels so good, to be filled after all his teases. My body flutters and pulses around him. This isn't the slow, blissful lovemaking I'm used to. He moves fast, only the briars' tight grip holding me in place. I cry out, tears running down my cheeks as he fills me.

I love you, he says in my mind.

And gods help me—

I love it.

I love the way he claims me with fury in his voice and worship in his thoughts. I love the way I can pretend to be used and ruined, when in truth, I've never felt more powerful.

So I play my part.

I cry out like I hate it. Like I'm ashamed. Like I'm helpless.

But inside, I burn. I ache for him. I take it all.

And I let them think the dark prince has broken his little flower.

Sweat drips over my body as he runs his hands along my breasts, fingertips digging into my hips hard enough to bruise. I clench, tensing around him.

"Oh, Cas," I cry out.

"Should we let her come?" he roars, bending over me, teeth nipping at my ear. "Would you enjoy that, pet? To come around your captor's cock like a good little whore?"

Tears of pleasure run down my cheeks as I give a needy sob. "Y-yes."

Caspian straightens and knots a hand in my hair. "Then let's give her what she wants."

The crowd is a blur of color and noise, their gazes searing my skin. Fae with golden irises and forked tongues. Goblins baring sharp teeth. Harpies with wine-stained lips and laughter like screams. They're watching, devouring me with their gazes, chanting Caspian's name, begging for more.

Some of them have begun engaging in vile acts of their own. It reminds me of the first Below party I ever attended. I never thought I'd be the one on the throne getting publicly fucked.

Or just how much I'd like it.

How much power I'd feel in surrendering to be his plaything, the thrill of being on display. Let the crowd believe I'm a pawn. A body to be taken. A prize to be defiled.

Caspian moves behind me, his hands gripping my hips with bruising force. The briars tighten, holding me fast, and I can feel him, gods, I can feel him, every thrust laced with rage, every movement a lie to them and a promise to me.

His voice rings out above the madness, cruel and sharp. "She likes it. She pretends she doesn't, but she lives for this. Being used. Being mine."

Gasps, laughter, more wine spilled.

You look perfect when you're bent over, my Rose, Keldarion's voice says in my head. *You're going to let him spill inside you and come to me filthy.*

Fuck, Kel, Caspian answers. *Your voice is going to make me finish early.*

I can't help but let out a laugh at the lust and pleasure racing through our bond. It doesn't matter that there are hundreds of people watching us. It's just the three of us.

"Cas, I can't hold on," I moan.

Tears prick my eyes. From the ache. From the euphoria. From the knowledge that we're being watched by the very monsters we plan to destroy.

Caspian's grip tightens. The pace builds. The heat coils. My body quivers against the throne.

"Come for me, Rose," he commands.

And I do.

My climax crashes through me like a storm of stars, hot and endless and utterly consuming. His hot pleasure courses through me. I cry out, shaking, lost in him. In us. In this terrible, beautiful lie.

The Below roars like they've won.

But they haven't.

They have no idea what's coming.

Caspian pulls out of me and releases the briars, dragging me to my feet. *Stars, I wish I could kiss you right now instead of—*

Roughly, he turns me to the crowd. "Look at her, dripping with me. Off to her husband she'll go so he knows who owns her. To be fucked again and again and again until he realizes the whore she is."

Stars, Rosie, I love you so much, he says in my mind as the briars of his and Kel's bargain rise through the ground and wrap around me.

As they drag me under, I see Caspian tilt his head to the dangling cage and smirk. "She's all yours, lover."

45

Keldarion

Briars crack through a corner of the cage, and Rosalina appears before me, naked, Caspian's seed running down her thighs. I grip one of the bars of the cage and hold myself steady. I don't think desire has ever sung louder in my blood than it does now.

Not only because of how delicious she looks but because of the pure need pulsing through our bond. She *likes* me seeing her like this, *likes* being sent to me, used and spent.

Rosalina blinks up at me. "Kel, I belong to you."

The bargain. I have to release her.

She giggles, then says lowly, "How strange. I know I belong to you, but it doesn't feel like it did before. I think breaking free of Caspian's bargain has lessened the effect."

Relief floods through me. "That'll make it much more convenient in the future."

"What, are you two planning to do this a lot?"

I only smile, and Caspian's voice drifts up from below. He lounges on his throne, black cape draping over him. "Keldarion," he croons, "do you like the state in which I've sent your mate? Do you smell her on me?"

I'm not the performer Cas and Rosie are, but I ram against the bars, closing my knuckles around them. "I'll kill you for what you did to her."

"No," Caspian says simply. "I'll kill you both if you don't do what I say. And because I doubt you grasp exactly what I mean, the first thing you're going to do is lick her pussy clean so you finally understand who she belongs to."

"You bastard!" I roar.

His voice drifts into my mind. *I knew you'd like that, pet.*

Rosalina gives me a playful look before running to the back of the cage. It sways with her movement. "No! I only want you, Prince of Thorns."

"The beast of Winter will do what I say," Caspian calls. "By whatever means necessary."

Rosalina gives me a desperate, scared look. Then a wink. *Catch me if you can, Kel,* she says in my mind.

A low growl sounds in my throat, and I charge after her. She's quick, dancing out of my reach.

"Caspian!" she shrieks as I grip her soft waist and pull her to the ground, cage lurching. Down below, most of the guests are watching us. Very few still seem interested in the rose. *It's working.* Of course it's working. Caspian knows these people well.

Rosie puts up a mock struggle, but I grab her legs and shove them apart, taking in a heady breath as I stare at her pussy. Perfect and pink, dripping with the evidence of Caspian's pleasure. Unable to control myself, I latch my lips over her inner thigh and bite.

She moans and throws her head back, fingers grasping for purchase. I work my way up, doing exactly what Caspian ordered. She spreads for me, not able to keep up her act of resistance. Her thighs tremble as I lower to her. The first taste of her, sweet and silken, is intoxicating, but beneath it lingers a trace of him. Caspian. It should make me rage. But it only makes me hungrier. I run my tongue along her center, soaking wet and dripping. I lap it all eagerly into my mouth.

So fucking delicious. I delve deeper, fucking her with my tongue, until she's crying out.

"Yes, my pet," Caspian calls from below. "Use that scum of a prince for your pleasure. The only reason for his pitiful existence is to serve you."

Rosalina moans, straining to reach down. With one hand, she grabs a fistful of my hair, pulling me harder against her center.

I'm in fucking rapture. I open my mouth wide, taking as much of her as I can, sucking, licking, wanting each piece of her. She writhes beneath my tongue, moaning into the dark, her fingers clutching the iron cage floor like it's the only thing anchoring her to this realm. And I taste her. Gods, I taste them. Caspian lingers on her skin, a haunting echo. It sends a bolt of heat straight through me. I love it. The wildness of it. The way our magic coils together in her, tangled and unrepentant. She's slick and sweet and soaked. I drag her to the edge, holding her open, savoring every shudder as she breaks apart, her words a delirium.

I pull back, her taste still warm on my lips. She is flushed, spent. Radiant.

I look down. The crowd is still watching. Dozens of them. Hundreds. Their eyes glitter in the torchlight like predators at the edge of flame. They watched all of it. Every gasp, every thrust, every cry of his name from her throat. They watched me take her apart with my mouth, the intent for her to belong to no one but me.

I growl and shift my gaze to the beautiful prince on the throne.

"Very good," he claps. "Now fuck her like the whore she is and send her back to me."

A predator's smile grows on my face as I stare at my wife, my lips still coated in her.

She's dazed, mouth parted, cheeks flushed with the kind of heat that could burn through Winter. Her legs remain open in an offering—or a dare.

The crowd holds its breath. Caspian watches with a lazy, wicked smirk, his knuckles propping up his chin. This is his stage. But I am no one's puppet.

"I said—" Caspian begins.

"I heard you," I growl.

Then I lift her.

My hands slide under her thighs, pulling her against me in one swift, savage motion. She gasps, eyes flying wide as I press her back to the cold iron bars, her spine arching against them. Magic crackles in the air. Mine, hers, his. A trinity of ruin and desire.

"You're mine," I murmur, not loud enough for the crowd but enough for her. "My mate, my wife, my Rose."

I feel her reply with every heartbeat, every breathless moan against my neck, every tremble of her limbs. We gaze at each other, both desperate. Below, the crowd jeers. Someone throws an empty goblet at the cage.

"Are you going to fuck her or stare at her, *beast*?" Caspian yells.

"Well, I suppose I'll get on with it." I smile at Rose and sink into her.

Her hands claw my arms, head thrown back against the bars, sweat-damp curls falling through them. And she *screams*, low and long, for every agonizing second it takes to slowly work my length into her. Her body strains to accommodate my size.

"You took him, you can take me," I growl, anger and possessiveness coursing through my words. A part of my act.

But I'm not expecting the thrill of desire that flows through our bond at those words. I drop my head to her neck and bite down. *You like it hard and rough, Rose?*

She does, Caspian purrs. *Don't go easy on her, Kel.*

Rosalina meets my gaze, taking my face in her hands. "He played with me, Kel," she says. "You can destroy me."

Something inside me snaps. My jaw clenches, breath ragged as I drag her tighter against me, the hard line of my body flush with hers. My eyes flick to the crowd, then back to her—only her. I brace a hand behind her head, the other running up her thigh with a reverent desperation. She wants this. She wants *me* like this. I want to ruin her beautifully.

"Let them watch. Let them see how you fall apart for me," I growl and bite her bottom lip between my teeth. "By the end of this, you won't remember how to stand, let alone *his* name."

My grip tightens on her hips, fingers bruising. My cock throbs with the need to claim, to prove. I slam her back against the bars, metal rattling with the force, and my mouth crashes into hers like a storm. I don't think. I just take. Because she asked. And because I can't fucking help it.

I move hard inside her. The world collapses into this: her legs wrapped around me, her fingers digging into my shoulders, her lips on my throat. The cage swings on its shadow tether, but I keep us steady. Below, the crowd watches like wolves starved for blood. But I'm not performing for them. Not anymore.

Because even with her soaked in another man's power, she shines like moonlight on snow, radiant and bright and mine.

I press my forehead to hers, our breaths tangling. Her eyes are soft, and they search my own.

"I belong to you, Rose," I whisper against her skin.

"No," she rasps. "We belong to each other."

And as I move—slowly now, reverently despite the sharp edges of need—the cage, the crowd, the prince on his throne all blur into nothing. Let the world bear witness if it must.

But what they see is not a claiming.

It is a covenant.

Her back arches against the iron bars, spine bending like a drawn bow, legs locked around my waist as I drive into her again and again, each thrust a vow, a punishment, a plea, an act. Her nails drag down my shoulders, a cry catching in her throat, and I don't know where she ends and I begin anymore.

The cage rattles with every movement.

I shouldn't be lost in her like this. Not with everyone watching.

But gods help me, I am.

Below us, Caspian gazes from his throne, wineglass lazily swirling in his hand, lips curved in a smile. He watches as if he's orchestrated the whole thing, and in a way, he has. We're dancing right to the rhythm of his strings.

But what a fucking wonderful dance it is.

"Kel," Rosalina breathes.

"You're not supposed to enjoy this, remember?" I whisper.

"I–I…" Her face scrunches as she tries to suppress a moan of pleasure. "But you feel so good."

I slam into her again, groaning as the tension builds in me, molten and brutal. Her head falls back with a gasp, her body trembling around me, pulsing with the heat of release just on the edge.

I grip the bars, my mouth finding hers in a kiss that's all teeth.

"That's it, pet," Caspian calls. "Milk the Winter Prince of his cum and fly back to me."

"Yes, Prince of Thorns," Rosalina answers.

"You're close," I whisper between her breasts. I kiss my way up to her lips. "Come with me."

And she does.

Her cry splits the dark, spine arching hard as she shatters around me, her magic surging like a storm. And I follow, thrusting once, twice more, and the world breaks open.

My release hits, molten and shaking, stars bursting behind my eyes. I bury my face in her neck, riding it out, trying not to fall apart entirely.

But I do.

We fall together.

Her breathing syncs with mine. Her magic twines with mine. The cage creaks beneath us, stilling.

And from below, Caspian smiles, soft and satisfied. “Well done, my wicked things.”

46

Rosalina

THEY USE ME UNTIL I'M SPENT, NOTHING BUT A WITHERING, trembling mess. Cas ties me up in thorns and fucks me fast and hard. I desperately clutch the bars of the cage as Keldarion stretches me within an inch of my life. Then I'm sent back to Cas, wobbly legged, only to have him throw me on the ground and shove his cock down my throat. Off to Kel after that, who tosses me around like a rag doll.

I'm dripping with the evidence of their love. It's over my lips, my pussy, my ass. I descend into a haze of blissful delirium. And the only thing that would be better is if my other mates were here to see me, to love me too. Oh, what they would think.

I love every second of it.

And thankfully, so does the audience. Their eyes are on us. No one's paying attention to the rose.

I'm riding Caspian's cock on the throne, fully on display for the court as he runs his fingers along my body.

This time, he says, *I'm not going to come, and you're going to briar yourself away.*

It's really time? I reply, almost sadly.

He kisses my neck. *We'll play later when we're all safe.*

I sigh as he reaches forward and circles my swollen clit.

"One more time, Princess. I want to feel you come around my cock one more time," he says, then spears me deep.

It's enough. I cry out, blissful waves of pleasure coursing through my spent body. "C-Cas."

"That's it, you dirty girl," he cries out to the crowd, tossing his head back as if in ecstasy. Then he throws his cloak around me. "Now, the Winter Prince will use you like the animal you are."

But it's not the briars of Caspian's and Kel's bargain that break through to grab me. No, I take control of his purple ones, wrapping them about myself and dragging me far away from here.

It's time for the plan to begin.

47

Farron

"In Summer, we fight to death in the arena, and we still have more dignified entertainment than the Below," Dayton growls under his breath.

My stomach twists as I force myself deeper along the narrow boardwalk of cages. Cryptgarden's menagerie is less a zoo than a prison. A decrepit ironwork sign looms overhead, the last E in MENAGERIE hanging by a metal thread. Broken, charred cobblestones line the way, cages crowding in on either side. Unlit lampposts jut like iron bars along the route. The whole cursed place presses inward, claustrophobic and grim. The cages lean against stony walls, and the path ends abruptly at a jagged cliffside. Though we're in the open—or as open as it gets in the Below—the only hint of freedom comes from the swirling, misty excuse for a sky.

We've walked the entire length of the menagerie, that sickening feeling in my gut growing stronger with each cage. There is all manner of depressed-looking creatures, from winged horses to dire foxes, each one seeming in worse condition than the last. The bowls of water have green film, and some contain bones long past the point of gnawing. Worst of all, when one of the creatures meets my eye, there's decades of sadness in their gaze.

"Sira will pay for this," Dayton snarls.

The twins, lagging behind us, give grunts of approval.

"One of many things," I agree. "But first things first. No Kel. They must have moved him."

I run my hands through my hair, mind spinning for our next move. I wish Ez were here, always so decisive, never overthinking as I do. But we separated from him and George in the tunnel right outside Cryptgarden.

Once we reached the city, it became clear we had at least one advantage: Cryptgarden is empty. From our vantage in the tunnel, we could spot Sira's tower, Nether Reach, in the far south. It appeared as if a great celebration was being held, and everyone's gone to attend.

We couldn't pass up such an opportunity. Ezryn and George headed to Caspian's palace to search for Rosalina and the rose while Dayton, the twins, and I made for the menagerie to find Kel.

"Don't get into trouble," I said to Ez as we separated.

"You're telling me that?" he responded, and I could practically see his brow arching from behind the underfae helm he wore.

We made it to the menagerie without incident. There'd been the odd goblin guard, but whatever's happening at Nether Reach has pulled the entire city's attention.

Approaching the very edge of the zoo, we stand on the cliffside and peer down. There are a few jagged outcrops of rock, but after that, nothing. What's deeper than the Below?

I turn to my party, their faces solemn. With no one around, we've ditched our underfae getups. Now Dayton and my brothers wear matching weary expressions.

Without Ez, I'll have to decide where to go next. "Kel's not here. If we hurry, we can meet up with Ezryn and George and help search the palace." I walk away from the edge of the cliff and start making my way down the path, trying to block out the moans of the creatures, the stink of feces and blood.

Dayton steps in stride with me. "Or we could investigate the celebration at Nether Reach. Something's happening there, and I bet Caspian's involved."

Dominic shadows my other side but stays silent, head downcast.

"Let's get out of here—" I begin but notice someone's missing.

Turning around, I see Billy standing rigid in the middle of the pathway. "Come on, Billy."

"We can't," he says. His hands have formed tight fists.

"What are you talking about? Let's go," I urge.

He crosses his arms and shakes his head back and forth. "We came to the Below to save people, didn't we? Well, then that's what we have to do. Nobody gets left behind."

Understanding dawns, and I look over at the cages. A wave of defeat hits me square in the chest. "I hate this as much as you do, but we don't have time."

Dom skitters from my side, running over to stand with his brother. "Rosie would make time. No one gets left behind with her. Not the people of Hadria, not the soldiers on Voidseal Bridge." He points a finger to a cage where a gryphon is curled in the corner, tattered wings wrapped around its body. "No one gets left behind."

I take in a deep breath, the scent of neglect heavy on the air. Rosalina's love hasn't only touched me. It's changed them, my brothers. Of course it has. Stories of the Golden Rose have spread across the realms.

And isn't this what she'd want? These creatures have been left to rot and be tormented for how many years. What would Rosalina tell me?

Compassion is stronger than hate. And when we lead with love, we become all the more emboldened by it.

I turn to Dayton and raise a brow.

He shrugs. "Your brothers. Your call."

I flick my gaze to the fierce faces of the twins. Little brothers. Boys. These words seem diminutive for the men they're becoming. "Alright," I grumble. "But if you free anything with teeth…run."

~

A chorus of roars, hoots, and whinnying fills the air. I'm surprised all of Cryptgarden hasn't come down on us by the racket we've made. Whatever's happening in Nether Reach has stolen their attention.

I squat back on my heels, panting. My hands are still hot from melting so many locks, and fur and feathers stick to my clothes. I wonder if this is how Aurelia felt when she first created the Vale with all its inhabitants.

We are surrounded by creatures. Even the ones that make my

hair stand on end, like the giant blue spider with its eight spying eyes, seem docile. Maybe they're all weak and underfed. But a part of me thinks they understand we're trying to help. A giant queen's winter fox, whose soiled fur I imagine was once a stark white, rubs up against Billy, nearly knocking him off his feet, while Dom sits on the ground, picking thorns out of a gryphon's paw.

"Hey! Over here!" Dayton calls. "There's one more."

I follow his voice behind a couple unlit lampposts and a tree crafted of obsidian. A small glass tank looms in the dark, so dirty the water appears black. But I catch glimmers of light within.

Dayton wraps on the glass. "Hello? Come to the surface if you can."

Slowly, a pale face, two pink eyes, and stringy hair appear. With her now motionless, I can make out a tail through the gloom. A siren.

"Are you really here to help?" she says, her voice low and raspy. Her gaze flicks over the pathway, filled with meandering creatures.

"We are," Dayton calls. "What's your name?"

"Megaera." She pulls herself up to the lip of the tank, then peers down, her eyes like glass orbs. "I know you. Son of Ovidius. Your father used to sail our waters."

"And I will return you to such waters as soon as possible," Dayton responds.

My eyes catch on her arm, hanging over the side. A steel band emblazoned with waves and stars winds around her forearm. A bargain circle.

"Are you trapped here?" I ask.

Her tail snaps with nervous agitation. "I made a bargain with a piece of scum that I'd sing on command until my feet touch land." A breathy laugh escapes her. "They haven't let me out of the water in years."

I push the sleeves of my tunic up to the forearms. "Let's see what we can do about that."

Pressing my hands to the glass, I move my palm in a circle. Orange light beams from between my fingers. Heat radiates through my body: the warmth of a bonfire, the dappled glow of sunlight through leaves. The glass begins to melt. With a crack, the heated circle fractures, shatters, and water surges out, pouring over our boots and the cobblestones. Megaera yelps, swept into the current, gushing through the hole and spilling onto the pavement in a heap of pink fins.

Dom, never able to resist a lady in need, rushes over with an old blanket and lays it over her. I catch a glimpse of her tail shimmering into pale legs, the blanket twisting around her as she lifts her arm. The steel band evaporates away like water droplets on a pan.

She stares at her skin as if gazing upon the sun. "My bargain… It's broken. I know a thousand songs, and none will ever capture this moment." She peers from Dayton to me, then to Dom and Billy, who has run over to join him. "Thank you. How can I repay this?"

"Maybe you could tell us, have you seen a man?" Billy asks. "White hair? Kind of looks like a giant mixed with an abominable snowman?"

"He was kept in the cage on the edge of the cliffside. But they moved him for the revelry day party at Nether Reach." Megaera winces, turning her gaze to the south. "Sira's throwing a celebration at her tower. And if I'm not the entertainment, then someone else must be. Go there to search for your friend."

Dayton helps her to her feet. "That's what I was afraid of. But we've got to figure out a way to get you all out of here."

She shakes her head. "You've done more than enough. There's a tunnel that leads to an underground river at the very back of the Gem. I remember it from many years gone by. It's a long road, but we can follow the riverbank. Eventually it flows into one of the lochs outside Coppershire. With the city emptied, I can make it there."

"What about them?" I ask, looking to the herd of creatures.

"I will lead them." She holds her hand out to the spider, which closes its eyes and presses a mandible against her, chittering. "We've grown accustomed to one another after all these years."

"Go then, quickly," Dayton says, face falling as he too looks to the south. "We don't know how long Kel will survive as entertainment."

Megaera grabs my hand. "I'll find a way to repay you one day."

"How about this?" I manage a smile and look over all the creatures, holding as many of their gazes as I can. "Should the Golden Rose ever call for aid, you answer. Deal?"

The siren gives me an odd look but smiles. "It is a vow."

Dayton, Dom, Billy, and I stand solemnly as we watch the strange flock of creatures follow Megaera's lead out into the city.

When the last of them have ambled out of sight, I turn to Billy and nudge his shoulder. "Look at you, hero."

Dayton ruffles his hair. "Practically Aeneas!"

"You too," I say, grabbing Dom around the shoulders. The boys' faces flush in the exact same pattern, starting from the apples of their cheeks and spreading over their noses.

A sense of pride fills me. My brothers, so strong in their convictions, brave and gentle.

That's the kind of leader my mother was.

The kind I'm striving to be. Not ruled by fear but by this all-encompassing love.

I put my other arm around Billy and pull them both tight to me. "Thank you," I whisper.

"For what?" Billy asks, words muffled in my shirt.

"For always teaching me."

The boys give awkward laughs and push away, but I don't want to let them go. Not yet—

"Fare?" Dayton's voice.

I look up from the red thatches of my brothers' hair.

Dayton's wandered a few steps down the path, his back to me. "Are you doing this?" he asks.

"What—"

Then I see it. And as a cool shiver runs up my spine, I know it's not me at all. For one by one, the lampposts of the menagerie flicker to life, burning with green flame.

"Draw your weapons," I say. "We have to get out of here."

But it's too late. We're pinned by the stone walls and cliffside as one by one, more lights flash green at the entrance of the menagerie. The lights shuffle into focus, and I see they belong to soldiers.

No.

They belong to the corpses of soldiers, wearing Autumn armor.

My soldiers.

48

Dayton

THE TRIDENT MATERIALIZES IN MY HAND IN A GLEAM OF TURQUOISE, the only other color down here besides the green flames. Just our luck. They may have emptied the city of goblins, but I guess the dead don't enjoy a party.

This army of undead is as horrific as the one we fought outside Coppershire, if not more so. They're not frozen like Perth Quellos's wraiths. These look like true corpses, their skin sallow and bloodless, limbs hanging at awkward angles. Their golden Autumn armor is dull and covered in blood. They shuffle forward, green flames flickering in their eyes and in their chests.

I assess our surroundings as I would the arena. What do I have to work with…and what's going to be working against me? The menagerie is a narrow causeway with jagged stone on either side. Behind us…

A steep drop into stars know what.

That means there's one way out of this, and that's *through.*

I twirl the trident in my hands. Fine by me.

Beside me, Dom draws his hand axe and Billy his falchion, their faces grim. "Dom, you and I will cut through the left flank," I say. "Billy and Farron, push the right."

"Yes, sir," Dom and Billy say in unison. But Farron says nothing. I turn to him for confirmation.

Farron has drawn no weapon nor taken a stance beside us. His eyes are wide and unblinking as he takes in the approaching army.

"Come on, Fare, wake up," I growl. "We've got to cut through this army—"

"My army," he whispers. "My soldiers. My fault."

There's no time to consider his words as the first of the undead approaches us. I charge into it, driving the trident through its rib cage with a yell. Then with a spin, I shuck the corpse off, knocking it into three more approaching soldiers.

At my action, Dom and Billy spring forward, diving into the army, their weapons flashing with deadly purpose. We move as a unit, ducking their attacks, breaking their defenses, and slicing through their ranks. My arms strain with each rapid swing and strike of my trident. I need to go faster. There are so many of them. Each time I lay one out, another takes its place.

Then I catch sight of why. Just like Perth Quellos's wraiths, these damned things don't die. I watch with sickening horror as Dom relieves one corpse of its head. The body slams to the ground…then clambers around until it grabs its skull, tendrils of flesh reattaching like two squids' tentacles reaching for one another.

Breath surges from my throat. The smell of rot and congealed blood clogs my nose. If we're not careful, we'll get surrounded. "Pull back!" I yell to the boys.

Farron's still standing by the edge of the cliff, staring at the army blankly.

I use my trident to block a corpse's spear blow. He abandons the spear and attempts to claw me, gnashing his teeth right in my face. One of his eyes has been ripped out, and there's only a bloody, messy hole. I shove him away and yell "Get behind me!" to Dom and Billy. Then I look at Farron. "Fare, you've got to do something. They don't die!"

"They're not dead," he mumbles. "Not really."

"You need to do the spell!" I roar. "The one you performed at Coppershire that made the wraiths pass on!"

Farron's expression breaks. "No. No, that would mean their deaths are permanent. I can still save them. I can bring them back. They're my people. I have to bring them back..."

"Cover me," I grunt to Dom and duck behind him. I grab Farron by the tunic and shake him hard. His feet stumble, and I realize how close we've been pushed to the cliffside. Pulling Fare away from the edge, I stare into his golden eyes. "Farron, listen to me. You can't control this. You're not meant to save them."

"Don't say that," he growls, pushing away from me.

"They have to die," I yell.

"No!" Farron screams, but he leaps into the fight, a torrent of red flames erupting from his hands. The corpses shudder, their skin charring, hair going up in embers. But they keep coming, walking through the fire as if it were cool rain.

I take a heaving breath, staring at the back of Farron's head. He doesn't understand.

They're not his soldiers anymore. They didn't choose this. They don't want to be *this*.

But I can't make him understand. So I rush to his side, protecting his flank as he changes to a steaming wind, trying to push a path through the chaos of bodies.

"Dom! Billy!" I scream. I see a thatch of red hair to Farron's right and yank on the shirt, pulling the twin tight to me, out of grasp of a corpse. It's Dom, who immediately gets his hand axe up, buying us some time with three quick swipes at the crowd.

"Where's Billy?" he gasps. "He was next to me."

"Billy? Billy!" Farron screams.

I spin in a circle, blocking with my trident, and peer through the horde. In my peripheral, I spot another flash of red. Billy, walking backward, falchion gleaming as he defends against a charging corpse.

"Billy, stop!" I scream.

But it's too late.

Billy blocks a sword strike, then takes a step back. There's no ground beneath him.

His other foot slips, and he tumbles over the cliff's edge.

49

Farron

There is noise all around. Metal clashing against metal. The moan of my soldiers, fallen yet forced to walk. Dayton crying out my brother's name.

But I hear only one sound.

Snap.

"Billy!" My voice is lost in the hiss of flames as orange fire envelopes my body. I fling myself over the cliff.

The propulsion of my blaze keeps me from free-falling as I search the dark and mist. There, sixty feet down. An outcrop of rock.

My brother.

Thatch of red hair. Freckled face. He's lying on his back, limbs splayed, hands up and open. A maple leaf with the edges curled, fallen too soon from its branch.

I land beside him, flames extinguishing, and collapse to my knees. "Billy!"

His eyes are wide and glassy, and they dart around before they find my own. He doesn't turn his head to look at me. A trickle of blood dribbles from his mouth.

"You…found me."

"Of course I did," I whisper, stroking his hair. "Of course."

"I can't…feel my…hands."

His voice. So wet and raspy. So familiar. I know the cadence of this voice because I hear it in every nightmare. My mother's voice, when her lungs were thick with blood.

No. No no no.

I won't let this happen again. I *promised* this would never happen again. I made sure of it.

"You're okay," I tell him, but my words snap in half. "I'm going to fix this. It's going to be okay."

The power is close by, as if it were lingering just around the corners of my heart, watching, waiting. The gift of the Green Flame.

I gaze upward through the mist. Green lights dance along the edge of the cliffside. In their glow, I can barely make out Dayton and Dom, desperately trying not to be overrun. They need help. But I have to do this first.

Knit him back together, Malekai Furiondemius whispers in my mind. *You can do it. Unbreak his spine. Pull the ribs from his lungs. Make him one of us.*

I can do it. I won't mess this up like I did with the soldiers. Billy will be just how he was, my brother, forever at my side.

The strange magic rises in me, blood humming. A cool heat

burns my eyes, flooding my vision with a green haze as I'm flush with the Baron's power.

Billy's golden gaze burrows into mine, pupils shaking. "Where's… my brother?"

"He's up top, with Dayton. Dayton will keep him safe."

"No." Though weak, his voice is fierce. "Where's my…brother? I want…my brother."

What—

I release my hold on the Green Flame's power, letting it drain out of me. My vision clears. "I'm here, Billy. I'm right here."

"Don't go. Stay…with me. 'Til the end."

I curl over him, tears falling from my face onto his. "No, no, no, Billy. You're not going anywhere. I'm going to keep you with me, okay? Okay? I'm going to fix your body. Fix you right up."

A smile twitches over his mouth. "I don't think…I need a body…anymore, Fare. Not where I'm going."

"*No.*" The baron's magic rises in me again. "I won't let you go. You're my brother. Mine. I have to keep you with me."

That's right, Farron, Autumn blood. Remake the world as you desire. It is yours to control.

Rage mingles with my fear and my grief. What did I do to keep losing them? Is this my punishment? Was it never the beast but rather a curse to watch those I love die and die and die again? I won't let it happen. I gave the Baron a part of me, and now Caspian can yank on it at whim. It has to be worth *something.*

"I won't let you die," I gasp, putting my hands on my brother's chest.

Billy's eyes are losing their glassiness, but somehow, he still finds a way to hold my gaze. "Do you feel it? The wind found…me, even down here."

"The wind?" There's no wind. Only the dark, miserable mist.

Billy closes his eyes. His voice quickens, breaths coming in sharp gasps. "Smells like the orchards. There're leaves. Do you see them? Yellow and red and orange. How'd…they…make it down here?" His eyes burst open, pupils huge. "It hurts, Farron."

"I'll make it stop." I dig my fingers into his chest, feeling the flow of the Green Flame pass through my chest, over my arms—

"No."

"No?"

Billy's staring straight up now, even though there's nothing there. "I…want…Mother…to recognize me…when I get…wherever I'm going."

"No," I say, because there is nothing else. "No, no, no."

"I'm gonna keep protecting you, okay?"

I want to scream. To beg. To plead. But I stoop over my brother until we're nose-to-nose, and I know, more than ever before, I must be brave.

Because he's going somewhere I can't follow. And he's said he'll watch over me there. So right now, in this last moment, I need to protect him.

Once again, I release the power of the Green Flame, willing it to become embers in the hearth that holds my magic. The baron's screaming at me, telling me this is my chance, I must save him.

And I will. In the way he's asked me to.

I close my eyes and listen. Listen for the wind my brother heard. It whispers out of his lungs, dancing around his body in celebration.

The last wind. We are the final breath of life as it passes into the beyond.

But it's not an ugly thing. In fact, it's beautiful. The changing colors of the leaves, their journey from tree to forest floor, the transitions to long nights filled with stars.

We are the grand adventure between life and death.

And as High Prince of Autumn, my job is to shepherd the journey.

There are other winds nearby. I feel them above me, snagged on bones too tired to carry on, caught in the half-life I trapped them in. They are thralls in a way. Thralls to life, which they no longer belong in.

Thralls to the Baron.

As I am.

"I'm going to protect you," I whisper over the constellations of freckles on Billy's face.

It's not a spell read from a scroll, as I did in Autumn.

It's a breath. My wind mixes with his wind. *I will see you to the arms of our mother. Wait for me. One day, I will join you. And in the meantime, go on grand adventures, and I will do the same. When I next see you, we will have stories upon stories to last us until the end of time.*

I keep breathing, one breath at a time. My wind flows with Billagin's and up through the dark cavern to meet those of my soldiers. *I will show you the way.*

I gave you a gift, a voice snarls in my mind.

This is no gift, I say back. *And I will not let it poison me anymore. For when it is my turn to join my family wherever the Autumn wind blows, I will have them look upon me and know my heart.*

I expect him to fight. To crawl into the cracks of fear that lace through my body.

But I have my brother's wind with me. For his last adventure in the Enchanted Vale, we blow together, filling my chest with all the strength and love of Autumn. And I feel something dark and evil within me extinguish.

Goodbye, little brother.

Up above, lights begin to wink out. One by one, the soldiers I cursed with the Green Flame blow away like embers on a wind.

The air becomes very still.

Now, knowing he is free of pain, I grab Billy's body and clutch him tight. My heart is shards, as shattered and jagged as bones dashed upon rock.

But it is mine, fully and completely.

"You did that," I whisper to my little brother, rocking him against my chest as if he were but a baby. "You gave my heart back to me."

I can't endure the thought of him down here in the dark. Orange flames envelop us as I propel up the cliffside.

Dayton and Dominic stand back-to-back, surrounded by the fallen bodies of our comrades. Free now to go wherever their families await them.

Dayton's breathing heavily. He rubs his chest and shakes his head, skin pale. "F-Fare..."

I lower Billy to the ground, and Dom lets out a horrid wail. In this moment, his soul, his heart, has forever been cleaved in two.

I collapse, burying my face in my dead brother's chest, and howl my grief into the abyss.

50

Rosalina

My briars part around me as I emerge at the back of Nether Reach tower, hidden in a cluster of rocks by the stream. Searching through the moss, I find the leather satchel I'd hidden earlier. From it, I pull rags and clothes, dark and simple, that won't catch the light. Quickly, I dunk a rag into the stream and scrub off all traces of the evening. The cool water bites my skin, but I don't care. I have to be fast. On the other side of the tower, the revelry churns with jeers and laughter.

A breeze brushes the back of my neck as I skulk to the side of the tower and look out. Caspian slumps in his chair like a predator who's grown bored with the game. His dark eyes lift toward the cage hanging above the celebration, where a cloaked figure clings to the bars. Keldarion, on the other side, observes the figure.

Me. Or what looks like me.

"You two can rot up there," Caspian calls, voice curling with disdain. "I've had enough whore for the evening."

Perfect.

They're all looking at the cage now, every pair of eyes locked on the illusion. Heidi, veiled by Caspian's shadows in my shape and wrapped in a black cloak, plays her starring role perfectly. None of them sees the real me move, the briars stirring at my feet as I slip from my hiding spot straight into the crowd.

I am shadow. I am thorn.

My heart drums against my ribs as I pass through them, close enough to smell their wine, their perfume. One step. Another.

The rose sits in the center of the courtyard, forgotten among all the revelry. No second thoughts. I have to be quick and quiet.

My fingers close around the bell jar. A wave of repulsion runs through me. Even through the glass, I feel its magic: cold, slippery. Like oil and ice. Wrong.

Tucking the jar into my satchel, I shove the unease down and dart through the crowd. Briars surge at my command, dragging me under the earth. No stopping.

I must get to Castletree. Caspian will follow with Kel and Heidi, and we'll all be—

Something hits me.

A tidal wave of grief so loud, so raw, it knocks the breath from my lungs.

Farron.

His pain is everywhere, thick in my throat, hot in my eyes. It's him—it's him. My mate. I feel it like a scream in my bones.

I don't think. I follow that pull.

He's in the Below. Close.

Why is he here?

I know I should get to safety. Protect the rose.

But my mate needs me.

I go to him.

51

Ezryn

GRIEF RIOTS THROUGH MY MATE BOND, A COLOSSAL TORRENT OF IT, enough to steal the breath from my lungs and bring tears to my eyes.

But it's an echo, not belonging to Rosalina herself but to one of her mates.

A mate of my mate is in terrible pain.

We haven't found Kel, Rosalina, or Caspian. Cas's palace was empty, his bedroom devoid of any clues, no sign of the rose. But I remember the direction Dayton, Farron, and the twins were headed when we left them.

George and I tear out of the palace grounds and into the main artery of Cryptgarden. The city, thick with strange mist that hangs over the black cobblestone, glows in jewel tones from the gems embedded in the buildings. The place seems to have deteriorated from when I last walked these streets. There are piles of rubble, and gleaming graffiti shines in back alleys.

There's no sign of goblins, underfae, or any of Sira's other servants, but even if there were, I wouldn't hide. I'd cut them down right here in the street if they dared try to prevent me from getting to my family.

George keeps pace with my sprint, and I'm once again impressed by his fortitude. Though he can't feel the sorrow piercing through the bond, I think he senses it in me.

Shapes appear in the distance, moving fast toward us. I touch my token, materializing the Hammer of Hope. "Get behind me—" I begin, readying an attack.

But it's not goblins or ogres or trolls barrelling our way. It's all manner of creatures, none known to be inhabitants of the Below. Many I've only glimpsed in the wild or heard about in legend. Dire spiders, gryphons, white elk, queen's winter foxes, firebirds, all in a stampede.

I grab George tight to my side, and we go still, letting the herd charge past. I glimpse a pink-haired woman, clad only in a dirty blanket, running amid the animals. Her large, webbed ears denote her as a siren.

She skids to a halt before me. "Don't try to stop us from leaving."

"I would not dare." I recognize her from Caspian's revelry day celebration, which feels like ages ago. Another prisoner of the Below. My hammer dematerializes from my grip. "Please, tell me have you seen a party of four fae? Three men of Autumn, one of Summer?"

She tilts her head, observing me for a moment before deciding I can be trusted. "They're at the menagerie. Very south of town. Keep following this street, then take a left when you see the cliffside."

"Are they safe?"

"They were when we departed."

I don't have time to ask how she met them or where she's going. Snatching George's vest, I yank him behind me. "Come on."

We bolt through the animals, leaving them to their mission and them leaving us to ours.

My lungs burn and my legs are on fire by the time we cross into the southern quarter. I don't know if I've ever run so fast. George is red-faced and wheezing, about ten steps back now. I suck in a deep breath and nearly vomit. The scent of death sits heavy on the air, thick and cloying. George is not so lucky, heaving over the cobblestones.

I give him under a minute to collect himself, then we're off again, heading straight into the fog of death. A broken sign hangs before us: MENAGERIE.

Dozens of corpses, days old by the smell, litter the ground, all clad in the golden armor of Autumn. My feet slow as I scan the narrow pass between two rock walls, lined with cages. At the very back, I catch sight of someone pacing.

Dayton.

He looks sickly, eyes hollow and struggling to focus, face a pale sheet. Behind him, one of the twins—Dom, must be, as a hand axe dangles from his belt—sits on the ground, arms around his legs, shaking and crying.

And Farron is curled over the thin body of a boy, who, if the world were fair, would never have known the taste of war.

"Oh no," George breathes. "Not the lad."

My chest echoes with anguish, Farron's sorrow passing into me like an unwanted visitor. *No, I've got enough of my own grief. Keep this. Keep it.*

A pained sob escapes Dom as George falls to his knees and wraps him in his arms. Dom clutches at George, burying his face in his chest.

I'm struck still, staring at Farron.

Something is different. Something about the echo in my chest.

I charge over to Dayton, grab his jaw, stare him in the eye, then look him up and down.

"Ez, stop," Dayton says, his voice cracking.

"What happened?"

"We were surrounded by Green Flame soldiers. Ones Farron changed himself. Billy..." His words shatter into a gasp.

"How did the soldiers pass on?" I say lowly.

Dayton squeezes his eyes shut. "I think Farron let it go."

It.

The Green Flame.

I grab Dayton's tunic and pull it up, burrowing my gaze into the skin of Dayton's stomach, right where the arrow wound was. The one that killed him. I have to make myself think the words. *Killed him*. Because I can't forget and pretend that him standing here is anything less than otherworldly. But no wound materializes.

"I'm fine," Dayton says.

My hands find the sides of his face, Spring's blessing rising through me, pouring into him. I reach for the flow of his body, desperate to feel that he's still here—

"Stop it. I'm fine." Dayton tears out of my grip and steps away. Another pained sound escapes him. "I'm *fine.* Go to him, please, please, Ez. Farron...he's the one who needs you."

I stare at him for a few moments longer. Then I turn to Farron. A thousand shards of broken glass all seem to pierce my chest at once. This grief...this is my own. Because Billy looks like such a little thing, just a young boy who should be riding horses and chasing girls and looking forward to all the life he has to live.

And Farron should not have to grieve another loved one. Not Farron. Not he who has always been the kindest, the cleverest, the most caring of us beasts.

Staggering behind him, I fall to my knees, then wrap my arms around Farron, squeezing him so tight, as if I could leach the pain from him and bear it myself. I can't help Billy. I can't bring Farron's mother back. But I can hold him and let his grief crash upon me, even if I can't do anything else.

Farron crumples against me, clutching at my forearms. I squeeze him tighter. "What was any of it for?" he gasps. "What was it for?"

I don't have the heart to tell him for nothing. Because I don't have the heart to tell myself that. The death, the pain, the homes we've lost, the families torn apart... This war *has* to be for something.

Doesn't it?

Doesn't it?

A crack sounds in the stone nearby, and golden briars erupt through the ground. Rosalina steps out of them. She wears pitch-black traveling clothes and carries a leather satchel, and even shrouded in sorrow, she is as radiant as the sun.

My breath staggers looking at her. How many sleepless nights did I spend, dreaming of seeing her once more? Worrying if she was okay, what horrors she had to endure down here in the dark, alone? But as she takes in the scene, her spine stays rigid.

She is stronger than Spring steel.

The horror in her eyes shifts to concern as she clutches her chest and looks at Dayton. Does she feel it? Farron's freedom from the Green Flame?

Does she fear what I fear?

She goes to him, touching him to make sure he's real, just as I did, then glides toward Farron and I, kneeling at our side.

I want to hold her, to clutch her to me and never let go. The strength of her love caresses me as she holds my gaze.

But grief swallows us all.

I release Farron, allowing Rosalina to take him in her arms. They embrace, become one entity.

Another crack sounds, and purple briars split open the nearby cobblestones. Kel and Caspian step out, followed by a small goblin woman.

I stand, drawing my hammer from the token.

"Easy now," Caspian says and puts a hand in front of the goblin. "This is Heidigog. She's with us."

"It's not her I'm worried about," I growl.

"He's himself," Kel says.

I take Caspian in, the clever gaze, the catlike grace to his movements, the way he hovers right at Kel's side. He *is* himself.

My hammer disappears. I reach out, grab Caspian around the shoulders, and hug him. There's too much pain in our world to let a moment of goodness pass by.

Caspian makes a purring sound in the back of his throat. "Missed you too, Metal Man."

"How did you find us?"

"I felt Rosie's briars travel here and followed those."

Wave after wave of grief sweeps through our bonds as I fill Caspian and Kel in. I can only imagine what they've experienced since we all separated, but that will have to wait. Dayton wanders toward us, but he doesn't talk, only paces and paws at his chest.

Dom has made his way beside Farron, and the two brothers hold each other, still curled over Billy. Rosalina and George embrace, then they walk over.

"The rose is in my bag," Rosalina says. "I've got it."

"It won't be long before someone notices and Cryptgarden is swarmed," Kel says. "We need to move now—"

George lets loose a cry. He clutches at his chest and falls to his knees. "Anya!"

"Papa!" Rosalina grabs his shoulders, steadying him. "What's going on?"

George blinks rapidly. "Pain… She's in pain. I saw her…moved from her cell. Sira's taking her somewhere. Anya…"

"Where, Papa, where?"

"Two crystals…black as pitch but flashing with green. She's strung between them…"

Rosalina gives a stricken expression. "I know where that is. Sira's doing it now—taking all Mom's power."

Kel grits his teeth. "We have the rose, and we're all together. We can't stay here—"

"And we can't go." Farron's voice cuts the air. He rises and walks toward us, face a blank mask. I can feel the pain he's hiding beneath it. "We need to finish what we started. Need to make this all mean something."

I take a step back, looking at my family. Each one of us, broken, jagged shards that will cut one another if we're not careful. But as George once told me, we still have a choice.

Now, to make the right one.

I turn to Rosalina. "You know where to find your mother?"

"Yes. And Papa can lead us there too. He feels her wherever she is."

The weight of the words settles over me. We've all known about George's connection with Anya, how he led Kel through the labyrinth…

But the pain he just felt in this moment—it was like how I can feel Rosalina's pain.

They're mates. The queen and a human. *The magic of the world never ceases to amaze me.*

And Sira will drain it all unless we do something.

Rosalina's stern voice interrupts my thoughts. "We'll send the rose to the surface and then end this once and for all."

I take Rosalina's bag from her and open it up. Within, there's a domed glass jar and inside, a glassy rose, petals slick and reflective like oil.

I pick up the jar and carry it over to Dominic, squatting down beside him. He doesn't look up.

"Dom?" I touch his shoulder. "There is no way we will ever take away the pain of losing Billagin or fill the hole in our lives where he once stood. But we need to finish what we started. The mission he believed in."

Dom turns to me. His eyes are red and swollen, gaze faraway. How young he appears. A bird with only one wing, the other torn off, never again able to fly.

I place my palm on his cheek. "Billy needs us to finish this. So there's something important you must do." I hold out the glass jar. "Rosalina will send you to Castletree. You're going to bring this to Marigold and tell her to keep it safe. Can you do it?"

He doesn't say anything but shakes his head no.

I lower my helm to his forehead, breathing deeply so he can match his breaths to mine. "You can do this. This pain you bear means you're fighting. You're a fighter, Dom. And so was your brother. And what Billy was fighting for is worthwhile, I promise."

Dom draws a raspy breath and takes the jar, clutching it tight to his chest. He nods once.

I squeeze his shoulder before slipping back to Rosalina's side. "We can't send him all alone," she whispers.

"I'll look after him!" a squeaky voice says. The goblin, Heidigog, tugs on Rosalina's pants. "I used to work in the crèche, helping hatch the wee squeakers, keeping them all warm and wriggly. Besides, I always wanted a peek at Castletree."

"You'll like the bloomies there," Rose says.

The goblin snorts a laugh. "You and your bloomies."

And I thought Caspian would be the strangest alliance I would ever make. But Rosalina's trust is good enough for me. I squat down, holding the goblin's giant yellow stare. Or at least attempting to. Her pupils go in two different directions, but I think she's looking at me.

"When you arrive, you'll meet a woman named Marigold. Tell

her Ezryn sent you. She needs to put the rose in the vault and prepare Billy for his journey home. And to look after Dom, please."

"Message received, shiny pants!"

Farron embraces Dom one more time, then kisses Billy on the forehead. In a sweep of golden briars, Heidigog and the twins of Autumn are swept away to the world we hope to save.

George, Kel, Caspian, Farron, and Dayton drift toward the exit of the menagerie, staring up at the mountain upon which Caspian's palace is built. Somewhere within, Aurelia is being prepared for the ultimate theft of power.

I move to join them when Rosalina pulls on my elbow. As I turn to her, she falls against me, burrowing her face in my stolen underfae armor. I wrap my arms around her.

"I'm sorry," she mumbles. "I just need a moment to be weak."

"No," I murmur into her hair. "Don't apologize. I've got you, now and forever. Your sadness doesn't make you weak. You are the strongest person I know."

She gazes up at me. Sadness and strength, wrapped together in radiance.

I remove the underfae helmet and let it fall to the ground with a clank. She strokes a finger over my jaw, my cheek, then laces her hand through my hair. Her breath is warm on my lips, a taste of the world above. Gently at first, then with a ferocity I can't contain, I sweep her in my arms and kiss her. She may think she's weak, but her touch gives me more strength than I could ever explain.

As much as I wish we could stay in this embrace, I pull away.

"Now," I whisper in her ear, "we go make this mean something."

52

Caspian

Of course there's more. There's always more to my mother than I anticipate. Layers and layers to her wickedness, and this cesspool is no different. The green water bubbles and pops.

We stand in the secret chamber within the mountain, the one only Sira and I are supposed to know about. She still has no idea it was I who led Farron here months ago, that we were the ones who destroyed her careful system that drained Anya's magic.

But I should have known nothing will stop her. Below the water, there's an even deeper chamber where she'll attempt to take everything from Anya—every drop of power, every ounce of her life. And if it kills Anya?

Then Sira will hunt Rosalina and Wrenley to the very ends of the earth.

"It's too dangerous to go in this way," I hiss. "The baron's magic is the strongest in that pool. He'll corrupt your mind."

"I made it through," Rosalina says, face twisted in determination. "But the water was dark. He wasn't present."

"We're not all as strong as you, sweetheart," Farron says, brow furrowed.

I search his face. *So the Autumn Prince found his way after all.*

Perhaps the Baron isn't as powerful as he wants us all to believe.

And if Farron found a way…

Let me follow.

"It's just a little water," Dayton says, stepping up to the lip. He holds his hand above the pool, jaw tightening. A pained sound escapes him.

"Careful, Sunshine," I say. Every instinct in me screams to stop him, but we're a team now. I have to trust them.

So I watch. This isn't water like the Summer Prince is used to. It churns in unnatural pulses, thick and glowing, a sickly green. Hungry. It bubbles as if it's alive.

Because it *is*.

Dayton clenches his fingers.

The pool reacts. With Farron's connection severed, it's only my father's presence in the Vale keeping him standing now.

The water quivers, and slowly, it starts to spin. A spiral forms, the green liquid dragging itself into a whirlpool, pulling down, deeper and deeper, until there's a tunnel carved straight through the middle. A passage.

"Day," Rosalina chimes, "you're incredible."

But Dayton is barely standing. His whole body's trembling now, and his knees buckle. My blood quickens at the way his jaw clenches, like he's stifling a scream.

"No time to waste. It's now or never," I call.

Kel moves.

The Winter Prince steps up beside Dayton without a word. His hand rises, mirroring Dayton's, and the magic answers. The swirling edges of the whirlpool hold firm, steadier now.

"You learned how to create snow for me," Kel says. "I can help you control a little water."

Dayton sways, but he doesn't fall. He just leans on Kel.

"Hurry, jump through before it closes." Rosalina turns to me. "Cas, are you ready?"

Ready to face my mother, knowing she can whisper any command into my mind? To confront my father, risk the Green Flame breaking through when we're at the source of his power in this world?

No, I'm not ready at all.

But I'm done running. If this is a fight to end it all, then I will be here at the end of it all.

Even if it will be the end of me.

"As I'll ever be, Princess," I say and jump.

~

I land in a catlike crouch, blinking as my eyes adjust to the inky darkness. The others drop down behind me.

A green glow flickers. Then a scream breaks the silence. The light flashes again, and this time, I see it.

Two giant crystal obelisks, pulsing with green. Lightning flickers between them, as if the obelisks are reaching for each other. And strung in the middle hangs the Queen of the Enchanted Vale.

Below her sits my mother, madness flashing in her eyes as she stares up at Anya. Ropes of phantasmic green energy bind the queen's wrists, keeping her suspended between the crystals.

"Anya!" George yells, but Keldarion holds him back.

Sira's really doing it, draining all Anya's power at once. *Killing* her. All to ensure the Baron can step through to our world...

"This is the moment you've been waiting for," I say softly, stepping forward.

Sira shakes her head as if coming out of a trance. "Of course, my love. When we take the Vale, we shall do it as a family. You, myself, and your father."

Well, now all the princes know of my cursed lineage. But the Baron isn't my family.

And neither is this monstrous woman before me.

I raise a set of briars and strike at her.

"You will not harm me," she sneers without flinching.

The lashes of the bargain snag me, and my thorns drop. Breath heaves in my throat as I stare at my mother. At least she hasn't figured out she can now give me more than one command.

"It is our shared desire, son, to bring the Green Flame home." Sira stands, dusting off her skirt.

"I have never once shared a single desire of yours," I snarl. No more pretending. She's gone too far. "And if you think the Baron will be on your side once you let him through, you are sorely mistaken. He wants the realms for himself. You as his equal was never a consideration. You stopped being useful to him after you bore me."

Sira ignores me, the truth bouncing off her. She takes us in, and not even a flicker of worry crosses her face as she stares at four high princes and the heir to the Vale.

And that worries me.

Rosalina steps forward, hair down and eyes blazing gold. "Enough, Sira. You're outnumbered. Outwitted. You cannot put another command on Caspian without dooming yourself."

Sira gives a tinkling laugh, as if being scolded by a child. "Oh, can't say I've missed this version of you, dear. What's a little flower going to do to me?"

"Caspian might not be able to kill you, but we can," Keldarion growls, stepping on my other side.

"Let my mother go," Rosalina hisses. "You are alone."

"Alone?" Sira licks her lips. "I'm never alone."

The green crystals flare, and the pool suspended above glows. Anya's scream pierces the air. Her back bows as spirals of light rip from her chest. A torrent of water shoots to the ground like a falling star. Then it rises, takes shape.

The shape of a man.

No, not a man.

A god.

Seven feet tall, with a sheet of white hair, ears unnaturally long, and armor of obsidian. Half-formed of light, not quite corporeal.

My father has arrived.

"Hello, Caspian," Malekai Furiondemius purrs, a familiar smile on his face. "Are you ready, my son?"

His words traverse my mind and race along my bones, the perfect cadence to unlock something hidden deep down.

I scream and collapse to my knees, ears ringing, a thousand voices screaming to get in. *Burn! The world shall ignite in flame.*

That power inside me rises like a caged beast, fighting to be released. I can't control it anymore. I can't—

"Get him out of here, Rose!" Keldarion screams.

Golden briars erupt from the floor and close around my legs, my arms.

Pathetic.

I suppose I'll have to teach my future queen another lesson.

53

Rosalina

Caspian destroys my briars in a rush of green flame. His eyes are too bright, his expression distant. Wrong. The edges of his body shimmer, his shadow stretching long and curling like smoke. He's gone. We're too close to the Baron for him to fight the Green Flame.

And my mother…

The first time I've seen my mother with my own eyes in over twenty years, and it's this? Suspended between the obelisk crystals, once black, now pulsing with green magic, face contorted in excruciating pain. Her head hangs low, brown hair drenched in sweat. I can't tell if she's conscious. The light winks off a jeweled ring on her left hand. A wedding band? But on her other hand, she wears another ring, a plain iron band.

Her bargain circle with Sira.

Magic crackles, snaring her wrists and ankles like webbing. The suspended water above us seems to reach for her, drawing her life force…

Making that *thing*, that ethereal glowing figure, more real, more here. It's him. Caspian's father. The Baron of the Green Flame.

"No," I breathe.

Shadows flood behind Sira. A tide of them.

"So many choices, little rose," Sira sneers. "But there's no time. Once Aurelia's fully drained, he will be free. The baron will enter this world fully—forever!"

My heart slams.

The baron has come. My mother is in chains. Caspian's being overtaken. Shadows are spilling like oil from the walls. Our magic is weak down here. Every breath cuts me from the inside out.

Which problem do I fix first?

I grit my teeth, eyes darting between all of them. My princes look to me. They look to me for answers.

And maybe I have them.

"Kel!" I shout. "Keep Caspian busy. Don't let him fall!"

Kel is already moving before I finish the sentence, ice leaping at his heels.

"Papa!" I face my father. "Help me. We free Mom together."

He meets my gaze with a nod.

I turn to Dayton, Farron, and Ezryn.

"The rest of you…kill Sira." My voice roars like thunder, and the moment ignites.

Steel flashes. Spells fire, washing the Below in light.

And I run toward my mother, praying I'm not already too late.

Sira laughs as the princes charge her.

Farron is first, his Lance of Valor blazing gold in his hands. Dayton follows, summoning the Trident of Summer in a crash of light and heat, its three-pronged edge gleaming. Ezryn comes last, his Hammer of Hope striking the stone floor with a deep, thunderous hum.

They move like dancers. Like gods.

Sira blinks in and out of puffs of smoke, dodging every blow. She slices at them with shadow blades. Farron's lance pierces her side, but she's gone in an instant, laughing again from across the chamber.

Dayton stumbles, his face pale, breath ragged. He lifts his trident for another strike, but I see the tremble in his arms.

"Day!" I shout, but Ezryn's already there.

He throws his shoulder into Sira's next blow, shielding Dayton, and counters with a swing so powerful it splits the stone beside them.

And still, she keeps coming.

The only one that's ever been able to hold her back is—

Cas. But he's fighting a war of his own. As I must.

"Help me!" I call to Papa and summon two golden blades of thorns, tossing one to him.

He catches it, twirling the blade in a practiced arc.

"I didn't know you knew how to use one of these!" I say.

He raises a brow. "Neither did I."

My mother's body jerks between the green crystals. Her lips move, but no sound escapes.

I slam the blade against the stone.

Nothing.

Papa's sword crashes into the other. It doesn't crack the surface.

Again and again, we strike.

Still nothing. Last time, it took Nori's mushrooms to destroy the crystals, but I'm not sure these obelisks are even the same thing. But I had been able to chip them.

They were black before. Farron would know more, but I can't distract him. Dayton looks weaker by the second, and Fare and Ezryn are barely holding Sira back.

Think! How would Farron view this? All those days spent in the library of Castletree, the research we did together…

The crystals in the chamber above are not the same as these obelisks, but Sira's using them as a substitute conduit. The words she spoke to the Baron days ago… *Tether. Connection.*

There's more here. There *has* to be more I'm not seeing.

Snarling, I drop my briar blade and slam my hand against the obelisk. *Sira*, I think. Magic flickers beneath the surface, and a single vision appears before me. Sira, younger, hair shorter and cropped in rough waves around her face. She sits cross-legged between these very obelisks, her fingers caressing them as if they're sacred. Her eyes shimmer, and then—he speaks. The baron. "You're not alone anymore," he tells her. And she smiles, tears running down her cheeks.

My throat tightens as the memory fades. The initial price she paid. A moment of her joy. This place, these stones, is where it all began.

This was where she first opened herself to him. These obelisks aren't just anchors. They're a door. A promise. A lie she wanted to believe.

"These stones," I gasp. "They're how he's anchored here. This is his connection."

Papa swings again, grim-faced. "Then we break them."

I bite my lip hard enough to draw blood. "It's too strong. Sira's created them with too much magic."

Keldarion and Caspian dance across the rocky ground, a sight I'm all too familiar with. My husband with his swords of ice, my love wielding shadows and flame.

The form of the Baron flickers into view below the pool, only half-formed, a silhouette rippling and pulsing with growing clarity. He turns toward me, and my blood freezes.

We're running out of time. He's drawing magic from my mother's body. Still shackled between the obelisks, her head lolls. Her light dims. The more she fades, the stronger he grows.

We can't free her without weakening the obelisks.

But the crystals are too strong. I can feel it in my bones. All the love of the Vale, poured into them for years.

That's how she's done it, I realize. It's not only Sira's magic. She's stolen joy from fae and goblins and Elderblood. Heidigog's bloomies. Aquila's stars. My wedding. Sira even stole her own happy memory of when she first met the Baron.

She's captured the most powerful force in all the worlds near and far.

Love.

And now with my mother's and the Baron's magic flowing through them, the obelisks have become impenetrable.

I turn, wild-eyed, searching for someone, anyone, to listen.

"They're fed by joy!" I shout, pushing myself to my feet. "The love of the Vale! We have to break the connection and stop this flow of magic."

But no one hears me.

They're all too busy surviving. Sira's laughter echoes like shattered glass as Ezryn is thrown across the floor. Farron shields Dayton with his own body. Green magic coils around Caspian like a second skin, and he's spinning too fast, too wild, his eyes green.

No one is listening.

And if I don't find a way to break these crystals…

We'll lose everything.

54

The Prince of Thorns

The Green Flame sings.

It coils around my spine, warm and alive, filling every weak space. I see. The truth, the future, the way.

Farron and Sira—what fools they are. Believing themselves powerful, important. But they're nothing more than stepping stones. Pawns to the Baron. To my father.

And he's coming.

Aurelia's death will open the gate. With her last breath, the final tether will snap, and he'll enter our world. The Enchanted Vale will burn, yes, but it'll be ours. Father and son. Green fire across the sky, smoke rising from the bones of weak princes.

Sira's purpose is complete. She was the match. Now it's time she's snuffed out.

I smile.

My father's will pounds through me like a second heartbeat. His hatred for the traitor burns brighter than mine. Farron, the unworthy heir. The coward who turned away. We'll start with Dayton, his precious Summer Prince. Make Farron hold him as he dies. Then the High Prince of Spring will fall.

Farron's life will be last.

He will beg.

I raise my hand, and the flame leaps with me, vibrant and wild, casting emerald shadows across the cavern. My body feels endless. Limitless. There's no fear anymore. No doubt. No love.

Only purpose.

Only fire.

And I am ready.

"And what of this one?" the Baron says in my mind but also from the flickering form. He's almost here.

I follow his gaze.

Keldarion.

Charging, blades of ice glinting in either hand. His expression is carved from fury, but there's something else under it, something I know all too well.

Grief.

"He too must die," the Baron says.

Flames coil over my body, forming a ball in my hands, one to launch at the High Prince of Winter.

"No," I yell, forcing myself out of the way, flames whooshing around me.

"Kill him," my father commands.

I straighten. "This one is my pet. Mine alone to break."

Make him kneel.

Something inside me shatters at the thought.

No. No.

Not my pet. My—

My love.

Thoughts crack like glass.

Cas. Kel's deep voice rings in my mind. I try to grasp it, grasp him, but it's as if I'm the stolen rose, trapped in a jar, pounding on the glass.

Kel looks at me. No. *Into* me. And I see him. He sees me. Just for a heartbeat.

Fire swirls at the edges of my vision. He will kneel before the Green Flame or die by it.

I move.

We clash, two storms, blades and flames, ice and fire. I drive him back. He meets every strike. His eyes never leave mine, even as green magic drips from my hands. I want to hurt him. I want to hold him.

And stars help me—

If I kill him, I'll die too.

55

Keldarion

I WILL NOT LOSE HIM AGAIN. I AM LEAVING THIS CURSED PLACE WITH the man I love.

With everyone I love.

It's not as it was before. I see him flickering in and out like stars, purple eyes, then green. I fight with the pure intention of holding him off.

"Cas, come back to me," I growl as he slams his shadow blade against my ice one.

Nothing.

Caspian's not only fighting me.

He's fighting himself.

And losing.

The baron's grip is deep now. Cas's movements are sharper, faster, less fae and more…something I don't understand. His blade sings with green fire, and behind him, the Baron's silhouette looms.

The bastard's got a sword the size of a damned tree. It looks like it could carve the mountain in two.

I wouldn't want to see it up close.

Too bad I don't have a choice.

Frost climbs my arms. My blades are light and quick. Good for slipping past armor. Good for making monsters bleed.

But Caspian's faster now.

I risk a glance across the chamber. Aurelia's still chained, hanging limp between the crystals. Her light flickers like a candle in the wind. Rosalina's driving briars against the obelisks, eyes wild. Not working.

Fuck.

Dayton's down. Collapsed in a heap, his trident slipped from his hand. Not moving.

"Damn it," I hiss.

But Farron's still up, wreathed in orange flame. Ezryn's beside him, hammer raised. They're driving Sira back inch by inch, matching her blow for blow.

A force knocks me away, and I crash against the wall, pebbles raining on my head. What—

A glowing figure steps in front of my vision. Towering, with long, white hair, eyes flashing green. He moves beside Cas like a second shadow, wielding a sword longer than I am tall and twice as heavy. It hums with power. The kind of power that splits worlds.

So he's got enough magic from Aurelia to be physically here, at least partly.

And father and son are coming for me.

I stand and parry left—Cas's blade. Block right—the Baron's. Ice sprays with every hit, frost trying to slow them down, but it's no use. I'm getting pushed back. One step. Then another.

Cas moves fast, brutal. No hesitation. And the Baron is not even fully here, and I still can't land a strike.

I duck under a slash, feel the heat of the green magic skim my cheek.

Too slow.

The Baron hurls a blast of energy, and I take it full in the chest. I hit the ground hard, the wind knocked out of me. Both my ice swords shatter.

This is bad.

Caspian stalks forward, face half-lit in sickly green. His eyes flicker for a heartbeat with something real.

Then it's gone.

"Damn it, Cas," I mutter, spitting blood. "Fight it!"

"The Green Flame cannot be caged, not by him. It is woven into his very blood. It *is* him." The baron raises that monstrous blade again.

I try to form a new blade, a shield, anything. There isn't time—

"Two against one isn't fair."

Ezryn.

He crashes down between us, hammer slamming into the ground with a blast of light. The shock wave ripples out, knocking the Baron back a step. Cas stumbles too, snarling.

Ezryn flashes me a grin. "Let's even the odds."

We fight, the four of us: me, Ezryn, Caspian, and the damned glowing form of the Baron. Blades and hammer and flame and shadow. Ice splinters underfoot, and green magic spits like venom.

Ezryn swings heavily, every hit a quake. I dart around him, cutting where I can, but the Baron doesn't falter. Caspian's not holding back anymore.

It's chaos.

And we're losing.

I'm losing.

I feel it in my arms, heavy now, slow. My breath fogs in front of me, coming too fast. Frost crawls over my shoulders, trying to brace what strength I have left. Even with my blessing, it's hard to reach its full potential in the Below.

It's not enough.

We can't win this.

Not like this.

Caspian leaps at me, all fire and rage and something I can't name. Our blades crash together, and I stagger from the weight of them. A twinkle of light flashes at the nape of Caspian's neck.

Rosalina's moonstone necklace, the one she gave Cas. One of five precious tokens, made for the first high rulers.

Images blaze into my mind. Carvings in a cave. The warriors of old etched into the stone. Justus's voice echoing in the dark. One hand to the chest. One breath. One release.

My hand moves before I think.

It drifts to my sternum, right over my snowflake token, fingers splayed, pressing hard. There is ancestral memory buried inside me. I inhale slow. Deep. The cold fills my lungs.

Then I lift my palm outward.

Fingers curl into a fist.

I hold.

Then—

I unfurl them. And I release.

The air shifts. No, it *snaps*. Magic jolts up my spine. Ice rushes up my legs, over my arms, wrapping me in something older than armor. Something given, not forged.

Magnificent sapphire plates form over my chest, edged in silver-frost filigree that pulses with light. Bracers shimmer over my forearms, carved with snowflakes. My pauldrons are wings of crystal, flared and jagged like frozen mountain peaks. A cloak of the deepest blue whips behind me, tethered by pins shaped into wolves' heads.

A helm curves around my head, leaving my face exposed.

The temperature drops.

Even the Baron hesitates.

I exhale slowly, mist curling from my lips. "Let's try this again."

56

Dayton

I'M ON THE GROUND AGAIN.

How many times have I hit stone tonight? My body's screaming. My arms are filled with molten lead. Every breath scrapes through my chest as if it's trying to escape me.

I didn't want to admit it before.

Didn't want them to see it.

But the truth is I'm empty.

I'd been running on the Green Flame. Whatever scrap of life the Baron shoved into me when Farron dragged me from death, it's almost gone now. A snuffed-out candle in a storm.

I'm flat on my back, still catching my breath, when Keldarion goes full divine warrior. There's a flash of blue light, and then *bam*, our High Prince of Winter is wrapped in enchanted sapphire like the walking night sky.

Snowflakes swirl around him dramatically. His cape flutters even though there's no damn wind.

"Right," I mutter, dragging myself up, coughing on dust. "Of course Keldarion gets the special armor. Sworn Protector of the Realms, Starbringer of Winter, Blades of Brooding—well, I'm just making shit up now."

No one's listening to me.

Doesn't matter.

Because Farron's roaring across the battlefield, flames coiled tight around him, and he's still going at Sira with everything he's got. But she's not slowing down.

He stabs his lance, and she disappears in a puff of smoke, reappearing behind him, shadows extending from her hands. He barely ducks in time.

I try to move, to help, but my limbs are sluggish. I grunt, pushing to my knees.

Light flares to my left.

Ezryn is *glowing*.

His fist is extended before him, and he unfurls his palm.

The air tastes sweet. Like the first breath of spring after a bitter winter.

Armor blooms over him in shimmering plates, starlight silver, edged in pink and green vines. A faint shimmer of petals bursts around him like confetti from the gods. His pauldrons are new buds curling open but with steel instead of petals. Unlike Keldarion, his helm covers his entire face, his T-shaped vizor edged with silver.

I blink.

"Okay," I whisper, grinning. "That's pretty."

I rise to all fours, and it feels heavy against my neck—the queen's token, that little shell nestled among all the normal ones and the piece of red sea glass that Farron strung for me.

Kel, shining like a glacier, and Ezryn, blooming like dawn, move against the Prince of Thorns and the Baron. Farron holds back Sira's blades, but his movements are slowing. She's too fast.

And he's too focused on her. Has he realized what's happened to Kel and Ez?

I know what I have to do.

I push to my feet, every muscle shrieking in protest. My hand rises, slow but sure. I press it to my chest, right over the token. *What did they do again?*

But I know. Know it in my bones, in my blood. Magic sings beneath my skin, and I don't think I could move any other way.

One breath.

I lift my hand and unfurl my palm.

The world ignites.

Light bursts around me, not soft like Ezryn's or sharp like Kel's but hot and fierce and full of life. Water and sun. Laughter and battle cries.

Armor slams into place, piece by piece, stunning teal and gold, edged with curling wave motifs. Coral embossing twists down my gauntlets. My shoulders flare with sunbursts, a swirling cloak trailing behind me, frothy as sea foam. Then the helm settles onto my head. Curved cheek guards, a sharp nose ridge, and, rising from the crest, a plume of shimmering gold and teal feathers.

I catch my reflection in the obelisks. I look like a prince carved from sunlight and summer storms.

And damn if I don't feel like one too.

I grin, wide and wicked. *One last fight.*

"Well," I say, summoning the Trident of Honor to my hand with a satisfying snap, "someone had to bring the flair."

Then I leap.

Sira's already mid-swing when I crash between her and Farron, trident meeting her shadow blade in a shower of sparks.

She snarls. I don't flinch.

"Come on, pup," I say, flashing Farron a wink. "Let's see you in some pretty armor too."

He blinks. Then smiles.

Farron steps back, examines us all, then lifts his hand to his chest.

He breathes in and glows like a harvest moon.

His armor roars into being, vibrant orange and burnished bronze, carved with Autumn trees and wolves, a flowing mantle of flame curling behind him. His eyes are sparking embers. A circlet of golden leaves adorns his brow, the color bringing out the red in his hair and beard.

"Show-off," I mutter.

Rosalina's standing by the crystals, staring at us like we've stepped out of a story.

Maybe we have.

But this story's not over.

Not yet.

Farron and I move in unison. We have to hold Sira back, kill her if we can, give Rosalina enough time to free Queen Aurelia.

My body aches, and my muscles scream in protest. But if this is the end, then I'll go out in a blaze of glory.

One last fight. I can give my friends one last fight. Sure, it's not the Sun Colosseum, but I couldn't ask for better teammates or a fiercer enemy. I mean, a cosmic god and the Queen of the Below? *My brothers will greet me with pride.*

But what of Delphia? A pang of hurt washes through when I think of my little sister. She never wanted to be high princess. But if we pull this off, then she can be a princess of peace, not one of war.

I flash a glance to Rosalina, so beautiful. My mate. She will lead them well.

Farron and I move as if we're two parts of one body. Fire and water, strike and counter. He feints high, and I sweep low. My trident flashes in a whirl of teal light while his lance blazes with ambered gold, both of us driving Sira back with unrelenting force. Her smoke forms falter under our rhythm, her shadows too slow to catch us when we're together. We don't speak. We don't need to. Every step, every blow, is instinct. Lovers. Warriors. A storm of Summer and Autumn crashing down on her like the end of a season.

And I know for sure now, once we defeat this psycho bitch, I can go in peace. Because they'll be okay. He'll be okay.

My little Autumn leaf has set us both free.

57

Keldarion

I've fought beside Ezryn thousands of times, but we've never fought enemies like this before. The baron towers above us, glowing and unnatural. His massive broadsword seems to arc across the entire cavern with each swing.

And beside him fights Caspian.

No. Not Caspian. Not really.

The Prince of Thorns comes at me with wild, brutal precision, green fire streaking off every motion. His blade is swift, his strikes sharper than I've ever seen. But his movements are too clean. Too perfect.

He's not fighting like Cas.

He's fighting like a puppet.

The baron must be watching me, because a cruel smirk crawls

across his too-perfect face. One that's becoming more material by the second. *Come on, Rose.*

"Let him go, Winter Prince," the Baron says. "There is no Caspian. Not anymore."

I snarl and drive my blade toward his chest. He blocks it with a lazy flick of his monstrous sword.

Caspian lunges past him, slashing straight for my ribs.

I dodge too slow.

The blade scrapes my side, burning cold where it cuts. I stumble, and Ezryn catches me, planting his feet and swinging his hammer in a wide arc, keeping the Baron back for a breath.

"We're losing ground," he mutters.

I grunt. "Noticed."

Across the cavern, I see Rosalina, her hands bloodied from trying to break the black stones, her briars coiled tight around them. But they won't move. Her mother still hangs in those cursed chains, her light growing dimmer.

And on the far side of the chamber, Farron and Dayton.

They've unlocked Justus's ancient memory as well. Day shines in brilliant teal with Farron beside him, his Autumn armor burning bright. Together, they fight Sira in perfect rhythm, pushing her back step by step.

And for the first time, I believe we can win this right here, right now.

Ezryn shouts, leaping into the air and slamming his hammer into the Baron's side with a crack of sound that shakes the cavern. The monster stumbles, only for a heartbeat, but it's enough.

I run.

Straight at Caspian.

He turns as I slam into him, and we crash to the floor. I land on top, pinning him, breath heaving. His sword skitters out of reach.

I press my forearm to his throat, then freeze.

Because his eyes aren't glowing. They're as lavender as the dawn. But terrified.

"Kel," he chokes. "I can't—I can't fight it. It's in me. And he's *here*. He's *here*. Always has been."

I drop my blade. My hands move to his face, cupping it gently. I kiss him.

He mutters something against my lips, broken and raspy. "I can't fight the Green Flame, Kel. I can't keep it caged anymore."

"You're not meant to fight it," I growl. "You're meant to tame it."

58

The Prince of Thorns

"The fire cannot be contained." Green flames rush out of me and blow the Winter Prince and his foolish words back.

He lands in a heap on the other side of the cavern and doesn't rise. His new armor resists even a single scratch.

Doesn't matter. Everything will burn beneath the Green Flame.

Tame it. The words pulse through me.

Kel's hurt. I run to him. To help, to destroy... I scream, my mind ablaze with this magic, this *power*, consuming everything I am.

"Kill him and free yourself," my father says as he makes his way toward Ezryn.

The Spring Prince won't be able to hold him back long, not with how fast Aurelia is fading.

My breath hitches. Who am I?

The Prince of Thorns? Caspian? Heir to the Green Flame?

I've been all three, but never all at once.

Tame it.

Keldarion rises to his feet, forming two ice blades in his hands. His eyes flick up to mine.

I rush toward him, feeling myself slipping, but manage to spit out, "I was born this monster, twisted and wrong."

"I know," Keldarion says gruffly. "And I've loved you every damn day of it."

A terrible scream tears out of me. This fool, this damned fool. A blade of thorns forms in my hands, and I slice at him. Ice chips and showers us.

My father drifts closer. "Do you think love will save him? Do you think it's strong enough to unmake me? He was created for destruction, Winter Prince."

Ezryn steps between us and the Baron, hammer raised again. "Maybe he was. But he gets to choose what he becomes."

The baron smiles, slow and cruel. A blast of green flame erupts from his palm, slamming into Ezryn and sending him shooting across the cavern.

"Ezryn!" Keldarion cries.

"You're getting stronger, Father," I say. "Soon, you shall be here with us fully, at the death of the queen."

"Two great powers ruling the Vale, one my mate and one his sire." Rosalina's voice carries across the chasm. I look over at her. She's kneeling beside Ezryn, but when she catches my gaze, she rises slowly, as if we have all the time in the world. As if all her other mates aren't about to perish.

I prowl over to her. "You'll be at my side, willing or not."

"I wonder who will truly rule." She places a finger to her lips. "The sire, who the power stems from but who is still and will *always* be a visitor to our world...or you?"

"My home is wherever I make it." Malekai turns his attention toward her.

Careful, my mate, I say in her mind. *Don't displease him.*

So we bow to someone? she replies in my mind before facing my father. "Where is your own home then? Why the need to claim ours?"

"All the worlds shall be mine," he snarls.

Rosalina tilts her head, curls falling over her brow. "I see. You don't have a home of your own, do you?"

I have never seen my father so much as flinch, but he stalls, only for a second, horrors playing across his face. Then he turns to me, the mask firmly in place. "Muzzle your whore, son, or I will."

But my mate's words are still spinning in my mind. *So we bow to someone?*

I turn to my father. Is his power greater than mine?

My gaze drifts to Farron and Dayton, his former pawns, now freed and facing my mother with their own magic. They were bound to his will, because he gifted them a seed of his power...

But I was born with it. It is in my blood.

"Caspian, listen to me," my father booms, ancient voice echoing off the stones.

"No," I say. Or the Prince of Thorns says. Something synergizes inside me. My two wills agree.

We are not his pawn.

His magic may run through my veins, but it is not his to control.

"Caspian!" Keldarion grips me by the shoulders.

I whirl. My face reflects in his armor: eyes green, then purple, then green. A ringing sounds in my head, and flames flicker up and down my arms. I cry out, briars breaking free from the earth and wrapping around my legs.

Rosalina yelps. The baron shoots a ball of green fire toward her, and she throws up a golden briar in time to block it. She calls up more, and Ezryn stands, swinging his hammer.

"Rosie!" Farron yells, he and Dayton still locked in the endless dance with Sira.

"Cas!" Keldarion growls, gripping my shoulders and forcing me to look at him. "They need us. Our mates need us. Need you. All your power."

Tears burn down my cheeks, and I feel it, something breaking inside me. The cage I've spent my whole life shoving the Green Flame into, locking it away. I thought control meant silence. Containment. Denial.

But every time I buried it, it only grew wilder. Hungrier. Until it wasn't mine anymore—it was his. My father's will. The lure of power. The promise of never being weak again.

But power always comes with a price.

And I've paid for it in pieces of myself.

"You've been fighting the Green Flame your whole life," Keldarion growls. "Time to stop. Tame it, Cas."

"What if I'm not strong enough?" I cry.

Keldarion's eyes crinkle at the sides as he looks at me, even now, with so much love. "You have to be."

As if it's that simple.

Because either I can wield it, or I can't.

Either I become the weapon, or I break beneath it.

The fire inside me surges, screaming for control, begging to be let loose. It wants to consume. To burn everything, starting with the ones I love most.

My fingers tremble. My breath shudders. "And if I lose myself again?" I whisper.

Keldarion leans closer, forehead pressing gently to mine, his voice a quiet storm.

"Then I'll be there to pull you back."

I believe him. With everything I am, I believe him.

"When the stars wove my fate," he murmurs, eyes closed, a surrender to me, to the Prince of Thorns, Cas, all of me, any form, "they made a tapestry of light and fire and frost..."

"One that always ends with me loving you."

I turn to Rosalina. The green shadow of my father draws closer to her, massive sword dragging on the ground behind him.

The Green Flame writhes beneath my skin, furious, untamed, alive. It's never been quiet. Not once. It's clawed at the edges of me, whispering with my father's voice.

I've tried to fight it. Tried to bury it. I thought that was strength. That if I locked it away, I could be good. Safe. Worthy of a prince and princess's love.

Because a monster could never have them.

But it was never the flame that made me dangerous. It was the fear of it.

The fear made me cruel. Made me cold. Made me run from the very things that make up who I am.

But Keldarion's here, holding me. Ezryn stands guard like a

mountain, unshaken. Dayton and Farron refuse to give up. And Rosalina looks away from death and stares at me.

In any form, I will love you.

And even George is here, tearing his hands apart trying to free the woman he loves. The woman who saved me once before.

"When you can't stop the storm," I murmur, "you find another way out."

They're still fighting.

For me.

I look down at the flames flickering along my arms. A birthright, a burden. *You decide what to do with the magic you bear.*

I take a breath and close my eyes.

Not to smother the fire. Not to cage it.

But to claim it.

I draw it in, deep and burning. It floods through my veins. It screams and thrashes…

But there isn't only fire in my blood. There is shadow and thorn too.

I bring it all to the surface, weave it together in a way my father never could. The magic of the Below, the magic of the Vale, and the magic of the world beyond, united.

And mine.

Keldarion stumbles away, the pulse of magic too strong even for him.

I scream. Flames and shadows and briars writhe around me like a storm. But if a camel can find her way out of one, then so can I.

You. Are. Mine, I cry to my mind, to my soul, inside and out. And the green fire along my arms begins to bend.

Change.

I gasp, back arching, as the magic inside me flares.

And for the first time in my life, I choose not to fear the part of me that burns.

The Green Flame yields.

My eyes open, glowing green and steady, reflected in Keldarion's armor.

"Hello, lover," I purr. And I see for a second that flicker of confusion on his face, that worry of just who he's talking to. And as much as I long to tease him, there will be forever to do that. "Let's go save the world. I'm tired of always letting you be the hero."

59

Caspian

MAYBE IT WAS WORTH THE DECADES OF TORMENT, OF LOVE MIXED SO well with hate I forgot what to call it, just to see the dumbfounded look on the High Prince of Winter's face.

"You really did it, Cas?" he asks softly.

"As if there's anything I can't do." I give him a wry grin. "Besides, you got that fancy new armor. Couldn't have you showing me up."

Keldarion takes my hand and places it over the moonstone rose token on my chest.

Could it be? I straighten my arm, the way I saw the other prices do. *Surely it won't work for me. I'm not like them. I'm not one of them.*

But with Kel's eyes steady on mine, I decide to stop being afraid. I unfurl my palm.

Light shimmers along my body. Armor appears, sleek and formfitting. Glittering pale moonstone reflects the light of Farron's flames and the green glow of the obelisks. A white cape flows behind my back.

Transfixed by my reflection in Kel's sapphire armor, I spy a circlet of moonstone roses cresting my brow.

Keldarion smiles at me. So damned beautiful. "Alright, Prince of Roses. Let's see what you can do."

A sword of briars forms in my hands, the blade sharp. The hilt blooms with lilac roses. *Interesting.*

I summon a deep breath and leap across the room. My sword clashes against my father's, intercepting a blow intended for my mate. Sparks of green flame clatter, and Malekai stumbles, a look of bewilderment across his face.

One that quickly turns to fury.

"Cas, you're…" Rosalina breathes.

"Beautiful? Elegant? An awe-inspiring hero?" I flash her a grin. "All of the above?"

Her golden briars rise. "Who I always knew you were meant to be."

Imagine all the heartache I could have prevented if only I'd figured that out when she did, I think.

"It's not possible!" Sira screams, disbelief etched on her face. "You're under *my* control! Caspian—"

Dayton strikes at her before she can utter a command.

Malekai's blade swings toward me again. It's colossal, shimmering with that sickly green fire. I meet it midair with my briar-forged sword. The impact rings through my bones like a song I was born to answer.

The surrounding shadows twist to life, dancing at my feet, climbing my arms. Green flames spark from my fingertips. Briars slither across the ground, growing sharper with each breath I take. I'll need every part of who I am to face him.

My father steps back, his eyes narrowing. "You dare stand against me, son?"

I tilt my head. "All that blathering about legacy, power, destiny, and you're mad I actually lived up to it?"

"I gave you everything. My blood. My power. My purpose."

"You gave me chains," I say, raising my free hand. Shadows whip forward like spears, slamming into his side. He stumbles but doesn't fall.

He growls, swinging again. His sword is so massive it seems to cleave the air itself, but I duck low, roll, and come up in a surge of thorns and green flame. My blade lashes across his shoulder. A clean strike.

"I gave you my power!" he bellows, magic crackling. "Without me, you'd be nothing."

I smirk. "Look at me now. Glowing. Gorgeous. Very much something."

My briars lash again, snapping from the floor like vipers. He burns half of them away, but not fast enough. I leap into the air, twisting in shadow, and slam down with a blast of green fire wrapped in thorns.

He bats it away with his sword but grunts. *That's new.*

"You're drawing on my power," he spits.

"No," I say, eyes locked with his. "I'm using what was always mine. This isn't some gift you can pull away. You, in your arrogance, passed your power down in my *blood*. Try to take it back. I dare you."

He roars, lunging for me.

But then ice whistles through the air.

Keldarion.

He flies past me in a blur of sapphire, blades of frost drawn wide, intercepting a bolt of shadow that had been arcing toward Farron. "Keep fighting, Cas," he shouts. "We've got Sira!"

I glance over. Dayton's plume flashes gold and teal as he pins Sira with a trident strike. Farron comes in hard beside him, the flames wreathing his body like a meteor. Keldarion joins them in the fray, and she finally seems to shrink away.

Good.

Because I've got my own monster to slay.

Malekai swings again, and this time, I welcome it. My shadows catch his blade, just long enough for me to slip through. My sword carves a line down his side, and I twist, letting the momentum spin me into a backhanded strike that sends a spray of embers across his chest.

He snarls. "You are still mine!"

"No," I cut him off. "I'm Rosalina's. I'm Kel's. I'm mine."

Footsteps sound behind me, light and sure.

"We're with you." Rosalina appears beside me, gold briars at the ready.

Ezryn flanks her, hammer blazing in his hands. "Let's finish this."

I smile.

We press him hard.

Ezryn's hammer crashes against Malekai, rippling out with blasts of spring light, forcing him back step by step. Rosalina's golden briars snap like whips, coiling around the Baron's legs, binding, tearing, holding. I charge through the chaos, blade of thorns blazing with green fire, and slash deep across his chest.

He staggers, movements slow.

His magic is still powerful, but it's faltering.

"You've got nothing left," I snarl, slamming my boot into his side and driving him back farther. "Your time's over."

He lifts his massive, gleaming sword with trembling hands, and I feel it break. Not just the weapon. Him.

This time, when I move, I don't hesitate.

My blade plunges into his chest, briars twisting, flame pulsing down the edge, shadows lashing outward like a scream made visible. A roar of pure shock erupts out of his throat.

His form begins to unravel, flesh withering. Light bleeds out.

He looks at me. And I see him for what he is. Not a god or a monster.

Just a man. A man murdered by his own son.

"For what it's worth," I snarl, "you were right about one thing. I am powerful."

Then he crumbles.

His body collapses into ash and green light, folding in on itself and vanishing into the air.

Ezryn exhales. "Is it over?"

Rosalina looks toward the crystals, her hands still glowing with magic. "Something isn't right."

I turn, scanning the chamber: Anya strung between the obelisks, George pounding against them. He's not even making a dent.

Then Anya lets out a wailing scream, back bowing. Her whole body is a firefly, flickering. George screams, reaching for her. Then the water above her stirs and pulses with light.

A low hum begins.

"George, get back!" I shout.

Too late.

The water explodes.

Green light bursts downward like a geyser, and from within it, he emerges.

The baron. Reborn.

"You didn't think it would be that easy to end me, did you, son?" He smiles. "I am tethered to this world as it is to me."

My stomach drops. "No."

Rosalina stumbles, wide-eyed. "Cas…"

Beside me, Ezryn's grip tightens on his hammer. "It shouldn't be possible."

From the other side of the cavern, Sira laughs. A burst of shadows explodes around her, knocking Dayton and Farron away.

"Yes!" Sira cries, spinning like a child at a festival. "She's almost dead. It's time."

My sword trembles in my grip. We had him. I beat him. And it still wasn't enough.

Ezryn rushes forward, slamming his hammer against the Baron. Kel pulls away from Sira to assist.

"Cas." Rosalina grips my arm, forcing me to look at her. "The obelisks are the tether. Sira has been stealing the joy from people to feed them for years."

So many secrets, Mother. So much pain. For what? *So you would feel less lonely? For one perfect creation?* I stare down at my hands. All this power, and it's still not enough to beat him.

"I chipped them before," Rosalina snarls. "But with the Baron's magic running through it, they're unbreakable. I can't control the

Green Flame magic. It's not of the Vale. We need to disrupt it somehow."

The words are thick in my throat. "I'll find a way."

Her eyes flash. "You break the connection. I'll break the obelisks."

"Alright then. Together, Princess?"

"Together."

With my father distracted, Rosalina and I rush over to the glowing green crystals. As soon as I place my hands on them, a surge of energy floods me, blowing back my hair, whipping my cape. Green light refracts across my moonstone armor.

It washes over me all at once, so many faces I know. Faces I've seen walking the streets of Cryptgarden, always joyless and empty. Each one of these moments is a sacrifice tying the Baron to this world.

And now Sira's using the strongest of all her crystals to channel both Anya's magic and Malekai's, all in order to bring him here.

Anya screams again, and George lets out a heart's cry to meet it.

"Hold on," I gasp, fingers curling over the stone. I told Rosalina I'd find a way to break the connection, but how?

If happiness tethers him here, what could disrupt that, if only for a moment?

Of all the magic I've been born with and given, nothing can compare to these raw emotions…

But maybe it's not magic I need.

It's something else my father's given me. Something my mother has too.

I grasp for a connection to the crystals, threading their energy with my own. But instead of giving it memories of joy…

I give it pain.

Every strike of Emberlash's whip. Every rejected glance and twisted word from my mother. Vespera's objects. Kneeling at my father's feet as he speaks of a world of flame and ash.

The memories wash over me, sucking into the crystal, each one flooding through me as if they were as fresh as the day they happened.

Sweat beads on my brow, and I scream, the sound ripe with grief and torture. In the reflection behind me, I watch my father swing his sword, sending Keldarion flying across the room. Dayton has fallen to one knee, Farron barely able to hold back Sira on his own.

"Cas!" Rosalina shouts.

I scream louder. The cage of fire. Watching Sira torture my sister in front of me. Saving my mate and having to leave her all in one day. *Take it all.*

Threads of memories fray, snap, and—

The green light flickers. The crystals drain to black.

"Get the hell out of our realms," Rosalina snarls.

Golden briars rise from the ground and pierce the now dark crystals. A spiderweb of cracks carves across the obelisks.

The baron turns from the fight and rushes toward us.

"No!" Sira shrieks, true terror in her voice.

A creak sounds as the cracks multiply, turning the crystals into a flickering kaleidoscope. Malekai reaches me. He drops his sword and instead grasps my face.

Those glowing green eyes crinkle, his hair falling across his brow in the same way mine does. "In all the hundreds of thousands of worlds, you are my only family."

The crystals shatter, scattering like a star shower. And he breaks apart too, into thousands of fragments of light, without so much as a scream.

I heave out a deep breath. "And I just saved my family from you."

He's not dead. Not really. But he has no more ties to this world. The Enchanted Vale is free of the Green Flame.

And the next world he decides to haunt better have a hero stronger than me to defeat him. Preferably several.

Anya drops to the ground, and George rushes to catch her in his arms, sobbing. "She's alive. She's alright, my Annie. Keep breathing."

Rosalina sprints over to her father, laying a hand on his shoulder and gazing at her mother breathing softly in her husband's embrace.

"Sira's gone," Ezryn yells. "Fled as soon as the crystals cracked."

"We can track her down. She's scared and injured," Keldarion says. "We have the rose. We have the power."

But a small voice breaks through. "Rosalina…"

It's Farron. He holds Dayton in his arms.

The High Prince of Summer's armor has faded away, and so has he.

60

Farron

He's so heavy.

He's so heavy in my arms.

Of course. Dayton has always been broad and strong.

But this is different. He's so heavy because he can't move himself. He can't even stand.

Golden and purple briars wrap around us, but I can't let go of Day. I *won't* let him go. We break through the earth to the surface.

Castletree. *Home.*

But it can never be home without him.

The other princes gather nearby. George is on the ground, Queen Aurelia in his arms. Rosalina rushes from their side to ours.

Not good, not a good sign, because then her mother must be okay, and Day is…

Rosalina drops to her knees and carefully pulls Dayton's head onto her lap.

He blinks up at her dreamily. "Got your mom back, Blossom?"

"Yeah, Day, I did." Tears pool in her eyes, and she looks across at me. "What's happening to him?"

"He was fine and then he…" I start. "He collapsed."

His skin is ghastly pale, breath shallow, sweat dotting his brow.

"Farron used the Green Flame to tie him to life," Caspian says, stepping forward. "When he gave it up, there wasn't anything keeping Dayton together anymore. I suspect when we destroyed the Baron's connection to our world, that was his last thread."

A bubbling sob bursts out of Rosalina's lips.

I hold Caspian's lavender gaze. His irises are specked with tiny dots of green. "But you can do it. You still have the power."

Caspian looks down at his hands. Green flames curl up and down his arms. "This magic…it's not meant for that. There was something *wrong* about the way he was brought back before. You felt that, Farron."

I turn away from the Prince of Thorns, because he's right. I did feel that. It's why I had to let Billy go—

"I can't lose them both," I choke out. My brother. My love. My heart's not built for this sort of grief.

"It'll be alright," Dayton murmurs, his voice so weak. "I don't want that fire inside me, Fare. Let me go like this, a hero. In a blaze of glory, like Dammy said."

"Day, no!" Rosalina sobs. Her hands on his chest are glowing, but from the look on her face, the fact that Ezryn is standing behind her, not even trying to heal him…

There's nothing they can do.

There's nothing to *heal*. The fire I fueled his body with has burnt out.

"I can't survive this." My hair falls over my brow, and I collapse over him. Eyes closing, I rest my head over his chest. His heartbeat is slow. So slow.

Every one is precious.

"Such a pretty color, like the brightest leaves." With the last of his strength, Dayton smooths a hand through my hair.

Hands that have protected me. Held me. Loved me.

Another sob racks through me. I clutch him tighter. A distinct and strange feeling runs through me. I notice it immediately because it's so different from the terrible soul-wrenching grief that consumes my body.

Something beautiful that burns in the most comforting way—the press of a high summer sun on your shoulders, the crackle of an autumn fire.

Something that burst into life that's been living inside me for a long time. And by the shocked gasp that escapes Dayton's lips...

He feels it too.

I open my eyes and pull away, blinking at him. He rubs his chest, a crooked smile on his face.

"Hi," he says.

"Hi," I reply.

The light bursts between us, blinding and brilliant, a tether of golden light hovering between our chests.

"Mates," Rosalina gasps, smiling.

This shouldn't be possible to see, but I follow the golden motes of dust swirling in the air to the queen. She's still held tight in

George's arms, her palm extended, glowing. Like she's pulling back the veil for us.

"Fare," Dayton says, running a hand along the golden thread, "I'll tell you the same thing I told Rosie."

"Yeah?"

"Always knew we were mates."

I laugh, because even at this moment, he can make me smile. "You do realize that this means we could have broken our curses a long time ago?"

Dayton throws his head back, another laugh echoing in his chest. "We still beat Kel. That's all that matters."

"Heh," Ezryn laughs. "Even Cas unlocked his mate bond before Kel. Wasn't hard."

Keldarion lets out a light chuckle, and the three other princes gather around us, bending down.

"You'll look after them," Dayton says weakly.

It's Keldarion who nods and places a hand on Dayton's shoulder. "With every beat of my heart. Thank you for all you've done, High Prince of Summer."

Tears run down Cas's cheek as he crouches beside Keldarion. "Guess I'm going to win our bet, Sunshine."

"Shame." Dayton still manages to smirk back.

Ezryn removes his helm and bends his brow to Dayton. "I will let Delphia know of the glorious hero her brother proved to be. I will guide and teach her how to be a high princess. I promise you, brother, she will never be alone."

A tear slides down Dayton's cheek. He's blinking more now, eyes growing glassy.

"No," I choke out, clutching tighter to him. We can't be doing this. "I don't know how to say goodbye to you."

"Then don't, Fare," Dayton says so faintly. Maybe I'm hearing it in my mind. "Just tell me you love me. And please, kiss me once as your mate."

I look across at Rosalina, her face as broken as mine, holding him so carefully in her lap. *I can't do this.*

What if this is our last kiss? I can't kiss him, thinking it will be our last kiss. I can't.

You can, she whispers in my mind. *For Day.*

I choke out a sob and lower myself to his lips, still tasting of summer and salt. *Tide-kissed forever.* He sighs against me, using one of his precious last breaths to love me.

"Through every season and every storm," I murmur against his cheek.

Stars, I can barely hear his heartbeat now. Every one that echoes through me feels like a miracle.

Don't go, don't go, don't go, I cry out in my mind.

Rosalina bends over next to us, and I reach out and grasp her hand as if it's a tether. She kisses Dayton's cheek, whispering in his ear, "You're the tide...and..." She chokes back a sob. "I love you."

"You..." Dayton begins, but there's no more breath in his lungs for words. *You two are the greatest treasure I ever found. I love you.*

So much light bursts around us it's almost blinding, all our threads intertwining. "Goodbye, Day," I gasp out. "We'll be woven together forever."

61

Rosalina

There's one thing that's keeping me from falling apart completely. His last moments need to be beautiful, held and protected and safe in the arms of the people he loves.

If only love was enough to keep him here.

So I hold my Summer Prince, basking in the glow of our bonds, a gift from my mother.

"Goodbye, Day," Farron gasps out, and my heart breaks with those words. That he was able to say them. "We'll be woven together forever."

Woven together.

Something about those words sticks in my brain, but now is no time to think. I need to be present for Day.

Woven together...

A memory sounds in my mind, a voice of darkness and despair:

Everything in our world is woven together with life and spirit. You only need pull back the veil from your mind to see the threads.

"To bind one's life to another," I murmur, and then I sit up.

My mother bound Papa's life to Castletree. *Pull back the veil.* My mother's already done that, and now I can see the threads around me.

I turn to her. I haven't even gotten a chance to look at her. Facets of Wrenley are visible on her face. Parts of myself too, I suppose. The same brown eyes. She's staring at me with sadness but also curiosity.

"Hi, Mom. Nice to meet you," I say. "Can you teach me something?"

62

Dayton

An endless sea and a milky pink sun wavering on the horizon. It's beautiful but a little sad.

I'm out here all alone.

There's a drop coming soon. I can feel it more than I can see it. Perhaps there will be others awaiting me: Decimus and Damocles, my fathers, and my mother. But *they* won't be there.

My mates.

Hopefully, they won't be with me for a long time. A shame. I wish I could float here a little longer, but I don't think that's a choice.

I'll really miss them.

The horizon creeps ever closer.

Two stars blaze in my vision to the right of the sun, then fall. Tethers of golden light streak past me into the water. One feels of fire, the other of life. I know it's my choice to hold on, to grasp this.

If I do, I might not be carried away by this peaceful current.

And I am at peace. The lure of the horizon draws me.

But…

I've never been one for good ideas.

Peace can wait.

I reach out and grab hold.

63

Rosalina

"I CAN FEEL HIM. HE ACCEPTS IT!" I CRY OUT.

"Careful, Rosalina," my mother warns, hand hovering over my shoulder. "If you lose hold for even a second, it will all unravel."

"I won't let go," I say, determination coursing through me.

I sit poised above Dayton, Farron across from me, eyes closed, as still as he can be, body and soul surrendered to me. To us.

As I bind Dayton's soul to ours.

Castletree is too weak to hold another soul. My mother warned me a mate bond was not a strong enough tether to tie two fae together. It's why she had to use Castletree to begin with.

But what of *two* mate bonds? Our golden threads burst with life. I will tether Dayton to Fare and I forever.

"Remember, I cannot help you," my mother says. She's pale and weak but somehow managed to crawl over to me. "Sira drew too much of my magic. This is all you, Rosalina. Pull back the veil until you see not only your bonds but your souls."

I take in a deep breath and concentrate in the same way I do when I harness the power of transformation. Light shines off Farron, flickering like embers in a hearth. A glow emits from me too, pulsing a soft rose gold. Around Day, it trembles in waves, but it's so faint, reminding me of mist dispersing under the sun's rays.

We don't have much time.

"I've done it." My breath rattles. Merely seeing this part of the hidden world takes all my concentration and strength.

"Good," my mother says, drawing closer. "Now, weave all the parts together in a single braid, strand by strand. But I warn you, Dayton has no life thread of his own. If you or Farron fall, it could mean the death of all three of you."

Farron opens his amber eyes, staring back at me. The choice throbs through our bond, as if there's no choice at all.

For our mate.

Furrowing my brow in concentration, I begin to pull pieces loose. It's sticky and slow, like the threads of our souls are caught in honeyed mist. Farron lets out a gasp of pain as we tug ourselves apart.

"Weave your mate bonds into the binding," my mother urges. "It will hold this all together. At least in theory." She pauses. "What you're doing has never been done before."

"Always such encouraging words," Caspian huffs at her. He paces like a caged animal above us.

"But she's your daughter," Papa says. "Rose, trust in your heart."

We braid slowly. My breath hitches as more of our essences

weave together, yet Day's soul slips further with each strand, vapor unraveling in the wind.

"We're losing him, Rosie," Farron whispers.

"No." I reach out and clasp Farron's hand. "He's staying with us. Do you hear me, Day? You're staying with us."

Strand over strand, Farron's warmth, my light, Day's misty blue, all twined with our glowing bonds. Again and again and again.

Black dots the edges of my vision. Sweat beads my forehead. But we're almost there, at the end of our tie. I can't tell where one of us ends and the others begin.

"Ready?" I whisper.

Farron's lip trembles, and he nods.

I let the veil drop. A gasp escapes me as I fall back to reality. Dayton lies beneath us.

With shaking fingers, I smooth the hair from his brow and watch his chest, willing it to move. Castletree is silent. All the princes' eyes are on me. My mother and father hover close. And behind them, Astrid, Marigold, and the rest of the staff watch us. I hadn't even heard them come in.

My gaze falls to Dayton, and I swallow the fear rising in my chest. He hasn't stirred.

"Please, Day," I choke out. "*Please.*"

Farron grasps his hand, tears staining his cheeks.

Then—

Dayton gasps. His eyes flutter open, and he's breathing. He's *breathing.*

He gazes at me, then Farron, and then the rest of Castletree. "Why's everyone looking at me? Just a little surface wound."

Farron's crying now, shoulders shaking with it. "Hardly the time for jokes."

"Jokes?" With a grunt, Dayton heaves himself up. "What jokes? I told you I'd always come back to you. I meant it, Fare."

One hand on Farron's neck, Dayton drags him in and kisses him, fierce and trembling.

And it's like I can see the life return to him, the color in his cheeks, the strength in his arms. Life, woven between all of us.

He pulls away from Farron and turns to me, looks me up and down with those teal eyes, and gives a shy smile. "Just when I think I've figured out all your tricks, Blossom."

I touch the side of his face. "This is a new one, Day. I sort of bound the three of us together. Forever."

"Hmm, forever with you two?" He smirks. "I can live with that, preferably for a long time."

Then he kisses me, soft and slow and golden.

64

Rosalina

The wooden stairs are slick as tree bark beneath my bare feet as I ascend the winding staircase up to the High Tower. It's deep into the night, and the castle is quiet besides the soft swish of my dressing gown.

I'd been unable to sleep, tossing and turning alone in my bed. Farron and Dayton are escorting Dom to Autumn where Billy's body will be laid to rest. Kel, Caspian, and Ezryn had all said they'd come to bed soon, but I'd heard them in the dining hall, laughing and reminiscing like three old friends in a bar.

Reuniting with my friends was sweeter than even walking the familiar halls or eating the delicious food here. Seeing Astrid for the first time since I broke my mate bond with Kel, freed from her curse, filled my heart until it was overflowing. They're all free, everyone in Castletree.

My mother faded into sleep after we brought Dayton back, and Papa carried her himself to the medical ward. Last I saw them, she was sleeping peacefully, looking like a princess from a fairy tale, while Papa sat vigil at her side.

Even the staff have settled down. Our return has sent them all into a fit. I'm not sure any of them recognize my mother, having been too young to have served during her reign, but Marigold couldn't take her eyes off her. Thankfully, she seemed distracted by her newest charge: Heidigog. I asked her and Astrid to take the little goblin under their wing. I'd overheard Heidigog going off about the bloomies in the Spring Wing, so her memories must have returned after we broke the crystals, as have mine.

The moonlight drifting through the slanted windows reflects off my ring. Kel's vows sing through my mind, and I can practically smell the cranberry and fir boughs from the wreaths that decorated our arch.

For now, we're safe. We're home.

Yet I could not sleep. Just like that fateful night after the winter solstice ball when I felt called to the High Tower, I feel a similar tug. I picture myself looking something of a ghost, white nightgown wafting in the breeze that sneaks through the windows, drifting up the stairs, drawn by a secret purpose.

I crack open the door and step into the circular room at the top of the High Tower. It's cool up here. Golden briars flush with flowers surround four blooming roses: dark blue, pink, turquoise, and orange. They have never looked so beautiful—

There's someone standing in the middle of the room, amid the roses. She could be my ghost's twin: long waves of dark hair, brown eyes, white nightgown, bare feet. Except she feels different.

Power rolls off her like the warmth of the sun as it breaks through the clouds: radiant, warm, and very, very ancient.

My mother.

I try to take her in, to truly soak in the fact that she's here before me. But even though I know she's real, it's like looking at a painting in a museum I don't comprehend the meaning behind.

Who is she?

Aurelia? Anya? A queen, an anthropologist, a wife, a leader, a coward, a deserter?

A mother?

Questions so endless I could fill a book with them have tumbled through my mind all the years I've been alive—so many things I wish to ask her, to understand about her life. But now that she's right before me, my throat is tight.

"Hi," I whisper. The word feels like an enormous feat.

"Hi," she whispers back.

"You're supposed to be in the medical ward resting."

She shrugs. The creator of the Enchanted Vale, *shrugging*. "I woke up."

"Where's Papa?"

"He fell asleep. I'm sure he'll find me here soon enough."

My brain doesn't seem capable of any more words, so I attempt a smile, then knot my hands in my nightgown, swishing it idly. Over two and a half decades of missing her, and now she's right here. Yet I still feel like my feet have sunken into the earth, and I'm staring up at the sky, trying to speak with a star.

Needing something to do, I shuffle over to the four colored roses. I bend down, pretending to examine them, though I watch her out of the corner of my eye. She opens her mouth, closes it. Knots her hands in her nightgown and swishes it.

"So, uh, do you—" I begin.

"Rosalina, I—" she says at the same time.

A beat of awkward silence follows, then we both laugh.

"The Good Lord in high leather boots," she mumbles under her breath. "I am a mess of a mother, aren't I?"

"Well, you didn't have much of an opportunity."

She wrings her hands together, gazes down at her feet. "I'm sorry about that. The bargain debacle with Sira. I'm sure you heard about it. One grand bungle after another, really."

I shrug. Guess shrugging is no more a princess thing than a queen thing, but I'm not sure what else to do.

"And the whole 'cursing your mates' bit. That was a tad impulsive on my part…" She chews on her bottom lip.

"I'm starting to learn impulsivity is kind of a you thing," I say, avoiding her gaze.

"You're probably more suited to this than I ever was." She lets out a sigh and waves her hand as if indicating the castle. "I get the impression you have your father's patience."

I stand and wipe my sweaty hands on my nightgown. "Well, as long as I don't snore like him, I'm okay with it."

She laughs, and I can't help but join in. My mother gives a large exhale and laces her fingers behind her neck, pulling on her hair. "Oh, Rosalina, there is so much I want to say to you. So much I want to *know* about you. And your sister."

My sister. Wrenley. Where is she? The raw, angry space in my heart cries out, *Who cares?* But when I close my eyes, draw in a shaky breath, I look at that space, that crying, aching empty space. It's saying *I care. I care.*

Because Wrenley is my sister. And I'm here with our parents and with Caspian, who was as good as a brother to her. And she's all by herself.

I wouldn't give up on them: Kel, Ez, Farron, Dayton, or Cas. And they never gave up on me.

What if I could show Wrenley there are people who care for her? That there's a family waiting for her to return? That no one needs to hide away in the darkness?

Isn't *that* what this is all for?

I stare into my mother's eyes, twin flame gazes burning as one. "We're going to see this through. The baron is gone. We have the rose and can control any of Sira's creations. The high rulers of Castletree have restored their power. And you and I are reunited. Let Sira come, bargain or no bargain. We'll face it."

My mother quirks her head. "You truly are suited to this." She glides toward me, and wherever her feet touch the ground, a rainbow of roses arises. My heart drums in my chest as I let my mother look me over, tracing a finger along the curve of my jaw, examining a piece of my hair. "May I..." she breathes. "May I hug you?"

I smile. "I thought you'd never ask."

For the first time in my remembrance, my mother embraces me. She smells of gardens and the pages of a new book and a beam of sunlight after a storm.

"My girls."

A warm voice echoes through the chamber. We both turn to look at Papa, leaning in the doorway, arms crossed, smile crooked on his face. Despite his salt-and-pepper hair mussed from sleep, clothes still dirty from the road, he looks positively dashing. And maybe it's because the four roses are blooming strong, because there's hope in Castletree's bones, but he radiates with life.

"George," my mother whispers.

"Anya."

"George!" She runs to him, this centuries-old, good-as-a-goddess queen, and leaps into his arms as if she were a girl.

And my father, who has traversed the world looking for her, holds her as if she were the greatest treasure to ever walk the earth. And to him—to us—she is.

I have flown on winged horses, swum with sirens, and created briars with gleaming golden roses.

But witnessing my father hold my mother for the first time in decades?

This is magic.

I slip out of the High Tower, letting my parents have this moment to themselves.

Tomorrow, we will decide the fate of the rose and thus the fate of the Vale. But tonight?

Tonight is for love.

Because *that* is what this is all for.

PART 4

Wicked Illusions

65

Caspian

GREAT BONFIRES OF YELLOW AND ORANGE CRACKLE, LIGHTING UP THE dark skies of the Autumn Realm. I watch from the tree line. Will there ever be a time when I don't observe everything from the sidelines, when I can finally be a part of life?

But like many things, such as figuring out who I am without my father's voice in my head, it'll take time.

For now, I'll honor Farron's brother from afar, listen to the cheerful music, the celebration in his name. I'll mourn him and the Autumn soldiers that fell to the Prince of Thorns.

Through it all, I feel a spark of hope. Farron and I are both free from the Green Flame in our own ways. And we'll use that freedom to help the Vale, to end my mother's tyranny for good.

But today, we celebrate Billagin in his home, to remember a life lost too young. The funeral crowd looks like a treasure hoard, all dressed in gold.

I feel her approach more than hear it. She did always have a way of moving unseen.

"Watching from afar as well?" I tilt my head to look up at Anya. She wears a simple gold dress with a hood.

She sits down next to me on a smooth rock. "I don't believe the Vale is ready for my return."

The world isn't ready or you aren't?

"Besides, Cas," she sighs as if reading my mind, "I'm tired."

I understand. Really, I do. As Sira's prisoner, her magic was siphoned for the last few decades. She spent all that time in the dark, never knowing the fate of her husband or her eldest daughter and having to watch Sira manipulate her youngest.

No, the queen has every right to feel bone-deep weariness, and yet…

"I don't think we have the luxury of being tired," I say. "Not yet."

She gives me a sidelong glance. "Unfortunately, you're right."

I run my hands over the moonstone locket that still dangles from my chest. "Do you want this back? You made it for George, didn't you?"

"Oh, I didn't know who it was for when we first forged it," Anya says. "I didn't think there was a mate out there for me. But fate never works how you imagine. My daughter gave this to you, so keep it. I thought you looked quite striking in that armor."

I roll my eyes and let the locket fall back to my chest. "Come on. You were half-dead. You didn't see anything."

She pokes me in the cheek, somehow finding a smile. "Are you calling me weak, princeling? I'll have you know, this magic almost brought an entire being from another world here."

"Far too powerful for your own good," I chuckle. Because damn, if I don't know the feeling. Lightly, I touch the golden bracelet at my wrist. "And this gift...the briars. I'll return it if you want. A lot of terrible things have been wrought with this magic."

She closes her hand over mine and the bracelet. "A lot of good as well. You're keeping Castletree alive and standing. It'll be a while yet before my magic returns to what it once was and you can release your briars."

"Even in the depths of the Green Flame's power, I never let Castletree fall," I say. "Maybe the Prince of Thorns longed to rule there, or perhaps there was always a part of me fighting to keep it standing."

"Well, it was quite smart of me to gift that to you. Without your magic, without your thorns keeping Castletree alive, all the magic in the Vale would be lost and..." Anya looks back to the festivities. "So would my heart."

I follow her gaze toward the celebration where George sits next to Dominic. George coaxes a smile out of the young fae, then throws an arm around him. What are they speaking of? Happy moments of his brother, or maybe just a silly joke?

"I always knew George would be a good father," Anya says.

Rosalina has mentioned how he wasn't always there for her. But when he was present, he was filled with love.

More love than my own father or mother ever gave me.

"How did you know?" I ask.

"Well," she says and gives me a smirk, "I saw how he was with you."

I gaze into the faraway flames until my vision turns blurry.

I can't remember the exact moment, but it was over a century ago when I packed all my worldly possessions in a bag—a cloak and a few of my favorite books—and stole off into the night. It had probably been after one of my mother's speeches about how one day I'd rule the Vale. Or maybe it was after the first time she brought me to meet my father. Regardless, I'd studied maps of the Below for weeks until I was confident I could find a path to the surface.

The tunnels were so twisted that I was half-starving and delirious by the time I felt a wind on my face. Of course, the path I'd found had led to the coldest, most barren part of the Vale. My journey would have ended right there, my body turned to a statue of ice, had I not run into another boy, not much older than me.

He had sapphire eyes and white hair as wild as the blustering storm. He gave me a cake of oats and dried berries bound with honey. He showed me a secret path, a way into the human realm.

And when I left, I realized there was now one thing in the Enchanted Vale I'd miss.

Of course, having never been out of the Below, I had no idea my body would start turning to rot in only a few months. Or how hard it was to be a child among humans. But what was there to care about? I had left behind the evil destiny my mother so desperately craved for me.

I also didn't realize how bound I still was to the Vale, how I was but a moth to the flame of our world's magic. That's what the queen was—a bursting signal fire whose energy drew me to Egypt.

And that's how I crossed paths with the anthropologist Anya and the archaeologist George.

I often wonder...without my adventure in the human realm, if I'd never gotten lost in the desert storm and known the love of two explorers, would I be different? Would Sira's claws have hooked me deeper if I hadn't had the chance to see what real love looked like?

Sighing, I dig in my cloak. "Let me give this back to you at least. It was a gift for you."

Anya holds out her palm. In it, I drop a small wooden camel. "Cleo," she says, running a hand over the figure.

"Thank you," I say, tilting my gaze from the flames to the stars. "She led me out of the storm one last time. And now I know how to shape my magic."

66

Farron

HERE AGAIN. STARING AT THE ALDER TREE, WONDERING HOW I COULD have gotten so many things wrong.

The funeral attendees have moved into Keep Oakheart. I'm alone in the grove. The surrounding trees, thick with orange and red leaves, bow in the breeze, filling the air with the smell of maple. The moon casts a radiant glow over the alder tree, making it appear more of a statue than a living thing. I swear I can see a face within the bark, watching me. Appraising.

I'm not sure what I'm doing here. My mother won't suddenly emerge from the trunk, and neither will Billy. They're gone from this realm forever, and I was the last one to hold their life threads.

It feels like such a burden and a blessing all at once.

I want to fall to my knees and beg for forgiveness. From whom? The tree?

Maybe I'll fall to my knees and scream at the moon, howling with rage and sorrow instead. But that seems an insult to all those I've hurt. What good is my grief to them?

They're gone. And I'm…

I don't even know what I am.

A rustle sounds in my peripheral, and I turn. Something large moves through the dark.

His name forms on my lips, but I don't speak it, afraid it will scare him away.

Thrand ambles toward me, his massive body lit up by moonlight as he steps out of the tree cover. Despite his size, there's a grace to him, his hooves barely disturbing the fallen leaves, antlers silhouetted by the sky's glow.

Not even a breath escapes me as he approaches and stops only a few feet away from me. Finally, I whisper, "Hello, old friend."

Thrand stares at me with those glistening black eyes. As always, I feel like he can see right through me.

To what?

I don't know who I am anymore.

There's nothing inside me.

Not even darkness. Just a gaping, empty hole that goes on and on and on.

Like the one Billy nearly fell into.

It's not caused by grief, this hole. Maybe I remember it because of the grief, but it's lived inside me for as long as I can remember. I've tried to fill it with research and obsession over the curse and finally with the Green Flame.

Take all that away and what am I?

Empty.

I close my eyes. It's not fair of me to ask anything of him. But with my fingers trembling, I extend a hand.

Nothing greets my touch. But there was no reason to expect differently. I doubt my elk remembers me anymore after all the versions of me I've cycled through.

Then—there's the press of coarse fur against my palm. I blink open my eyes.

Thrand nuzzles against my hand, then takes a lumbering step forward and bumps my shoulder.

A choked laugh escapes me. "Thrand..." I rub his head, then scratch the spot beside his ears that he loves. He licks my cheek with a rough, sandpapery tongue, then snorts.

"You don't like the beard, eh?" I chuckle. "Fine. I'll shave it."

Sighing, I lean against him. *So you remember me. Even with this emptiness.*

My gaze drifts upward, over Thrand's antlers and through the branches of the alder tree to the night sky beyond.

Maybe it's not a hole inside me. Maybe it's a cloudy sky. One I can explore. And eventually...blow the clouds away.

I'm not the person I was the last time I visited this alder tree. And I'll be different the next time I visit too. I guess I get to choose who I am from here on out.

But the question is: Who do I want to be?

A leaf floats down in front of me, bright yellow, edges curling on the side. *Who do you want me to be, Billy?*

I know what he'd say. He'd look up at me, a sneaky grin on his face, and tell me with all the confidence of someone who lives fully in the moment, "Don't ask me, dummy! How should I know?"

A breath escapes me. Great question.

Who will I be? A coward, a leader, a tyrant, a pacifist? A murderer, a savior? A beast, a ruler? A brother, a son?

I have been all these things. They make up the vast emptiness—no, the sky—that is me.

Closing my eyes, I decide to look at it. This sky within me.

And it's not so dark. In fact, some of the clouds are already starting to drift away. And all the facets of me start to twinkle. Stars making up the light map of my life.

They shine like the constellations of freckles across Billy's face.

"You're still protecting me, little brother," I say. Then I wrap an arm around Thrand's thick neck and walk with him toward the keep, where the warm glow of Autumn's hearths calls me home.

67

Dayton

Giving a yawn, I stretch, my arms knocking Rosie and Fare on either side of me. Pale light streams in from beneath the curtain. It must be very early morning.

Fuck, I love this giant-ass bed. It's been a crazy few days since we made it out of the Below. All our focus went to supporting Farron and his family as we prepared for the funeral. The day after was quiet. Mostly, we all went our own ways with our own reflections.

But last night, all six of us ended up in here, each staggering in at different hours. There are so many decisions and plans to be made. But for this moment? I'm just going to enjoy being surrounded by my family.

Farron gives a huge yawn and throws an arm over my waist, letting his cheek rest on my chest. I tug him in closer.

Farron, High Prince of Autumn. My mate.

The first time we made love after that discovery was something I'll never forget. Stars, the memory of me contained in the orb of ancestors will boast about it for centuries to come.

He's a part of my soul now, the life that keeps my heart beating and the blood pumping through my veins. A soft whimper sounds on my other side, and Rosalina curls in, her leg slinging over mine.

And so is she.

My mates, my life in every sense of the word. Could a man ask for anything more?

Movement rocks the mattress as someone turns over. Ezryn, on the left edge of the bed, hooks himself around Rosie's waist. On the right side, Cas shuffles, subsequently elbowing Farron and nearly pushing Kel off. Kel gives a rumbling groan and pulls the blankets over his face.

Well, I could ask for brothers, for friends I'd trust with my life.

I truly am blessed, far beyond my magic.

"What you thinking about, Day?" Farron blinks up at me.

"How lucky I am to be here with all of you," I reply. And I feel it. *Life.* Safely tucked between my mates, the soft press of silken sheets on my skin, the warm touch of the morning sun…

"We're so lucky to be with you," Rosalina says, her voice welcome as a sunrise. She pushes a strand of hair out of my face and kisses the corner of my mouth.

Her lips linger a beat too long. Then another.

A spark flickers in my chest.

Ezryn hums low in his throat. "It's too early," he says lazily, but his hand slides beneath the sheets, dragging across Rosie's waist. She arches, breath catching.

Farron grins, his palm splayed over my stomach. "Too early for what?"

On the far side of the bed, Keldarion groans dramatically. "If you lot start without me again, and I wake up with Rosie over me…"

Cas sits up and runs a hand in Keldarion's snow-white hair. "You liked that."

"And I'm pretty good at not being enthralled anymore." Rosalina presses on my chest to look over at them.

"Shall we test it?" Caspian raises a brow.

Ezryn's pillow hits him square in the face. "I swear to all the gods, if you ruin this bed with your little thorns—"

A briar snakes up from the ground and wraps around Ezryn's bare forearm. "My briars are anything but little, Ez," Cas purrs. "Rosie's had them inside her. You want to see if you can take it like our girl can?"

Ezryn growls and breaks free of the briar, but I meet the Prince of Thorns's gaze.

The corner of his wicked mouth raises. "Or you, sea puppy?"

I give a long chuckle. "There are some things even I'm not brave enough for."

"What if *I* was controlling the briars?" Rosalina says, then erupts into a fit of giggles.

I catch her around the waist and drag her away from Ezryn and pull her onto my lap. "All I'm hearing is our little Rose and Thorn are feeling very playful this morning. And I think that should be rewarded."

The air shifts, tension growing.

Rosie drops her lips to my neck, and Farron's fingers slip lower on my stomach.

Ezryn sits up to whisper in Rosie's ear. "Then let's make this morning memorable for our girl."

68

Caspian

I COULD GET USED TO MORNINGS LIKE THIS.

The kind where I don't wake up choking on flame. Where no one's bleeding out, making plans to kill me, or deciding what torture I'll get for stepping out of line.

The kind where I wake up tangled in limbs, Kel's arms wrapped around my waist, my face buried in Fare's hair that smells like cinnamon and apples.

Rosalina's laughter rings in the air, and I can't stop staring at her, tucked on Dayton's lap, mouth against his neck, cheeks flushed.

I shift on the mattress, still half-hard from the dream I was having. Farron's hand is under the sheet now, probably feeling up Dayton. Lucky man. And Ezryn is watching Rosie like he wants to paint every part of her with that tongue of his.

And me? I'm just grateful.

Grateful that the flames are quiet. Grateful that when I reach for my power, it listens. That when I look at my family, I feel the truest version of myself I've ever been.

"You're smiling," Kel says beside me, voice still hoarse with sleep. His hair is a mess and his arms are crossed, but he's watching me.

"I know. It's gross, isn't it?" I lean in, pressing my shoulder to his. "Must be the afterglow of not being an emotionally repressed monster."

He huffs a laugh but doesn't move away.

I glance across the bed again, at Rosie, at Dayton, at Farron's hand, which is definitely not still.

My body hums. I want in.

I crawl closer, the sheet dragging low on my hips. "Well, if we're starting the morning with a bang," I murmur, "I'd hate to be left out."

Rosalina glances at me, eyes heavy-lidded, lips slick from whatever she's done to Day's throat. "And what do you want, Caspian?"

"Everything," I say. "But I'll start with you."

Her breath catches. Farron growls low. Ezryn's grip tenses on her waist. Kel shifts behind me, and the air tightens with promise.

Rosalina watches me with those big, dreamy eyes, lips parted. I crawl closer, leaning over Farron and bracing myself with a hand on Dayton's thigh. I cup her face.

"Tell me to stop," I whisper, brushing my thumb across her bottom lip.

She doesn't.

Instead, she leans forward and kisses me.

Soft at first. Testing. Then she presses deeper, her fingers tangling in my hair, pulling me in. Her mouth opens against mine, and gods, I sink into her like I've been starving. Like she's sunlight and honey and everything I never thought I'd be allowed to touch again.

When we break apart, breathless, I don't move far. I press my forehead to hers.

Dayton lets out a low, amused hum. "You're going to make Farron jealous."

I look below me. There's Autumn's golden prince, flushed and biting his lip like he wants to say something but isn't sure he should.

My heart skips. Because I want him too.

I turn to Dayton and Rosalina. "May I kiss your mate?"

Rosie doesn't even blink. "Yes."

Dayton's smile is lazy, but there's a fire in his stare. "If he'll allow it."

I shift again, crawling back until I'm facing Farron. He sits up, breath shallow, his gaze darting from my mouth to my hands to my eyes.

"You sure?" I ask.

"I'm sure," he says, barely above a whisper.

I hold his face, warm and familiar. He's shaved his beard and looks much more like the prince I first met all those years ago. The one I always thought had such an adorable charm.

So I kiss him.

It's different from kissing Rosie. Where she melts, Farron meets me. He pushes back, lips parting, hand sliding to my waist. It's warmth and hunger and a flicker of something wild. His fingers knot in my hair, and he groans against my mouth, tugging me in like he's waited a long time for this.

And maybe he has.

The kiss deepens, slow and scorching. It's his own heat, not that of the Baron, and damn if that isn't a powerful thing.

When we part, I drag my tongue along his jaw. "You're delicious, like cinnamon and pumpkins."

Farron gives a breathless laugh, pulling me in until we're nose-to-nose. "And that's just my lips."

Rosie sighs and Dayton murmurs something profane. Ezryn shifts closer. The bed moves behind me, a low growl vibrating against my spine.

A second later, I'm dragged backward by the waist, a strong arm yanking me flush against a very familiar chest.

"Mine," Kel mutters, voice rough with sleep and something else entirely. His hand sprawls across my stomach, fingers digging in like he's afraid I'll vanish if he lets go.

I smirk, not turning around yet. "Jealous?"

"You're crawling all over the bed kissing everyone but me," he grits out. "Of course I'm jealous."

His hand trails lower, sliding over my bare skin with maddening slowness. Mapping every inch of me he missed in the months we were apart.

And fuck, I let him. I crave his touch.

"Thought you were too tired," I murmur, tilting my head back enough to feel his breath on my neck. My long hair sprawls over his shoulder.

His lips find my throat, kissing the skin right beneath my ear. "I'll never be too tired for you."

His hand drags up my chest, splaying wide across my heart

before slipping down again. The other arm tightens around my waist, pulling me flush to his hips. And gods, he's already hard.

"You kissed Rosie like you worship her," he whispers. "You kissed Farron like you've dreamed of it for years."

His touch slips lower. Lower.

"What about me, Cas? How will you kiss me?"

I turn my head and meet his eyes, frost-blue and burning with desire.

"You?" I whisper. *I'll kiss you like I love you.*

His mouth crashes against mine before I can say another word.

It's fierce and hungry, like he needs to prove I'm his. The kiss is teeth and tongue and breathless groans, his hands moving over me like they can't decide where to land.

And maybe they don't need to decide.

They land everywhere.

Over my ribs. Down my thighs. Palming my ass and yanking me tighter against him until there's no space, no breath, no room for anyone else but him.

I can barely think. Barely breathe.

He breaks the kiss, panting against my lips. "Next time you kiss someone else," he rasps, "I expect to be invited."

I grin, biting down on his bottom lip. "Next time, you'll be first."

He growls and pushes me beneath him in one smooth motion, pressing down until I feel every inch of him.

"Damn right I will."

Kel plants his hands on either side of my head, his body a wall of heat and muscle and need. The ice in his veins might be cold, but against me, he burns.

"You going to let me take my time with you?" he asks.

I arch up, wrapping my legs around his waist. "You're already taking it, aren't you?"

His mouth finds mine again. Rougher. Like he's trying to carve himself into me from the inside out. His hips grind against me, slow and deliberate, his hand sliding up my chest, over my ribs, then down, down, until he throws off my pants and grips my cock. It's so hard now.

I gasp, my back bowing. "Fuck, Kel—"

"I want to see you fall apart," he mutters against my skin. "Do you want everyone to witness how you come?"

Gods, I do.

He grips a hand along my thigh and lifts my hips. I feel the tip of his cock at my entrance. Are the others watching us? I don't know. I can't look away from his gaze.

But even through the haze of pleasure, I catch it.

Movement.

Soft sounds. Breathless ones.

I turn my head to see Rosie's eyes fluttering closed, Ezryn's hand cradling her jaw as he kisses her. His body is curved protectively around hers, fingers tracing a slow path beneath her sleeping gown. He meets my gaze.

"Alright, Prince of Thorns, I'll give it to you," Ezryn growls, collaring Rosie's throat with his massive hand. "You do look pretty when you're about to be fucked."

Fuck the High Prince of Spring. If he makes me come early, I'll kill him. "Pretty enough to kiss?"

He ignores me, tongue halfway down Rosie's throat. Beside

them, Farron has disappeared. He's under the covers now, curled between Dayton's legs. Dayton's head is tossed back, but he's watching me, mouth open in a soundless moan as his fingers twist in the sheets. His other hand reaches for Rosie, finds her thigh, squeezes.

It's a mess of limbs and mouths, all of us out of control.

Kel pulls my focus with a low sound. He slides inside me with one smooth, devastating thrust.

I gasp, sharp and involuntary, and he stills, just for a second, watching me with those storm-blue eyes.

"Mine," he whispers again, voice cracking with something deeper than lust. "Always mine."

"Yours," I breathe, dizzy with it. "Fuck, Kel, I'm yours."

He moves, really moves, each thrust sending sparks shooting up my spine, grounding me even as the world spins. My nails dig into his back, my breath shattering against his shoulder. I give myself over to him, to the rhythm of his body against mine. He knows how to touch me from all our years together. The bed creaks beneath us, sheets twisting as Kel drives me higher, faster, until my vision blurs.

The bed rocks. Ezryn moans. Dayton gasps.

But all I can think about is the way Kel's kissing my collarbone like he's sorry for every time he ever hurt me. The way he grips my hip like I'm the only anchor he has left in the world.

And the way I love him for it.

Kel's rhythm deepens, rougher now, more purposeful. Each thrust strikes a chord in me I didn't know I had, unraveling me bit by bit. My body arches, chasing him, needing him.

"Fuck, Kel—" I gasp.

I'm close. So close. My perception narrows to the places our bodies meet, to the sound of his breath in my ear as he desperately whispers my name.

He lifts his head, brow slick with sweat, hair a tangle. His voice cuts through the haze, sharp and low.

"Rosalina. Here. Now."

I barely have time to blink before she moves. Flushed from Ezryn's touch, dazed and beautiful, she slips across the sheets. Unfortunately, still clothed in that nightdress.

Kel doesn't stop moving inside me. If anything, he fucks me harder. But he reaches out, grabs Rosie by the hair, and pulls her in for a brutal, claiming kiss.

She whimpers, body trembling. "Yes, Kel?"

"Lips down here," Kel growls, dragging her head with gentle force, guiding her mouth lower. "He's close."

She doesn't hesitate.

Rosie slides between us, eyes flicking up to meet mine, and I swear the moment her lips close around my cock, soft, warm, perfect, I shatter.

It's too much.

I can't last much longer.

Rosie's taking me in her mouth, her tongue circling as she hums softly. Kel's hand is fisted in her hair, holding her in place, knowing she's his to command and mine to worship.

I come with a broken, ragged cry, Rosie's name on my lips, Kel's name on my tongue, my whole body convulsing as white-hot pleasure explodes through me like lightning splitting the sky.

Kel kisses the side of my face. "That's it," he whispers. "Let go, Cas. Let us have you."

And I do.

I give them everything.

Rosalina pulls off me, pearly white coating her lips.

What will happen with the bargain?

Ezryn's watching her like a hawk to see if any briars will pop up through his perfect bed, but just as the last time she made me come here, she's too close to Kel for that.

A slight haziness clouds her vision, and she shakes her head. "I told you I'm getting better at resisting it."

I look at the frosted bracelet on my wrist. I'll never fall out of love with him. I'll have this bargain for the rest of my life. But we'll find a way to make it work.

I'm still trembling, when Kel kisses my temple, slowly moving inside me. His deep, deliberate thrusts cause me to whimper from the overstimulation and the craving for more all at once.

"You thought I was done?" he murmurs against my throat, biting the skin. "Not even close."

Rosalina licks her lips, hand running along my sweat-soaked stomach. "You can take it, lover."

I groan, touching her neck, fingers sliding down to her breast. My hips lift to meet every punishing stroke. I'm wrung out, but fuck, he makes me feel alive, like the world could collapse around us and I'd still be here, shaking in his arms, begging for more.

I'm moaning again when Dayton gives a sudden, gasping cry, his hips bucking, body arching off the bed.

Farron's head emerges from beneath the covers a second later, smug and flushed, his mouth shining.

Dayton drapes an arm over his eyes and laughs breathlessly.

"Gods. Remind me to forget everything I ever said about hating to get up early."

My cock is hard again, pulsing, muscles clenching with each stroke. "Ruin me the way no one else can."

Kel loses it.

His rhythm falters. His grip tightens. He buries his face in my neck with a raw groan and shatters inside me. I hold him through it, nails dragging down his back, whispering his name.

"Cas," he breathes. "You feel so good."

The room is thick with heat and breath and the gentle shifting of bodies. Sheets tangled. Skin slick.

One by one, every gaze turns to her.

Rosalina.

Lying beside me, her hair a mess of curls. Her chest rises and falls in steady anticipation. Ezryn's eyes are locked on her. Dayton reaches to brush her knee. Farron turns his whole body toward hers.

All of us are looking at her.

Wanting.

"Well, Princess," I say and drag my lips to her ear. "Tell us all. What do you desire?"

69

Rosalina

The world is quiet in that sharp, electric way it gets before a storm.

Bodies surround me, warm, sweat-slick, rippling with muscle. I can still taste Caspian on my tongue, feel the hum of Ezryn's touch on my skin, the ghost of Dayton's moan echoing in my bones. Farron's lips are swollen. Kel's chest heaves with the remnants of release.

And every single one of them is looking at me.

Caspian's mouth is at my ear, his voice low and reverent. "Well, Princess," he says, dragging a kiss along the shell of it, "tell us all. What do you desire?"

A shiver runs down my spine.

Because they'll give it to me, whatever I ask. Because in this bed, at this moment, I am theirs. And they are mine.

I take a breath. My fingers curl into the sheets—I need to anchor myself against the storm I'm about to summon.

"Everything," I whisper.

Ezryn's hands form fists. Farron makes a sound low in his throat. Dayton sits up, eyes dark, hungry.

"I want all of you," I say, louder now. "At once."

Kel groans behind me, already leaning forward over Cas, his teeth at the back of my neck.

"I've been good. Haven't I?"

"You're always perfect," Ezryn says, voice like velvet.

"So let us worship you properly," Farron adds.

And just like that, the storm breaks.

"Let's start," Keldarion says. He reaches around Caspian and grips my waist, pulling me so I'm cradled between him and Cas. Ezryn moves to the end of the bed. He parts my thighs, his hand warm and deliberate as it glides up my leg.

"You helped Cas," Ezryn murmurs, stroking slow circles against me. "But now it's our turn to help you."

Dayton moves closer and mouths at my breast, tongue swirling over the fabric, teasing over a nipple. Caspian presses kisses along my shoulder. And Ezryn, controlled and precise, slides his hand under my dress and pushes two fingers inside me.

My head falls back against Kel's chest with a moan, body arching as the pleasure rolls through me. "Please—"

"Shush," Kel says in my ear. "Take it, Rose. You asked for everything. Let us give it."

Ezryn's mouth finds my inner thigh, kissing beside where his fingers work me open. He looks up at me through thick lashes, his lips so close, his breath like wind through the trees. The stubble of his cheek rubs against my sensitive skin.

"She's shaking," Farron breathes. "Such a good girl."

Dayton lowers himself between my legs and replaces Ezryn's fingers with his tongue. Damn, it feels so wonderful. I've been so turned on all morning, watching how roughly Kel took Cas, Dayton coming in Farron's mouth, and Ezryn's teasing touch all over my body.

The world explodes in sensation, Dayton's tongue, Ezryn's hands, Caspian's mouth at my neck, Farron whispering praises against my skin, and Kel holding me together like I'll break if he lets go.

I cry out, the pleasure ripping through me like lightning, my thighs trembling, my hips bucking. And still, when it's over, when I'm panting and limp, blinking through the aftershocks, I know it's only begun.

Because now their eyes are all on me again.

Waiting.

And I want more.

They descend upon me, hands roaming, lips brushing, bodies crowding close.

Dayton runs his fingers along the hem of my nightdress. The fabric clings to my skin, damp with sweat and pleasure, thin enough that every peak and curve is visible.

"She's still clothed?" Caspian teases. "What an oversight."

"An offense, really," Farron agrees, sliding his hands up my calves with reverence. "We should be punished."

Kel hums low, his hand stroking over my hip. "Take it off her."

Dayton lifts the nightdress. He grazes my thighs, my stomach, my ribs, and I shiver as the fabric peels away inch by inch.

Caspian helps from behind, pulling it up over my arms as Farron presses soft kisses along the path it reveals. When the dress slips over my head, they all pause.

Staring.

Their gazes roam over every inch of me, bared, glowing in the morning light filtering between the curtain and through the cherry blossom tree. Petals drift through the air, catching in my hair, and I feel like something out of a myth. A goddess unwrapped.

Dayton leans over Cas and Farron to press a kiss between my breasts. "So damn beautiful."

Farron trails his tongue along my side, teeth grazing my ribs. "Can we taste all of her now?"

But before I can answer, Caspian flashes a wicked grin at Ezryn.

"What about you, stoic prince of restraint? Are you content watching from down there forever, or are you working up the courage to give me a welcome home kiss?"

Ezryn raises a brow, unimpressed. "You want a kiss, Caspian?"

"Well, it's only polite." Caspian shrugs, but he's already shifting down the bed toward him, mischief in every line of his body. "Unless you're scared you'll fall in love."

"Please," Ezryn says, but he leans forward anyway, bridging the distance.

Caspian meets him halfway.

Ezryn holds his gaze, cool and unreadable, but stops moving closer. "I think you've had enough kisses for one morning."

Caspian lets out a low laugh and throws an arm around my waist instead. "Can't blame me for trying." He shifts his focus to Dayton. "I really want to win our bet."

Dayton's brows raise as if he's remembering something. "Right, fuck. I should have asked Kel for a kiss on my deathbed. Aren't you so delighted by my presence that you'd give me a little smooch, mighty Prince of Winter?"

Caspian glares. "Don't you dare, Kel."

Keldarion rolls his eyes.

"Ah well, I suppose you'll do, Blossom." Dayton's hand slides between my legs again.

"I'll do?" I raise a brow. "For that, you're going to watch me while not touching yourself at all."

Two golden briars rear from behind the bed and clasp my Summer Prince's wrists, holding them over his head. Instead of looking disturbed, a grin appears on his face, and his thick cock stands to attention. "Do I get to choose who touches you next?"

"I suppose." I can't help but grin back at him.

"I want Farron and Cas to fuck you at the same time." Dayton's smile turns devious. "In the same hole."

70

Farron

Every part of me ignites at the suggestion.

My mate knows me, down to the deepest desires. And my desire right now is to be here, with all the people I love, seeking our pleasure together.

I turn to Caspian and find he's already looking at me, eyes blazing. Kel runs his hands through Cas's hair. "You'll fill her so well." He settles against the headboard next to Dayton.

Ezryn's also watching. As he crawls up the bed, he grabs Rosalina's face and kisses her. "You're going to be a good girl."

He doesn't phrase it as a question but as a command, and she mumbles a part moan, part sigh against his lips.

"Farron," Ezryn says, "lie back on the bed."

I do, my cock already hard with anticipation.

"Alright, Rosalina, now get on all fours over Farron," Ezryn instructs, all dominance as he orders us into position.

She nods, climbing over my lap. Her breasts swing in my face, and I can't help but arch my neck and capture a sweet pink nipple, sucking it between my lips.

"Farron," she moans, sinking her body against mine. Her soft curves brush my abs.

"Inside her," Ezryn says.

I look up at my perfect woman, my mate. Then I brace a hand on her hips and slide into her. We both moan, but it's Dayton who lets out the deepest groan, arching his back, cock straining.

"Yes, I'm the mastermind, and Ez is the puppeteer." Dayton smirks.

Ezryn shakes his head and nods toward Cas. "Here."

Caspian's brows shoot up, and he crawls closer. "Whatever you say, Da—"

"Don't." Ezryn shoots him a glare. "Unless you want to get smacked."

"We'll save that for later," Cas says.

Rosalina is still above me, and I fight the urge to pulse inside her. Instead, I relish the sensation of her warmth surrounding me.

Caspian kneels behind Rosie, then looks back at Ez. "Here?"

"Lower," Ezryn says.

Caspian rests his hands on Rosalina's hips. "Here?"

"Too low."

Caspian gives a sigh and adjusts himself again. "Here, oh great Spring Prince?"

Ezryn grabs Caspian on his bare hips and lowers him an inch. "*Here*."

Caspian grins, then arches his back, ass brushing Ezryn's fully clothed body.

"You little shit," Ezryn growls.

"I couldn't figure it out without you," Caspian purrs.

"Come on, Cas." Rosalina cranes her neck. "I *need* you inside me."

"Give the woman what she wants." From the top of the bed, Kel leisurely strokes his cock.

"Anything for my princess," Cas says and looks past her straight at me. "And my prince."

Fuck, he's beautiful, eyes flashing like a violet storm. I can't stop staring at him as he enters our mate. Can't stop staring at him as I feel every inch of his cock slide against my own.

"Oh my god," Rosalina whimpers, arms trembling as she braces against my shoulder. "Both of you feel so—"

"Nice and slow, Flower," Caspian says soothingly. "Just get used to us."

I slam my head back into the pillow, needing the words to calm myself, needing to free myself from his entrapping gaze. Stars, the feeling—my cock pinned between his and the warmth of her inner walls.

"You still with us, Fare?" Dayton asks.

"Huh? Yeah," I gasp, twisting to look at him. He's watching with an entrapped gaze of his own. Cock untouched and dripping precum, briars tight around his wrists… Fuck, that's hot too. "We're going to give you a good show, baby."

"You better."

Rosie starts to move, showing us she's ready. Cas braces himself on her hip and pulses in and out. I start to piston my own hips. And stars, if I thought just feeling this was going to throw me over the edge, the friction of it all will send me to another universe.

The slide of his slick and rock-hard cock against mine, her wet, warm pussy embracing us both... "Fuck, you feel so good," I gasp.

Caspian's hair falls over his brow. Rosalina cries out, her own hair wild, and digs her nails into my shoulders.

"Yes, stars, yes," she moans.

"Slow down or you'll pop out," Ezryn commands.

Caspian obeys, slowing to an agonizing rhythm. Every part of him is an experience, from the ribbed veins to the slick head. "You feel so good against me, Fare."

"I think we can get deeper," I challenge, gazing at him from over Rosalina's shoulder.

He raises a brow. "Together?"

I nod.

At the same time, we drive into our mate, hitting deep against her walls, stretching her out in the most delicious way. She trembles, tears shining at the corners of her eyes.

"Yes, oh god," she whimpers.

I reach up and cup her face. "You're doing so well, sweetheart, taking both our cocks. Do you like being filled by us?"

She nods, and I pull her down to my lips, kissing her, tongue slipping inside her mouth. The angle spears our cocks deeper until her walls are pressing Cas's and my cocks so tight against each other, I think I might explode into pure bliss.

She is fire and silk and sunshine between us—and I will worship her like this until the stars burn out.

71

Rosalina

I've never felt this full.

Every nerve is alight, every breath shallow, and every thought—what little I can hold on to—is tangled in the overwhelming sensation of them.

Farron lies beneath me, his auburn hair fanned against the sheets, eyes glazed with pleasure. He grips my thighs, grounding me as I rock against him. He's deep, all burning Autumn heat and reverent touch, whispering my name like a prayer.

And goddamn…behind me is Caspian.

Caspian, kneeling, wild and wicked and unhinged, his hands braced on my hips as he thrusts into me from behind.

I can't describe it. The stretch. The pressure. The sensation of being claimed.

And the way they react to each other?

Devastating.

A low groan slips from Farron's lips as he grinds upward, Cas's thrust sending both of us spiraling.

"Fuck," Cas pants, voice ragged. "You both feel so good."

"Such a pretty cock," Farron bites out, his fingers digging into my thighs as his hips stutter. "In Rosie's pretty pussy."

The sound they make together, lost in me, nearly undoes me completely.

I try to speak, to moan, to beg them not to stop, but all I can manage is a broken whimper. My arms tremble, shoulders burning, but I can't move. Can't think. Not with the way they're filling me—grinding against each other inside me, drawing out every ounce of sensation I didn't know I had.

And all around us, the others watch.

Ezryn kneels at the edge of the bed, his jaw clenched. Dayton has drool running down the corner of his mouth, eyes locked on where we're joined. Keldarion is still, his hand tight at the base of his cock.

None of them touch me.

Not yet.

They watch. And god, I love it.

I love being open and taken, filled and treasured, loved and ruined in front of them.

For them.

I let my head fall back, caught between Caspian's wild rhythm and Farron's desperate thrusts, and I moan, raw and wrecked and shameless.

"More," I gasp. "Please. Don't stop."

Farron groans like the sound is dragging him to the edge. Caspian leans forward, his chest pressing against my spine, his lips grazing the shell of my ear.

"You feel so fucking perfect," he growls. "Tight and wet and ours. Taking everything we give you."

And I do. I feel perfect.

Because right now, in this moment, I belong to them. To all of them.

"She can take more." Dayton grins.

We all turn to him.

"Her ass and mouth are free." His smile widens. "I think Ez and Kel will know what to do."

Oh, that bastard. He's making me regret tying him up.

The room stills. Then Kel moves.

He prowls across the mattress, his muscles taut, eyes locked on me, on us. I feel Farron twitch inside me beneath the weight of that stare. Cas groans behind me, burying his face in my neck.

"Stars be damned," he breathes. "You are trying to kill me."

Caspian straightens and Kel kneels over me, one long leg on either side of my waist, his hand settling on my lower back. "You sure about this, Rose?" His voice is a low rumble.

Kel's massive cock in my ass? No, not sure at all. But being filled by my mates? That I'm sure about. I want everything they can give me. "Yes."

He doesn't need more.

I feel him line up, sharing space with Caspian, then there's the thick, deliberate press of him against my ass. My body tenses, anticipation crackling like lightning across my skin.

Slowly, Kel presses in.

I cry out, the stretch intense, burning and perfect and full. Caspian swears behind me, hips bucking instinctively.

"Fuck," Cas hisses. "Gods."

"Be quiet," Kel growls, voice low and feral against my back. "She's taking all of us like a goddess."

His hips roll, burying deeper—and I feel it. The unbelievable fullness. Kel in my ass, Caspian behind him, still thick inside my core, Farron hard and throbbing beneath me.

I can't move. Can't breathe. Can barely think.

"Shit," I gasp. "I'm so full."

"You're doing so well, sweetheart," Farron says, hands trembling on my thighs as he looks up at me, awestruck. "You're perfect like this."

Caspian moans, his hands tightening on Kel's hips. "Kel, your ass is brushing against my chest," he mutters. "Gods, it's such a perfect ass."

"Fuck!" Dayton calls, grinning. "You all look so damn hot."

"We fucking do," Caspian groans, thrusting shallowly. "Gods, we're going to break her."

Kel growls above me, trailing a finger up my spine to fist in my hair, pulling to arch my back more. "She can take it."

He thrusts again, deep and punishing, and I scream. Not in pain. In pure, overwhelming ecstasy.

Their bodies press in from all angles, hot and solid and relentless. Farron below me, Kel braced above me, legs on either side of my hips, and Caspian behind him, sharing my pussy with Farron. I'm nothing but sensation—lips parted, skin flushed, tears slipping down my cheeks from the intensity of it all.

Ezryn still watches from the foot of the bed, eyes like storms ready to break.

"You next, Ez," Dayton says, voice rough. "Let her choke on that bloom budding in your pants."

Kel growls possessively, stilling inside me. "You're going to come for us all, Rose."

And stars help me—

I will.

Kel thrusts into me again, deep and brutal, and the sound that tears from my throat isn't even human. Caspian groans behind me, gripping Kel's waist like a lifeline, while Farron moans beneath me, bucking his hips as he tries to keep pace.

Everywhere I look, every inch of my body is being touched, filled, claimed.

And then Ezryn moves, finally throwing off his pants.

Silent and sure, the Spring Prince kneels on the top of the bed by my head, his cock thick and flushed, already slick. His eyes meet mine, and he cups my jaw, tilting my face toward him.

"You're still sure?" he asks, voice low and steady.

I nod, unable to form words.

He leans forward, pressing a kiss to my forehead, and guides himself to my mouth.

And I take him.

Slowly at first—lips wrapping around him, tongue swirling along the tip. He groans, fingers tightening in my hair.

"You look like a queen," he whispers. "With all of us inside you. Taking everything. Giving everything."

I moan, and the vibration draws a sharp curse from his lips.

Behind me, Kel's rhythm deepens, his massive body pressing flush against mine as he drives in harder, his breath hot against the back of my neck.

"Fuck, Rose. So good, so perfect," he grits out, his thrusts growing more ragged.

Caspian groans with each stroke, grinding against me "She's going to ruin us."

"She already has," Farron breathes beneath me, placing kisses over my breasts.

My vision swims. My body trembles. But I've never felt more powerful.

I am a star being pulled into orbit, burning, breaking, becoming something new.

And then Dayton… My Day.

He's watching me from the edge of the bed, his gaze fixed on my lips sucking Ezryn's cock. His skin is flushed, his mouth parted in awe.

I let the briars fall away and reach out my hand. He rolls closer.

Even with my arms shaking, I curl my fingers around his length. He lets out a strangled sound and thrusts into my palm, his head falling back, golden curls damp with sweat.

"Fuck, Rosie," he breathes.

I take Ezryn deeper, stroke Dayton harder, and feel Kel tremble behind me.

"Now," Caspian groans, voice cracking. "Now, I'm—fuck, I'm going to—"

It happens like lightning.

Keldarion growls my name, slamming into me one last time as

he explodes, heat flooding inside me. Caspian cries out, his body shuddering violently as he follows. Keldarion's fingers dig into my hips so hard they bruise. Beneath me, Farron swears, his own climax tearing through him as his arms lock around my waist.

Ezryn gasps—low and desperate—and I taste him as he spills into my mouth, my tongue coaxing every drop. Dayton comes in my hand seconds later, his seed warm on my wrist as he moans something I can't even hear over the roar in my ears.

And when I finally break, it's like a million stars shattering inside me. Feeling all of my mates' pleasure coat me, inside, over my skin, down my throat…It's an indescribable pleasure.. My whole body shudders with waves of ecstasy.

We collapse together in a tangle of limbs and sighs, breathless and boneless, our bodies sticky and glowing in the golden spill of morning light.

My heart pounds. My skin hums.

Caspian is the first to speak, his voice low and reverent as he brushes my damp hair from my face. "You're so good, Rose," he murmurs against my shoulder. "So good."

Farron nuzzles into my side, pressing soft kisses beneath my breast. "Our perfect girl."

I smile through the haze, letting my head fall on Caspian's chest, his heartbeat steady beneath my cheek. Gentle fingers trail down my spine. Dayton, probably, and someone pulls a blanket up over my bare hips.

"I don't think I can move," I mumble.

"You don't have to," Ezryn says, his cool palm cupping the back of my neck. "Just rest. Let us hold you."

Keldarion's arms wrap around me from behind, solid and sure, his chin hooking over my shoulder. "You did so well," he murmurs, kissing the crown of my head. "So strong. So brave."

Their voices blur together, low praise, soft laughter, the occasional teasing groan from someone shifting too fast. I feel Ezryn press a kiss to my temple. Farron intertwines our fingers. Dayton mutters something about swallowing a cherry blossom. Caspian brushes the side of my knee.

I sigh in contentment. I've never felt so safe. So full. So utterly, undeniably theirs.

Ezryn's hand finds mine beneath the covers. "Sleep, Rosalina," he whispers. "We'll be here when you wake."

Even as my body begins to drift, I feel them all pressed close, warm skin, soft kisses, tangled limbs. My mates. My loves. My family.

Home.

72

Rosalina

GOOSE BUMPS RIPPLE OVER MY ARMS. I'M WEARING ONLY A WHITE T-shirt and black leggings, with the boots I haven't touched since I first entered the Enchanted Vale, though Marigold's shined them up. I take a step backward, trying to get out of the shadow and into a beam of sunlight filtering through the thick canopy of thorns that makes up the Briar.

Kairyn shifts with me, and once again, I'm engulfed in shadow.

Scuffing my toe in the dirt, I chew on my bottom lip, wondering if there are any words that will make this experience less awkward. I don't believe so, so I might as well embrace it.

"So, uh, what do you think she's doing there?" I ask, looking up—*way* up—to catch his red gaze.

Kairyn keeps staring straight ahead, into the thick tangle of thorns, blossoming with black roses that shimmer with prismatic colors, like an oil slick. "I don't know."

Okay, so that won't be our conversation starter. I let out an exhale, blowing away the curl that's fallen in front of my face.

I never pictured myself deep in the Briar with only my mate's brother, the same man who imprisoned me, forced me to fight in his twisted games, and tried to take over the Spring and Summer Realms, but I've come to expect the unexpected. A strange truce has formed between Kairyn and me—one that began when I saved his life in Hadria and he passed the blessing of Spring to me—and he and Ez are working to mend the decades of hurt between them.

So when Kairyn knocked on Castletree's door early this morning saying he knows where Wrenley is, I was the first to invite him in.

Even though he won't meet my gaze, I keep looking at him. He has Ezryn's rugged handsomeness, but there's a youthfulness to his face Ez has long lost. His hair, longer than his older brother's, curls in a similar way, and his tawny skin is streaked with dirt from the road. Regardless of the strange underfae features—horns, red eyes, and enormous size—he's still beautiful.

Maybe sadness suits him.

I exhale again. I'm stalling at this point. Facing the rosebush again, I stare into its depths. *Hello, old friend.*

It's not the same rosebush I entered Castletree through; Kel destroyed that a long time ago. But another has bloomed within the Briar on the outskirts of Castletree, this one heavy with roses, luminescent as Wrenley's briars. And Kairyn's heart has led him here.

"Sure you don't want to come with me?" I ask.

He shakes his head, horns swinging. “A monster in the human realm? I would be hunted before I ever found her.” Finally, he meets my gaze, his own shining. “I just want to know she’s safe.”

I nod. “Okay. I’ll meet you back at Castletree soon.”

Then I fall to my hands and knees and crawl into the rosebush.

My heart pounds against my ribs as I push through the thorns, and my stomach twists. This doesn’t feel like going home; it’s like trying to step into a black-and-white photograph, my colors too bright to fit in again.

Not that I ever did.

But what is my sister doing here? Wrenley never lived in the human realm. Never stepped foot in it, as far as I know.

I keep scrambling beneath the thorns until a gleam of light shines up ahead. Pulling myself through the last briars, I emerge in a familiar forest with a familiar scent. The air tastes like eating a candy I haven’t tried since childhood.

Briarwood Forest.

I follow paths I traced as a kid, walking past trees that grew up with me. Gray light washes over my skin as I step out from beneath the forest canopy into a drizzle. A wooden sign with a cartoonish orca greets me. A speech bubble above the caricature reads WELCOME TO ORCA COVE!

Home.

But not home.

Because while this is where I was born, my heart was always split in five directions across the realms of the Enchanted Vale.

Why is Wrenley here? What could possibly draw her to a tiny village in the human realm?

Fixing my hair so my pointed ears are hidden, I wrap my arms around myself and walk into town, head down, eyes averted. I'm good at becoming small. I did it all my years living in this town.

My heart pounds, and goose bumps rise on the back of my neck. It's like my body knows I'm not supposed to be here. It's funny; I didn't realize it until now. When I first came to the Enchanted Vale, even though I was imprisoned by four cursed fae, I never felt small.

They changed me, my princes. As I changed them, and they've changed each other.

Love is transformative. I'll never be able to make myself invisible like Orca Cove wanted me to be. And that's okay. I've got the Vale, my true home.

And it's Wrenley's too.

Nothing is too different since I left. The Seagull's Gullet Book Emporium is empty as always, and I glimpse my old boss, Richard, sitting behind the counter, staring into space. At first, I don't know if I'll be able to look up at the Poussin Hunting Lodge, but I do at the last minute. Missing posters line the windows, and Lucas's face stares back at me, a haunting ghost.

I pause, drawn in by the familiar smile, the handsome figure that once possessed me. With all the horrors he inflicted on me and the ultimate retribution I made him pay, it is his parents who will forever suffer, never knowing the fate of their son.

There's no way to tell them of the monster he became. They could never see the monster he was in this world. Still, I take a stuttering breath, wishing them peace.

I keep walking, passing the abandoned building I'd once dreamed of turning into a library. The Poussins had converted it into a tacky gift shop, but it is empty once more. The windows are boarded up, and there's caution tape over the door.

Some things will forever be frozen in time in Orca Cove. Lucas will remain the town hero. But there are no missing posters for me or for Papa. We will fade from memory, as if we were never here at all.

I stop at the willow tree. Papa always said it was Mom's favorite. I place a hand on the bark. A wave of energy passes through me, warm and bursting with life. My magic is so much more attuned to the living world now, but even back then, I knew this was a good tree.

My feet carry me unconsciously up my old street, down the long driveway, and to a cottage, easy to forget it ever existed here.

It's dark, but of course it is. No one's been around to pay the electrical bill. The cottage was never in great shape to begin with, but without Papa's occasional patch-ups, it's fallen into disrepair. The porch groans under my step, damp leaves stuck in the corners. One of the shutters has come loose and knocks against the siding. The air smells like wet wood.

I lift the soggy mat, find the key, and put it in the lock.

My breath catches. The door's not locked.

Slowly, I turn the knob and step inside.

The house is only lit by the gray light casting in through the windows. I can almost see them moving through the rooms like ghosts, hear their voices as echoes: memories of Papa and me, in the life we lived before. Me following him from room to room, writing notes as he reads from a text. My old routine of plopping down at the bench by the front door, pulling on my boots, readying for the walk to work. Sitting in the seat by the kitchen window, waiting for someone to return.

I narrow my gaze, examining that particular ghost. But it's not a memory at all. There's a person in the rickety wooden chair right where I used to sit, legs all curled up, head leaning against the windowsill.

But her hair is short and wavy, eyes like our father's sapphire blue.

My sister turns to look at me. She wears clothes that are far too big for her—black sweatpants and a navy hoodie with a bleach stain down the front. My clothes. Swamped in fabric with bare feet and tucked into a ball on the chair, she looks so fragile, like a bird fallen from its nest.

Her blank expression doesn't change as she takes me in. "Oh," she says quietly. "How disappointing." She returns to staring out the window. "I was hoping it was someone who would finally kill me."

I swallow in a dry throat. Look around the kitchen. It's a mess, strewn with pried open tins of beans and peaches and foil packages from various pantry goods. A leak must have sprung in the roof, and a puddle has formed on the floor. There's other clutter too, stuff that doesn't belong in the kitchen: books piled on the microwave, my old diaries flung open and left on the floor, old letters of Papa's hung on the fridge by magnets.

"How long have you been here?" I ask, my voice barely above a whisper.

She shrugs. "Since the Winter Realm." Then she mumbles so low I can hardly hear her, "No place in the Vale for me."

"How did you find it?"

"I know more about you than you think," she spits, that old

venom creeping back. Then she sighs and says, "Small town. Easy to find."

So this is where Wrenley's run off to. I itch to start tidying up Papa's papers or take a seat in the kitchen with her, but I'm struck still. What was she searching for in the pages of my childhood diaries or the ramblings my father jotted down?

"I came looking for you," I say. "Caspian's worried. Kairyn's worried. They want to know you're okay."

She squeezes her eyes shut. "Cas is gone—"

I move, scooting into the chair beside her. I reach out my hands to take hers, but she pulls away, huddling more into herself. Because she hates me? Or because she's afraid of me?

I clasp my fingers together to resist the temptation. "He's okay, Wrenley. He fought the Baron and won. Caspian's himself again."

Wrenley nods and her breathing quickens. Her gaze rises upward, and I see how shiny her blue eyes are. "That's good. I'm happy for him. Really, I am."

I bite the inside of my cheek, then go for it, lightly resting a hand on her shoulder. She stiffens beneath my touch. "Everyone's at Castletree. Me, Caspian, Kairyn. And our parents. We all want you to come home."

A half sob, half laugh erupts out of her throat. She whips her head to look at me, and I jerk back against the chair, her gaze withering. "That's great, Rosalina, really great you've got your whole happy family at Castletree. You keep on playing princess and leave me out of it, okay?"

"You can't stay here," I whisper.

"Why not?" She stands and paces to the back of the kitchen,

slamming her hands on the counter. "'Cause this is your precious little home, and I'll only infect it? Is that it? I can't even have your dregs?"

"No." I stand. "Because your place is with your family."

"I don't *have* a family," she spits. "What don't you understand about that?"

"Caspian's your brother—"

Her lips pull back like a cat in a hiss. "He's not my *real* brother. And he jumped ship as soon as he could to be with you."

"Kairyn… He's your mate—"

"Argh!" She claws at her chest. "It's not real! It's just stupid star stuff! It's not real! I ruined his life enough already. I'd tear the thing out of me if I could."

My heart is pounding now. I need to get through to her, need her to understand she is part of all this. "But Mom and Papa are at—"

Wrenley glares at me like I'm a bag of trash. "I don't *have* a mother who made a bargain to protect me. And I never got a dad."

"He wants to get to know you."

"It's too late." She turns her back to me. I watch as her shoulders heave with each word. "Can you possibly understand how badly I wanted a father? All those nights when Sira forced me to sleep in a pool of cold water or struck my face because she didn't like my eyes?"

"I'm sorry," I whisper.

"I made a dad up in my head. Talked to him even." A choked laugh escapes her. "His name was George. How did I know that? Did Sira let it slip? Or maybe Cas did. But in my imagination, he was good as a king, brave as a hero. I'd picture him fighting down to the Below, rescuing me. But he never came. Why?" She looks over my shoulder at me, and in the gray light, it's striking how much she resembles him. "Because he was with you. Being your dad. Being your hero."

A sad laugh escapes me. "George was no hero. He was gone more often than he was home, and even when he was here, he was lost in a grief-fog. Everything, *everything,* was about our mother. I couldn't count on him to remember my birthday let alone to feed me on the regular. No, I didn't grow up in the dark like you, Wrenley, but I still grew up alone."

"You're not alone now. I've seen the way he looks at you. Like you're every star in the damned sky."

"We've both changed. I had to learn to forgive him. And he had to learn to forgive himself. But I still carry it, that feeling I had as a kid. Why wasn't I enough?"

She scoffs, sharp and bitter.

"I mean it," I say and take a step forward. "You should have had summers swimming in the lake and drying off in the sun. I shouldn't have had to forge my own permission slips or tuck myself into bed each night. And we both should have had a sister to grow up with. To tease and laugh with and love more than anything."

"You're delusional."

"It's not too late," I say softly. "Not for me. Not for George."

She spins, face contorting with pain. "It's too late for *me*!"

"It doesn't have to be this way." I take a step toward her, reaching out my hand. "Please, Wrenley, there are people who care for you."

She makes a sobbing sound and buckles over, hugging herself. "How can you stomach it? I couldn't stomach it…"

"What?"

"Giving all those people so many ways to hurt you."

I stare at her, a crumpled piece of paper of a girl. "It's called love, Wrenley."

Tears flow rampant down her face now, but she grits her teeth like a wild animal. "You must be sick with it."

"It makes me strong." I take a step toward her. "And there are so many people who love you."

"No!"

"Caspian." I take a step. "Kairyn." I take another step. "Mom and Papa." I lift her chin to look at me. "And me. You're my little sister, Wrenley. I love you."

"You don't know me!" she shrieks, smacking my hand away. She staggers backward to the very end of the kitchen, now pinned in by the cupboards, wall, and fridge. Her eyes dart wildly, as if looking for a way to escape, before finding mine once more. Her pupils blow. "And if you did, you wouldn't. I'm horrible and hateful—"

"And I wish I could go back in time and steal you away from whoever made you believe those things," I say. "But I can't. So I'll tell you what I see. Someone who is strong and passionate and still fighting to stay alive. Someone with my mother's smile and my father's eyes. And I bet you have my sense of humor, because Caspian tells me you're funny as hell, and you know what? So am I." I've never had to be this brave. But I fight for my family, so I will fight for her. "Let me get to know all the other parts of you. Please, I promise I'll keep them safe."

A beat of silence. Then Wrenley lets out a wail, throws open the cupboard, snatches out my SUPPORT LOCAL LIBRARIES mug, and hurls it at the wall by my head. It wasn't meant to hit me, but the glass shatters loud enough to make me jump.

I take a deep breath. Close my eyes and choke back the tears. When I open them, she is curled in a ball in the corner of the kitchen, clawing at her shoulders.

"Go away," she says, a whisper and a sob. "Please."

So I do.

I walk out the door, down the street, and back to the rosebush. Stroking the soft petals of her prismatic roses, my own bloom entwined: gold and black, briars weaving together.

"Whenever you're ready, I'll be here," I whisper. "I'll never stop fighting for you."

73

Ezryn

I sit at the long table in Castletree's dining room, feeling strangely at ease.

There's noise everywhere. Staff duck in and out, laughter bounces off the stone and wooden walls, feet tip-tap on the floor, and silverware clangs. The whole place is alight with motion, with warmth, with a kind of joy I haven't felt since...

Well, since Rosalina arrived.

Though there was no grand announcement, it wasn't long before the staff figured it out. Of course they did. Aurelia and Rosalina could be twins after all. And Aurelia emits such a presence, it's like basking in the sun itself.

The Queen of the Vale has returned, and Castletree is alive with the ecstasy of it. Caspian's thorns still hold up its structure. I can only imagine it will take a while before the queen's magic has restored enough to heal Castletree.

Before me stretches out a feast fit for a coronation, even though it's simply teatime. The chef, Oliviana, has summoned the full strength of the kitchens, and Marigold has pulled out the finest tableware.

It's like a culinary map of the Enchanted Vale spread before us. There are maize cakes topped with salsa, served alongside stuffed blossoms filled with smoky beans and roasted peppers, some of my favorite dishes from Spring.

From the Summer Realm, traditional baked barley loaves brushed with oil and fig skewers drizzled with honey are plated on a terra-cotta platter. I can't resist tearing off a chunk of a loaf, just for the warmth of it in my palm.

Autumn's fare is richer, with oat pies and roasted root vegetables with blackened edges. The apple cakes are nearly gone.

A rich smell creeps up from Winter's dishes, reminding me of my many childhood adventures spent in Frostfang with Keldarion. Dark rye, sharp cheese, and lingonberry preserves are all on the menu.

I even notice a row of ink-black mushroom tarts, a staple in the Below. It seems like Oliviana wanted all the realms to be represented. I'll have to tell Marigold to save one for me. She always makes a separate plate that I can eat in private, when my helm is off.

Tearing my gaze away from the food, I look across the room. Dayton's pulled out a pair of wooden training swords and has somehow baited Kairyn into a sparring match. Marigold dashes past them carrying a steaming dish the size of a small basin and shrieks,

"Get those swords *out* of my dining room before I flay you with them!" Dayton grins and ducks as Kairyn swings at him.

Trailing after Marigold, her large feet flapping on the floor, is Heidigog. Why am I not surprised Rosalina befriended the most peculiar of creatures? It seems Marigold's been tasked with taking the goblin under her wing. Heidigog struggles to keep up, nearly tripping over her dress, a pink, floral puffball of fabric. Flavia's handiwork, no doubt.

To my right, Keldarion, Farron, Astrid, and Eldor are locked in a card game. Judging by the victorious smirk on Astrid's face and the gleam in Keldarion's eye, I'd wager they're on the same team. They're not gloating, but I catch a few nods and nudges. Meanwhile, Farron's groaning into his cards, and Eldy looks ready to upend the table.

My heart swells seeing them all like this. It's been so long since everyone's been able to relax, to remember that there is goodness in the quiet moments. And it's all thanks to Rosalina. She promised she would bring her mother home, and she did.

I peek over my shoulder to look at her: the Queen of the Enchanted Vale. Aurelia leans against the wall, effortlessly graceful. There are still dark circles under her eyes and a sallowness to her complexion, but it does not detract from her beauty. At once natural and at home in this hall, there's something also...strange about her. A legend materialized from the words of a story.

She hasn't been able to have a quiet moment since she arrived. Even now, she's pinned in on both sides. On her right by George, who I don't think has let go of her hand once. And on her left by Justus.

Dayton sent word to him about Aurelia's return. He's the only soul outside the castle who knows. Centuries ago, he went by the name Aeneas and traveled with Aurelia throughout the realms, finding the mythkarite that would one day form the divine weapons. She named him the first high ruler of Summer.

When Aurelia is ready, we'll let the realms know about her return. But until then, it felt right that Justus be informed. He'd shown up at the castle a day after we sent the letter. I guess he was eager to see his queen once again.

Now, Justus looks far more groomed than I've ever known him to be, his gray-white hair flowing over his shoulders, beard trimmed. He wears the traditional garb of Summer, a sheet of pale fabric clasped over one shoulder, revealing his toned arms. I can only hope I maintain such form at his advanced age.

He leans toward Aurelia, a wine goblet in hand, his grin easy. "I must confess, I wasn't entirely sure you were real. Dayton's letter made it sound like a story told in a poem. '*She's returned from the darkness, as radiant as the cosmos themselves. Unchanged by time.*' That's how he wrote it. Very dramatic, that boy."

Aurelia lifts a brow. "And yet here I am. Unchanged by time… and as unimpressed by flattery as ever."

Justus chuckles. "I was hoping to at least earn mild amusement."

She sips from her own goblet, a twinkle in her brown eyes. "You'll have to try harder than that, Aeneas."

"Stars, I haven't heard that name in a century." He tilts his head toward her. "You remembered."

"Hard to forget the first high ruler of Summer."

George shifts beside her, arms crossed, trying not to scowl. "He's not a high ruler anymore."

"I never claimed to be," Justus replies smoothly, his eyes never leaving Aurelia's. "And yet she remembers me fondly."

"Fondly?" George cuts in. "I doubt *that's* the word she'd use."

Aurelia turns, slow and deliberate, placing a hand on George's arm. "Relax, love. We're all friends here."

Justus raises his glass. "Some of us are *very* old friends."

George doesn't answer, but the muscle in his jaw ticks.

Aurelia smiles sweetly between them. "You boys keep this up, and I'll have to make you duel for me."

"Is that an invitation?" Justus asks, giving a grin that reminds me of Dayton.

"I'm not sure either of you could handle it." Aurelia waltzes off, hips swaying, to a new spot: right over Farron's shoulder. She leans down and whispers in his ear: "Play your moonstone prince. It'll kill the deck."

Now Justus, George, *and* Farron all seem to be blushing messes.

I snort and shake my head, barely disguising a laugh. Justus can try all he likes, but he doesn't stand a chance. Not when Aurelia gazes at George like he's the stars, the moon, and the sun all wrapped up in one. That kind of devotion doesn't unravel, not even with hundreds of years between them.

Caspian's sitting beside me. I notice him watching the interaction as well, and he chuckles into his wine cup. He looks relaxed, lounging, one leg crossed over the other, an arm draped over the chair next to him. There's a stillness to him, not brooding or braced for a fight. Just…quiet. At peace, in a way I don't know if I've ever seen before. I feel the same thing in him that I feel in myself: that rare and fragile sense that, for a breath, we are allowed to just be.

His gaze remains on Aurelia, and he says lowly, only for me to hear, "With her home, it's as if a great weight has been lifted off my briars. Like I can breathe properly for the first time in years."

"You don't have to keep Castletree standing anymore."

He shakes his head. "She's not at full strength yet. Until she recovers..." He trails off, but I can hear the unspoken words. *Until that day, it's still on me.*

"You're not alone," I say softly.

His violet gaze pierces through my helm, but he doesn't fight me. He nods. We fall back into our easy quiet.

But because it's Caspian and it's me, I need to ask, "What do you think Sira's doing now?"

His expression darkens. "I don't know. But whatever it is, she hasn't given up. She's not out of tricks, not by a long shot."

The air around us feels colder for a beat. I glance toward the doorway, half expecting to see someone appear.

"Rosalina's due to return soon," I say, more to myself than him. "Perhaps your sister will be with her."

"I don't think my little Birdy will ever fly home." He lets out a humorless chuckle. "There's no way everything in my life can be perfect."

I search his face, the sadness tucked behind those words. A laugh rings out across the room. Kairyn's on the floor now, pinned by Dayton, who's grinning like he's won a war. Kairyn kicks him off but accepts Dayton's hand up, then demands a rematch.

A smile forms beneath my helm as I watch them. "It doesn't have to be perfect," I say. "Maybe it can be messy. And that's okay." I pause. "Maybe it's better."

Caspian lifts a brow, then smiles. "I suppose you're right—"

Something shifts.

Kairyn, mid-swing with his wooden sword, goes still. Not tired or winded. Still. Like a statue frozen, head cocked at an unnatural angle, breath held.

Heidigog drops the platter she was holding. It crashes to the floor with a clang. Carrots scatter. A bowl rolls and spins, spins, spins...then stops.

Silence.

Then I see their eyes.

Kairyn's first. Flooded with darkness, black as pitch. It spills across the whites of his eyes like ink dropped in water, swallowing everything.

Heidigog's too. Her little hands curl into claws at her sides, her pink dress bouncing up and down as she shakes.

I rise from my chair slowly, finger trailing up toward my token, heart pounding even as my voice stays calm. "Kairyn, what's going on?"

They move. Stiff, jerking movements, like puppets on invisible strings.

And then they attack.

74

Rosalina

I BRIAR INTO CASTLETREE AND STRAIGHT INTO CHAOS.

The dining hall is a blur of movement and magic, chairs overturned, plates shattered, walls riddled with flame. A table flips and crashes inches from my feet as I duck.

Heidigog and Kairyn are attacking.

Their eyes are pitch-black, soulless voids that don't blink, don't waver. They snarl like beasts, lunging at Ezryn with unnatural strength. He throws up a shimmering wall of wind to block a chair thrown at him.

"What's going on?" I scream.

Justus grapples with Kairyn near the hearth while Farron tries to catch Heidigog, who scrambles away from him.

"Careful," Caspian says. "They're not themselves."

Dayton holds a silver platter as a shield to block a butter knife

Heidi throws at my father. Kel responds by shooting a sheet of ice beneath Heidi's feet, sending her skittering.

Caspian is right. They're not themselves.

My mother steps forward, spreading her arms at her sides. "I have had enough of this."

Her eyes glow gold, brighter than I've ever seen, and magic coils around her like a storm about to break. She lifts both hands and slams them to the ground.

The air shudders.

From the cracks in the stone floor, golden briars explode upward, thick and gleaming like sunlight. They twist and weave with terrifying precision, slamming into Heidigog and Kairyn and yanking them backward. The vines wind around their limbs, pinning them in place midair, then snap into a cage, sealing them inside.

The cage crashes to the ground. They thrash. Snarl. But they're trapped. Their black eyes lock on me. There's no recognition there.

"What happened?" I ask, breathless.

Ezryn's jaw is clenched tight, his arm still raised defensively. "They…turned. Suddenly, with no reason."

"One second, we were all chatting," Farron adds, his voice shaken. "The next, they decided we would be better off dead."

"Something is wrong," Caspian says.

Inside the golden briars, Heidigog and Kairyn don't blink. Don't speak. They pace, eyes still black, shoulders tense, fingers twitching like they're waiting for someone to give a command.

"It's like they're being controlled…" I whisper. My chest tightens. "The rose."

"No," Marigold says, charging toward me. "The vault was locked tight. I checked it myself this morning."

But I'm already moving.

My feet thunder down the hall. The others trail me. I don't speak. I can't. My heart's beating too fast, dread curling in my gut like smoke.

I go down the steps into the very depths of Castletree, to a place I hardly go. The air becomes colder. Through the cellar, past the secret door. A vault door looms ahead. I throw it open with a burst of briars.

Inside, the rose sits where it always has in its bell jar.

I let out a sigh of relief. Sira doesn't have the rose. *But what else could control both Kairyn and Heidi, two of Sira's creations?*

I slow, my fingers reaching toward the glass.

I lift the lid.

My hand brushes the stem. Inky and cold…the feeling is…familiar.

The rose flickers, then dissolves into a pool of shadows.

Just like the food Sira tried to serve me in the tower. Like how Caspian changed Heidi's form.

"Shadows," I breathe. "An illusion."

Kel steps up beside me. "If we have the fake…"

"That means Sira—" Ezryn starts.

A voice whispers through the hall, slipping into my ears like poison laced with honey.

We all spin, running for the entrance.

The great doors to Castletree groan open, just a few inches, and shadows pour in, coiling about my limbs, dragging warmth from my skin.

“Rosalina, step back!” Caspian screams.

But it’s too late.

She’s here.

Sira.

She emerges from the shadows, cloak billowing, a wicked smile on her lips. Her arms snake around me, and the cold kiss of a blade presses against my neck.

“Oh,” she purrs, voice mocking, “is something wrong with your little rose?”

75

Caspian

AND JUST LIKE THAT, MY MOTHER HAS IMMOBILIZED ALL THE MOST powerful fae in the Vale with a single move.

I pride myself on being ten steps ahead of everyone else, but my mother always has one more on me.

But not this time. Rose or not, bargain or not, she will answer today.

"Don't move or I'll kill her," Sira purrs.

She stills us all with a look, then sweeps her gaze from me to Anya.

"How sad," she continues. "My two little pets have flown the coop. You do realize you still belong to me."

Anya's face turns into a vicious snarl. "Even rotting in the white bark of the Evergrove would be too good a punishment for you, Sira."

"You'll never take my wife again." George steps protectively in front of Anya, who puts a hand on his shoulder.

Sira gives a dark chuckle. "Bold words, human, figuring you are the cause of her imprisonment. You and that unnaturally long life. But alas, all things must end."

"Don't threaten my family," Rosalina snarls, twitching against Sira's grip. "The Green Flame's reign is over. You have no god or army to help you."

She leans down, her voice a soft whisper. "But I do have an army. One your own father helped me gain."

My ribs feel too tight. She has the rose, which means when she took control of Kairyn and Heidigog, it was part of something greater. All those creatures I recruited as the Prince of Thorns… She's truly done it.

They could be marching now, on Castletree, on the realms, on all the Enchanted Vale.

Nausea roils in my gut.

I can't let that continue.

"The Green Flame isn't gone, Mother," I say as I step forward, letting fire dance along my arms. "Let Rosalina go, return the rose, and perhaps we'll allow you to live out your miserable existence back in the Below. Yes, you can command me, but remember, you only have *one*. Choose wisely."

"Oh, my darling boy." Her smile widens. "I only need one command. And it's not even for you."

A pit drops in my stomach, and I feel twenty steps behind.

"Aurelia." She turns to Anya, then gestures to me. "Turn that wretch under my control into a human."

Into a human.

Into a human?

The years I cried myself to sleep wishing for that. The hours I pleaded outside Anya's prison for her to turn me human. All so I could rid myself of the Green Flame.

But now I have mastered it, along with my thorns and shadows.

"No." I throw a line of emerald flames up to protect myself.

And I'm not the only one. Keldarion raises a shield of ice, Ezryn a wall of rock, Farron a torrent of fire, and Dayton a barrier of water.

The queen's magic bursts through them all as if they were as thin as a butterfly's wings.

A beam of light strikes my chest and throws me to the ground. The other princes fly back, slamming into the pillars.

"Caspian!" Rosalina screams.

Light explodes in my vision, and I make out the queen, hands outstretched, tears running down her face. She's screaming at George and Justus.

And then I can't concentrate on anything more. It's like I'm being struck by the sun itself.

I try to summon my magic, but it's no use. This isn't something I can fight. Not with shadows. Not with thorns. Not with flames.

It sears straight through me, slicing open everything I am. My ribs burn, my blood turns to ash, and there's a sound—gods, a sound like a dying animal.

I think that's me screaming.

My magic writhes, snarling, trying to hold on. But it's being pulled from me, one thread at a time.

I rise to one knee.

"Anya," I manage. Her name scrapes my throat like broken glass. She's crying. Stars above, she's crying. But she doesn't stop. Her hands tremble, but the magic doesn't falter.

The light tunnels deeper. I can feel it now, what it's doing. Twisting the core of me into something…less.

"No," I rasp. "No, no, no—"

I'm unraveling.

Everything that makes me fae—my thorns, the shadows in my soul, the pulse of distant flames—is slipping away. Being scorched clean.

It's like being flayed alive from the inside out. Not just pain. Loss. Someone's carving out who I am and leaving a hollow shell behind.

There's chaos around me. Distantly, I hear Rosalina's voice.

And then—

I can't feel the briars anymore. The veins I've dug into the earth surrounding Castletree, all leading here, weaving through its halls, strengthening its bones, protecting the home of those I love…

I can't feel them.

My golden bracelet falls to the ground.

Castletree trembles.

The briars at my feet wither and turn to dust. My connection to them is severed. For over twenty-five years, I have been holding this castle up…and the connection disappears in an instant.

Aurelia isn't yet strong enough to keep Castletree standing. She told me so herself.

My briars drop off the walls, raining down in a shower of purple dust. The tree groans and shakes.

Castletree is going to fall.

"Don't cry, my darling boy," Sira says. "Isn't this what you always wanted?"

I scream.

And it sounds human.

76

Rosalina

I CAN'T MOVE. SIRA'S MAGIC HOLDS ME FAST, FROZEN LIKE A DOLL IN A nightmare. Her shadow knife is at my neck.

But I can see everything.

Caspian screams.

The sound tears through the air. His green fire flares, but it can't protect him. A beam of light pours from my mother's hands straight into his chest. Her face is soaked with tears, lips trembling, but she doesn't stop. She *can't* stop.

I want to scream. Want to claw free, run to her, run to him, do *anything*, but I'm trapped.

There has to be *something* I can do!

Caspian is shaking. His fingers dig into the earth like he's trying to hold himself in this world, but I can see the light burning through him. I can feel it too. Like it's ripping the faeness right out of him. His glow is dimming. His scream is breaking—

Kel lets out a mournful cry. He collapses to his knees. The bracelet on his wrist, his side of the bargain, splinters and falls. Caspian's does too. It clatters to the ground, icy thorns melting away.

He clutches his wrist, a sob ripping out of him, sharp and strangled.

I know the words they said. *And if ever there is no love between us, let this bargain melt away like snow under rain.*

No.

No, it wasn't that.

I shake my head, blinking past the tears. "It's not that you don't love each other," I whisper. My voice trembles, but my heart is screaming.

I look at the melting bracelets, at my mates kneeling in ash and light, at the beam still pouring from my mother's hands. Her sobs, his pain.

I feel my own fury.

And then the words fall from my lips, quiet and certain. "A human cannot make a bargain with a fae."

Sira's command echoes in my mind. *Turn that wretch under my control into a human.*

She didn't say my son. She didn't say Caspian.

That wretch under my control.

One of the first lessons I learned in the Vale. One the Prince of Thorns taught me. *It pays to be specific in bargains.*

My heart stutters.

If a fae is made human…

They can't be bound anymore.

My breath catches.

We don't have to stop my mother's magic. We don't even have to stop Sira.

We just have to stop the bargain.

I snap my gaze to her, my mother, Queen of the Vale, drowning in her own magic. She meets my eyes through the glow.

I scream the only truth that can save us. "A human cannot make a bargain with a fae!"

Her lips part. Her throat bobs.

All my life, we've been apart. But do we think the same? *Understand. Please understand.*

The queen closes her eyes.

And turns the magic on herself.

"No!" Sira screams, but it's too late.

The light arcs, twisting and bending like a serpent devouring its own tail. It slams into my mother's chest, and she jerks back, arms flung wide, mouth open in a silent cry.

And I take a moment to realize what a sacrifice this is. My mother, one of the few fae left of the Above, the most powerful fae in the Vale, sacrificing her magic to save us.

Her shining chestnut hair dulls to a mousy brown. The gold flecks in her eyes twinkle out. And her pointed, regal ears blur at the edges, curl in. The simple iron band wrapped around the ring finger of her right hand cracks in half, then plummets to the floor.

Her power vanishes. I feel it drain from the air as if someone's stolen the moon.

She falls to the ground like a petal from a dying flower.

77

Caspian

THEY'RE GONE.

I can't feel them anymore.

My thorns, my beautiful purple thorns, that for so long have felt like an extension of my own self. Who I am.

The Prince of Thorns.

Without them, who am I?

My thorns wither to the earth. Briars I dug deep into the earth, raised up through the bones of Castletree to protect Kel, to protect this place I love…

I can't feel them anymore.

They shrivel, curling in on themselves. My beautiful briars. The only good magic I've ever had.

Gone.

Castletree groans, the structure shaking without the support of my briars. The ground quakes, and I nearly lose my footing.

Sira's scream splits the air. I lift my head, breath ragged, every bone in my body aching. And my own scream echoes inside me.

Anya's spell stopped before she completed it.

I'm still fae. Still me.

At least most of me is. My briars are gone, and my bargain with Kel. My heart aches.

But there's still magic running through my veins. I'm weak. What magic I have left feels like an empty well, and I don't know how long until it refills.

Kel's got his hands on my shoulders, his voice frantic as he pushes my hair out of my face. I want to tell him I'm fine. But I'm not. Not even close.

My mother still has Rosalina at knifepoint.

The shadow blade presses to her neck, kissing her skin. Sira's hand trembles, not from fear but from fury.

She lost control over me *and* Anya.

And the only reason she still lives is because she's using Rosalina as a shield.

I glance toward the others. Farron, Ezryn, Dayton, Justus—they're all frozen in place, rage burning in their eyes but held in place by that one command: if you move, she bleeds.

Anya lies motionless in George's arms. A queen made mortal. And Castletree groans, more of my thorns withering.

I've failed them.

Sira bends close to Rosalina, and I catch the wild shine in my mother's eyes. "You stole my bow," she snarls. "You banished my god. You turned my queen into a mortal. But I still have you, child of the Above."

I meet Rosalina's gaze across the wreckage.

Even now, with blood on her throat and shadows at her heels, she looks at me like I'm something worth saving.

"She's not yours, Mother," I rasp. "She's mine."

Sira sneers. "Then choose. Come with your mother and this girl, or die in this collapsing castle, weak and magicless." She leans in closer. "My horde is coming. They will not stop until every last one of you is dead."

Shadows rise around us, licking at the stones, hungering.

"What can you do?" she croons. "Your little thorns are gone, Prince of Nothing. You have no choice but to return to me."

The choice she's always offered me. And the one I've always taken. Back to her, back to the Below.

Maybe I would follow again…if a beautiful human girl hadn't crawled through a rosebush to reach me.

If a wild Winter boy hadn't shown me the path beyond the thorns.

If a stoic knight hadn't shown me how to use cleverness in a game.

If I hadn't laughed, truly laughed, at the sun-haired gladiator's ridiculous jokes.

If I hadn't seen my own fire mirrored in the eyes of someone more afraid than me—someone I *had* to save.

If a stubborn camel hadn't led me through the heart of the storm.

I rise. Kel reaches to steady me, but I shake him off. My legs are trembling, hands soaked with dirt and blood. I stare down at the briars, *my* briars, wilting, crumbling…dead.

"Yes. My thorns are gone." My voice breaks. "They were never mine. Only a gift."

Then I lift my chin.

"But shadows…" I whisper. "Shadows are in my blood."

The air shivers. Something deep inside me stirs to life after nearly being ripped away. I raise my hand, fingers trembling, and call the shadows to me.

They answer.

Gods, they answer too well.

They pour through me like fire made smoke, searing up my spine and down my arms, veins alight with darkness.

The blade against Rosalina's throat dissolves into mist.

Sira screams as black tendrils surge from the shattered stones, thick as ropes. They lash around her wrists, her arms, her waist. She thrashes violently, teeth bared, spitting curses that curdle the air. But I don't flinch.

My knees nearly buckle. My vision swims. Sweat beads along my brow, soaking into my tangled hair. My chest heaves like I've run a hundred miles.

She's fighting me.

I feel the moment her will strikes mine. Her rage tears into my magic, trying to reclaim it. To bend it back. The shadows hesitate, pulled in two directions—mother or son, creator or heir. I grit my teeth and shove harder. I cannot let her win. Not again.

Not when Rosalina is still in her grip.

I only have seconds. Just seconds before Sira rips through the magic and takes it back. She's older. Stronger. She shaped these shadows long before I ever touched them. The only reason I'm holding her at all is because she didn't expect me to fight.

Or because I'm fighting for her.

For my mate.

What are you fighting for, Mother?

Power? Control? Love will always prevail. Rosalina showed me that. And I will not let her down.

I wish I could hold Sira long enough for one of the others to strike. But I won't last. My magic is weakened, frayed from the spell that nearly made me human. I can barely keep the shadows from collapsing in on themselves, let alone attack.

The only thing that matters now is getting Rosalina free.

If Sira drags her down to the Below, I don't know how we'll ever get her back.

So I hold.

Every muscle in my body shakes as I anchor the shadows around my mother. My vision blurs at the edges. Blood drips from my nose. But I don't stop.

If I fall, I'm taking Sira with me.

In a rush of darkness and wind, Rosalina breaks free and stumbles away from the shadows.

"Farewell, Mother," I whisper.

My shadows drag her under, into an abyss of my making.

I guess I can create too.

And then it's just silence. Crumbling briars. The scent of ash and roses. My knees buckle, and Kel catches me before I hit the ground.

"I didn't have the strength to kill her," I rasp, "but she'll fall in darkness for a while."

Rosalina's arms bind around me, holding tight.

"You're still fae?" she whispers.

I nod. "Anya never finished the spell. My shadows and flames are still here. Weak but here." I cup her face, my thumb brushing the tears from her cheek. "The briars, though…they were hers. I can't feel them anymore, Rosie. They're gone. Castletree is—"

A quake jolts the floor. Above us, a branch crashes down from the ceiling.

"Without Cas's thorns," Farron says grimly, "and without Queen Aurelia's magic…Castletree will fall."

"No," comes a voice.

We turn. Anya pushes herself up in George's arms.

She looks different now. Not like the radiant Queen of the Vale or the imprisoned fae we found Below. No, she looks real. An anthropologist in the desert. Human.

"My magic is not gone from the Vale," she says.

"But, Your Majesty," Justus starts.

"I may be human," the queen says, "but my daughter's not. She will save Castletree."

78

Rosalina

Me? My mother wants me to save Castletree?

"Mom," I whisper, clutching her hand. It's cold.

Her eyes burrow into mine, deep brown. No glow left but full of fire.

"You have to save it," she rasps. "Castletree's still alive. Only you can save her."

"What about Papa?" I gasp. "You used your magic to tie his life with Castletree's. But if you're human, does that mean…" I can't bear to utter the words.

"His lifeforce is woven with Castletree's. The magic within the tree has long become its own. Of the high rulers. As long as the tree lives, so does your father."

My heart pounds like a war drum in my chest. It's not just a castle. Not just a home to dozens of people.

It's a lifeline to all the magic in the Vale. It's *Papa's* lifeline.

I swallow hard, chest tight. All around us, the vast, hollowed-out interior of Castletree shudders. It's like being inside the bones of a dying god. Briars crumble from the walls, and chunks of bark fall away. I feel the tree's heartbeat, faint and failing.

"I don't know if I can," I whisper.

A deafening crack splits the air.

The front doors erupt in a storm of splinters, blown inward by a force that reeks of rot. And through the shattered threshold, creatures pour in, snarling, clawed, and unnatural.

A monstrous horde of goblins and trolls charges into the chamber. Their growls reverberate through the roots, shaking the ground.

A screech sounds above, and the high stained-glass windows shatter in a spray of color. Harpies dive through, shrieking, wings like torn parchment, talons outstretched. Their eyes are wrong—completely black, no pupils, no whites. Just void.

Even from afar, her order to her creations still stands. They're under Sira's control.

The air fills with howls and beating wings and the sickly scent of rot.

They're coming from all sides.

"We'll protect you!" Dayton roars, summoning his trident in a flash of ocean-blue steel. He charges forward, meeting the first wave of goblins head-on with a wild grin.

"We need to save the staff!" I cry. "What if I can't—what if I'm not enough?"

"You *are*!" Mom says. Even as a human, her voice rings with command.

"I'll evacuate the staff," Farron says, and he's already gone, vanishing down one of the curved wooden passages.

"We'll buy you time, Rose." Keldarion crafts a blade of ice, shimmers into his armor, and runs straight into the fray beside Dayton, his sword carving arcs of frost through the air.

Ezryn steps between me and the chaos, his cloak billowing, hammer glowing in his hand. "No one touches you," he says, calm and deadly.

Caspian falls to his knees, weak but upright, trembling with effort. Justus and George press close to him and Mom, guarding us all.

Alright, my turn.

I stare at Castletree. The walls crack. The great boughs groan overhead.

It's all falling apart. But it's not gone. Not yet.

I sink to my knees and press a hand to the bark coating the ground, reaching for its essence beneath the crumbling stone and thorns.

It pulses. Weakly.

Alive. Calling out for help.

I feel you.

I've always had a connection to Castletree.

And I'll be dammed if I let it fall.

79

Keldarion

So the fight has come to Castletree. As we always knew it would.

I fight, as there is nothing else to do. To my left, Dayton moves like a dancer, teal armor glowing, trident loose in his hand, each swipe creating a wall of water that sends goblins scattering to the floor. I've created two long swords of ice and freeze a dozen that pile through the door, causing another group to trip and fall over.

A shriek sounds overhead, and a flock of harpies soars through the roof. I toss one of my swords in the air, and it explodes around them in a shower of ice, piercing their bodies.

"Kel!" Dayton cries.

Another wave pushes through Castletree's entrance. They don't stop coming.

Summoning a second blade, I dash beside him. We stand

back-to-back, Dayton concentrating on the opening, me on finishing the stragglers that make it through.

Mostly goblins form this assault. Sira's outfitted them in crude armor and jagged swords. Their eyes are pure black, revealing they're all thralls to the rose.

The rose we never had.

Behind us, Justus and Ezryn have created a perimeter around Rosalina, Aurelia, George, and Cas. No goblin can break it.

Rosalina is on all fours, hair wild, hands digging into the ground. I can *feel* more than see the magic radiating from her. She's making a connection with Castletree.

"We have to push out the door," I say to Dayton. "Let's see what we're dealing with."

Dayton and I fight our way through the splintered entrance, blades flashing, monsters falling at our feet. The air reeks of rot and burning bark. Behind us, Castletree groans.

We burst outside.

"Fuck," I say.

The bridge is swarmed. Goblins, trolls, harpies, grinjaws—every nightmarish creature Sira could summon is crawling toward our home like ants over a carcass. And beyond…

Armies.

Tents and siege towers stretch as far as the eye can see, all camped along the edge of the briars. Or what's left of them. There's a hazy mist in the air, but it's just Caspian's briars fading away.

Dayton slows beside me, his trident dripping with dark blood. "How are we ever going to fight them all?"

I turn, and my chest clenches.

Castletree.

The great trunk groans, its bark splitting open with a sound like thunder. Towers crack and spiral downward, crashing into the earth with bone-rattling force. Vines shrivel to ash as they tumble from the heights. Stone walls, once cradled in living wood, shear away and plunge into the roots below. The whole structure is coming undone.

Without Caspian's briars, without the queen's magic…there's nothing holding it together anymore.

It's dying.

Rosalina is truly our only hope. She must tap into the magic of her birthright, but she's so young, so new to the Vale. My Rose has only just begun to understand the depths of her power… and to save Castletree she'll need to descend further than before.

And I need to give her the time to do this.

I grit my teeth, the wind howling through the ruins behind me.

"We fight them," I say, turning back to the horde, "one at a time."

Then I shift.

Bones crack. Fur bursts. The cold surges through me, glorious and wild. The wolf takes hold.

And I charge into the fray.

80

Rosalina

"It's up to you, Rosalina," my mother says. "Save Castletree."

Placing my hands on the bark, I let my consciousness seep into Castletree. A gasp escapes my lips.

It's weak, so very weak. But there is still life here. Life I can *save.*

Like a tether snapping into place, I feel Castletree latch on to me and begin to drink. The gates of my magic open and flow into the tree.

It's similar to when we transfer our magic to the roses, only… more intense. With the roses, it feels as if I'm getting something back. But Castletree has nothing left to give, and it's sucking power from me at a rapid rate.

I gasp, sweat dotting my brow, the sensation unnerving. I'm a tap that can't be turned off. My arms shake, but I hold on to the connection.

A bloom of dust showers to my right as another tree branch falls into the entrance hall. Ezryn is swift as the wind, dancing around me, making sure no one breaks past his barrier. On his other side, Justus moves masterfully with his trident. My parents hover on either shoulder.

I can't think too much about what this means for Papa. There's a growing fear inside me, and if I give it too much slack, it will cover me completely. *No.* I need to focus. Need to believe in myself.

Caspian has managed to get to his feet and moved to the entrance, orienting the staff members that Farron finds and attempting to lead them to safety. But where is safety in all this chaos?

"Don't lose concentration now, Rosalina," Mom says, placing a hand on my back. "I can see Castletree knitting to life around you."

I wipe the sweat off my brow. Yes, yes, the tree is healing beneath me, bark turning a bright brown. Still the walls are an ashy gray.

"You have to push your magic deeper," she says. "Into Castletree's roots."

I heave in a breath and close my eyes. Something's glowing deep below the earth. Castletree's roots, like branching tendrils of light. But they fray, shatter. The light cuts off where it should lead to the Winter wing.

Oh no. The Winter wing has collapsed…

Other junctions of light split, then disappear as Castletree falters.

And for the first time, I realize how much Caspian has poured himself into Castletree. It was never just his briars holding up the structure. He flowed his magic into the tree as well, an ever-present stream.

He's so powerful, I think, even when he was giving up nearly half his magic to this. To protect Kel and my mother's legacy. To protect my father, whose life is tied to Castletree.

Now it's my turn.

I scream, pouring more of myself into the tree. Great gushes of power leave me. I won't let Caspian's sacrifice be for nothing. It's up to me to finish what they started.

My heart is racing so fast it's pounding in my ears. I'm unable to take in enough air.

"Dig deeper, Rosalina." Mom's voice pounds in my head. "Castletree is the source of all the magic in the Vale. The source of the high princes' magic. You cannot fail."

My arms shake, and I fall to the ground, cheek pressed against the bark and broken marble, tears running down my cheeks. I can't let go of my connection. Not now.

If I fail… High Tower will crumble, and all the princes' roses will die. After all we did to break their curses, their magic will leave them. I won't let it happen. And also, my mother said Castletree is the source of all magic in the Vale. If the tree falls, what happens to the realms?

Shouts and cries sound behind me. I heave in a breath and cough. More dust. Caspian's briars withering.

Castletree sucks in more of my magic, but it feels like trying to fill a pool with an eyedropper. It drinks ravenously until I'm feeling like a husk—one of Caspian's briars, shrunken and wilted on the ground.

And with horrifying clarity, I realize I don't have enough magic.

I don't have enough power.

I blink my eyes, gaze at the dusky surroundings. Ezryn's armor is spattered in blood. He and Justus have made a pile of monstrous corpses around us. Caspian leads another group of frantic staff out through the back gardens, concealing them in shadows. But still, more of Sira's black-eyed horde pours in through the door. Keldarion and Dayton are outside. I catch a glimpse as they shift from their wolf forms into their armor and back again, destroying dozens of goblins at a time.

Castletree shakes as the remnants of Caspian's briars fall away in droves. They could be nothing but shriveling leaves under a blazing summer sun.

I cry out, feral and desperate. Golden briars sprout through the floor and crawl up the walls, trying to strengthen the foundation as Caspian had.

"It's holding," I gasp. "I can…I can reinforce the rest of the castle."

A crease furrows between my mother's brows.

A wall shatters, my golden briars crumbling in on themselves. A hole breaks open, revealing an array of trolls and goblins standing in the castle gardens.

"On it!" Caspian shouts from his position at the door and throws up a barrier of green flame. His skin is ashen. He can't keep this up for long.

"Keep your connection strong, Rosalina," Mom yells. "You won't be able to save Castletree by structure alone. You must heal the tree *inside*."

My vision grows blurry around the edges. "I can do it," I whisper, though the words barely leave my cracked lips.

I throw myself back into the connection.

And it hurts.

The tree drinks like a dying animal gasping for air, and I give it everything. Every drop.

My heart pounds in my chest, wild and thunderous.

But then…

It falters.

A beat skips. Another comes slower, then slower still.

A strange hush falls over me, as if the world has dipped beneath water.

My breath catches on the edges of my lungs. I try to draw in air, one deep breath, but it rattles, thin and useless. It doesn't reach. I try again. Nothing.

Why can't I breathe?

The bark under my hands swims, turning soft and unfocused.

I blink, and the castle spins.

There's a ringing in my ears now. No, not ringing. Silence. A perfect, terrifying silence.

And through that silence, a cold truth unfurls inside me.

I'm dying.

The thought doesn't scare me. Not yet.

It lands with a dull, faraway clarity, like I'm watching myself from the other side of a mirror.

I gave too much. I let Castletree take it all.

And it still wasn't enough.

My body is here, trembling, broken on the stone. But my soul is already fading, pouring into the roots of this ancient tree. The tether has become a noose.

What will happen to Dayton and Farron? Our lives are tied together. If I…

If I die. I make myself think the words.

I need to be strong for them, but I can't. Their love is so powerful. Maybe it will be enough to keep them going without me…

I feel my heartbeat stutter again.

Once. Twice. Then slower.

Thump.

Thump.

It shouldn't feel peaceful. But it does.

My vision narrows to pinpricks of golden light. I try to dig deeper, to reach the tree's roots, but I'm more likely to find a way to swim through stone.

"Rosalina!" Mom's voice slices through the haze. "Keep going! You can do this!"

But I can't. I can't.

My fingers twitch once, then go still.

Someone seizes my shoulders, pulling me from the ground and breaking my tether to Castletree.

Magic surges through me. Not mine.

Ezryn's.

A flash of Spring, bright and sharp, rushes through my veins, and I gasp, a ragged, raw sound as air floods back into my lungs.

Ezryn's voice, hoarse and furious, booms above me. "You almost killed her!"

"She's my daughter!" my mother snaps. "I know what she's capable of!"

"And she's my mate!" Ezryn bellows.

Everything stills.

I wasn't enough.

The castle groans. Another tremor splits the stone beneath us. The air chokes with dust and ash. The tree's branches curl inward like dying fingers.

I blink through tears, my body trembling violently now, and I know.

There's nothing I can do.

Even with Ezryn's power inside me, I'm just a drop in a boiling ocean.

Castletree will fall.

81

Farron

I RUN.

The halls of Castletree split apart around me. The roots groan and stone screams as it cracks. I leap over a fallen beam and duck under a tangle of vines and broken masonry. Magic hangs heavy in the air, wild, raw, and wrong. My lungs burn with smoke and dust.

Most of the staff are evacuated. I led them to Caspian, who has wrapped them in shadows so they can hide in the back gardens.

But two are missing.

Mandaria. Paavak.

Where are they?

I turn, boot skidding on loose stone as I barrel into the Autumn wing. The temperature shifts. It's warmer, like the heat of a long-burning hearth. My chest tightens. No—

My feet carry me faster until I burst through the double doors into the library.

Gods.

The library is falling apart.

Golden light streams through fractured windows, dancing across the leaves that gust up from felled trees. Books tumble off shelves. The floor is littered with torn pages. The fireplace still burns somehow, casting a soft orange glow over the worn velvet couch in the corner of the room. Half the tables are overturned, stools broken under fallen branches.

"Mandaria!" I shout, voice raw. "Paavak!"

A cough. Then another.

I rush toward the sound, dropping to my knees and peering beneath the splintered remains of a table. Two figures huddle there, covered in dust, eyes wide.

"There you are," I breathe. Relief crashes into me.

"High Prince Farron," Mandaria whispers. "We didn't know where to go—"

"Come now." I haul them both out. "Straight through those doors. Caspian's leading everyone to safety. He'll get you out."

Paavak hesitates. "What about you?"

"Run!"

They do.

I make to follow but hesitate. How can I leave my library like this?

The ceiling groans, then cracks, caving in dust and debris from floors above, right in front of me.

A shadow falls across the floor as the redwood bookshelf, one of the tallest—the one I used to climb to reach the poetry on the top shelf when I was only a kid visiting here—splinters free from the wall and crashes to the ground.

I stagger back, coughing, arms raised as the air explodes in dust and falling pages.

I can see the exit, but I can't make myself leave.

When I return, it won't be the same. What if it's all gone?

"No." My fingers brush the shelf's shattered edge. The wood is warm, still alive. But only just.

What if saving our home is too much, even for Rosalina?

Another crack splits the ceiling. A beam falls. The leaves on the remaining trees curl inward, blackening at the edges. Flames lick higher in the fireplace, and the reading couch catches.

I stand there, frozen, helpless.

This place, this room…it's mine. The heart of the Autumn wing. Where I learned to read. Where I first heard stories of heroes and fools, gods and monsters. Where I found peace.

It contains all the histories, every story, every legend, every encyclopedia. It is lives upon lives upon lives within the pages.

And now it's dying.

The grief comes so fast I can't stop it. I press a hand to my chest, trying to catch my breath, trying to—

Trying to do something.

But all I can do is watch as the place I love most in the world crumbles before my eyes.

"Farron!" a booming voice yells. "Farron!"

Then a monstrous shape leaps over the broken beams and lands before me. Dayton, the High Prince of Summer, the golden wolf.

"Day—" I say, breaking into a sob.

He gives a little whimper and nudges his wet nose against my cheek. "We need to get out of here, Fare."

"I can't." My face burrows into his neck, tears sticking to his fur. "I can't lose this too. All the stories, the knowledge... I've lost so much—"

"I know you have, my love," Dayton says. "Your life is worth more than this. The great thing about stories is we can tell them again. They live in the hearts of people."

My fingers wrap tight in his fur, and I blink through my tears. A shelf has fallen in front of the fire, and it's catching the books.

I sat by the window and looked at the gardens with my siblings and read them stories. Nori, Dom...Billy. They loved the library.

And Day—we made love on that couch, surrounded by the smell of woodsmoke and the sea. I thought I was going to die of happiness.

And I fell in love with Rosalina between the pages of these books where we first saw each other's souls, our twin flames of curiosity.

"I can't lose this place," I sob. "This is our home."

There's a flicker of magic, and my arms are grasping cold armor. Dayton sits as a fae before me.

He gasps, surprised, and looks down at himself. "What happened? I didn't mean to change."

We stare at each other.

Dayton's teal eyes widen. "Fare... I can't feel my magic anymore. Or my wolf."

A hollowness echoes through me, like a piece of my very being has been stripped away. I hold out my palm, but the idea of a flame forming there feels as impossible as flying.

"Our roses," Dayton gasps.

"They're dying," I say. "Like Castletree."

82

Rosalina

It's over.

I've failed.

What else can I do?

Castletree will fall. Our home, destroyed.

I wasn't strong enough to stop Sira. .

Beams of wood break around me. Stones skitter over my skin. The air shakes with the sound of creatures roaring and screaming. But I can't even raise my head off the floor.

We were prepared to protect the realms. All our armies wait at the ready. But there's no one to protect Castletree. No one except me.

How stupid they all were to put their faith in me.

"We have to get out of here!" Ezryn roars. "The entrance hall's about to collapse!"

I'm yanked to my feet, Ezryn's grip bruising. There's panic in his voice, unlike anything I've ever heard.

My father wraps his arms around my shoulder. "Steady now, Rosalina. We're going to have to move quickly. I've got you."

But who's got Papa?

What will happen to him if Castletree is nothing but debris? His life is tethered to its magic. Without it…

His hands tremble, and there's a raspy quality to his breath. *I have to save you…*

Caspian backs up until he's standing near us. He looks up at my mother, and it's as if a silent conversation passes between them. "Fine," my mother whispers. "We go."

A crash explodes through the air, and I'm only kept on my feet by Papa. Slivers of wood and stone shower over us. I blink through the dust to see a hole in the wall. Standing in the wreckage is a massive ogre, twelve feet tall and snarling. His body appears to be made of boulders, skin meshed with rock, eyes red with grit. In his hands, he's holding a club. To my horror, it's one of Castletree's branches. He might as well be wielding one of my limbs.

Ezryn makes a low growl and steps in front of us. "My wolf will see to this."

A moment passes. Nothing happens.

"Ez?" I whisper.

Ezryn staggers backward. "What's happening?" He holds up his hands, staring as if they've betrayed him. "My magic…"

My mother's face empties of color. "It's their roses." She clutches my wrists. "Rosalina, we have to save their roses!"

"Go. We'll hold them off," Caspian says, stepping up beside Ezryn.

Ezryn clutches his token. Gleaming armor envelops him, and the hammer appears in his grasp. "My token is unaffected. We can handle this. Hurry! Go!"

There's nothing to do but run. My father drags me by the wrist, charging out of the entrance hall. The stairs are completely blocked; a huge pile of rubble has collapsed over them.

"We'll take the staff stairwell. Follow me," Mom says.

Papa runs at my heels, but his breathing is ragged. Stopping to rest isn't possible. The roses…if they're destroyed…

I can't think of it. Won't even imagine it. All I can do is run.

We navigate the labyrinth that Castletree has become. Walls crumble, covering us in debris. We scramble over fallen beams, huge as tree trunks, and find holes between piles of rubble that block our path. My lungs ache, and I'm drenched with sweat. I swear I'm one heartbeat from collapsing, but we don't stop.

Finally, we sprint up the staff stairwell and emerge into the junction between all four wings on the upper balcony of the entrance hall. The door to the High Tower is just ahead. A massive chunk of wooden wall has fallen across our route.

"Together now!" Papa cries.

Mom and I get on either side of him, heaving with all our strength until we push it out of the way.

There! The door—

And before it, a snarling, grotesque creature. I've never seen one before, but I've heard the princes talk of them. *Gargoyles.* With leathery skin, translucent wings thick with veins, and a maw like a vampire bat, this monster is something out of my childhood nightmares.

It spots us, black eyes shining. It gives a delighted hiss, revealing row upon row of jagged teeth.

I look around, trying to see if there's anything we can use for a weapon. How do we fight this? Two humans and one powerless fae.

I hold my breath. The gargoyle snarls, then beats its wings, legs tensing to leap—

A sickening crunch echoes in the hall as an arrowhead erupts through the creature's skull. It lets loose a moan, wavers, then falls.

And standing behind it, bow drawn and blue eyes flashing, is my sister.

Wrenley.

83

Rosalina

She's not the Wrenley from Orca Cove, swamped in darkness and oversize clothes. Neither is she the Nightingale, with her prismatic armor and stolen bow.

Instead, she wears tight black pants and a shirt—typical wear for under armor—and her face is bare. No mask. Just her, with her short, wavy hair, round cheeks, and eyes like lightning.

She lowers her weapon. I don't recognize it, but it appears to be a standard short bow, wooden with a quiver of arrows on her back. Something she could have pilfered off a soldier or a goblin.

Beautiful and deadly and angry. And even though Sira tried to beat it out of her, an O'Connell. Even if she doesn't know what it means yet, I do, and I see it in her every move.

"You came," I whisper.

Her lips curls. "Would have been here sooner, but my briars

gave out." She stalks over. The shortest member of our family, she looks up at Mom with an expression of complete derision. "What's wrong with you?"

Mom crosses her arms. "If I answer that, we'll be here for weeks, and none of us have the time." She sighs and relaxes her stance. "Look, we need to make it up to the High Tower and save the roses. Can you help us?"

Wrenley looks at Mom, then me, and finally Papa. Her gaze softens as it drifts over him. Then it jerks to the floor. "I can get you there."

"Come on." I kick the dead gargoyle out of the way and wrench open the door.

Up, up, up, we round the spiraling staircase. Mom leads, with Wrenley and Papa in the middle, while I take the rear. My body is still so weak, and my head swims with each step.

Papa falls to the ground. I tumble over him, scraping over the rough stone.

"Are you alright?" I gasp, grabbing his shoulder.

He heaves in a breath, sweat dotting his brow. "Yes, my girl. Let's keep going."

Once we secure the roses, we'll figure out a way to save Papa. Maybe we can find a seed of Castletree's, or I can find a way to transfer his life force to something else. I won't give up.

I help my father up, and we catch up to Mom and Wrenley.

"Here!" Mom cries, gesturing us all into the chamber at the top of the High Tower.

What breath I have left escapes. No. *No.*

The room...this felt like the place where magic began. A place so sacred, nothing could ever touch it. But it's as destroyed as the rest of Castletree. The beautiful murals of starfall and winged orbs lie in chunks of painted rock across the floor. The briars that once gleamed golden with blossoming roses are now withered husks. And the stained-glass windows are a shattered rainbow on the ground.

Through the broken panes, I see outside is a warzone. Harpies and gargoyles dive-bomb through the air, and goblins skitter across the branches like maggots over a corpse.

But there, in the middle of the chamber, are four roses, still blooming, still holding on despite everything. Blue, pink, turquoise, and orange, all shimmering with a golden glow.

I'm transported back to a tale told in a monastery, before I ever knew how woven I was into the history of the Vale. How when the Above was falling, Aurelia saved four roses from the Gardens of Ithilias and, with that, kept magic from leaving the world.

"Castletree's not protected anymore," my mother says, running over to them. "We have to remove them and take them somewhere safe."

I draw in a shaky breath. So I will be like my mother. I will steal this magic away from its home and plant it somewhere new. Someplace where it has a chance.

I fling myself down beside my mother. She rips off a chunk of her skirt and lays the fabric out. "We'll wrap them in here. Carefully now, carefully."

I lace my fingers into the dirt, feeling for each root. It's like the threads of my mates' power, each one sacred.

My mother and I work in tandem. Slowly, we unearth Keldarion's sapphire rose and lay it in the fabric. "I'll keep you safe," I whisper.

Then we begin toiling on Ezryn's pink rose.

Wrenley paces nearby us. Papa saunters up to her. "So, uh, you're Wrenley?"

Wrenley jerks her head to look at him. I expect her to make a cutting comment. To sneer and say "*That's my name, don't wear it out*" or, knowing Wrenley, something more clever and mean.

But instead, she averts her gaze to the floor again. "Yeah."

"I'm George. Nice to meet you." Papa holds out his hand to her. It's shaking.

A bright red flush creeps across her nose and into her cheeks as she takes his hand. She doesn't say anything else, and he doesn't push her.

My heart thrums against my chest as we work the roots free and place the pink rose beside Kel's. Two more.

Guttural screams echo up the staircase. In a single swift movement, Wrenley draws her bow, an arrow poised at the door. "Hurry up. I don't think we have much time."

I force myself to stay steady as we place the turquoise rose with the others. One more.

Together, my mother and I free the orange rose. I stare at the empty plots where they once withered and blossomed. A home for our love story.

Wherever we are is home, I think to the roses, even as tears sting my eyes. *I'll protect you.*

Mom squeezes my shoulder as I carefully bundle the roses in the fabric and clutch them to my chest.

I rise to my feet. "Okay, let's go—"

It happens so fast. The blink of an eye, the beat of a heart.

There's a chittering sound, familiar from the Briar.

A goblin appears in the window, standing in the pane, heedless of the shards of glass. He raises a bow, his arrow trained on Wrenley.

She's facing the door. She doesn't see. I scream her name.

It's too late. By the time she turns, the arrow's flying through the air.

But Papa's not too late. He leaps, throwing his entire body in front of hers.

The arrow makes a squelching sound as it pierces his chest, and in that blink of an eye, that beat of a heart, I am drenched in my father's blood.

84

Rosalina

WHAT DO YOU TELL SOMEONE WHEN YOU ONLY HAVE ONE MOMENT left with them?

Do you try to recall your happiest memories, spinning images into words of a life well-lived?

Do you take the last opportunity to curse them out for all the pain they wrought upon you? To remind them of all the ways they hurt you?

Do you lament the lack of a future together? Cast your wishes into their well so they might carry them, wherever they're going?

Or do you simply tell them the truth: *I loved you. I love you. And I always will.*

These are the questions that assail my thoughts as I fling myself down to the side of my father.

The arrow juts out of his heart. Brilliant red blood sputters from his mouth and paints the front of his white shirt. For the first time in my life, my father looks afraid.

I wish I could burn the image from my mind.

A strangled roar tears out of my mother's throat as she charges the window, shoving the goblin with all her might. He tumbles backward with a screech.

Then she's next to me screaming. Screaming like a woman undone from the inside out. Wrenley's collapsed on his other side, shaking him and wailing over and over: "Why did you do that? Why did you do that?"

I want to cover my ears and shut my eyes and curl up in a ball, but I can't.

Because my father is dying, and I have one moment left.

I grab Papa's hand, but it's too limp to squeeze mine back. His gaze is faraway, out the window. It's almost like he's searching the sky.

My useless body is completely devoid of magic. There's not even an inkling of healing energy left within me. So what do I do? *What do I do?*

This...wasn't supposed to happen. My mother bargained away our freedom to make sure time would never claim him. To learn how to bind his life to something eternal. But there's no way to bargain with the crack in his ribs, with the blood gushing from his heart.

There are more things I need to say to my father than there are stars in the sky. Hurts I want to scream, apologies I want to utter, and memories I'm desperate to make. It's as if I can see them sputtering out around me, like candles in a rainstorm.

Papa gives a gasp, and he squeezes my hand once, tight.

There's no coming back from this. I know it not because of the slowing of his heart but because the world tilts and nothing feels safe anymore.

My mother shrieks, Wrenley lets out a keening sob, but there's only silence in my head.

"Why? Why?" Wrenley shrieks again.

Papa's eyes blink wildly, but somehow, they find hers. His voice is barely a breath. "Because you're my girl." His fading gaze trembles over Mom before resting on me. "My girls."

I need to say something before there's nothing left. *Say something. Say anything!*

But Papa's heart beats once, twice, and then stops.

It is as if Castletree can't bear to be in this world without him.

Everything collapses.

The ground shakes. The walls crumble. Branches and stonework rain upon us.

And I don't think any of George's three girls would have moved if it weren't for the army of underfae barreling up the staircase. Faustrius leads the charge. Unconsciously, I slip the bundle of roses into my shirt before I'm yanked out of the collapsing tower and, along with Wrenley and my mother, clamped in chains.

One moment. I thought I had one moment. A breath, a second, I would take *any* of it…

But I didn't get to yell, to tell him I forgive him. To tell him I *love* him and what a beautiful adventure he set me upon.

Now, there are no feelings in me as Faustrius and his soldiers pull us out of Castletree, over the bridge, and into the Briar. It's as if my nerves have gone dead, my mind a vacant hum.

I might as well be one of the flecks of dust billowing around me.

Let me waste away in this nothingness. Let it swallow and consume me. I'm so *sick* of the pain…

But I guess the world thinks I can handle more, because when I cast a final look back, I see my home crumble to root and ash, taking my father's body with it.

85

Rosalina

THE WORLD IS NOT THE SAME.

The Briar, once a labyrinth of thorns thick as tree trunks, now feels like walking between the bones of a skeleton. Caspian's briars are withered. Rotten. Dead.

Castletree is gone. Not only was it my home, but it was the source of my magic. Wrenley's magic. The princes' magic.

All magic.

Now there's simply a thin sensation in the air, the world around us matte and gray.

We are captured, all of us. Walking in a line, hands clasped with steel. The underfae army had been waiting for all those who escaped the collapsing castle. The staff, Justus, Kel, Ezryn, Dayton, Farron, Caspian. Mom and Wrenley. We march, manacles clanking.

I don't know where Kairyn and Heidigog are. Probably

somewhere amid the other legions of Sira's possessed creations, their wills stolen.

Faustrius and his soldiers walk beside us, carrying heavy bows, spears, and swords. Their eyes differ from the rest of Sira's army, still shining various shades of red, yellow, and green. So she hasn't stolen their wills.

Where are they taking us? I have no idea. We've been marching for hours.

And I don't have the strength to stop the voice that mutters: *Who cares?*

My father is dead.

I will never hear his boisterous laugh or listen to his crazy theories or watch him fall in love with his Annie all over again.

There isn't even rage inside me. There's just nothing at all.

Mom's been screaming for hours. I think her voice must be close to going out, but it doesn't stop. Brutal, guttural cries that can only be from the very darkest corners of her heart.

One of the underfae guards walked over to her about an hour ago, told her to be quiet. Without hesitating, she lunged at him, knocking him to the ground. The heart's cry had become a battle roar, and I swear she was going to tear his throat out with her teeth until another guard pulled her off.

She's gagged now, but I can still hear her screams through it.

The princes have all tried to catch my eye, but I can't tell them what happened. I think I could still speak in their minds if I tried—the only bright magic left within me are my mate bonds—but I don't have the words.

Instead, I walk with my sister. Wrenley drifts like a wraith beside me. My mind imagines us as twin ghosts floating through the briar husks.

I haven't heard her speak since we were imprisoned, so when she whispers, "It doesn't make sense," I look around, sure it must have been a voice on the wind.

Her sapphire gaze burrows into me. I meet it. This is the only place I'll find my father's eyes now.

"That arrow was coming for *me*," she spits. "We'd only just met. Why would he sacrifice himself for me? I don't get it."

I sigh, the answer so painfully obvious. I'm too numb to feel sympathy for her. "Because in that moment, he *knew* you. And that's what family does."

Wrenley slows her pace after that, and we fall out of step. I don't look back at her.

The only comfort to me is the press of the roses against my chest, hidden by my white T-shirt. I'm still in my human clothes. Leggings. Boots. I look so much like I did when I first came to the Vale.

I wish I could say I felt different. I'd thought I'd changed.

But I'm still as weak as I was then.

Up ahead, Faustrius raises a hand, and we halt. The huge underfae, his slate-colored skin shiny with sweat, begins to walk the line, checking the faces of the prisoners. Kel yells at him as he passes by, but Faustrius ignores him.

A shadow stretches over me. I drag my gaze up until I'm face-to-face with the antlered warlord. Once a fae of the Above who chose to become one of Sira's monsters, he is as ancient as my mother. I wonder if he ever knew her. Perhaps he does not recognize her as a human, thrashing and muzzled. And I do not think she recognizes anything but her grief.

"So," I say, my voice devoid of any emotion, "is your vengeance now sated, prince, pauper, king? Thrainn of Winter refused you a home. You've destroyed ours."

He stares at me for a long time, the ribbons attached to his antlers swaying in the breeze. "No. It does not seem to me justice has been delivered." He pulls out a large silver key, grabs my wrist, and unlocks my manacles.

"What are you doing?" I breathe.

"Quite the escape attempt you organized, out here in the Briar. Freeing your party without killing a single member of my guard. Most impressive."

"Escape? We haven't escaped—"

Faustrius silences me with a glare. "I have been complicit in the destruction of two worlds. One, I helped orchestrate. The other was forced upon me when my people were frozen, left to remain entrapped forever. My people deserve a place on the surface, and if that means upending the old order for a new one, so be it." He inhales deeply, nostrils flaring. "But I will not let Sira dictate which lives I take. That will be my own choice. And you and yours deserve to live." He steps away from me and holds up a hand. "Let them go!"

Steel clangs as his soldiers wrest the manacles off each prisoner's wrists.

My words are a breath. "Why free us?"

"You are their leader." Faustrius reaches into his heavy black cape and pulls something out.

A stuffed, winged lion. Aeneas, the toy I leant to Aquila.

"If you treat your people with the kindness that you treated mine, then I wish you a chance at life." He drags his gaze from me to Kel, to Caspian, and finally to Ezryn, Day, and Farron. "Do not think this means your safety. There is nowhere in the Enchanted Vale that Sira won't be able to find you. She will hunt the six of you until you're dead." He holds me still with a stare. "I'll give you as much time as I can. Find your people shelter. This is only the beginning."

With a snap of his cape, Faustrius turns.

I reach out and snag his arm. "Wait. Why do you follow her?"

He gazes at me, red eyes soft. "She promised me a new world. If I stop now, it will all have been for nothing."

I stay rooted to the spot as Faustrius and his soldiers form a new line, marching back the way we came, leaving the people of Castletree adrift in the dying bones of the Briar.

His words rumble in my mind. *It will all have been for nothing.*

Farron's grief from days before echoes behind it: *What was it all for?*

And my own question joins the fray.

If we don't stop it, who does?

86

Caspian

The human realm. It's different than I remember. Though the last time I was here was decades ago, when I was a youth. I'd left home, thinking there was a way for me to outrun my affliction. To outrun my destiny.

I look to Rosalina, eyes vacant, mouth a thin line. Little did I know my destiny was going to find me.

Magic is dying in the Enchanted Vale. I could sense it draining out of the earth like blood pouring from an opened artery. Castletree is the wellspring of the seasonal realms' power. Without it…

Well, it may very much feel like this place soon.

This place. A cloud of damp mist shrouds the towering fir trees in a gray veil. Lights begin to wink on in wooden cabins, the quaint atmosphere shattered by a terrifying bug-eyed depiction of an orca on a sign.

Orca Cove.

Kel, Ezryn, Dayton, Farron, Anya, Birdy, and Rosalina stand in a line, no one quite prepared to take the first step into town. Not with what it will signify.

Defeat.

Fleeing the Vale.

Because Faustrius was right. There's nowhere in the Enchanted Vale where Sira won't look for us. And with only my weakened shadows and green flame—the only magic left between us—we had no choice but to run.

After Faustrius, the proud, self-righteous bastard that he is, decided to let us go, we had to move quickly. We five princes and the three O'Connell women have fled to the one place beyond Sira's ambitions. Marigold, Eldy, and Justus have taken charge of the rest of Castletree's orphans with intentions to lead them to Spring and seek sanctuary in Keep Hammergarden.

Marigold had been in a state at first, insisting we come with them. But Rosalina silenced her with words so filled with darkness, it didn't seem like my Flower speaking at all: "If we go with you, Sira will hunt us down. We're a liability. Sira won't stop until we're dead. And we can't protect anyone. *I* can't protect anyone."

So Marigold and Astrid hugged her tight. She didn't hug them back.

Justus stopped us as we turned to leave. "Your tokens. You won't need them in the human realm. But I might be able to think of something. There are a few tricks in this old bird yet."

So we handed them over to the first High Prince of Summer. Kel's snowflake, Ezryn's wooden trinket carved with cherry blossoms,

Dayton's seashell, Farron's leaf, and the moonstone rose gifted to me by my mate. It felt like giving up the last of my faeness.

The eight of us cut our way through the Briar, finding the rosebush Birdy had made. Brown rose petals and stems running with black veins of rot adorned the weak portal.

I'd been the first to step through, feeling the cool shiver as I crossed from one world to another. One by one, they followed me, each in a deeper pool of despair than the other. Kel and Ez, stoic as ever. Farron and Day, visibly exhausted with grief.

Then my girls.

How badly I wished to take Anya's hand. I have seen her in fits of laughter, red with rage, and howling with sorrow. But this… whatever *this* is that's overtaken her…

It is as if she is nothing more than skin and bone, forced to move, her expression as numb as a doll's.

I can't let myself feel it: George's death. He was good to me in ways no one ever has been before and no one will ever be again. And if I let myself *realize* it—realize that I will never sit opposite him at a fire, discussing philosophy, or see the sparkling effect he has on those around him—then I have no idea what kind of animal the grief will turn me into.

I need to stand. Need to tell them which way to go. To watch out for roots so they don't trip. I need to be a shore they can crash upon.

Birdy shivered out of the portal next. We hadn't spoken, not once. But when I reached out to take her hand, she stumbled slightly, and I pulled her to my chest.

"You're okay," I mumbled into her hair.

She didn't respond, just stood like a wooden board in my arms. Then she melted against me, fingernails scratching my back. "I'm sorry, Cas. I'm—"

"None of that."

She stayed there in my arms for half a moment before pulling away—which is a lifetime to get to hold Birdy.

Lastly, Rosalina crossed the veil between the worlds, her body trembling with radiance in a way it never will in this realm. She didn't take my hand, nor did she look back. But her eyes burned with a familiar fire, one I have only seen in tapestries and paintings.

The light of the fae as they fell from the Above.

My magic is weakened after Aurelia's spell. I don't know if it'll ever fully return, but I was able to use a rush of green flame to incinerate the rosebush. *No one can follow us now.*

We stand on the edge of town, the rain dripping down my spine and settling on my eyelashes. I look to them: Rosalina. Kel. Ezryn. Farron. Dayton. Birdy and Anya.

All the people I've ever loved in my life who still draw breath.

I finally had everything I wanted. A home. A family. And my mother's dark heart destroyed it.

My gaze settles on Rosalina. Her throat bobs, and I wonder if it is only rain painting her cheeks.

She takes the first step, then heaves a breath. "Well," she whispers, "I'm back."

I don't tell her this, not yet, because she's too deep in anguish to hear it.

But she's not back. Not by a long shot.

None of us are.

Instead, I stand beside her and squeeze her hand. Someone takes mine on the other side. I look down. Birdy, a wren with feathers too drenched to fly. On Rosalina's other side, Farron has taken her hand, and Dayton his. He reaches out for Ezryn, who takes his hand and extends his own to Kel. Then the Sworn Protector of the Realms offers a hand to the Queen of the Vale. Anya takes it.

I have been beaten and tortured and stripped of all hope. But I know how to claw it back. So I'll teach them. For all the things they've given me in my life, I'll give them this.

And when the queen, the princesses, and the princes of the Enchanted Vale rise again, nothing in the seven realms or the worlds beyond will be able to break us.

87

Faustrius

NIGHT IS FALLING OVER THE ENCHANTED VALE, BRINGING WITH IT THE crisp breeze and bite of cold.

Long have I dreamt of this: walking with my people under the stars that once housed us. A new home. A new life. A place to bask in the remnants of magic, as we once basked in its full glory.

But there is no magic here. At least not much. It's wisping away, like water boiled too hot.

I stare at her, sitting upon a makeshift throne of rubble and wood. She lounges with her legs over one armrest as if it were made of silken pillows and gold plating instead of destruction. Somehow, she's still able to make the whole thing luxurious.

But Sira has always had this quality. To take something vile and put it to purpose.

Despite having only just escaped the shadow prison her son

trapped her in, she is as striking as ever. Victory suits her, carving her lips into a semblance of a smile. Her hair is a silky black curtain down her back. Though there is only ash and blood on the wind, I know how it smells, the heady blend of jasmine and frankincense that would overtake my mind with a flick of that black curtain over her shoulder.

But a beautiful crown does not make a beautiful queen.

"You've killed the tree," I say, hand tightening on the hilt of my sword.

"And you've lost my prisoners," she snarls.

"This was never our arrangement." I step toward her, voice rising. "What of the magic?"

She waves her hand flippantly. "Who needs Aurelia's dregs?" Her gaze shifts to the ground, and she says through gritted teeth, "Besides, for one pesky weed, her roots run deep."

I shift from foot to foot. The fabric tied around my antlers—remnants of the clothing of a family, long passed—sways with the motion. "Then you've got what you wanted. You are the queen of Castletree—"

"No." Sira sits straight up, fingers digging into the armrests made of cracked wood. "What I *want* is Aurelia's head on a pike, next to her little daughters and those cursed princes! Instead, you've gone and lost them. *All* of them. Isn't that quite the coincidence?"

Who is this woman? I wonder, not for the first time. Is she still the same one I followed down from the Above? That industrious, enlightened woman with a vision of a new world? The one who would not let anything stop her, not even her broken wings? I resist the constant urge to scratch my shoulder blades.

I would have done anything for that woman. I *did* do everything. Gave up my home, rallied my people, became this…thing.

And this is what it's all come to. A queen of rubble and rot.

"You will find them and kill them," Sira says.

The word comes out of me as a breath. A word I have not known in an age. "No."

"No?" Her eyes go wide, and she lets out a shrieking laugh, as if in disbelief.

I do not relent.

When all I do is stare at her, her gaze narrows, as piercing as a snake's strike. "Aquila!" she screams.

My second-in-command comes into step beside me. Her face, now healed of its burns, is ashen, and she stares up at the sky. Once a priestess who communed with the stars, she has only known the dark for so long. I had thought possession of the surface would be a boon to her.

Maybe it will be. She seems more herself these last few days, ever since Sira lost connection with her Green Flame god.

"Due to Faustrius's insolence, you are now the commander of the Elderblood. Hunt down the prisoners, and relieve them of their heads."

My throat tightens. Sira can't do that. I was chosen by my people. She has no say over our ranks.

Aquila holds her head high. "No. My loyalty is to Faustrius and Faustrius alone." That teasing grin creeps up her face. "And the stars, but they don't answer to anyone down here."

"We are not your servants," I growl to Sira. "We were to be equal allies. That was the arrangement. Your bidding should be reserved for your own subjects, which we are not."

"If we are allies, then why do you betray me so?" Her brows knit together in a facade of hurt.

"I told you. The prisoners escaped. Regardless, it is you, Sira, who has made the first betrayal. The boy you turned in the fires of Mount Rhuvenmark. He is one of us, yet you forced him under your control. Free him."

"There appears to be a misunderstanding. You are not in a position to negotiate." Sira goes very still, except for her eyes. Her irises shake, and the pupils seem to change in size, large, then pinprick small. "If you cannot be trusted to act in the best interest of my queendom, you force my hand."

A dark shiver creeps down my spine, like someone's poured ink on my bones. "No, Sira. Don't do this."

"Fausty," Aquila murmurs, grabbing my arm. "Fausty, she wouldn't—"

But it's too late. Sira reaches into the shadows that curl around her like eels and pulls out the last living magic of the Above: the rose from the Gardens of Ithilias. Long had we thought it lost, and for the best that was. But when Keldarion and the human retrieved it from the ice, we Elderblood knew better than any what a danger it was.

The magic of creation. The magic of *control.*

It pulls at the edges of my consciousness, like being swallowed in dark water.

"I will free the boy from my control," Sira whispers, "as an act of good will. But know this, Faustrius of the Elderblood. If I question your loyalty again…" She holds up the rose, examining it. "I will take measures to ensure I never need to in the future."

Dread, colder than even my imprisonment in the ice, floods through my veins.

So. I am a thrall regardless. Awake and with the illusion of choice.

With a short bow, I dismiss myself and walk back toward the tangles of withered thorns.

My options lie before me. Disobey Sira and condemn my people to thralldom.

Or serve her, condemning us anyway.

My gaze stretches far over what once was the Briar. Somewhere within that husk flees our only hope.

The words whisper out of me, a plea and a prayer all at once. "Long live the Golden Rose."

Acknowledgments

When we set out to tell Rosalina's journey across the Enchanted Vale, we knew it would be a tale of redemption. Sharing Caspian's story of forgiveness, inner strength, and the undying power of love has been one of the most rewarding parts of this whole process. When the world seems most dire, our beloved royals of the Vale will need someone who has walked through the shadows and come out into the light to guide them forward. What a joy it has been to bring Caspian to the point where he can be the true leader he was always meant to be.

What a privilege it is to work with a powerhouse agent like Susan Velazquez Colmant. Not only does she have our back through all the highs and lows, but she also knows our characters inside and out. It is a gift to tell stories with someone who understands the world as deeply as you do. We'd also like to extend our thanks to the whole JAB team, with a special shout-out to Christina Zobel, who has allowed Rosalina to travel around the world in so many different languages, as well as Destini and Valentina for all of their support.

A very big thank you to editor extraordinaire, Christa, who has poured so much love into this series and into us as authors. How lucky we are to have someone like you. Thank you for believing in us.

To Madison: creative, kind, and an absolute blast to work with. Thank you for putting up with our essays, our random thoughts, and for giving us opportunities to live our dream.

Thank you to Sabrina, who is not only a sentence and story wizard, but should also be named the Official Historian of the Enchanted Vale. Thank you for the care you put into our world and for putting up with all of our little idiosyncrasies.

To Sarah, the final line of defense against our rogue typos—thank you for your eagle eye!

Thank you in full to the incredible team at Bloom Books. We have had so much fun working with such a talented group of creatives. A special shout-out to Brittany, Deanna, Jaelyn, Jianna, Julie, Kylie, Letty, Rebecca, Shannon, and everyone else who has helped bring these stories to so many readers.

Thank you to Christina and the incredible Canadian team at Raincoast Books! Your support means so much to us— as well as getting to share in accomplishments that others might not understand, like seeing Bonded on the BC Ferries!

Stefanie Kay and Robert Hatchet, the voices in our heads… we love you both more than words can say. We can't believe how lucky we are to have made so much magic together over the last few years. You bring so much emotion, passion, and honesty to our characters in your performances, and we're forever grateful for your talents.

Thank you to the indie bookstores that have championed the Beasts of the Briar series. Whether you've invited us to meet your beautiful patrons, carried our books, or partnered with us to bring something special to our readers, we are endlessly grateful for everything you do for the book community.

Anne, Beate, Camille, Kaylee, Lindsay, and Sarah—your suffering is noted!! Seriously, thank you for being here through it all. The ups, the downs, the strange hand placements, the cringey lines that will probably still end up in the final book because that's just the way we are… We love you so much.

To the three people who not only keep the Elizabeth Helen engine running smoothly, but keep it running at all: Amanda, Chelsea, and Zara. Thank you for your creativity, your energy, your support, and for sharing your incredible talents with us. We are so grateful to have you on our side.

Thank you to our family for their unwavering support of this series. Mom and Dad, thank you for all of your encouragement throughout the years. Mom, I'm sorry Farron keeps misbehaving!

Graeme, I'm so glad we finally got to bring Malekai to life in a published book. He still has many worlds left to try to conquer, so he'll be back in another universe. It is a joy telling stories with you.

The final thank you goes to our readers. Without you, Rosalina would have stayed in Orca Cove forever. Now, she has a chance to return to her first home…and maybe find her way back to the Vale. Thank you for reading books. Thank you for loving books. Thank you for being here.

One final journey ahead. Are you ready, Roses? Rosalina's seventh adventure will take us across the realms and into the sky. Look up, past the clouds, past the stars… We'll meet you there.

About the Author

Elizabeth Helen is the combined pen name of sister writing duo Elizabeth and Helen. Elizabeth and Helen write fantasy romance and love creating enchanting adventures for their characters. When they're not writing, you can find them snuggling their cats, exploring their rainforest home in British Columbia, Canada, or rolling the dice for a game of Dungeons & Dragons. You can connect with them on TikTok, Instagram, or Facebook.

TikTok: @authorelizabethhelen
Instagram: @author.elizabeth.helen
Facebook: @elizabethhelen